INDIGO

INDIGO

CHRISTINE WESTON

THE REPRINT SOCIETY
LONDON

THIS EDITION PUBLISHED BY THE REPRINT SOCIETY LTD.
BY ARRANGEMENT WITH WM. COLLINS SONS AND CO. LTD.
1946

TO

MY PARENTS

PRINTED IN GREAT BRITAIN
BY COLLINS CLEAR-TYPE PRESS: LONDON AND GLASGOW

PART ONE

I

It was a February afternoon and they were watering the garden ; the smell of water among the flowers reached young Jacques St. Remy where he stood in his bedroom door, lazily allowing himself to be dressed. This was his fourteenth birthday and for fourteen years this fragrance had come up from the garden into his body, stirring a precious disquiet. Perhaps at the hour of his birth this same fragrance had touched his mother's face and his own.

" Lift thy foot," said Hanif sharply. He knelt before Jacques, tying the laces of his white buckskin shoes. " The other one—place it here, on my knee."

Jacques laid his hand on Hanif's head for support, but he did not take his gaze from the garden which lay in a haze of sunlit dust, twittering leaves and odours of moisture and flowers. Beyond the boundary of cactus and lantana bushes rose the dark mass of the mango grove whose limp russet leaves would soon turn a crisp green. Beyond that stretched the fields. The vats and huts and boiler-rooms of his mother's factory lay out of sight beyond the trees, but as he listened Jacques could hear, above the creak of a well wheel and the voice of the gardener, a distant hum and stir of machinery.

" Must you pull all my hair out at once ? " inquired Hanif plaintively.

Jacques' gaze drifted to the young man who knelt at his feet. Hanif was twenty, slender, beautiful in his own way. A velvet cap set off his curled and jet-black hair ; he wore a velvet waistcoat over his white kurtha, and his long legs were hidden in immaculate pantaloons. Hanif was a dandy who spent all his wages on clothes when he did not squander them on luxuries less innocent. An orphan whose parents had died in the last great famine, he came from Monghyr where they speak a shriller tongue than up-country, but when he sang his voice dropped to a minor key, and he sang a good part of the time.

"This cap," murmured Jacques. "It makes seven at least. There is the red one and the purple one and the grey one and . . ."

Hanif replaced the boy's foot on the ground and rose, setting the cap at an angle above his black velvet eyes. "It was bought solely in honour of your birthday. Shall I proceed about my duties looking no better than a chamar, or am I to appear decently clad in your mother's sight?"

"Where is the butterfly you promised me?"

Hanif removed the cap and from its perfumed interior plucked a crumpled object which he laid on the dressing-table.

"That!" exclaimed Jacques scornfully.

"I chased it until I was exhausted. I ran and I ran."

"The only time I saw you run was when the buck goat chased you."

Hanif retorted with an unquotable jest on the character of buck goats, then gravity descended on him once more. "Alas! Your hair, my child."

Jacques regarded himself in the glass. His own face always interested him, for it appeared always as the face of a stranger. He wondered sometimes what his soul looked like—his soul, that hidden separate self. He had discussed this question with his friend Hardyal but they never arrived at any satisfactory explanation. "My father," said Hardyal, "is not orthodox. He does not believe in the persistence of the soul as Father Sebastien believes or as Madame St. Remy believes. My father has made his ideas quite clear to me and he is happy that I share them."

"But your family!" Jacques had reminded him. "Your grandmother and your aunts! Aren't they always afraid that if they misbehave they might be born again as fleas, or turtles?"

Hardyal shrugged scornfully. "What can one expect from women?"

Hardyal's heresy did not trouble Jacques very much; nothing about his friend troubled Jacques, except perhaps an occasional twinge of fear lest something happen to separate them.

"Stand still," commanded Hanif. "You cannot appear thus before the photographer."

" I don't want to appear before him at all—in these disgusting clothes." His bottom itched in the new, tight drill.

Hanif dipped a comb in a bowl of water and drew it through the boy's light brown hair. Jacques knew that in her own room his sister Gisele was also being tricked out for the occasion. The ayah squatted on her haunches with Gisele crouched on a stool before her, and clawed the girl's golden fleece, eliciting screams of wrath.

The house was filled with the excitement of a party ; bare feet pattered over the china-matting, bead curtains clashed and tinkled, there was a scurrying between the cookhouse and the back veranda. Jacques heard the familiar sound of Father Sebastien's arrival and saw the priest's fat pony led away to the stables. In a few hours, he thought, this day will have ended like all the days I can remember. When light fades, the crows will fly westward to roost and the flying foxes will flap across the garden to feed in the tamarinds. From all over the plain dust will rise into the air, stirred by homeward moving feet ; there will be a smell of wood smoke and food cooking, and all the special evening voices. The Hour of Cowdust, Hardyal called it.

" There ! " exclaimed Hanif. " Now you are beautiful ! "

Jacques' hair stuck to his head as if it had been varnished. Singing under his breath Hanif began to set the room in order, shaking the mosquito curtains above the bed, picking up and smoothing the discarded clothes.

In an hour the guests would be here : Mr. Wall the Engineer, Doctor and Mrs. Brown, Hardyal, and the railway inspector's two dull little girls, invited because there were no other white children in Amritpore. The inspector's little girls were not wholly white, and neither Jacques nor Gisele liked them, but Madame St. Remy insisted that their company was better than nothing. Perhaps they would all bring presents, thought Jacques, brightening. Except for Hardyal he didn't care whether they came or not. Hardyal and Mrs. Lyttleton . . . he wandered across the room to examine his collection of butterflies. In the cork-lined case under heavy glass they looked like a jeweller's window, and for some minutes he stared at the great Cat's Eye moth which Mrs. Lyttleton had given him.

Hardyal and Mrs. Lyttleton ! These were his friends. Why, why since he loved them equally had he not been allowed to invite Mrs. Lyttleton this afternoon ? He knew that his mother disliked her, but his understanding stopped there. It confused him to feel that he must not love Mrs. Lyttleton, that he was not even supposed to be friends with her. She was old and kind and full of marvellous stories. She lived in a fascinating house from which he was allowed, at any time, to take anything he liked. She was the sort of friend one might dream about . . . and yet, and yet . . .

Wheels ground up the long avenue of shisham and he saw an ekka jerk to a stop, its dejected pony hanging its head. A shrill duet started up between the driver and his passenger, and Jacques began to laugh. Hanif joined him and they watched delightedly as Mr. Boodrie the amateur photographer dismounted from the ekka. In his anxiety to unload the camera and its apparatus safely he'd managed to entangle himself in the black cloth ; blind and frustrated he groped about under it while the ekka-wallah sat callously grinning.

Jacques exclaimed : " I hope it all goes to smithereens ! "

Hanif laid his hand on the boy's neck. " No running off. No climbing trees. Come ! "

2

IN A CORNER of the veranda overlooking her rose garden Madame St. Remy sat talking with her old friend and confessor, Father Sebastien, a tall, stout Franciscan with shrewd eyes and ruddy cheeks above his black beard. Ten years before, Father Sebastien had acquired Auguste St. Remy's taste for Trichinopoly cigars and Madame obtained them for him regularly, long after her husband's death. Father Sebastien smoked one of these now while he listened to her clear, quick voice.

" I think Ganpat Rai is mistaken in putting so much faith in Aubrey Wall."

"Because Wall is an Englishman and the English have a quality of maggots. They devour everything they come in contact with."

If in 1757 the Frenchman Dupleix had triumphed over the Englishman Clive it is possible that an historic effulgence might have warmed and sweetened somewhat the character and destiny of Madame St. Remy, one hundred and fifty years after the Battle of Plassey. But on this February afternoon she still cherished resentment against that ancient humiliation : whenever she was ill or angry her antipathies escaped into the open disguised as history.

The priest, who rather liked Aubrey Wall, said gently : "Your judgment is sometimes very sweeping, Madame."

"That is because I know them so well."

Madame could not afford to be wrong ; mistakes and shortcomings were reserved for God, via the accommodating ears of Father Sebastien. God and His vicar knew her to be chaste, a devoted mother, loyal to her traditions and bedded in her faith. Believing in God, cynical of men, she managed to combine submission to the Church with a refined tyranny over human beings. But Father Sebastien knew that she was a lonely woman, capable of a mysterious increase of spirit to any degree which ambition might demand of her. When Auguste St. Remy died, leaving her his two children and his indigo, Madame's genius for enterprise had emerged to astonish all who knew her. The indigo industry was wavering under the threat of German coal tar inventions, but to Madame it seemed inconceivable that anything so ancient and so well established as indigo should lose its market. She had learned much from the misfortunes of other planters, many of whom were Indians, and she was convinced that the European's flexibility was what made for his success against the native. She had observed, also, the waste and tedium of old methods, and two years after Auguste's death she imported machinery from England and built a new factory with a steam plant for the tanks and power for stirring and pumping. She bought up the pulse and millet fields of her neighbours and put them to indigo ; nor did she forget the old cry of the peasants : If you sign an indigo contract you won't be free again for several generations ! It was an echo from the days when men

inherited their fathers' and their grandfathers' debts. So
Madame wrote a new contract by which she bought, not
their product, but their labour. Under her genius the factory prospered and five years after Auguste's death she was
rich enough to build a chapel for Father Sebastien, and a
year later, a school for his Indian converts.

In the big green-washed drawing-room of Madame's
house there hung a portrait of Auguste St. Remy made ten
years ago. Fish ants had channelled down one aquiline
nostril, down the lips into his beard ; but his eyes, which
his son had inherited, gazed across the room to a pencil
drawing of his birthplace above Nonancourt in Normandy.
Madame St. Remy, never in love with her own middle-
class heritage, sometimes confused her children by references to Nonancourt as her own birthplace and to the
stone house among the plane trees as her father's house.
In France, measured by her own standards and mislaid
among her own kind, she might not have stood a fair chance,
but in India it was different. Indians were impressed by
greatness, nurtured on arrogance ; India was a vast theatre
for the struggle of the Church—and of Madame—against
the usurping Bloomsbury British. And when she spoke of
the British, Madame used the word *sinister*, and the word
formidable with ominous French sibilance.

She returned to the subject of Hardyal. " They are determined, between them, to send him to England and turn
him into a sahib." She laughed, but Father Sebastien
frowned. After a slight hesitation he said : " We must not
forget that there is a ruling power in this country. For
better or for worse it is part of our own power. It is our
protection too. We must not forget that. Jacques must not
be allowed to forget it."

" On the contrary nothing would please me better than
that Jacques might one day become lieutenant-governor of
the Province ! "

He gave her a quick glance, then laughed. "Ah,
Madame ! "

Madame stared into her garden where the most fragile
of her roses had shed their petals under the day's heat. She
said : " Talking of Aubrey Wall, you understand I am not
inspired by rancour. It is just that I mistrust his intentions.

One can never be sure what he is thinking. But you know as well as I that the most insignificant Englishman never loses sight of his object, which is the extension and preservation of the empire. They never submerge their identity, as we are always willing to submerge ours, in the soil and culture of a foreign land. The English will not even learn to speak another language with the proper accent. They actually pride themselves on their incapacities. Have you ever heard Wall trying to speak French? *Exécrable !* "

" Yet he has taught Hardyal to speak excellent English."

" Yes," she sneered. " And boxing—and cricket ! "

Father Sebastien surveyed his sandalled feet. " This question of race . . . how then do you account for a woman like Laura Lyttleton ? "

Madame's hands clenched in her lap. " I am not obliged to account for her. I am not obliged to invite her into my house. I am in no way responsible for her existence . . . nor am I constrained to admit, even, that she does exist ! "

Her passion alarmed him. " But Madame, who ever suggested . . ."

" Jacques ! "

He stared. " Jacques ? "

Madame brought her feelings under control. " Yesterday there was a scene. I asked Jacques whom besides Hardyal, he would like to invite here for tea. I realise how little Amritpore has to offer in the way of amusement and companionship for the children. And you know . . . for his age . . . how serious he is, how discriminating. It is not natural in a child, this quality, this capacity for love. It has always troubled me, for my feelings are deeply maternal."

He nodded, and she continued rather breathlessly : " What was I to think when he looked into my eyes and asked for Mrs. Lyttleton ? "

Father Sebastien was silent, frowning in his turn. He would have liked to say that he understood Jacques, that he knew the boy as intimately as she knew him, but the truth was he did not know Jacques. Gisele yes, he knew Gisele ; knew her mind, her heart, even her fate. He was himself, in a sense, the instrument of that fate.   But on Jacques' account he suffered strange forebodings.

Madame went on : " You know that I have scolded him for running over there as he does behind my back. I have warned Hanif to see to it, but Hanif is lazy. I have an idea that he might even connive."

" Then you should dismiss Hanif."

" It would accomplish nothing. Jacques can turn any servant round his little finger."

Father Sebastien chewed his cigar. He would not, if he could prevent it, lose the son as he had lost the father. " You believe, then, that Jacques really cares for Mrs. Lyttleton ? "

She forced herself to say it : " Yes."

" It would be fatal for him to come under her influence ! "

" As his father did," murmured Madame St. Remy with stinging bitterness. Presently she said in a calmer voice : " In a little while Hardyal will be gone and Jacques will feel deserted. Though he does not confide in me, though he tries to exclude me from his thoughts, I can read them. But what is one to do ? Children are so unpredictable."

The priest tossed his cigar into the garden. " Perhaps it would be better, then, if we were to do what I have often suggested—send him to France for his education."

She made a small, despairing gesture. " Ah, not yet ! When he is older . . . when I have taught myself to bear the thought of parting from him ! "

Father Sebastien started to say something, but he was interrupted by the appearance of Boodrie. " Madame ! Will you please come to assist me in taking Jacques' photo ? I have tried and tried. He will not stand still. He will not do one single thing which I ask. He falls down. He crosses his eyes. He makes indecent motions. He laughs. Hanif laughs. Gisele laughs. Junab Ali comes all the way from the cookhouse to laugh. They all laugh. Ah, Madame ! Father ! "

Madame rose, and she and the priest followed the demoralised half-caste into the house.

3

THE GUESTS assembled on a veranda which faced the big pipal tree in the centre of the lawn. They sat in cane chairs and sipped tea and nibbled sandwiches and cake. Madame had taught her Mohammedan cook something of the art of making French pastry, but how he did it in an unventilated kitchen over a reeking charcoal stove in a black hole of an oven remained a mystery bordering on the miraculous.

Every one talked in English, but the voices of the St. Remys were distinguished by a quirk of accent which lent their English and even their Hindustani a separate character. Father Sebastien sat at Madame's right and was waited upon by Gisele and Hanif. Mr. Wall the Engineer sprawled in his chair ; slight, sandy, genial, always at ease, always like most Englishmen taking up as much room as he possibly could. Madame St. Remy's ill-concealed antagonism amused him. He had never brought himself to like her, but he was fond of her children. Their beauty had a curious effect upon him : it touched and moved him as few things had ever touched or moved him in his life.

Doctor Brown and his wife were kind and prosaic, washed out after five summers on the Plains. Their children were in England, and something wistful crept in and out of Mrs. Brown's eyes as she looked at Gisele or Jacques. At other times her gaze rested wonderingly upon their mother. A remarkable woman, reflected Mrs. Brown, without envy. Indigo was planted in March and harvested in June when the heat was at its worst. She had seen Madame under an enormous mushroom of a solar topi, supervising the carting of the green crop by bullock cart to the factory ; she knew that Madame spent hours in the blanching heat, that she left very little to the discretion of her foreman or her coolies. When the drying and pressing of the dye was finished she rushed to the hills for a brief respite, but in August she was back for the second crop. How did she manage it without breaking down ? Doctor Brown thought he had the answer. " Ambition, my dear —ambition ! "

The Railway Inspector's two little girls had arrived,

escorted by a tyrannical servant ; they now sat huddled together, munching or retreating into a trance when they were spoken to. Jacques attended to them with a stiff, drilled politeness, but he felt sick at heart. Hardyal had not come. What could have happened ? Perhaps it was just that he had misunderstood the time, perhaps even the date. But that was not like Hardyal. At any rate he should have sent word, declared Madame, and to this every one agreed.

"Perhaps the little devil ran off to the bazaar," suggested Wall.

"Hardyal's father," said Madame, "does not permit him to frequent the bazaars. The family is exceedingly superior."

Gisele stared at Aubrey Wall. Whenever he spoke she made a tiny, involuntary movement, almost a start. There was nothing particularly arresting about him, yet she could never be indifferent to his presence. Perhaps she sensed the effect of her own presence on him. She thought of his unfailing sweetness to herself and to Jacques, and how once, last year, he had kissed her. It was at Christmas time and she had not been able to get the incident out of her mind.

Hanif, demure in his finery, handed round plates of pastry and pink toffee. In passing through Madame's dressing-room on his way to the veranda he'd paused long enough to anoint himself with her Eau de Cologne.

One of the Railway Inspector's little girls suddenly shrilled :

"There was an accident to-day at the junction. My father said."

Jacques revived momentarily. "What sort of accident ? "

"An awful accident. A woman threw herself under the train and it cut her up into mince. My father said."

"Mince ? " echoed Gisele.

"Potted meat, don't you know," said Wall. Madame frowned and the little girl retreated into another trance.

Hanif passed the sandwiches and the petits-fours and the Napoleons. He passed cigars to the men. A trivial and well-bred hum set up around them. Evening sank towards the garden, sifting the glare of the sky, and to take his mind off Hardyal Jacques began to think about his presents. They had, on the whole, been disappointing, except for the beautiful little riding crop which Mr. Wall had given him. Even while Madame thanked him she was annoyed that she had not thought of this herself, for it was impossible to miss Jacques' dazzled smile.

Gisele looked up suddenly. " Here is Hardyal."

They watched a phaeton drawn by a bay horse come down the drive, Hardyal's green-coated coachman riding high. Relief surged through Jacques as the phaeton stopped and Hardyal alighted. He was, perhaps, six months older than Jacques, a little stronger and taller. Like the others he'd assumed an especial finery for the occasion, and now he came towards them in his white dhoti and gold-bordered shirt, an embroidered cap on his head, and crimson slippers on his feet. Behind him walked a servant carrying a flat basket filled with fruit and flowers, globes of sugar spun on a thread, little boxes of white Persian grapes nestling in cotton wool, and a dish filled with Jacques' favourite sweets, the sugar-coated *gulab jamuns* about which he sometimes dreamed.

All whiteness and brownness and lightness and brightness, Hardyal approached and Jacques went to meet him. Side by side they walked back to the veranda, and Hardyal paused to discard his shoes before the lowest step. He was perfectly poised as he salaamed the company with both hands, and Madame St. Remy thought, with regret : What a pity he is not a Christian ! But Aubrey Wall reflected complacently : How well the English training stands out !

4

THEY PLAYED games until it got dark and the mosquitoes began to bite, then—gorged and exhausted—the party broke up and Father Sebastien's pony was brought round. He tucked his brown skirts round his waist and trotted massively away between the shisham trees, his groom loping barefoot after him, brandishing a fly whisk.

When they had gone—all except Hardyal—Madame took Gisele's hand and retired to the house. For the next hour Gisele would sit beside her mother's couch, patting Madame's forehead with Eau de Cologne and reading aloud in French.

Jacques turned to Hardyal. " Let's go to the mango grove."

They walked down the garden as the stars exploded along the length and breadth of the sky. It was dark under the trees ; bats flitted everywhere, the gloom was sweet with the scent of flowers. The boys came out at the end of the grove and sat down on a crumbling brick wall. Before them the plain lay dim in the vanishing light. To their left were the sheds, the huts, and the chimneys and vats of the factory. Some of the powdered blue carried by wind or on human feet lay in the dust beside them ; it was in the sky above them, too—the vast indigo sky which sloped towards the farthest limit of the plain. Fires glittered among the distant buildings, figures passed and repassed before the flames. They heard voices, a smell of the evening meal reached them with the scent of smoke which, as they watched it, ascended in a fine web between plain and sky.

" Why were you so late ? " asked Jacques. He spoke Hindustani as a relief from the precise English which he'd used all afternoon.

" I stopped to see Mrs. Lyttleton, and she delayed me."

" Oh."

" She asked for you, she sent you her love. Shall we go there for a little while this evening ? "

Jacques stared at the distant fires, knowing that each warmed and fed a small human clot. He felt, in all his pores, the still, warm, sensuous night, and out of it there emerged suddenly the face of Mrs. Lyttleton with that special look which was, he knew, for him alone.

He said thickly : " I can't go there this evening."

" But why not ? "

" I don't know . . . yes, I do know." He ducked as a tiny bat flitted past his head. " Maman doesn't want me to go to Mrs. Lyttleton's. There was a scene yesterday. I promised that I would not see her to-day, though I said nothing about other days."

"Mrs. Lyttleton made lemonade with wine in it. We were to drink your health."

"There is no use to speak of it."

"No use?"

"Not to-day." He plucked restlessly at the breast of his new suit. The plain darkened as the sky deepened in colour and each star spread its fire. Jacques longed to confide in Hardyal, to ask him questions, but loyalty to his mother came between them now as it had in the past. They sat, each wondering about the other's thoughts; then the mosquitoes set upon them and they rose. "Will you ride to-morrow?" asked Jacques. He felt the great day slipping into oblivion, and he hated to let it go.

"To-morrow I must spend with my grandmother."

"Oh." Blankness.

"But I could ride the day after to-morrow."

Jacques' spirit lifted. "Early, then—before breakfast. Before anybody is awake."

The thought exhilarated them. They left the grove and came out into the lighter air of the garden. Lights were shining in the house, and Hardyal's coachman was waiting.

"Good-night, Jacques!"

"Good-night. . . ."

5

NEXT DAY a light shower drifted across the plain and laid the dust for an hour. Aubrey Wall, riding home from an inspection of the new government canal, turned in through the gateless pillars of Mrs. Lyttleton's compound and trotted up a grass-grown drive between flower-beds turned to jungle. In Amritpore allusions to Mrs. Lyttleton usually centred on one of the three adjectives: Extraordinary, Eccentric, Impossible. They might with equal justice have applied them to her house, a huge sandstone affair which she had acquired for a song and a touch of blackmail from its original owner, a maharaja deposed by the English more than forty years ago. General Lyttleton had supplemented the torture chamber and the harem with bathrooms, gun-rooms, pantries and an aviary. When he died, his widow buried him near the loquat tree in the north-west corner, beside his infant daughter and his three favourite dogs.

As Wall dismounted under the porte-cochère a slovenly servant appeared and led away his horse. He went up the sandstone steps into a veranda crammed with furniture in varing stages of dilapidation. From the walls an assortment of stuffed heads stared down at him ; oakum and cotton wool oozed from their seams, here and there a glass eye drooped from its socket, little gray lizards played among the antlers.

As Wall came up the steps an Indian in European clothes rose from one of the crumbling settees. "Oh, hallo, Wall ! "

"Ganpat Rai, how are you ? "

Wall sat down and stared at the transmogrified menagerie. "Lord ! "

Ganpat Rai the barrister smiled. "Cheer up ! Yesterday when the water buffalo fell down and burst, we discovered a nest of scorpions."

Mrs. Lyttleton appeared and greeted her visitors. "How kind of you to come ! Has that lazy swine offered you anything to drink ? " Without waiting for an answer she lifted her voice piercingly : "Jalal ! "

The men had risen, and waited until she was seated. She looked at the barrister. "Well, what luck ? "

There was an expression of restrained triumph on his dark, intelligent face. "I won my case."

"Ah, congratulations. But I never doubted that you would." She turned to Wall. "And what have you been doing ? "

"Sweating as usual. They mixed *kankar* with the cement and an entire sector had to come down."

"What did you do ? "

"I told the contractor he could go to hell, I fined my headman, and gave his deputy a damned good hiding."

She frowned. "Aren't you rather free with your hidings, Aubrey ? "

"Well, it works, it works." He stretched his legs. "Since then I've dreamed of the long, cold brandy-peg which awaited me here ! "

"Jalal!" screamed Mrs. Lyttleton again. "Jalal!"

He appeared, dirty, red-eyed, with a slightly demented look about him.

"Brandy," said Mrs. Lyttleton. "In the cut-glass decanter on the sideboard. And water. And the cigarettes which are beside my bed. And hasten lest death overtake you suddenly!"

She sat back with a sigh. "Opium. I'm sure of it. You can see it in his eyes, but what can I do?"

"Kick him out," suggested Wall lightly.

"His grandfather served my father. How could I kick him out?"

"You are a fearful sentimentalist."

Ganpat Rai shook his head. "No, it is just that her heart is golden."

"Thank you, Ganpat Rai!" Mrs. Lyttleton laughed. "I've often wished it were—then I might live for ever."

Mrs. Lyttleton had lived in India most of her life. Now, at seventy, she was shrunken and brittle, the blood had thinned in her veins but it had not soured. Her once bright hair was sparse and white, pinned to her head by a tortoise-shell comb set with rubies. No one remembered, now, whether she had ever possessed beauty, but she gave that impression and they took it for granted. Because she had never fought India, India had preserved her from much of the bitterness of exile and the contradictions of the usurper. Essentially feminine, she had not ruined her complexion or her system by exaggerated exercise and unnecessary exposure to a ferocious climate. Aristocratic, it had never occurred to her that she had anything to lose by adapting herself to a way of life scorned and feared by her compatriots. Now in her old age she felt more comfortable in native dress, and kept better health by eating native food, and she was less lonely because she could speak their language as well as she spoke her own. No wonder that in Amritpore there were people who considered her eccentric, extraordinary, and, by their standards, impossible. She had been altogether too high-spirited to escape slander, but she was fond of remarking that whereas in her youth she might have resented the tales which were told about her, now that she was old she rather enjoyed them. She would, herself, have been the last to deny that she had always liked men and that she preferred warriors to all others. And if beauty had vanished, her spirits died hard. She missed people, she missed the excitement of days when Amritpore was a garrison and the sentry-boxes at the fort housed soldiers instead of bats. She could, of course, have returned to England, but the prospect of eking out her old age on an army pension in Norwood or Chelsea was not to be thought of. India was in her bones, and her bones would remain in India to sweeten, a little, some corner of its tortured soil.

Ganpat Rai had known her for twenty years. She was the only white woman with whom he could feel wholly at ease, although there were occasions when her directness disconcerted him. He had spent some years in England and greatly admired the English ; he was eager that his son Hardyal grow up as nearly like an Englishman as possible, but he was slow to realise that the English are a race of contradictory elements, profoundly, even tragically, paradoxical. Ganpat Rai sometimes found it difficult to believe that Mrs. Lyttleton and Aubrey Wall should belong to the same *jat*. Wall himself, though long since won over to a grudging admiration, never quite forgave Mrs. Lyttleton her native ways, nor could he understand that—in her own way—she remained as true to the paradox as he did in his.

Age and climate had tired her bodily, and she cared little now for her garden or for her rambling, magnificent rooms through whose lonely reaches she wandered by herself, tinkling and twinkling in her priceless jewels at all hours, attended by a retinue of dogs and cats, tame squirrels, and the birds which flew loose through the house. In addition to her pension she enjoyed the revenue of several villages which bordered the estates of Madame St. Remy, and which Madame would have liked to own if Mrs. Lyttleton had not been so perverse about selling. Mrs. Lyttleton's villagers trespassed on the indigo fields ; they stole Madame's mangoes and threw their dead grandmothers into her wells to save funeral expenses. Mrs. Lyttleton, when she heard of these outrages, rolled her eyes piously and derived a secret zest from the situation.

Jalal appeared with a tray and Wall sighed with pleasure.

"I must admit that this is more to my taste than yesterday afternoon."

"What about yesterday afternoon?" She refused the brandy but selected one of her Egyptian cigarettes.

"I went to Jacques St. Remy's birthday party." He glanced at her quizzically. "Why were you not there?"

"I was not invited." She smiled. "Madame honours me with her mistrust!"

They laughed, and Ganpat Rai said: "But that Jacques . . . he is charming."

"Both children are charming. I feel sorry for them." She hesitated, frowning. "One cannot help wondering what will become of them."

"Madame is rich, her children are clever and beautiful. Why wonder?"

Mrs. Lyttleton shrugged. "You have no imagination."

Ganpat Rai waited tactfully for the conversation to proceed. He never felt quite as much at ease in Wall's presence as he did in Mrs. Lyttleton's. Observed together, the English struck sparks from each other's armour; their wit, which lacked his conception of delicacy, sometimes bothered him, though for this he blamed himself, his own ignorance and slowness of understanding. With Hardyal it would be different. Hardyal would grow up among them, he would learn to know them in their own country. Even now they were impressed by the boy's manners, his quickness and intelligence.

Mrs. Lyttleton said abruptly: "Poor little Jacques!"

"Oh, I don't know!" Had she said "Poor little Gisele" Wall might have aspired to know more. Mrs. Lyttleton's face had a gentle, bemused look. "I miss him. But perhaps when Hardyal has gone, Jacques will come to see me more often."

Wall laughed. "Do you know, I believe you are in love with him!"

"I have never tried to conceal it."

"No wonder Madame St. Remy . . ."

Mrs. Lyttleton studied the diamonds on her hands. "It is a case of history repeating itself, isn't it? Madame has never abandoned her suspicion that I might at one time or another have tried to seduce her husband."

" Well," said Aubrey Wall slyly, " nor have we ! ' "

Mrs. Lyttleton laughed, her clear blue eye meeting his. " Auguste St. Remy was twenty years younger than I."

" And like the rest of us he liked to come here and talk and listen, in the long afternoons during the rains." The barrister smiled at her. " You are always gay, always kind. With you we are free to speak our hearts. It is natural that women should be jealous of you."

Wall was a little put out by this fervour and by the flush which it brought to Mrs. Lyttleton's unregenerate cheek. A compliment could make her look a dozen years younger.

" Madame," said Mrs. Lyttleton slowly, " is really a fool. Imagine wanting to bury one's only daughter in a convent ! "

Wall put down his glass. " I don't think she meditates doing that, does she ? "

" I am sure of it. After all, it would solve the problem of Gisele, would it not ? Short of putting her in purdah with Ganpat Rai's ladies."

The barrister laughed. " Purdah solves no problems, I assure you. It is itself a problem."

. Wall was frowning. " I don't believe . . ."

" I do. I've seen it coming. Gisele's beauty, Gisele's youth . . . here in India . . . how would you expect a woman like Madame to cope with the situations which—in Gisele's case—are almost bound to arise ? "

Wall persisted obstinately : " What situations, for instance ? "

" Adolescence, love, marriage—all the rest of it."

" But good Lord ! Why is Gisele's case unique ? I don't see it."

" Given her mother's temperament—given her own, and her quite extraordinary beauty, you still don't see it ? "

" Ah," said Ganpat Rai, nodding. " Were she one of us she would already be married, her life—her future, secured." When the others remained silent he added rather shyly : " With us, beauty is never a problem. It is an asset, a treasure."

"Yes," agreed Mrs. Lyttleton, rather sombrely. "There are many things in which you are wiser than we." She turned suddenly to Wall.

"I wish you would use your influence to have Jacques sent to England with Hardyal."

"My dear lady, I have no influence with Madame."

"With Father Sebastien, perhaps?"

"Hardly!"

She made a gesture of despair. "They'll send him away to be educated among all those twittering priests, I know!" For a second or two she brooded unhappily. "I believe in secular education. After all, what is possible for a Brahmin should be possible for a Catholic."

"You must remember that I am not orthodox," replied the barrister. "And Catholicism is not an exclusive educational system as Brahminism is."

She brushed this aside with a glitter of diamonds. "What has all that mumbo jumbo to do with governing India?"

"Perhaps everything," said Ganpat Rai softly. It was during these conversations that pride in his own achievement, his own liberation, rose to comfort him. Enlightened though he was, modern, a sceptic, he had his secret hours of doubt, even of terror. True, he had accepted the West with all its promise—but had the West accepted him? And he remembered other conversations, not as happy as this one—conversations with his friend and colleague Abdul Salim. "The English," he once said with bitterness, "belong to the category of men who leave welts on the flesh of history."

But Ganpat Rai believed that a lasting civilisation must come from the West, and that the East must go to meet it. Religion—Salim's own religion—was the great stumbling block, as it had always been. Three hundred years ago Akbar the great illiterate tried to solve the problem by welding Hinduism, Mohammedanism and Christianity into one. He concocted a new faith and died its only convert.

"Perhaps," said Ganpat Rai, hopefully, "perhaps Jacques and Hardyal will provide a solution."

"Perhaps," assented Mrs. Lyttleton. She looked at

Wall. "But in the meantime they will go away. You too will go away. India is the scene of farewells."

He shrugged. "Of course, one goes home."

There was a brief silence, then she threw off her gloom and turned gaily to the barrister. "Now do tell us about the case of Naiko versus Empress."

6

JACQUES AWOKE in the cocoon pallor of his mosquito net and saw the stars framed in the upper half of the Dutch doors. It was still night, but from the colour of the sky he guessed that it would soon be morning. He heard the jackals crying and remembered Hanif's interpretation of their refrain :

> Ek murra Hindu !
> Ka-hahn ?   Ka-hahn ?
> Ya-hahn, ya-hahn, ya-hahn !

> One dead Hindu !
> Where ?   Where ?
> Here, here, here !

Jacques pictured the gaunt shapes skulking outside sleeping villages or nosing among the funeral pyres beside the river. Mr. Wall and Doctor Brown had promised to take him on a jackal hunt. This meant riding them down with hog spears and a pack of dogs. Perhaps Hardyal would come, though he was not very fond of killing things.

Jacques thought of Hardyal : then, more wide awake, he thought of Father Sebastien, who had talked to him for a long time after lessons yesterday. Queer, that all he should be able to remember now was the sound of Father Sebastien's voice, and nothing else. He clasped his hands behind his head and stared into the gloom of the mosquito net ; he liked sleeping in a net, which made him feel mysterious, like a little spider. It brought him the same sense of inscrutability which he'd attained by accident a year ago when he found that he was never, actually, obliged to

answer questions. At that time his mother had taxed him
with some minor wrong-doing : confused, he engaged in a
private summing up of facts and circumstances, but mis-
reading his silence, she had broken into expostulations and
accusations. Jacques' silence held, it took root, it grew.
He found himself contemplating it with a sort of impersonal
wonder. Madame went on and on, mystified, aware with
a little inward shock of fright that he had discovered a
means of eluding her.

The same thing happened yesterday with the priest.
Jacques could not remember the question which had
brought on his own sudden refusal—for that was what it
amounted to, a deliberate refusal to commit himself. The
question was not important, it was no more than one of
those small prying remarks to which Father Sebastien was
sometimes given. He'd repeated it in the form of a query ;
then, arrested by the new quality in Jacques, made the
question direct.

The boy stood before him, silent, listening to an inward
pæan : " Even if they were to light a fire on my stomach I
wouldn't answer ! "

Jacques knew that they would come back to it ; not his
weakness but his strength would set his fate in motion,
forcing those who controlled it to take steps. In the meantime Father Sebastien's voice continued in the distance ;
it went on and on like the hum of a mosquito, and Jacques'
eyes closed. When he opened them again he knew that it
was time for him to get up.

Dawn was just emerging and a ribbon of colour rested
on the garden's edge as he hurried across the compound to
the stables. A cock crowed ; his dogs barked and were
answered by a pi-dog in the distance, but it was still another
hour or two before a general rousing.

Jacques went into the stable and led his horse into the
open ; it whinnied and laid back its ears as he slid the
bridle over its head and eased the bit between its soft lips.
Then Hardyal appeared, cantering along the turf which
edged the drive. He had exchanged his gold and muslin,
his crimson slippers, for English boots and breeches and a
solar topi. They greeted each other, then turned to see a
figure emerge from the house. It was Gisele, also dressed

for riding. She came up, pale, her eyes still heavy with
sleep. " I heard you. I'm coming, too."

Her hair was braided and she carried the skirt of her
habit over one arm. " Will you saddle the mare, Jacques?
I'll hold Robin."

A change fell on the boys' spirits ; neither liked Gisele,
but Jacques felt sorry for her. Hardyal had dismounted,
and between them he and Jacques led Gisele's half-breed
Arab from its stall and saddled and bridled it. The three
animals greeted each other in an electrifying whinny, and
from the servants' quarters burst a medley of groans and
coughings. Hardyal held the mare while Jacques helped
his sister to mount. She flew upward like a bird, her spine
resilient to the mare's lightning turn. Then all three trotted
across the compound through a break in the cactus and
lantana bushes. The plain lay in sallow light and a smell of
dew rose from it as the horses sprang forward, a night's
energy stored in their marrow.

They rode without speaking until the house faded into
the trees behind them. Now there was nothing but the
unending plain, the gallows-structure of wells and darkness
of mango groves. They passed a village swathed in smoke ;
there were other villages hidden in contours of the earth,
yet the plain seemed empty of life except for a quail which
flew under the horses' feet, and a jackal which stole away
among the shadows.

Gisele pulled ahead, her mare stiffening into a canter,
and the boys followed, one on each side. They exchanged
brief smiles, sheer physical exhilaration drawing all three
into a simple comradeship. The Fort, their favourite objec-
tive, lay five miles away in a bend of the Gogra River.
They swept three abreast over sown fields, recklessly aware
that they should not. The earth flew behind them, and
with a sudden tremendous clatter two peafowl rose and
clambered into the air, the cock's tail streaming fire.

In a little while they were riding knee to knee and the
first ray of light struck their faces and glittered on the chains
and buckles of their harness ; it brought forth, unaccount-
ably, shivering half-clad figures of myth and testament.
White bullocks swished their tails beside a well, a naked
child salaamed, crying " Maharaj ! "

Women repairing the little canals which fed the fields rested their bangled arms and smiled, the younger ones instinctively drawing their veils over their eyes. The children rode on and their passage left a dark ripple in the acres sown and unsown. More than a hundred years ago the peasant folk had watched these children's ancestors ride across the plain to give battle at the Fort. Their own fathers had taken part in the ceaseless struggles for the plain and the ghat and the nullah and the prince's house among the trees. Portuguese and Dutch, Danish and French and English—and before these, stalwart hordes from the North-West, and the élite from everywhere, all converging upon the rich and inviting centre. For gold or for jewels, for that fertile strip or for this strategic temple, for shittim wood or for cotton to bind up wounds ; for silk, for pepper, for jute and tobacco, and for the blue dye of sailors' livery. It had always happened ; it would go on happening though those about to die exhorted otherwise, and for these at any rate it was the last time.

The Fort was built of unbaked brick crumbling everywhere but still impressive above its shallow moat. The children rode across a hollow-sounding bridge under the portcullis, into a quadrangle broken into doorless rooms and quarters whose original use was lost to their ghost-believing eyes. The sun had risen, and under it the Fort lay silent and deserted. Here in the middle of the last century Mahrattas under their French officers had fought and lost to the English. The children had long since explored every cranny for old bullets and bloodstains, but all that remained to them now were scorpions and the sloughed off skins of snakes.

They hitched their horses to a thorn tree and wandered across the courtyard to a ruined stair which led to a favourite sentry-box. Below them lay the moat, green and formal as a park, under stunted acacias where a child was grazing a flock of goats whose bleating mingled with the incessant whistle of green pigeons.

Gisele said : " I'm going to see if I can find a snakeskin. I want one with the eye-holes complete."

" Look out you don't find one with the fangs all complete, too," Hardyal warned her jokingly.

He always found it difficult to joke with this girl, whose coldness chilled him. Her beauty, her sex were, for him, mysterious and remote. The boys sat on a crumbling balustrade beside the sentry-box and watched her walk away. At fifteen she was almost a woman, and though neither mentioned it they were glad when she left them. They removed their hats and the breeze stirred their hair.

Jacques said suddenly : " Next year we shall come here for my birthday."

Hardyal's eyes had a heavy look. " Next year ! " He was in an odd mood. " Do you remember the day we watched a cobra stalk a dove down there in the moat ? "

" Hanif killed it with a stone."

" And the year when Father took us to see the Magh Mela at Allahabad ? "

" Yes," said Jacques, looking at him. Hardyal would not meet his eyes, but went on in the same strange voice : " You wanted to bathe in the Jumna with all the others but Hanif wouldn't let you. I remember . . ." He broke off, frowning. " I've been remembering and remembering . . . sometimes it seems as if there was nothing that I had forgotten . . . nothing." Jacques waited, troubled by his friend's manner.

" I remember an evening when we went to Mrs. Lyttleton's and she told us about the Mutiny and how on certain days, in broad daylight, guns are heard here in the Fort. I remember so much . . . so much ! "

Jacques watched Gisele, who was walking along the pediment below them. She had found her snakeskin and wore it draped about her shoulders ; he heard her singing under her breath, and as she passed below them she glanced up. " Let's ride out to the river. I'll wait for you near the horses."

Jacques bent to examine a small funnel-shaped contrivance in the dust beside him. It was the circumference of a man's thumb and of finest sand. At its steeple-sloping bottom something minute and alive lay hidden. He captured an ant and rolled it down into the funnel ; at once there followed a microscopic upheaval as a pair of tiny fangs appeared, and the lion-ant seized the bait and snuggled down with it out of sight.

When Jacques looked up he saw that Hardyal's eyes were full of tears.

" What ? " he whispered. " What is it, Hardyal ? "

" I must tell you. . . . Father said I should not, because he promised Madame . . ."

Jacques sat motionless, and Hardyal went on in a thick voice : " You know that I was supposed to go to England soon . . . but I didn't know . . . I didn't even think, how soon. Now I know. It is to be in a week. I shall spend this summer with Mr. Wall's people in Sussex, then I shall go to school. In a week . . . in a few days."

Jacques captured another victim and fed it to the lion-ant.

Suddenly Hardyal broke down. " Hum nahi jana mungtha ! "

I shall remember this, thought Jacques. I shall forget nothing, nothing, least of all that cry : I do not want to go ! And suddenly everything that was familiar to him rushed away and stood at a distance. Hardyal was his earliest friend ; he had slept in Hardyal's house, they had talked and walked and ridden together, and although he'd been told often enough that the day would come when Hardyal must go away, Jacques had never quite believed it. " I remember so much," Hardyal had said, ". . . I remember so much ! " Jacques, too, remembered, for in a flash memory had become more important than the future, more important than the present. He thought of the summer when they had not gone to the Hills as usual, and the loo had blown red and scorching across the plains, while he and Hardyal played chess in the drawing-room and shouted to the punkah coolie to pull harder on the great frilled punkah over their heads ; he remembered the lazy swims in Hardyal's swimming pool among shoals of startled goldfish, and Krishna, Hardyal's servant, bringing them a dish of ripe figs as they emerged cool and dripping into the warm air. He would remember a summer when a break came in the rains and millions of tiny red velvet spiders appeared from nowhere, and all the frogs in creation chanted together : Port, Port, Port ! White Wine, White Wine, White Wine ! Sherry, Sherry, Sherry ! Seasons would come and go but one's friends stayed beside one for ever !

Gisele's voice reached them from the courtyard. " It's getting hot. We better start home."

As they rose, Hardyal whispered : " Do not speak of this."

Gisele was waiting for them beside the horses. Jacques looked at her questioningly. " What's the matter ? We've only just come."

" My head aches."

She looked white, and as Hardyal held the stirrup for her he felt her blue flowerlike glance on his face ; her lithe weight rested for a second on his shoulder, but the warmth which this contact kindled in him died at once. He dared not weep before her, he dared not touch her, nor dared he respond when she touched him, for the world which was soon to come between Jacques and himself had always stood between himself and Gisele.

They rode out into the bright sun and left the Fort to its cobras and its ghosts.

7

MADAME ST. REMY, on her way to the factory, paused at her son's door. Jacques was bending over his collection of butterflies and for a moment she stood quietly watching his absorbed face. There were occasions when his remoteness frightened her and she suffered the jealous pang of an intruder. " Jacques ? "

He rose and faced her. " I'm going to the factory. Would you like to come with me ? "

" I have my geography lesson, Maman."

She came and put her arm round him, the scent of her clothes touched his face. When she was gentle as she was now, Jacques was flooded with a passionate love. He was not proof against tenderness, but the storm was always interior—he contained it and remained still.

" Did you have a pleasant ride this morning with Gisele and Hardyal ? "

He murmured something, and she put her hand under his chin, lifting his face. " What is it, Jacques ? "

" Nothing."

" You looked as though you were going to say something."

When he stayed silent she asked: " What did you three talk about ? "

" Talk ? We didn't talk, much, about anything."

His eyes could look like the eyes of a young lion. Madame hesitated, then said lightly : " I had a note from Hardyal's father. He wants you to play tennis at his house to-morrow. You may go if you like."

" Thank you, Maman."

On her way to the door Madame paused to admire the butterflies in their cork-lined case. " Where did you get that big one in the centre ? "

" I caught it."

He could not bring himself to tell her that Mrs. Lyttleton had sent it to him by Hanif, but when she had gone away his mind pursued her, knowing how she must look sitting upright on the black leather seat of her carriage, her brown eyes concentrated on the eternal problems of dye, taxes, wages, revenue. He suffered a slight twinge of conscience : perhaps he should have gone with her to the factory. He knew that she liked to have him show an interest in the business, liked to have him ask questions and to appear excited when she spoke of the future when he would be old enough to help her. But Jacques hated the factory, he hated the smell of indigo, the steamy smell of the machines, the reek of coolies and attendants. He did not as yet fully understand his own aversion to all this, nor why he shrank from the tired look of the men and women who worked for his mother.

Madame St. Remy drove briskly over the short dusty distance to the factory, which stood in a large compound bordered by trees. On cool days she transacted much of her business under the shade of these trees, on an elevated structure called a chabutra. The process of hiring, of dismissing, paying off and making cash advances to her labourers sometimes consumed several days and invariably left her with a splitting headache. She might have spared herself by delegating authority to her factory foreman, but it was against her principles to trust subordinates. Madame knew that when her workmen were paid Mr. Boodrie exacted his commission—a percentage which bought or preserved his good will. After Boodrie loomed the figure of Ramdatta the moneylender, without whom no one could hope to survive, since there never was a wage which, of itself, did more than keep breath in one's body. Madame knew this moneylender well, and rather liked him. He was not really a villain—he was part of India, its fifth limb. Not for nothing do her gods and goddesses boast a plethora of arms and legs, for to endure at all one must sprout desperate tentacles.

Ramdatta was a big suave man who reminded Madame of Frenchmen she had known at home ; he was, in fact, thoroughly bourgeois. Orphaned at fourteen, penniless, he left his village and disappeared in the general direction of Bombay and its cotton mills. There among the gins and shuttles he worked as a sweetmeat vendor and somehow managed to save money. Naturally, inevitably, he slipped into the rôle of usurer, and when he was forty he came back to his native village and set up as moneylender, charging a seventy-five per cent interest. Gradually but by no means sluggishly he acquired his neighbours' fields and their flocks, even their homes. A gloss appeared on his skin, benevolent dimples at the corners of his full, childish lips. He cherished a profound admiration for Madame St. Remy's acumen and longed to lend her money, to install himself in her graces, for like all parvenues when a certain opulence has been reached, he now craved prestige. Madame was rich, she stood well with the local government ; his lands adjoined hers, and he permitted his miserable tenants to work for her during the sowing and harvesting of indigo. As for Madame, although she heard numerous stories to his discredit, she had always found him deferential and obliging.

Above the earth and the tops of the ripening crops, above the preoccupation of struggle and death, stood the Burra Mem ; beyond her hovered the carrion figure of the factory foreman, and beyond him again, the moneylender, and staunchly behind all three of them towered the invisible and all-powerful Sircar. No, there was nothing Madame St. Remy could do about that look in her labourers' eyes ; there was nothing that the moneylender could do about it, for he too had to live, and it is never enough just to live—a fact which he'd discovered for himself. There was nothing that Boodrie the foreman could do about it : he longed for a new and expensive camera. And the ryots and the coolies and the unschooled mechanics who were always putting Madame's machines out of order could do nothing about it either. There were too many of them, too many just like them. Unlike the land itself, which had reached a degree of exhaustion beyond which it could not go, the end for these people was the burning-ghat or the grave—and even to die involved expense. One's children took up the burden where one left off. There remained the Sircar and the Sircar did what it would here and there : it set up a dispensary, built a canal, staved off famine, fought cholera and made a stab or two at education. But its exponents were a handful in a territory of roughly one million seven hundred miles, among a population of three hundred million. The Sircar lifted its precise English voice in a huge unlettered silence ; it attempted in clumsy Christian fashion to impose incidental welfare on these miles and these millions, but when all was said and done the Sircar remained in India for reasons that were not very different from those of Ramdatta the moneylender himself. Madame St. Remy, too feminine to mark the illogicality of her own point of view, often remarked to the Father Sebastien that the Sircar was simply old John Company in metamorphosis . . . not entirely unrecognisable.

This morning a big table was set on the factory chabutra under the trees. Madame seated herself and one of the factory servants held a parasol over her head. Beside Madame stood Mr. Boodrie, arranging and rearranging ledgers, dispatch cases, fingering big braided sacks filled with coins. Nearby—relaxed but watchful—lounged two stalwart Sikhs, the factory policemen who wore Madame's livery.

Mr. Boodrie spilled the coins from their sacks and arranged them in symmetrical towers the length of the table. These towers varied in height, and behind the first row stood another—the lesser coin of annas and pice. The

B

eyes of every one except Madame flickered like bees over
this metal architecture. Brooding, speculative, their glances
computed the sum of rupees, annas, and pices in each tower,
but the total remained a cloudy dream which had little
relation to individual lives—wealth beyond computation,
beyond imagination.

They gathered, men, women and children, barefooted,
their clothing splashed with the olive and orange and the
final intense blue of indigo. They arranged themselves in
a semi-circle before Madame's table and there squatted,
coughing, murmuring, exchanging glances and small signals
of expectancy, complacence or despair. Some of the women
had brought their babies, and the spleeny stomachs of these
little creatures stood out brown and naked, their great eyes
opened like wet black flowers.

Madame St. Remy took her spectacles from their velvet
case and drew a ledger towards her ; Boodrie tilted his
dirty helmet back from his forehead, revealing his greasy
curls, and the people massed in the dust before him swayed
as though the wind had moved them.

Boodrie consulted his roster. " Mirban ! "

An elderly man rose and advanced towards the chabutra.
The foreman deftly sliced the top off one of the pyramids of
rupees and counted them into Mirban's hand. Mirban too
counted them, counted them with passionate attention as
though he might by sheer excess of hope multiply them into
a sum adequate for his limitless burden. Of the ten silver
coins which Boodrie handed him one would go back to
Boodrie, who had engineered the advance ; five would go
to Ramdatta to pay back a fleabite on the mortgage which
the moneylender held on his millet field ; the remaining
four rupees must somehow be spread over food for Mirban,
his wife, his mother, his two sons, and his bullocks.
And when the advance was used up Mirban must work
for a month for nothing, unless the foreman would
obtain a further advance, or unless Ramdatta would make
a further loan. In the meantime Mirban knotted his
money in a corner of his shawl and retired into the crowd
to brood.

" Adhira Bhai ! "

The name rose, fell, rose again. A slight scuffle ensued,

followed by a reassuring voice : " Go, go, child—no one
will hurt you."

" Adhira Bhai ! " cried Boodrie again, impatiently.

A little boy crept from the protective mass and one of
the Sikh policemen volunteered : " Adhira is ill. This is
her son."

Madame glanced at the child. " Come," she said gently.
" Can you be trusted to take your mother's money ? "

Dumb with terror, he stood before her.

" Hold up your head—the Burra Mem does not eat
children ! " cried the policeman encouragingly.

" What is your name, little one ? " inquired Madame.
He reminded her distantly of Jacques, and as her son's face
rose before her Madame picked up Adhira's share of rupees
and gave them to the child. " Don't be afraid. Take these
to your mother."

He gave her a single desperate glance, then took the
money and bolted back to the safety of the crowd.

A pock-marked Mohammedan wearing a cast-off English jacket rose and thrust himself towards the chabutra.
He began to talk in a high, excited voice, but Boodrie cut
him short. " Hakim Ali, you are dismissed. It is of no use
for you to keep coming back. Now go ! "

" My wages ! I am owed seven rupees eight annas in
arrears. . . ."

" You are not owed a single damnable cowrie. Go.
Depart ! "

Murder stood out in Hakim Ali's face, but before he
could take a step a lathi blow caught him behind the
shoulders. The Sikhs closed in and he was shoved and
hoisted across the compound and flung through the gates
into the road. The crowd watched passively. Two or three
laughed.

" Golam Hosain."

No one answered, no one came forward.

" Golam Hosain ! " repeated Boodrie. " Where is
Golam . . . ? "

" He is dead."

There was a brief silence. Then Boodrie stared at the
crowd.

" Dead ? "

" Dead."

Madame removed her glasses and wiped them on her handkerchief. Over her head in the branches of a nim tree a green pigeon whistled. One of the policemen turned aside and spat into the dust. He said in a sonorous voice : " Golam Hosain is dead. He died last night."

Boodrie reached across the table and removed an inch of silver coin from one of the pyramids, setting it aside.

" Kullu ! "

It would go on through the morning, through the afternoon, it would go on throughout the next day. Small lines would engrave themselves on Madame's features and her attention would waver, then from that reservoir which remained a mystery to the people who knew her best would spring a fresh resolution, a new strength, and the business would proceed unflaggingly, relentlessly. Boodrie might wilt in his stiff drill suit, Golam Hosain die of the consumption which had racked him for the past three months, but all the life in Madame would gather to burn with renewed vitality in her dark, expressive eyes.

She thought, now, about Jacques. Perhaps if he showed signs of missing Hardyal too much she would send him to the Hills earlier this year. But already he seemed stronger than he used to be ; like most Frenchmen he would mature early, unlike the hooligan English who clung so to their youth. When Madame thought of her son's future she saw the circumstances and surroundings as remaining unchanged, herself still young and in full possession, while round his head flowered all the blessings and all the banners.

" Behari Lal ! You are fined fourteen annas for permitting water to drip on a seed rack. Behari Lal ! "

8

When his mother had gone Jacques stood looking down at his butterflies and making unselfish resolutions. Then the bead curtains chimed in their arched doorways and Gisele came in. " Are you busy ? " His glance went at once to her bare feet. " You might step on a scorpion or get a splinter."

She went to his bed and sat down, drawing her feet under her. She said slowly : " The punkah coolie's baby is dying."

" Which punkah coolie ? "

" Kanhya. It's been sick and it's dying." Her voice trembled.

Jacques said : " Does Maman know ? "

" She says there isn't anything to be done about it now. It's too little and too sick. Jacques . . ." She broke off, staring at her hands, and Jacques hoped that she would not cry. Her crying always unnerved him. There was a strange quality to it, a grown-up quality.

" Jacques, it's terrible that anything so little should die unbaptised."

" Perhaps Father Sebastien . . ."

" He told me not to worry. He said that God's infinite mercy would take care of Kanhya's baby."

" Well, then."

" I know. But it won't nurse any more. It doesn't even cry. It just lies there panting. . . ."

He saw the tears fill her eyes. " It looks like a little dry twig, except that its heart . . . its heart . . ."

" Shall we send for Maman ? "

" No one can stop it dying now."

He was silent, thinking about Kanhya, the casteless Habura and his black wife. They were semi-nomadic, untrustworthy people, but Madame employed them out of pity. Gisele went on : " I've prayed and prayed, I've even walked about without shoes."

" Ah ! You shouldn't."

She stared at him with tear-filled eyes. " One must make an offering. I didn't see how God could refuse. Look ! " She thrust out a foot and he saw that there were spots of blood on the white skin. " It's an act of faith, but it isn't enough. I even kept myself awake all night, on purpose. And when I was dying to go to sleep I forced myself to get up and ride with you and Hardyal."

He stirred uneasily. " If you've done all that . . ."

She shook her head. " You could help if you wanted to."

" I'll pray," said Jacques. " Now, if you like."

" Would you do more than pray ? Would you do something really difficult ? " When he was silent she went on quickly : " Make an act of faith. Give something you love . . . something it would hurt you to give up. Perhaps if we both did, He'd hear us and take pity."

Jacques asked gently : " Well, what, for instance ? "

" Would you be willing to give up Mrs. Lyttleton ? "

" What do you mean ? "

" It would hurt you, wouldn't it, never to see her again ? But if by doing so you could persuade Our Lord to save Kanhya's baby ? "

" I'll give up something else."

" No, *that*. It would hurt you, it would be a true sacrifice. Please, Jacques ! "

His eyes were suddenly hard as beryls. " Is this . . . did Maman . . . ? "

But he saw from her expression that his suspicion was unjust. Now suddenly he hated Gisele, he hated this situation and everything behind it. They were always driving him into corners, making impossible demands on him. How different they were from Hardyal, from Mrs. Lyttleton, who asked nothing, who gave so much . . . whose mere existence was in the nature of a gift !

Gisele was watching him. " I see. Then tell me this : Do you adore Him, as you should ? Would you die for Him, as He died for us ? "

Jacques stayed silent, staring at the floor.

" You don't," said Gisele. " You wouldn't."

He wanted to speak, to protest, but his will remained quiescent as he listened to the sound of her voice falling away inside him.

" You've always loved other things too much," said Gisele. " You love Mrs. Lyttleton and Hardyal and Maman. You love your horse Robin. You loved that baby bat you once had, that the spiders ate. You love anything, everything—but you do not love Him."

Jacques knew that he should answer this, but her words bore his denial downward into a void.

" You know that if Kanhya's baby dies, it will be your fault in a way. At least I've done everything . . . everything. But you don't care. You won't lift a finger even for a little sick helpless baby."

He burst out at that : " I'm not God ! "

She went on inexorably : " You leave Him out on purpose for fear that He may interfere with what you want to do. And every time you take Communion you commit a sacrilege."

Revulsion swept through Jacques. He got up and went to the door, seeing the garden lie there colourless under tides of sun. Presently he heard Gisele get up and leave the room ; he heard the bead curtains clash softly behind her and knew that she was going away to cry. Left alone he felt a slight prickle on his skin. On Sunday it would be his turn to be one of the servers for Father Sebastien : he would carry the cruet of wine and water and ring the bell at the Elevation. But if it were sacrilegious to accept Communion without belief, was it not proof of belief to reject Communion for fear of sacrilege ? Besides, he did believe . . . he did ! It was only when Gisele came to him with her accusations that he felt doubt and confusion rise up within him.

He sat down and tried to go on with his geography lesson.

9

THAT NIGHT Kanhya's baby died, and in the morning Gisele carried the little body into the house and dressed it in her old doll's clothes and laid it in a white cardboard box. She had watched while the parents dug a hole under a tamarind tree at the edge of the compound. " Deeper," she exhorted them, thinking of the jackals. " Deeper, deeper ! " Madame had made her *orgeat* and bathed her forehead in cologne and put her to bed, but Jacques was unable to escape the sound of Gisele's weeping, nor could he forget the look she's given him when she came into the house with the tiny body clasped against her breast.

It was a relief when Ganpat Rai's carriage came to fetch him and they drove away, Hanif perched aloft beside the driver, and Jacques reclining on the hot leather seat. Hanif, decked out to kill in a sapphire waistcoat, glanced over his shoulder. " Do we stop at the bazaar for sweets ? "

" First we stop at Mrs. Lyttleton's." Jacques stiffened

as he spoke, anticipating an argument though he knew he could always cow Hanif by a display of autocratic fury. The coachman, however, interposed by informing them that Mrs. Lyttleton would be at Ganpat Rai's house this afternoon.

Jacques sat back, suffused with happiness. For him these moods of anticipation were the purest luxury ; no matter that reality seldom measured up to hope, his imagination was kindled, and the thought of Hardyal's departure, remembrance of Gisele, his own guilty doubts—all lost their importance and their torment. He knew well enough that they would return, at any rate, but this afternoon was his own.

To reach the Hindu barrister's house one drove through the bazaar, and before that one drove along a white road under dusty nim and mango trees. One skirted the sun-baked Maidan where native youths were playing cricket, and glimpsed the English club set among palms and green lawns. One passed Mrs. Lyttleton's house, its sandstone minarets towering above the tangled garden which used to be the boast of Amritpore. Then one saw the Indian houses, and these had gardens also, though they were different from those of Madame St. Remy and Mr. Wall and the Browns —different even from Mrs. Lyttleton's, where the jungle failed to obscure an original formality. The Indian gardens suffered from a sort of architectural miscegenation ; they were broken into cubes and lozenges, the flower-beds set out in coleus and marigolds, porte cochères muffled in bougainvillea or the even uglier purple railway creeper. But after this came the bazaar, which Jacques loved. He loved its aromatic smells, its swarms of yellow wasps, its starved dogs, its privileged bull, and its insolent monkeys which slipped down the trees and helped themselves to sweets and parched gram under the owner's nose. He loved the turgid vitality which survived filth and disease and starvation. Here, everything that lived was sacred. The boy's innocence was proof against these contradictions : so little was ever concealed, it would have been strange indeed that he should have been called upon to marvel or to protest. When a beggar, half blind and covered with sores, held up supplication hands, Jacques looked away not because he was horrified but because he knew that this was one of a million such beggars. Once when he and Hardyal had driven through the bazaar they bought peanuts and bread to feed the infant monkeys whose tender sunlit ears caught their fancy while, near-by, the beggars and the dogs looked on.

The coachman halted the carriage beside a sweetmeat stall and Hanif leaped down to buy a big cone-shaped leaf filled with syrupy stickiness. They usually paused at this vendor's, for motives which were not always connected with the purchase of jelabies or gulab jamuns. An upstairs window was ajar and from behind the shutter feminine voices hailed Hanif. Chaff of a dubious nature flew back and forth, and the coachman's ears twitched. Jacques listened ; although his education on these lines pursued a dim and reluctant course, not all the jokes were over his head. Presently he looked up and cried : " Do not be misled by his beauty—he is knock-kneed ! "

Laughter rained down and there was a great tinkling of silver and glass : Jacques knew that he was being keenly scrutinised from behind the shutters.

" Proceed ! " cried Hanif, springing up beside the driver. " If the Memsahib were to learn of this it would be as much as my life is worth."

" Rather late in the day for the awakening of your conscience," said the coachman, flourishing his whip. Hanif burst into song as they left the bazaar behind them and turned down a road which wound towards the river and Ganpat Rai's house. Parrots rose from the poppy fields. Sometimes Jacques had seen these birds hang drowsy with opium among the white flowers and once Hardyal caught one in his hand. " Look ! " he exclaimed. " The little drunkard ! "

Ganpat Rai's house was painted blue with pillars and arches of a dazzling white among the date palms and banana fronds which bounded his garden. Anxious to evade the vulgarity of his less educated friends, the barrister had taken European advice on the laying out of his garden. Here were no funereal marigolds, no coleus border, no bougainvillea, no atrocious magenta roses. Beyond the tennis court, beyond the embankment of Mr. Wall's new

canal, lay the river which, when the sun rose and when it
sank, turned to the colour of pearls. On its muddy banks
at almost any hour of the day there rose the smoke of a
funeral pyre, and Jacques and Hardyal sometimes followed
the funeral parties when they went down to the water's
edge with their burden. " Ram Ram ! " breathed Hardyal
in a troubled whisper, and Jacques, out of deference to
something of which he was not quite sure, echoed : " Ram
Ram ! "

He saw now that the big blue stop-curtains were raised
on the tennis court, and as he left the carriage he heard the
thud of tennis balls and Hardyal's voice calling the score.
Ganpat Rai, wearing flannels and a striped blazer, emerged
from the house and greeted Jacques.

" They are playing singles. Later, you and I will take
on Mr. Salim and his son." He put his hand on the boy's
shoulder and they strolled towards a group of chairs drawn
up beside the courts. There were some of Ganpat Rai's
colleagues whose wives were in purdah, but who had
brought their young sons. Jacques saw Mrs. Lyttleton. As
a sop to public opinion she'd compromised with her cos-
tume to the extent of adding a pair of kidskin boots and a
hat overflowing with chenille roses. From under its faded
brim her mischievous face peered out at Jacques. " You
have not been near me for a week ! "

She made love to every one, even to children. He gave
her a bright look. " I was going to stop at your house this
afternoon, but they told me I'd find you here."

He lowered himself on the grass beside her chair and
they watched Hardyal and Wall engage in a spirited volley.
Mrs. Lyttleton said softly : " You and I are going to miss
Hardyal."

She managed, somehow, to make almost anything
bearable when she spoke of it ; he had never known her to
dodge a painful subject or to launch into discussions from
a dry sense of duty. Why had his mother not spoken of
Hardyal's going ? Why had she been at such pains to prevent others telling him?

Now Mrs. Lyttleton spoke to Jacques of her conversation with Hardyal's grandmother and his aunts and the
numerous female cousins who kept strict purdah and who

violently opposed this breaking caste and going away across the black water. Hardyal's mother was dead, but that didn't simplify matters for Hardyal or Ganpat Rai. Mrs. Lyttleton repeated what she had already said to the inconsolable women : " It will not be for long, and he will come back for the holidays."

Jacques thought of Hardyal's words when they had gone to the Fort :

" First a whole year must pass."

" Years are not long," said Mrs. Lyttleton, laying her hand for a moment on his head.

" Well, even if they were what could one do ?

She glanced at the young cheek, at the deep hazel eye near her. There was, in Jacques, something which stirred a troubled tenderness in the old woman ; sometimes she thought she recognised the child of fortune to whose singularity all men bow, whose way is always made a little easier. But she could not be sure, for to her as to Father Sebastien and even to his mother, the boy was still an enigma. How strange, now, to remember Auguste St. Remy and their old affection ! Auguste had not possessed this latent fire, this brooding. His charm had been of a different order—a melancholy, questioning spirit. When Jacques was two years old Auguste had carried him in to see her and had expressed the hope that his son might be different from himself.

" I hope that he will be ambitious," said Auguste. " Ambitious and even ruthless. He will suffer less—those who will love him will suffer less."

Auguste brought her his verses and his drawings and played for her on the cracked piano in her drawing-room. They talked of an England and a France which both had left behind them a long time ago ; each was drawn to the other by an ineradicable loneliness. Mrs. Lyttleton had said of Auguste that he was one of those delightful ineffectual men produced by a great civilisation, but for whose special talents no government seems yet to have found a function. Poor Auguste ! So far from being a fool, so far from being ruthless, or even ambitious.

Wall and Hardyal finished their game and came over to the chairs, flinging themselves on the grass near Jacques.

The other Indians drew a little closer and a murmur rose, hesitant, a little guarded because of the presence of the English. There was a flush on Hardyal's cheek and his black eyes shone. The first shock of his impending departure had passed ; it recurred only at intervals between the excitement and bustle of preparation. He took pride in siding with his father against the women, although when, at night, he reviewed this angle of things fear and grief drowned him in tears. But Ganpat Rai had ordered trunks of clothing from Calcutta ; there were presents, letters, farewells, speculations on the new life which awaited him in England. Of his father's friends the Mohammedan Abdul Salim alone held aloof from the prevailing air of congratulation. " You will take much luggage with you, and you will come back with much," said he to Hardyal, and tapped his own forehead with a cryptic gesture. " If you succeed in putting any of it to use afterwards—you will be a lucky man."

Hardyal knew that Salim disliked the English and this fact made the big, black-bearded Mohammedan interesting in his eyes. " Why do you not come with me, Salimji ? We will walk in Hyde Park and look at the Thames River. . . ."

" I would rather walk on the Maidan and look at the Ganges," Salim interrupted with a flash of temper. " I have little use for piebald personalities, English or Indian. Were you my son you would stay at home and grow up like the rest of us."

Hardyal was not offended, for he had listened to endless wrangles between Salim and his father on the same question. Afterwards Ganpat Rai gave it as his opinion that Salim was a jealous and frustrated man. " He is his worst enemy, for he is totally without discretion."

Now Abdul Salim sat at a little distance from the others, listening with an air of sardonic boredom to their trivial chatter. Hardyal leaned over and whispered to Jacques : " Do come and look at all my new things."

They rose and walked away towards the house, followed by the other little boys, and Ganpat Rai lifted his hands and groaned. " Such a day ! My mother and my sisters ! I shall be thankful when it is over and he is gone."

" Will it be over then ? " asked Mrs. Lyttleton gently.

" Merciful heavens, I hope so. It is so bad for Hardyal, all this weeping and grieving."

" But consider your pride when he comes home a pukka sahib ! " observed Abdul Salim sarcastically from his corner.

" You would not send your own son to Cambridge if you could, perhaps ? " inquired another Indian, with equal sarcasm. Ganpat Rai intervened with a suggestion that they make up a foursome for tennis, and a cousin of his rose tactfully to the occasion. " Salim, you and I will play against Mr. Narayan and Mr. Ram Chand. They are fat, but you and I are old. Is that fair enough ? "

Tension dissolved, and when the game was under way Mrs. Lyttleton turned to Ganpat Rai. " Do not fret about Hardyal. He will like England."

" Of that I am not afraid. But I wonder . . . will he adjust himself quickly and successfully ? I did, but then, I was older."

" The English are easy to adjust to, in their own country. They are perhaps the most aped people in the world." Aubrey Wall caught himself up swiftly. " Hardyal is young—there is more danger of his being spoiled than homesick."

Mrs. Lyttleton stared across the garden. " What is all this ? "

A little procession was approaching across the lawn, white-turbaned men bearing baskets and garlands. Ganpat Rai went to meet them, and after a short conversation waved them towards the house and returned to his guests. " They were from my old client Naiko. He insists on sending me presents though I have asked him to stop."

" Naturally, he is grateful to you for getting him off ! "

The barrister smiled. " Naturally, considering his guilt."

They stared, then laughed. Ganpat Rai shrugged. " That is our English law. But those presents should really go to the prosecuting counsel. *He* deserves them."

Ganpat Rai watched his guests playing tennis. The little half-clad ball boys scurried beside the stop-curtains, the players' voices rose cheerfully on the warm and pleasant air. Abdul Salim seemed to have forgotten his bad temper and already in his heart Ganpat Rai had forgiven his friend's sarcastic remarks. After all, Salim was poor and could not afford to send his own son to England to be educated ; he was also a man of intelligence and energy, and he felt himself to be wasted in a small cantonment station like Amritpore. Ganpat Rai thought, generously : " I shall give him Naiko's *dalis* to take home. He is proud, but I shall put it on the score of his children, and he will not refuse."

The boys reappeared, Abdul Salim's young son capering rapturously. Two walked sedately ahead, and their appearance arrested the conversation. " What on earth : . ." began Aubrey Wall, and he began to laugh. Hardyal and Jacques had exchanged clothing ; now Hardyal wore Jacques' white drill suit which was too tight for him, and Jacques was resplendent in Hardyal's gold embroidered muslins. Wall stared at Ganpat Rai's son. By Jove, he thought, the boy will make a very presentable Englishman when we've done with him. But Hardyal's garments on Jacques seemed to him effeminate and unbecoming.

Mrs. Lyttleton gazed at them long and intently. Their youth, their vitality, their extraordinary good looks stirred her to the depths. Where were they going, and what was to be their fate ? At the moment they gave her the impression that they were equal to anything, but she was old, and she had seen the beginning and the end of youth, of vitality, of beauty. When Jacques' eyes met hers she caught her breath, unable, for a moment, to utter the necessary trivialities.

Wall broke the spell. " I'll tell you one thing, my boy," he drawled, looking at Jacques. " You simply can't play tennis in a dhoti ! "

10

THE CORRUGATED tin on the station roof cracked from accumulated heat and a variety of smells and sounds escaped from the population which milled about on the platform. Threading this polymorphic mass were the usual complement of starving dogs and veiled, sidling women. The hot breath of the train and the steaming breath of humanity rose to a blue heaven where the everlasting kites wheeled and circled.

Hardyal stood beside his father ; his heart was beating violently, his smile was fixed, great tears kept rising and subsiding in his eyes. Ganpat Rai would accompany his son to Calcutta and there Hardyal would be placed in the care of friends who were taking the same steamer to England.

" You'll like Colombo," Wall had told him, encouragingly. " The Galle Face, where a brown sea rolls up the beach . . . and when you pass the Island of Socotra think of the pirates who still prey on coastal shipping. You'll go up the Red Sea into Suez, and you'll look at the Mediterranean, and the Straits of Messina with the land olive-green in the early morning and Naples. . . ." Homesickness had made Aubrey Wall poetic. But to Hardyal everything seemed very far away. The tennis party of a few days ago might have happened last year. An age had rolled over him, he felt stranded on a reef of loneliness.

The train was disgorging passengers and freight in an intense panic-stricken confusion directed by a fat white station-master and his thin black assistant. Water-carriers and food-pedlars wandered through the crowd, their voices rising in the peculiar cries of another species—they sounded like birds, or like frogs after the rain. In a flash of anguish, Hardyal remembered the farewell to his grand-mother, who, now that the inevitable had arrived, found herself dry of tears. She had caressed his face with her jewelled hands and stared at him with unbelieving eyes. " I am old. I shall not see thee again."

" Yes, yes ! Soon—next year ! "

" Nay, I shall never see thee more. Our lives part on this moment. Let me touch thee, let me bless thee ! " He felt that she was dying in his arms, this old familiar woman who had nurtured him all the years of his life. His father's oldest sister had cried bitterly : " What good can come of this separation ? You will come back to us changed, a stranger, as your father came back years ago. You will look upon us with scorn for our ignorant ways—what is worse,

you will try to change us, too ! And for what reason ?
Why ? Why ? "

One by one the servants came and fell at his feet,
Krishna, his favourite, clinging to his knees, begging him
not to leave them. Then Ganpat Rai appeared and scattered them with a look. " Come, my son."

Hardyal did not look back as the carriage rolled past the
tennis court between the gardenia hedges, past the women's
arbour where all was silent, through the gates, past the
poppy fields and the bazaar, to the station. Now he stared
past the end of the train to a tossing grey-green of trees.
Beyond them lay Amritpore and everything he knew and
had ever known, but already it had passed out of his reach,
already it was immersed in itself, excluding them. How
cruel the world is, thought Hardyal for the first time.
Babies go on crying and sucking, children scream in the
dust, women tinkle their glass bangles, men wash their teeth
and spit beside the well. . . . I am forgotten, forgotten !

The crowd near him parted and he saw Mrs. Lyttleton
and Mr. Wall and Abdul Salim coming towards him, wearing determined smiles and waving gaily. He sensed his
father's pleasure : How good of these friends, what an
honour !

But where was Jacques ?

Mrs. Lyttleton put her arm round Hardyal. " Don't
dare to cry because if you do I shall, and that would disgrace me in the eyes of the world."

He tried to smile. " Why would it disgrace you ? "

" Because I put rouge on my cheeks and tears would
make it run."

Wall thrust a package under Hardyal's arm. " Something for the journey. You must write me news of my
family. Make them take you to see Arundel when the
daffodils are out."

Abdul Salim smiled at Hardyal. " I shall look for
changes when I see you again, my child ! "

Where, where was Jacques ?

Mrs. Lyttleton tightened her clasp of his shoulders.
" He will come. He would never let you go without saying
good-bye."

Ganpat Rai interposed. " Madame St. Remy sent me

a note this morning, saying that perhaps it would be better if Jacques did not come, since the farewell might be too painful for both of them. Hardyal knows this . . . it is silly for him to go on expecting."

Mrs. Lyttleton had flushed under her rouge. " Damn Madame St. Remy ! "

The others looked utterly shocked by this outburst, but she turned and clasped Hardyal in her arms. " I know how Jacques will feel about this. Can I give him a message, Hardyal ? "

He tried to think of something to say, but his head and his heart were in confusion. Ganpat Rai and Salim were talking in hurried undertones about some case ; Aubrey Wall, dreading a scene, lighted a cigarette and began to hum. Only Mrs. Lyttleton, then, really cared. . . .

" Tell him . . ."

A shudder ran through the train, a flexing of all its iron muscles, and with a despairing howl the crowd surged towards it.

" Tell him . . ." whispered Hardyal. Suddenly he forgot everything except that he did not want to go away.

" Come," said Ganpat Rai. Their luggage was already installed in a carriage which they would share with a venerable Hindu gentleman on his way through Amritpore to Calcutta. For the past few minutes this pundit had leaned on his window watching the little scene. He was touched to observe the happy mingling of English and Indian, though he was too much of a sceptic to place much faith in its significance. Still, how delightful, really, to see tears on that old woman's face under the preposterous hat, and the sensitive expression of the Englishman.

" Good-bye, Hardyal ! "

" Tell him . . . tell him . . ."

The sound of a whistle tore the moment into shreds as the train began to move. Those who were not going fell back and watched the great thing crawl over the rails and steady into its meshed and intricate flight. A cry rose from it and pierced their hearts with its strange, perpetually disturbing and incomprehensible message.

" I'll take you home," said Wall, giving Mrs. Lyttleton his arm. They turned to look for Abdul Salim, but he had

disappeared ; the thread which tied their awareness to him
and his to theirs had stretched and thinned : now it snapped
in the final glitter of the vanished train.

Gisele laid her hands on the organ keys and the voices
of Father Sebastien's native choir swelled and died round
her. Below the carved teakwood balcony she could see the
kneeling figures of her mother and the Browns. Jacques,
in gown and surplice, knelt on the altar steps beside Mr.
Boodrie. The candlelight swayed under the weight of the
hymn and the incense-laden air was as close-woven as silk.
Every head bent for the moment of Benediction : Jacques
raised the censer and its fragrance drifted towards his bowed
face. From under his lashes he saw Father Sebastien, in
alb and chasuble, lift the gold Monstrance. Except for the
thin voice of the bell in Boodrie's hand there was no sound.
Then Jacques heard the train far away, its voice flung in
an arc, a rainbow of sound across the brown miles.

> *Laudate Dominum omnes gentes ;*
> *Laudate eum omnes populi . . .*

Outside in the oleander-bordered compound Madame
St. Remy and her daughter waited for Jacques and Father
Sebastien, who were changing their vestments. As she
watched the little congregation drift away, Madame
smelled the nim blossoms and knew that the hot weather
would soon begin. Beside her on the carriage seat Gisele
sat rapt and bloodless.

" You played beautifully this afternoon, darling," said
Madame.

Father Sebastien appeared, followed by Jacques, and
they seated themselves on the little seat facing Madame and
Gisele. The coachman twitched his reins and they wheeled
out of the compound into the road towards Madame's
house, where Father Sebastien would dine to-night.

Madame linked her arm in Gisele's. " The nim
flowers ! " she exclaimed.

Father Sebastien lighted a cigar. " Summer's in the
air. I heard the brainfever bird."

Jacques said suddenly, " I shan't be able to go to you

for study to-morrow, Father. Hardyal is going away and I promised to say good-bye to him at the station."

Father Sebastien took the cigar from his lips and held it in his strong plump fingers; each finger wore a little overcoat of black hair, but the nails were like polished almonds.

Something in the silence which followed his words made Jacques look from one face to the other. "May I not, Maman?"

It was Gisele who answered him suddenly, in a stifled voice: "Hardyal has gone."

"Don't be silly. He doesn't go until to-morrow."

"He has gone. Ganpat Rai had business in Calcutta, so they went a day sooner than they had arranged." Her blue eyes stared at him from the pale oval of her face. "Hardyal has gone . . . gone!"

Madame pressed the girl's arm against her own, then she too looked at Jacques. "I would have told you . . . but I thought it better to spare you and Hardyal the grief of parting."

Jacques stared at them with utter disbelief. "But how could he have gone without my knowing it? He would have told me."

"Ganpat Rai sent me a note . . . I replied that there was hardly time . . . we all thought it best to avoid a scene." It was costing her more than she had expected, as Father Sebastien had known that it would. He looked quietly at Jacques. "Had we heard in time perhaps something could have been arranged. On the other hand, your mother is right: these partings are unnecessarily upsetting."

Jacques replied in a stony voice: "I don't care if they are upsetting . . . he is my friend. . . . I wanted to see him again."

"Jacques, darling . . ."

"How could you have done it, Maman?"

Gisele began in a high, excited voice: "It serves you right! You're too fond of people! Anyway, Hardyal had gone. You won't see him again . . . not for years, for ages."

The boy sat quite still and stared at the brown hummocks of Father Sebastien's knees. Grief and rage had ignited him, he felt that his very blood was on fire.

Madame leaned forward and touched his hand.
" Jacques, darling ! "

But he sat like a stone, not looking at any of them. He
listened to the sound of the horses' hoofs on the hard road
and their rhythm knocked dryly against his heart. Madame and the priest engaged in a discussion of church
affairs, Gisele sat and watched her brother's white face.

Clip, clop, clip clop, went the hammer strokes against
Jacques' heart. The carriage turned into the shisham
avenue and its misty columns met over their heads. Down
this familiar avenue Hardyal had ridden to see him, and
he had ridden back along its flickering shadow to call on
Hardyal. They had grown up together, sharing laughter,
sharing thoughts, visions, hopes. Who, now, would there
be to talk with, to confide in ? He saw the house, white and
low and thatched, and memory blew through him softly
like the sound of a horn. He leaped from the carriage and
without once turning his head or heeding the plaintive cries
which pursued him he ran through the lantana bushes and
the cactus, across the quelds towards the road and Mrs.
Lyttleton's house.

Father Sebastien glanced at Madame and shrugged.
" Let him go. Later, we shall have to come to some decision."

Jacques took all the short cuts and at last, dry in the
throat, he found himself in Mrs. Lyttleton's garden. She
was there, as he'd known she would be—as his father had
often found her walking under her trees in the brief Indian
twilight. When she saw Jacques she waited, a palm-leaf
fan hanging lightly from her hand.

. For a little while he stood before her, trying to get his
breath, then he stammered : " Hardyal . . . they let him
go . . . they never told me."

" I know." She took his arm and turned him towards
the house ; they went up the steps together, greeted in
silence by all the stuffed relics of that great hunter, the
General her husband. On a little table beside her chair
were set glasses and a big jug of sherbet ; there were little
cakes, and a plate of Jacques' favourite sweets. She had
known he would come, and now as he sat down beside her
she smiled, humour and tenderness making her face young

again. " Do you remember the day you and Hardyal stole my cigarettes? This time you and I shall smoke one together."

II

THERE WERE still two weeks before the break of the southwest monsoon ; the earth lay breathless under heat which seared the fields and seeped up the brown trickles of water which fed them. Buffalo carts and bullocks creaked between acres of indigo, lugging the freshly cut stock to the tanks where air and water would combine to beat it into a primary orange and ultimate blue. Everywhere people crawled like fleas seeking the living blood.

On the headwork of his canal, at a point where the river eddied past the locks, Aubrey Wall was fishing for crocodiles. It was an original sport, one invented by him in the deep boredom of the season. A coolie crouched above the locks and dangled a dead pi-dog at the end of a rope. Hideously enticing, the dog hung just above the brown water, while the hunter sat on a camp stool with his rifle across his knees, waiting for a glimpse of the blunt snout and hooded eyes of his quarry. Wall's cotton suit was dark with sweat, he felt brittle from weeks of intense heat. Now a cool breath rose from the water and there were fragile shadows under the acacias which had sprouted beside the embankment. Night, when it fell, would fall abruptly, but it would bring little respite to the overburdened air.

Father Sebastien sat near-by, smoking his cigar and taking an occasional sip from a bottle of lemonade which stood in a bucket beside him. A little distance away under the trees Wall's tonga waited, the syce stretched on the ground beside his unharnessed ponies. Wall watched a few Pity-to-do-its dipping and nodding along the shore ; they looked like women with painted eyes and coifs of shiny black hair stepping fastidiously among the charred pyres and refuse of the river. Beyond, the fields rolled towards the pallid sky ; mango groves rested like dark clouds on its edges and the mud walls of villages trembled as though they might collapse under the impact of human vision.

The canal cut its rigid line towards Amritpore ; its tributaries fed the tanks of Ramdatta the moneylender, the cisterns of Madame St. Remy, the reservoirs of the bazaar and the railway station. It revived with a lukewarm sweetness the few miles of exhausted soil which still continued, miraculously, like a buried corpse, to put forth a sort of subcutaneous verdure.

Wall stared at the glittering line which his labour had traced across the parched land. Well, there it stood, for whatever it might be worth. There were days when he felt well pleased with what he'd accomplished, but to-day was not one of them. With the approach of the hot weather just before the rains broke, his nervous system suffered a kind of accumulated shock, a reverberation of all the disappointments, dreams, hopes, despairs and resignations which had piled up during the year. Now loathing possessed him, loathing for the place, for the climate, for his work which he saw as a mere drop in this bottomless bucket of poverty, superstition and disease. He was haunted by memories of his home in Sussex, of his kind and civilised family, by tastes and sounds and familiar scenes. Their inaccessibility made him hate his exile.

Father Sebastien tilted his topi and mopped his rosy forehead with a large silk handkerchief. He'd been silent for some time, musing on the sacrament which he'd recently administered in the village whose grove of mangoes he could see from here. The recipient was young, a widow, and out of terror of the new God her family had sent for Father Sebastien. The priest knew well enough what would happen as soon as his back was turned—they'd carry her down to the river and complete the rites after their old fashion, and tie bits of rag to poles stuck in the sand—thus leaving nothing undone to pacify her restive shade. He sighed and hitched his camp stool close to the headwork. "Raise the animal somewhat—do not let it sink out of sight," he admonished the coolie, who roused himself and gave the bait an enticing wriggle.

"There were three of the brutes last week," said Wall. "But they've probably become wary."

"Would you like some lemonade ? Not cold, but refreshing just the same." He poured the liquid into a cup and gave it to the Engineer, noticing, without appearing to, the slight tremor of the other's hand.

The coolie gave an exclamation and all three craned forward, Wall lifting the big double-barrelled Greener. Something moved sluggishly in the water, slid up against the masonry headwork, rolled over and bared its devastated human face. A charred arm saluted them from the current, than sank.

" No mugger this time," sighed the priest, relaxing.

" Neither *Crocodilus Palustris* nor *Gavialis Gangeticus*," Wall agreed, in disgust. " Merely Homo Sapiens somewhat the worse for wear. One of your flock ? "

" Hardly. We bury ours."

" In consecrated ground, no doubt."

" Naturally ! "

" Do the jackals respect it ? "

" Well, we do employ a watchman."

Both smiled, amused by their grisly exchange. Then Wall rose.

" God, if only the rains would break ! "

" But the malaria," murmured Father Sebastien. He stood, impressive in his white summer robes, and stared at the river. " I cannot persuade the children to swallow quinine. They hate the bitter taste."

" Perhaps they'll find that death tastes sweeter," remarked Wall, with unaccustomed irony. He had little sympathy with the priest's calling, but both men respected each other and got along well.

The syce had come to and harnessed the tonga ponies ; the coolie hauled in his ugly bait and cut it free. It fell and disappeared, then rose a little distance away, and vanished in a vicious swirl that was not resurrection. Wall fingered his rifle. " Damn ! I knew that brute was somewhere. We'll get him next time."

They slid down the embankment to the waiting tonga, followed by the coolie carrying their camp stools and the rope. Wall took the reins and the priest sat beside him, while the servants rode behind. They started down the road in the late sunshine, and passed Madame St. Remy's creaking bullock carts laden with indigo. Boodrie, driving a dog cart, passed them at a smart pace and they had a glimpse of his shoddy tussore suit and his face like a melting chocolate-drop. Wall closed to allow the dust to settle. " Swine ! I can't stand these half-castes."

Father Sebastien realised that there were many things and many people Wall could not stand these days. He ventured, gently : " Boodrie is a good servant. It's hardly his fault that he is a half-caste."

" They're no good. I've never met one I'd trust round the corner."

" Nevertheless, you will admit their social predicament ? "

" Oh yes, I know, I know ! The sins of the fathers and all that. But it isn't my fault either."

Father Sebastien glanced at him. " Come to my house and have dinner. I am alone. I would like it."

" Thanks, Father, but I must get home. I have work to finish and I go into camp to-morrow."

" Camp in this weather ? "

" I have no choice."

The priest nodded. " No, we have no choice. We must sacrifice, suffer, endure, forgive." He sounded contemplative rather than minatory, and Wall laughed. " I belong to the opposition shop, if to any. But there are times when I wish I could share your charity. You fanatics possess an endurance the rest of us lack."

The priest smiled. " Well, you dig the canals and leave the rest of it to us fanatics."

One of the ponies pecked a little and Wall lashed it with his whip. They tore along for a few minutes, then he muttered in a choking voice :

" This bloody country ! "

The priest remained silent. Presently the green of the little civil station opened before them—carefully plotted gardens, shady trees, a scent of flowering hedges and watered grass. They drove past Madame St. Remy's factory and saw her carriage waiting inside the gates. Wall asked abruptly : " Tell me, what news of the children ? "

" Jacques seems to have adjusted himself to St. Matthew's School. Gisele, as you know, is with the Sisters of St. Mary, in Gambul."

" Rather young, isn't she, for all that ? "

" Fifteen ? And she is, I think, mature for her age."

Wall hesitated for a moment, then : " I miss them—
the children. They made this place endurable."

" You should marry," said the priest kindly. " You'd
make a good father."

" Marry ? " He laughed. " Leave my wife and children
in England or in the hills, or force them to swelter down
here with me ? "

The priest shrugged. " There are many who have
learned to make the best of it."

" There is no best. There is merely compromise and
boredom. I know. I've watched it. No, thanks . . . I'll
wait until I retire, if I don't pop off with dysentery or
enteric before then."

He suffered from a curious onset of emotion which
speech could not relieve. Presently they were at Father
Sebastien's little house in the church compound, where a
water-carrier was sprinkling the ground before the dusty
oleanders. Father Sebastien got out of the tonga and stood
for a moment looking at the Englishman. " I enjoyed our
little expedition. If you should want me at any time, I
shall come. At any time, and always as a friend."

Wall smiled dimly. " Thanks, I'm all right, you know."

He wheeled out of the compound and drove home.
After the day's heat he craved a bath, a drink, the month-
old newspapers at home—an unequivocal surrender to his
mood.

The Civil Engineer's bungalow was government-owned,
well kept but rather bleak. Wall had left it much as he
found it, a state of mind typical of men who have been
brought up by devoted women and who have never learned
the knack of making themselves comfortable. There were
several white-washed rooms filled with tasteless cane furniture, yards of stiff matting and rep curtains out of which
scorpions and tarantulas tumbled at unsuspected moments.
Lizards stalked flies along the floors or fell and lost their
tails which went on wriggling for an hour afterwards. The
drawing-room mantelpiece was crowded with photographs
to which Wall had recently added another, one of Hardyal
in striped blazer and snake-buckled belt, a straw hat tilted
over his eyes.

Bathed and refreshed, Wall examined this photograph with a faint smile. It had been taken by the village photographer at Bognor, under the supervision of his sisters. They had written how much they liked Hardyal, and Wall could picture them—well bred and kindly, hovering over the small dark stranger. After three months Hardyal showed the faint signs of integration and response : his eyes had the level focus of English eyes, his lips seemed less full and sensuous, his whole face seemed thinner and keener— or so Wall believed. The photograph had induced a wave of remembrance, and he saw himself at that age ; youth surged upon him with its reminders of time flying, of life slipping, slipping away like that poor charred relic of the fires, down the Gogra River to the crocodiles and the sea.

He carried Hardyal's picture to an armchair and stretched his legs on the wide leg-rests. Over his head the frilled punkah flapped jerkily and he heard his servants moving about the other rooms, lighting the lamps, rattling dishes. In a little while his Mohammedan bearer brought him brandy and cigarettes, rolled up the cane screens and closed the lower half of the Dutch doors.

" Do not light the lamps in here for a little while," Wall ordered. " And tell that brute of a coolie to *pull* ! "

When the man had gone and the punkah had taken a new lease of life, Wall sat quietly, refashioning the past. He was a lonely man and whatever was most important to him seemed to have receded beyond his reach for ever. What he'd said to Father Sebastien was true—he missed the St. Remy children, who had gone to the hills soon after Hardyal's departure. Something sweet and indefinable had fled Amritpore with them, and what remained seemed stale and hopeless. He found himself bored by his own generation—the Browns, Madame St. Remy, even by Mrs. Lyttleton whose age had seemed to set her in a special category. But the children had been like bees rifling what honey there remained in this parched country. He had not dreamed that he would miss them like this . . . that he would miss Gisele, dream about her, conjure up her face at odd moments of the day. Something vivid sprang through him when he thought of Gisele.

One evening before they had gone away he went to dine at Madame St. Remy's with the Browns and Father Sebastien. It had been a pleasant evening, pleasanter than many evenings Wall could remember. Madame exerted herself to be friendly, and after a while it had dawned on him that the shadow of the children's departure hung over them all. When it came time for Wall to take his leave he walked out through the back veranda, past their two little beds shrouded in mosquito netting. Obeying a friendly impulse, he'd stopped beside Gisele's bed and peered through the snowy screen, seeing her lying there mysterious and wide awake. Her hair, all loose, stood about her head like the love dance of some strange bird, and he bent closer, murmuring :

" Gisele ? "

She stirred, her eyes huge in the surrounding pallor, and it seemed to Wall that she lifted her arms towards him. He raised the mosquito curtain and knelt down to bid her a friendly good-night, as he had done once or twice before in their casual acquaintance. But she put her arms round his neck and drew his face towards her and offered her lips, cool and sweet. She held him so he smelled the lovely youth of her neck and breast, the perfume of her extraordinary hair, and before he knew it he had kissed her again and again, felt her trembling in his arms. Then he freed himself and went away, shaken and thoughtful, more than half inclined to turn round and go back. But go back . . . to what ? And why ?

The punkah flapped at slower and slower intervals and stagnant heat swarmed upon him. He shouted at the punkah coolie to pull harder, and the punkah jerked madly to life again. Somewhere in the outer darkness a drum rattled, a voice sang for a minute then fell silent. Wall finished his brandy, desire and despair flushing and draining him. Presently he called his bearer, and after a slight hesitation, gave him curt instructions. The servant stared discreetly at the dim outlines of his master's feet. He'd often wondered why this sahib had seemed different from others ; perhaps he attributed the difference to eccentricities hidden in white flesh. Now, reassured and privately amused, he took his orders and went away to the bazaar, to a shuttered room above the sweetmeat stall, a room well known and dear to the heart of Jacques' servant, Hanif.

12

HANIF AND GISELE's old ayah accompanied the children to the hills. They left Amritpore just as the hot winds were starting to blow, and their train came from a direction opposite to the one which had carried Hardyal to the sea.

From his slippery leather bunk beside the window Jacques watched the brown plain unroll ; seen thus the country was both familiar and strange. He'd gone to the hills in other years but this time it was different ; when he and Gisele had been delivered over to their fate the servants would return to Amritpore—Jacques would be alone. He brooded over the drab miles with their interminable mango groves, their wells, their mud-walled villages. Amritpore was soon lost, but there gleamed the river, and in another minute he saw the Fort : how thin the acacias looked from here, how toylike the sentry-boxes where he and Hardyal liked to sit and watch the goats grazing in the moat below ! Jacques more than half expected to hear a salute from those silent guns, and to catch a glimpse of the torn banners and the warriors so often resurrected by Mrs. Lyttleton.

The train dashed into a gully, plumed grass brushed the windows and the earth came up close like something seen through a magnifying glass. He had a glimpse of a separate, teeming world which went its way indifferent to trains and the life which they carried in their angry bellies.

Hanif prepared tea and produced a tin box of sugar-coated biscuits, smuggled into the compartment at the last minute by Mrs. Lyttleton. The train's rocking spilled the tea into their saucers and sent suitcases skidding across the floor. It slammed the lavatory door tight shut with the ayah inside it, and Hanif laughed heartlessly at her panic-stricken outcries as he worked on the lock. " You will be there until we reach the hills, Umma ! That is, unless you suffocate." Gisele did not share in their merriment. She sat, by herself, in a corner of the compartment, staring out at the flying miles. Jacques saw that she was crying—not the familiar childish tears of homesickness, but in a strained, suffering, grown-up way which hurt him.

At night Hanif retired to his own third-class compartment, leaving the liberated ayah in charge. Jacques lay staring at the round glow of the ceiling light behind its green baize cover ; he listened to the wheels singing their monotonous song and imagined the shining tracks stringing events on their bright cord. The metal tracks joined land with land and life with life, and the thought brought him a sudden sense of being utterly at their mercy, at the mercy of people and of circumstance : no matter what he said or did, he was powerless—powerless ! He wondered whether that was the thought which troubled Gisele, and longed to ask her, but the sound of her crying held him motionless on his own bunk. He thought of Kanhya's baby and wondered whether the jackals had burrowed after the tiny body in its white cardboard box. He closed his eyes and saw the Fort, and then he thought of the soldiers who died there in some forgotten cause, blood bursting from their bodies and drying as he'd seen blood dry, swiftly in the famished dust. He felt that he was part of these mysterious events whose memory persisted into the present ; the sensation became frightening, became unbearable, and he pressed his face to the window and saw the Indian sky alive with stars.

He had not intended to fall asleep, but he did, at last ; and when he woke again the air tasted fresh on his lips. He rose and lowered the dash and peered out. The train had described a perfect arc and he could see the little engine puffing up a gradient through low-growing forests of dhak. The flowers were open, fiery among their pale silver leaves, and he knew that men came here to hunt tigers. But now all he could see were the flowering trees and the little sandy openings and patches of plumed grass. Slowly the mountains materialised under his gaze, and then they came striding towards him out of the mist—towering, imperial. He lost them as they rose far above the angle of his vision and the train crept at a lowered speed under their shadow.

13

WHILE Madame St. Remy moved among her scorching
fields and Father Sebastien and Mr. Wall angled for crocodiles off the canal locks, Jacques sat behind his desk in the
fifth standard classroom, waiting with bored longing for
the dinner bell. He listened to his neighbour, the Raja of
Jhori, read aloud from a history of the Plantagenet kings.
The Raja was the titular head of a tiny kingdom in the
south-west, and his own ancestry was a matter of purest
conjecture ; but he accumulated learning as a parrot
accumulates swear-words, and he loved to read and to
write long sentences in English.

Jacques' thoughts were elsewhere. It was almost three
months since he left Amritpore and came to St. Matthew's
College. Nostalgia had given way by degrees to the fascination which people and places always aroused, but of one
thing he was quite certain : he detested St. Matthew's and
almost every one in it. Perhaps it was inevitable that he
should find, in this heterogeneous collection of boys—white,
native, and Eurasian—something essentially hostile to his
own nature and his own way. On the day of his arrival
they had ducked him in the great drinking cistern and
almost drowned him. Jacques was not unprepared for what
might lie in store for him ; he'd listened while Mr. Wall
instructed Hardyal in the peculiarities of public-school
behaviour, and Father Sebastien had dropped a few additional hints. Nevertheless, Jacques was not prepared for
the ducking. For hours afterwards he'd brooded on this
first violent affront to his youthful dignity, wondering what
Hardyal would have thought, wondering whether the same
outrage had been practised on his friend. No one had ever
struck Jacques, no one had shouted at him, laughed at his
clothes or sneered at his accent. Nor did he consider himself less of a man because of these deficiencies in his experience. He'd lived among adult human beings and
friendship had come to him all too easily. Now he found
himself forced to strike and to strike hard against strangers
whom he'd come prepared to like. When, later, they approached him with overtures of reconciliation, he had
nothing to say to them, and they went away disgruntled.

There were about two hundred boys at St. Matthew's ; the school was run by a Catholic order of Irish Brothers, and from a distance Jacques rather admired this group of apple-cheeked men who looked like sportsmen and who joked and laughed a great deal while they strove to beat a semblance of scholarship into their charges. But if Jacques was no longer prepared to like he was more than prepared to hate, and it was not long before he found an object in his class-master, Brother Doyle. This man was unlike the other Brothers ; he was lean and sallow, his features were coarse and his eyes like cold blue stones. Between Brother Doyle and Jacques there sprang an antipathy which, as the weeks passed, developed into outright antagonism.

Viewed from the perspective of St. Matthew's, life at Amritpore recurred in a happy carefree glow. At St. Matthew's there was no freedom, no privacy, no solitude. His letters were read, he moved in an inquisitorial atmosphere of study, prayer, pranks and hostility. At night he slept in a long bleak dormitory with twenty-five other urchins before whom he was obliged to dress and undress, wash, brush his teeth. Sometimes he wondered whether all this was visited upon him by way of retribution for the death of the punkah coolie's baby.

Gisele's convent stood across the lake from St. Matthew's, and on alternate Sundays Jacques was expected to visit his sister, although neither enjoyed these meetings. He would have liked to compare notes with Gisele but they were separated, now, by more than physical distance. Gisele adored her convent, and from Madame St. Remy, Jacques learned that his sister enjoyed special privileges among the good Sisters. No, Gisele would have little interest or sympathy with his tribulations. On his rare Sunday visits their conversation was confined almost entirely to accounts of her studies, her devotions, her aspirations—all seemed dizzyingly beyond his reach or his desires. Once she had given him a letter and asked him to post it for her ; turning it over in his hand, he saw that it was addressed to Aubrcy Wall at Amritpore, but when he was leaving Gisele suddenly asked for the letter back. She had changed her mind about sending it—then.

After a long silence a letter came to Jacques from

Hardyal, who was spending his midsummer holidays in Sussex. "We are on the sea and when the tide goes out we can hardly see it—it lies like a piece of wet string under the sky, and the sands come to life with very small crabs and things. I now find that I can swim quite well. We ride when I stay with Mr. Wall's cousins, on the Downs. I wish you were here. In school some of the fellows call me ' Wog.' A Wog is a kind of black doll with button eyes and hair of wool. I do not think that I look like a Wog. I wish you were here."

The original occupant of the seat which Jacques had usurped now returned and Jacques moved down the aisle to a seat at right angles from the prodigal whose profile was sometimes visible between all the others. Jacques was too self-absorbed to pay much attention to John Macbeth who, like the Raja of Jhori and a few others, was lucky enough to be a day scholar. But in a little while his sensibility registered a change in the atmosphere—something fresh, humorous, singular, animated it and attracted his attention. He drew his breath and cast about him for a cause and a reason, and immediately encountered a pair of grey, incurious eyes. As their eyes met, Macbeth smiled. That was as far as their acquaintance progressed for the time being. As suddenly as he had appeared Macbeth disappeared, and a note was brought by a mounted orderly from Colonel Macbeth, to say that his son was again indisposed and would not attend class for two or three days. Funny, reflected Jacques ; Macbeth didn't look in the least delicate. Now that indefinable Something which had stirred this stale and defeated air vanished once more, and he found himself staring at the empty seat across the aisle and trying to refashion the shape of a neat brown head and a sharply tilted profile.

A week passed and Macbeth returned, but still they did not meet. Perhaps a mutual attraction interposed its queer barrier ; at any rate Jacques was still too disillusioned and suspicious to venture an overture. What was more, he thought he recognised in Macbeth a trait which Madame St. Remy would instantly have stigmatised as *formidable*, even *sinister*. Just as there are certain plants and certain animals which enjoy a peculiar invulnerability, Macbeth was held in obvious respect by his fellows; even Brother Doyle treated him differently. Jacques himself was in no mood to take chances, and between Macbeth and himself there grew a self-conscious reserve—they went out of their way to ignore each other; but before the logic of their relation could declare itself Macbeth disappeared once more, and once more the mounted orderly appeared with the by now familiar crested note for Brother Doyle.

"What's the matter with Macbeth?" Jacques so far demeaned himself to inquire of his neighbour, the Raja.

"They say he has worms."

"No, fits," said someone else.

The situation between Brother Doyle and Jacques was becoming steadily worse. Jacques suffered spasms of terror, fear of the Brother, fear of some invisible force which operated against him through Brother Doyle and perhaps without Brother Doyle's awareness. Hanif would have said that the man possessed the Evil Eye and certainly there were moments when Jacques was sure of this. As for the rest of the class, the unequal struggle provided them with a happy release from boredom. They had a taste of Jacques' spirit, now they watched with vengeful fascination while Brother Doyle dealt with that spirit. Jacques' accent came in for special attention: "This is not a French lesson, Remy. If you want to show off your abilities as a linguist, save them for Brother Vincent." Or it was: "Remy, have you filled the inkpots? Ah, I forgot! St. Remy. Naturally you can't be expected to fill inkpots."

One day the nagging had gone on for the better part of an hour and the class waited feverishly for something to happen. Jacques looked as though a touch would shatter him, and perhaps Brother Doyle recognised the extent to which he'd succeeded, for he played the dogged little fish to a standstill, then prepared to let him go. Jacques had been summoned to the dais and stood now in full view of the class. Brother Doyle smiled at him with sudden radiance. "Very well, that will be all. You may go back to your seat, Remy."

Jacques did not obey at once; he lifted his head and gave his class-master a long, steady stare. Brother Doyle flushed.

C

" Wait a minute. What was it you were about to say ? "
Jacques was silent.
" Did you hear my question, Remy ? "
Silence grew in Jacques, it obsessed him.
" Remy ! "
The windows sparkled and Jacques could see butterflies
fluttering in the school gardens.
" Will you answer me, Remy ? "
The others craned forward as Jacques' silence fed theirs,
fed their silence as a spring feeds a lake, increasing with
every second, deepening, involving them all in its conspiracy. But Brother Doyle had no intention of drowning
in it himself. He struck Jacques a light, glancing blow.
Reeling, the boy caught the edge of his master's desk and
his fingers closed on a round glass inkpot which stood there.
What happened then happened as inevitably as the arc of
a reflex—his hand flew upward and the inkpot crashed
against the blackboard, missing Brother Doyle by a few
inches.
    Then Jacques fled, down the aisle between the desks and
out through the great doors across the terrace. He fled as
a deer flees, or a colt. The terrace ended in a steep drop
which he took in his stride, flying through the air for an
intoxicating second which ended in a bed of bracken.
Through this he scuttled, twisting and turning until he
found himself on the little path which ran below the play-
grounds to the hill road below. He had no idea of where he
was going or what he intended to do, but he was sure that
there could be no more St. Matthew's for him.
    The path along which he was half running, half walking,
dipped between the rhododendrons to the road below, and
sauntering towards him, carrying a butterfly net, was John
Macbeth. They came to an abrupt halt, doubt and suspicion drawing a resemblance between them. But some
genius for gauging situations must always have distinguished
Macbeth ; he shot a swift glance up and down the road,
then said :
    " Come on, I know a place where they can't find
us."
    They scrambled up the path, Macbeth in the lead. Here
the trees were heavy and their feet made scarcely a sound

on the leafy ground. The school was out of sight, they heard a voice or two in the distance and the singing of a hillman far down the road.

Macbeth paused, glanced at Jacques over his shoulder, then plunged down the hillside into a mass of ferns. They were now amongst an outcropping of rocks where purple orchids clung to the moss blanket ; here, suddenly, Macbeth vanished as though jaws had swallowed him. His voice reached Jacques from a green dimness at his feet : " Jump ! "

Jacques jumped, landing beside Macbeth in a sort of dell through which a little stream rustled on its way to the lake. The ferns had closed over their heads and the sun filtered down in splinters of light ; there was heat, and a smell of leaf mould and flowers. Macbeth crouched beside the stream and drank, and Jacques crouched beside him, plunging his face into the water. Then they sat back on their heels, embarrassment engulfing both. Macbeth took the initiative :

" I often come here when I'm fed up. No one else knows about it."

" How did you happen to find it ? "

" By accident one day when I was chasing a moth."

Jacques saw the butterfly net propped against the wall of their den. " I have a collection at home."

The ice was broken and they made themselves comfortable. Macbeth removed his hat and took a butterfly from under the sweat-band. As Jacques examined the exquisite creature remembrance took him by the throat. His birthday . . . Hanif taking a butterfly from his cap and laying it on the dressing-table. His mother, Hardyal, Amritpore. . . . He laid his head on his knees and stayed motionless, holding on to his tears.

Macbeth waited. He recognised home-sickness when he saw it, and he had, from the very moment of setting eyes on Jacques, liked him and determined to know him. In a little while the paroxysm had passed and Jacques sat up. He smiled waveringly at his new friend. " I thought you were supposed to be ill."

" I was, but I'm all right now."

" Jhori said you had worms."

" *He's* the one that has worms ! "

"Well, but what can it be, then? You're absent so often."

The tacit admission that his absence had been noticed and regretted thawed Macbeth completely. "If I tell you, do you swear not to give me away?"

"I swear!"

"I just take Cascara."

"Cascara?"

"It's quite harmless, but it makes you go to the bath-room like anything."

"Cascara," repeated Jacques, entranced. "Fancy!"

"At first my family kept sending for old Das, the assis-tant surgeon. He gave me things to stop it and I had to go back to school. It doesn't worry them as much as it used to, and I'm very careful not to take too much at a time."

Jacques gazed at him in admiration. Then Macbeth said suddenly:

"But what about you? Shouldn't you be in class?"

"I should, but I threw an inkpot at Doyle."

"What?"

"An inkpot."

"Heavens! Did you hit him?"

"No, worse luck."

"Heavens." It was Macbeth's turn to stare in wonder. "You did, actually? Then you'll probably be expelled."

Jacques was startled. Somehow the thought of expul-sion had never entered his head, he had not really thought of anything except blind escape. He began to see, now, some of the angles of his predicament.

"They can't very well expel me if I don't go back."

Macbeth was frowning. "I say, you could put the fear of God into old Doyle if you liked. You could write him a letter—I'd post it for you—saying that you'd decided to commit suicide." His grey eyes glittered with excitement. "You could leave your shoes and coat on the shore near the lake. Someone would be sure to find them. Just think what it would do to that——" And he used an expressive native epithet.

Jacques revelled in the thought for several seconds, then

cold reason intervened. " What would be the use ? In the
end they'd find out that I hadn't committed suicide."

" Yes. I suppose they would." Macbeth relinquished
the idea with evident reluctance. " Well, then, what are
you going to do ? You're in a proper fix, you know."

They were silent as little by little the ominous and
reasonable world intruded its logic upon them. " Of
course," Macbeth said finally, " you might be let off with
the most terrific bumming."

" Bumming ? "

" Thrashing. Duane, the head, always gives the important ones."

Jacques turned white. " No, I couldn't . . ." He jumped
to his feet.

" I couldn't . . . couldn't stand that."

Macbeth stared. " Lots of the chaps have had it. It
isn't so awful, you know. Better than being expelled."

" No !" Jacques' reassurance had vanished completely,
and Macbeth rose too, startled out of his complacence.
" Look here, I don't mean to say that you *will* get a bumming. As a matter of fact Duane hardly ever thrashes any
one. It's only for chasing after the Convent girls or for
stealing and things like that."

Jacques was not listening. He seemed to feel once more
the grasping hands of enemies when they hurled him into
the tank and held him under the water until his breath was
ready to die in his lungs. But those enemies, at least, had
been his equals. How could he expect to stand up to giants
like Brothers Duane and Doyle ? He had heard about those
public thrashings—they would take down his trousers and
whip him with a leather strap; and yet, it was not really
the prospect of pain which frightened him. He remembered
something that had happened a long time ago in Amritpore when he and Hardyal watched Aubrey Wall thrash
a groom for stealing the horses' grain. It was not a spectacle
which either he or Hardyal had ever been able to forget.
The man offered no resistance as Wall beat him almost
senseless with a riding crop. Jacques remembered his own
feelings as he watched—feelings of terror, of queer, creeping excitement that was not wholly disagreeable. He'd
even laughed rather hysterically when the groom's turban

fell off, but Hardyal had turned away, shivering. Ah, to be beaten oneself, to submit to a beating—he couldn't stand it, he couldn't, he couldn't !

He stared at Macbeth. " I'm going back to ask them to expel me."

" What ? "

" Yes. I won't let them touch me. I'd rather be expelled."

He turned and scrambled up the side of the little dell and ran down the path towards the school. Again as when he'd bolted half an hour ago he had no very clear plan of action : he merely followed the dictate of his blood, which warned him that anything was better than indignity. There was still an hour before the class ended, and no one had been sent in pursuit of him. Round the end of the buildings and across the gravelled yard he ran, under the bored eyes of a few strolling Seniors.

Brother Doyle was standing beside the blackboard as Jacques walked down the aisle to the dais and faced his class-master. A stir went round the room, but no one spoke as Brother Doyle looked at this single envelope of flesh and blood.

" I came back to ask you to expel me. If you try to— to touch me I shall kill you, or kill myself. But you can expel me, if you want to."

The saving grace to which his vows and his black robe fully entitled him, now came to Brother Doyle's rescue— and perhaps also to Jacques'. The Brother laid his hand on the boy's steamy forehead. " Go to the infirmary and tell Nurse I sent you. You're to stay there until to-morrow."

When Jacques had gone, Brother Doyle addressed the stupefied class :

" We shall hear no more of this incident. It is finished. I think that our young friend had just a touch of fever."

14

A PAIR of Scotch missionaries struggling over the final hill of their long journey were, it is said, the first white men to look down on Gambul's bright blue lake. That was many

years before Victoria became Empress, but news of the
latter event and of all the ferocious events which had preceded it were long in reaching this shadowy crypt set half-
way up the ladder of the Himalayas. It was in May that
the missionaries came, with their noses like pointer-dogs
lifted unerringly in the direction of strayed souls. They
retrieved a few, although competition must have been
rather one-sided, a native faith having got there first.

On the north-western shore of the lake a Hindu temple
rounded itself like a fat pearl on the rim of a blue shell, and
the missionaries who pitched their tent at a discreet distance
went to bed with the sound of conches in their ears and
awoke to the same summons. There were no real houses,
merely huts of mud and stone with grass roofs, and little
paths beaten clean by generations of bare feet. People kept
goats and sheep and planted a few crops on their rough
terraces ; they fished from rafts or waded with spears after
the mahseer whose shapes the missionaries could see when
they gazed down from the nearby cliffs. No one molested
the newcomers although theirs were the first white faces to
appear in the region. The hill people were too busy with
their own affairs and the temple priest too preoccupied
with his to indulge in inquisitive attitudes. The missionaries
spoke only English and the natives spoke only Pahari, so
a braying of temple conches, the plangent voice of the
sambhur and the short grunting cough of leopards were
for a long time the only argument heard in Gambul. There
was room, then, not only for the houses of men but for an
architecture which would house their ideas. Sambhur and
leopard watched the builders from afar, and in a little while
strange reverberations disturbed the ancient solitude and
pealed echoes from the hills. The missionaries had brought
firearms and they lived well off the pheasants which flew
and roosted everywhere. Then everything wild, everything
lively and incurious, lifted its head and retreated a step.
New and restless gods had arrived just in time to praise a
vision of rhododendron flowers shed by the wind, floating
above the dark shallows of the lake, and to bring a bundle
of flower-tinted feathers hurtling out of the sky.

But all this was a long time ago. Years exercised a sort
of molecular action and before Queen Victoria was dead

Gambul had gathered to itself much of the substance of a self-conscious civilisation. No one remembers what happened to the missionaries. More came after them. Paradise retreated another step or two but the idea of it remained captive in several churches and within the original undisturbed temple on the shore. When men had put their notions and their families safely under cover they set out after fresh adventure and further problems. Leopards and deer, birds and beetles were, unknown to themselves, invested with identities in Latin; rocks acquired dynasties, trees assumed titles, and Paradise faded—mute and intestate.

Colonel Macbeth had built his house on a speck of Empire which once supported only the missionaries' tent. He pushed away the deodar forest and laid out his English garden. A plum tree flowered suddenly among the primeval ferns, ivy swarmed up the north wall, a chastened sunlight distilled the perfume from great purple pools of heliotrope. Whenever the Colonel returned from his campaigns he discovered some patch of earth which might be persuaded to yield something better than stones or lizards.

The house itself was large and two-storied, and stood on a small hill flanked by larger hills. Here, all through the day, cicadas made music and fat moths hung damply beside their discarded chrysalises. Behind the house the hillside fell in terrace after terrace and one could see, through a cleft in the farther hills, a wide view of the plains two hundred miles away. Among the grasses and rocks of the lower terrace Jacques and Macbeth lay, resting their exhausted bones after a long afternoon in the sun. It was a Saturday and the morning classes had ended with the Raja of Jhori stammering his way through English history. To-day was a half-holiday, theirs to waste as they would.

Jacques had leave to spend the week-end with his new friends, and the boys had exchanged butterfly nets for catapults; each wore on his hat the bright wings of some murdered bird. Far below them the monsoon clouds were gathering, leagues of vapour shaped by wind into immense and intricate architecture. Wherever a warmer current of air pierced this mass the boys had a glimpse of the lower hills, the thickets of the Terai jungle and beyond them the tense level of the plains. Somewhere in its indistinguishable patterns lay Amritpore where people were dissolving in their own sweat, where their minds tightened like wet bow-strings. But for Jacques Amritpore was already retiring to a limbo out of which in his decreasing moods of loneliness he plucked an occasional bitter fruit. His mother wrote that her foreman Boodrie had come down with dysentery and as a consequence she saw no prospect of escape to the hills until later, perhaps not at all. Father Sebastien, too, had been ill ; the Browns had gone to England, Aubrey Wall sometimes called to ask after the children, and she had seen Ganpat Rai, who spoke of Hardyal's life in England. Hanif had boils, which made him irritable and sulky. Never mind, the summer would pass, and early in December Jacques and Gisele would come back to Amritpore.

Mrs. Lyttleton had not written, but Jacques did not expect that she would, for he remembered her declaring once that pen and ink were poor substitutes for flesh and blood. He was, however, learning to draw the past close to him, to turn over the hoarded occasions and to ask himself just what it was, now, that he wanted. Did he really yearn for Amritpore? To return and find Hardyal gone, himself cut off from Mrs. Lyttleton and confined to the companionship of his mother and Father Sebastien? To go back—to June's white heat and a long-drawn existence inside the house under a flagging punkah, reading for the hundredth time *The Count of Monte Cristo*, or arranging his butterflies, or riding alone in the early mornings and late afternoons? The truth was that for Jacques life at St. Matthew's had taken a turn for the better. The Macbeths, of course, were the deciding element in this. John had brought his new friend home one week-end after the episode of the flung inkpot and had presented him to his parents. Jacques found Colonel Macbeth to be a tall, angular soldier with drooping moustaches and pale eyes like his son's. The Colonel combined a passion for soldiering with a passion for gardening, and it was difficult for Jacques to picture this gentle giant killing anything larger than an aphis or a caterpillar.

Mrs. Macbeth was a tiny woman with big eyes and

numerous golden freckles. She fluttered from room to
room, from house to garden, rather like one of the moths
which her son was for ever pursuing, or like the little bird
which he brought down with his catapult. For Jacques,
busily engaged in building his secret honeycomb and storing
up his secret honey, life at the Macbeths was as far removed
from the uncouth existence at St. Matthew's as St. Matthew's was remote from life at home in Amritpore. With
the Macbeths he had discovered a different charm, something which he was later to define as a character grown out
of the accumulation of history at its deepest point. From
the very beginning he detected in it a resemblance to
another character which he knew very well : a kinship to
that authority which was larger than men. For the Macbeths this authority was history—it was, essentially, English
history. For Madame St. Remy it was French *esprit* and
French *espoir* inescapably merged with God. Whatever it
may have been for Colonel Macbeth's sepoys in their curled
beards, their fringed turbans and gold-frogged chapkans,
was not for any one to say—not yet. History had not
accumulated to a point where they, or Jacques, were finally
to stand and say it.

In the meantime there were gay happenings in the big
house up there on the hill ; much playing of the piano and
singing of Braga's Serenade by Mrs. Macbeth and any one
who would sing with her. There was a great deal of coming
and going of the younger officers from the garrison, some as
mild as milk, others as fierce as wart-hogs. Macbeth was
himself the centre of much of this attention, which had the
effect of making him a possessive and jealous friend—lacking in generosity, but poised, vain, and intelligent. He hated
to hear others praised, something which Jacques had discovered at the very beginning of their friendship when he
spoke of Hardyal.

" Hardyal ? " Macbeth frowned.

" His father is a barrister in Amritpore. A—a very
enlightened man," added Jacques, not quite sure what that
might mean, though he'd heard the term often enough.

" Ah, *educated* ! " Macbeth shrugged. " Father says that
the educated native is worse than all the others put together."

" Well, what about your father's soldiers—doesn't he like them ? "

" They are different. They are men."

Jacques tightened. " So are Hardyal and Ganpat Rai men. So is my bearer Hanif a man."

Macbeth replied coldly : " There's no use in sticking up for natives. Sooner or later they let you down."

" So do a lot of white people. Those beasts at school, for instance."

" How would you have liked it if they'd been natives ? "

" Don't be silly. No native has ever touched me."

" If it wasn't for the Army, they might."

They argued, now, as children argue—and as they had heard their elders argue. Jacques stammered : " Well, what about the Mutiny ? They gave us a run for our money then, didn't they ? And they nearly beat us, too."

Macbeth's smile became tense. " A lot of howling niggers—beat *us*? I suppose your Hardyal, for instance, could beat *me* ? "

It was a challenge, but Jacques missed it. Quite suddenly he felt the question to hold an interest above and beyond his friend's vanity. Could Hardyal have beaten Macbeth ? Would he have tried ? He thought of his Indian friend, slender and very strong. When they wrestled Hardyal could throw him on his back, but in boxing Jacques had the advantage. The argument with Macbeth ended there, and on this Saturday afternoon the air was clear between them as they lay propped on their elbows and watched the great clouds foregather. Sounds reached them strained by distance or magnified on the nearer winds—the high note of a bugle-call from the barracks and from the road directly below the guttural voices of Bhotiyals driving borax-laden sheep down to the foothills.

Macbeth removed his hat and examined the plumage of a Paradise flycatcher which adorned it. " That was a damned good shot I made."

Jacques agreed, rather sleepily.

" Once," said Macbeth, glancing at him sideways, " once I killed a pigeon on the wing."

" Jove ! "

"And once on the plains when I was quail-shooting with Father, I got a right and left which he missed."

"Did he like that?"

"Oh, he was sporting about it. But don't mention it before him, will you? I'd hate him to think that I was bragging."

After a brief pause Macbeth said: "Wonder what it feels like to kill a man?"

Jacques replied that he had no idea. "Has your father killed a man?"

"Hundreds." For Macbeth numbers were infinite. "Only don't mention that I told you. He's frightfully reserved about such things."

Jacques was, by now, fairly accustomed to these emendations.

"I dare say," Macbeth continued, "that some time I may have to kill men myself."

"Good Lord, why?"

"If I go into the Army, like Father."

"I thought we were both going to be taxidermists!"

"I haven't quite made up my mind."

Slowly, the clouds travelled up the mountainside and the retreating sun bathed them in colour. Presently they must collide with the higher peaks, shatter, and rain down to the earth. Already from a single escaped cloudlet directly over their heads the boys felt the first hard, cold drops. Macbeth got up and stood on the edge of the terrace, stretching his arms. "Look!" he cried. His shadow was flung far across the sea of vapour, and as Jacques rose and stood beside him they stared in awe at their two slight bodies extending and growing ominous in the freakish light.

Macbeth exulted. "We're huge! Look at us! Look at us! We're miles!"

Jacques rose on his toes and watched the elastic air add a cubit to his stature. Were his head and shoulders at this moment in Amritpore? Down there on the plains could those crawling fleas look up and see the dark, gigantic angels?

More rain fell and from the pulsing mass below them a mutter rose, a vein of light played and vanished. The boys turned and scuttled for the shelter of the house.

15

THAT EVENING the Colonel and his lady were dining at Government House. Mrs. Macbeth had spent the greater part of the afternoon in bed, with the curtains drawn, and later when Jacques saw her emerge from an arbour of still, white orchids into the golden light of the drawing-room, he gasped. She looked ethereal, hardly human, reminding him more than ever of some rare and fragile moth.

"Do you like me, Jacques?" she asked, and tilted her head so the tiny jewels in her hair gave off sparks of fire. He could not have said whether he liked her or not, whether she pleased or frightened him; her femininity was too complete and self-sufficient for his understanding.

She turned to her son. "Do *you* like me, darling?"

"Yes—except for your earrings."

"My earrings?" She raised her hand to touch one, an emerald giving off its strenuous fires. "Why don't you like my earrings?"

He stared at her with concentration. "I don't quite know. Whenever you wear them you look as if you were going away and never coming back." At once Jacques saw what he meant; the earrings changed her expression, her whole air, they transformed her china delicacy into something dubious and disturbing.

She had flushed at her son's remark, but now she laughed. "Silly! These are very precious. When I'm dead you shall give them to your wife."

He replied coldly: "I won't have a wife."

"No? But I thought you intended to marry your cousin, Elizabeth."

Conscious of his friend's embarrassment, Jacques turned away, glancing as he did so at a portrait which stood on the piano; it was a photograph framed in silver of a young girl, and now her eyes seemed to meet his and to hold them in a close and subtle glance.

Mrs. Macbeth smiled from one face to the other. "Go along," she said. "Both of you. Help your father tie his kummerbund, John."

They left her for the Colonel's dressing-room which

smelled of leather and brilliantine.   Jacques perched unobtrusively in a corner and watched the Colonel's servant
helping his master to dress, while John Macbeth lounged
round the room touching things and asking questions.   The
Colonel, in blue trousers with a red stripe, and a stiff white
shirt, stood before the mirror tying his little bow tie.   Behind
him the servant was carefully smoothing the starched collar
of a mess jacket, and suddenly Jacques found himself remembering Father Sebastien vesting himself for the Mass.
First came the amice, then the alb . . .

The Colonel turned, lifting his arms, and his son wound
the crimson sash round the Colonel's lean waist.   The
cincture . . . (" Gird me, O Lord ! ") then the maniple and
the stole.   The Colonel clutched his stiff cuffs in his fists and
turned his back on the servant, who slid the jacket deftly
over the extended arms and eased it up the straight back.

" Receive the priestly garment, for the Lord is powerful
to increase in you love and perfection. . . ."

Jacques felt the Colonel's eye on him.   " What are
you thinking about, young 'un ? "

Jacques came to.   " Nothing, sir."   But he had been
thinking of the sacred corn of the Brahmins, of amulets
containing passages of the Koran, carried by some Moslems,
and of the copper bangle worn on the left wrist of the Sikhs.

The Colonel was dressed at last—booted, spurred,
armed against a world unarmed, his own impressiveness
like his wife's beauty, a shield between them and the devil.
Jacques felt that he himself had absorbed much of this
splendour : he felt the sparkle sift down into him, lighting
him like phosphor.

The rain had stopped.   A rickshaw with hood raised
waited, its runners in regimental livery squatting on the
gravel beside it.   A groom was walking the Colonel's horse
to and fro under the trees.

Mrs. Macbeth embraced the children.   " Good-night,
my darlings ! "

They had gone at last, lighted by a runner with a lantern, and their passage glittered away like a swarm of fire-
flies down the road under the trees.   The boys turned back
to the house, all theirs, now.   The sense of liberation went
to their heads, and Macbeth rushed to the piano.   " I'll be

Mother's friend Mrs. Sykes," he announced.   " You can
be Captain Ponsonby. Here goes ! "

Neither he nor Jacques could play or sing a note between them. Macbeth brought his hands down on the
keys in a frightful discord and Jacques struck an attitude
beside him.

" O qua—li mi ri-sve—glia-no . . ." Jacques bellowed
after the style of Captain Ponsonby.

" Dol-cis-si-mi con-cen—ti non li o-di O . . ." shrieked
Macbeth.

They were applauded from several doors by the grinning
servants, and from her silver frame on the piano Macbeth's
cousin Bertie Wood seemed to smile and to listen.

16

THE school year ended in December.   After Christmas
Macbeth came down to Amritpore to stay with the St.
Remys. Madame was curious to meet her son's new friend,
but she found little to reassure her. Macbeth's precocious
self-possession and rather lordly manner were an offence in
her eyes, for she read in him every vice which she held as
being peculiar to the English. What was worse, he was not
Catholic and his influence on Jacques might lead to almost
anything. But happiness in her son's return tided Madame
over her disappointment in his choice of a friend, and she
exerted herself to be gracious. During meals she discoursed
at length on the charms of her estates at Nonancourt, of
Jacques' ancestors, of her own, and of the prosperous future
of indigo.   The children listened respectfully as Hanif
handed round the silver dishes and interrupted the conversation with comments on the food and reminders to Jacques
of this or that event, past and to come.   Macbeth was
cautious and slightly puzzled, but he betrayed nothing. He
had taken an instant dislike to Madame and to Gisele and
looked with suspicion on Hanif, for he was not accustomed
to servants who behaved as though they were members of
the family. Living with the St. Remys was like living in
another country ; their mixture of prosperity and piety
fascinated Macbeth, for although it had a foreign character

he felt that it was a character which merged more steeply in this Indian setting than did his own or his parents'. Except when he was alone with Jacques, conversation with the St. Remys struck him as being dull and strained. This was not like being at home where people said what they liked and usually liked what they said. Jacques and Hanif seemed to be the only people who really laughed, and to Macbeth there was something wrong about that also, for one does not hobnob with one's servants.

"You don't understand," said Jacques afterwards. "Hanif isn't exactly a servant. My mother adopted him when his parents died in the great famine. He's been with us since he was five years old."

"Is that any reason why he could give you a shove when we were leaving the dining-room?"

"Oh, that? Well, I did step on his foot."

"Give them an inch and they'll take an ell," said Macbeth, quoting something he'd heard from a disgruntled elder. "And why on earth does Hanif cover himself with *scent*?"

Jacques was reflecting: "It's a different life. Macbeth's life is the army, all cut and dried, where no one dreams of going beyond certain limits. Every one has his appointed place, they don't have to make allowances or to try hard to understand anything. For us it's different . . . for us this means home. This is our country. Hanif is our friend." But although Jacques felt these things keenly enough he was unable to translate them into a language which would be acceptable to his friend. Macbeth liked his own world and had no intention of exchanging it for another—faced with such a prospect he became more than ever himself, hard, clear, and assured. He found the factory far more exciting than Madame's household, but Jacques, though pleased by his friend's interest, suffered the old revulsion as soon as he entered the gates and smelled the acid dye. Boodrie bustled round the two boys, pushing the coolies out of his way, cursing them when they were slow to move.

"It belonged to my father," Jacques explained to Macbeth. "I suppose it will belong to me eventually." He looked depressed at the thought. Boodrie gave a short

laugh. " If the bowels don't fall out of indigo in the meantime. In which case, who will pay for the boilers, I'd like
to know ? "

" Aren't they paid for ? " inquired Jacques, surprised.

" Oh my ! With last year's *gaud* still lying unsold in the
Calcutta godowns ? "

" Then shall we plant as much this year as we did last
year ? "

" Madame says yes, but it depends on whether that old
bitch Mrs. Lyttleton will sell her chunna fields."

It was late afternoon when the boys left the factory and
took a short cut across the grounds towards the house.
Jacques was smarting under the foreman's insult to his old
friend ; he had longed to make a fierce retort, but Macbeth's presence restrained him. Now he said with a sudden
air of desperation : " Would you like to call on Mrs.
Lyttleton ? "

" The old bitch ? "

" She's my friend. I'm going to see her. You can come
if you like."

He had waited ever since his return from St. Matthew's,
waited perhaps unconsciously for something like this to
happen, for some spur to his love and loyalty.

Macbeth looked at him in surprise. " You've never
mentioned her before."

" I can't explain, exactly, but I'm not supposed to
know her."

" But doesn't your mother know her ? "

Jacques hesitated. " They don't like each other. It
doesn't matter, does it ? She has always been my friend
and Hardyal's."

The thought of forbidden fruit made Macbeth's face
light up. " I say, is she pretty, or something ? "

" I don't know about that. Let's go and see her."

They sauntered unobtrusively in the direction of the
road, taking pot shots at jays and hoopoes on the way.
Macbeth's catapult hung from his hand as they passed
between the sandstone pillars of the garden ; there, perched
enticingly on a branch, was a small green parrot. Macbeth
brought it down with a perfect shot just as Mrs. Lyttleton
came down the steps of her house to greet them. She rushed

forward and picked up the crumpled bunch of feathers, turning a face of fury upon the murderer. " How could you ? "

He recoiled, and she turned to Jacques. " Couldn't you have stopped him ? "

Jacques explained incoherently that he'd not had time and that upon his word his friend intended no harm. Macbeth, flushed and frightened, looked on with a defiant air, then pulled himself together and apologised. Mrs. Lyttleton listened grimly, stroking the dead bird and twisting the tiny silver bracelet on one of its feet. " I'd had him for years," she said at last, bitterly. " He knew my name, and always greeted me by shouting ' Laura, Laura,' when he saw me. He almost died last year when he had the moult, but I saved him. I gave him brandy and did him up in flannel and he slept beside my pillow. Now you've killed him. How could you ? Oh, how could you ? "

Jacques trembled. " He didn't mean to . . . he just didn't know it was a tame parrot. Did you, Macbeth ? "

Macbeth mumbled something, and Mrs. Lyttleton lifted her fierce gaze to his. " Macbeth ? Where do you come from ? "

He told her, and her face softened a little. " There was a Macbeth who was killed at Kabul, with Major Cavagnari."

" That was my uncle."

" Ah ! " Tension lessened. " That Macbeth had a brother; as I remember. Tall, fair ? "

" He is my father," said Macbeth, secretly wondering how he might gain possession of the dead parrot and remove the offence from her sight.

Mrs. Lyttleton said reflectively : " I remember the Macbeth brothers when they were young—very young. But heavens ! There were so many, and they have all vanished." She smiled faintly. " There, I forgive you, you little brute. But first we must bury Arthur."

They paused beside a weedy flower-bed and the boys knelt, scraping a hole with their hands. They worked diligently and with intense seriousness while she looked on ; then, the grave completed, Jacques laid Arthur in it and covered him with earth. Macbeth toyed with the idea of plucking a flower for the hallowed spot, but a revived self-respect intervened. They rose, brushing off their knees, and Mrs. Lyttleton led them up the driveway to the veranda. She put her hand through Jacques' arm. " I knew you had come home. Now it will be like old times, except for Hardyal's absence."

As they reached the veranda Macbeth stood in respectful contemplation of the stuffed heads. " Someone *did* kill things," he observed, pointedly.

" My husband was a great sportsman, but not given to knocking off little birds with a stone."

" My father has a lot of horns too." And he added, generously—" Though not as many as your husband."

She gave a sudden laugh. " It's all a matter of luck, my dear."

The boys realised dimly that some cryptic witticism had passed over their heads. Then she conducted them into the house where canaries fluttered and a new generation of dogs and cats frisked over the tattered matting. Macbeth had never seen such a house ; it smelled rather like a zoo, and it was crammed with weapons and trophies of all kinds. She showed them the underground zenana where the original owner had hidden his women folk when Amritpore was stormed by the Moslem hordes, and the torture chamber where he had practised on his captured enemies. These ancient events seemed to have left their echoes among the damp walls and crevices, and the precise English voices sent them fluttering and whispering into dim corners, and roused a sonorous protest from the heavy stones.

When the boys had seen all that there was to be seen, Mrs. Lyttleton led them back to her favourite corner in the veranda, where her servant brought them refreshments. Macbeth stared when his hostess lighted a cigarette ; it was the first time he had seen a woman smoke and the spectacle rather scandalised him. She caught his eye and laughed. " Have one yourself. They're quite mild."

Both boys had smoked before, making themselves ill on cheap native tobacco. Now they lighted up and lolled in their chairs like old roués while Mrs. Lyttleton told them stories of what had happened in Amritpore during the past few months. Like most people who live much alone, she loved to talk, and like most children Jacques and Macbeth loved to listen. Now she recounted the story of a dacoity at Ramdatta's village, when thieves broke through the wall of Ramdatta's house, beat Ramdatta's servant to death with a brass pot, and escaped with much booty. The police gave chase, and the thieves took to the trees in a big mango grove. It was a dark night, and they bided their time until the constables with their high-caste inspector tracked them down—then they all excreted into their hands and rained the foul volley down upon the lordly heads in the darkness below. The policemen all fled in disorder, and the dacoits were still at large.

There was another story about the Assistant Magistrate's horse. A thief crept into the stable and burrowing under the straw and litter, managed to loosen the wooden peg to which the beast was tethered. But the horse stirred, wakening the groom who slept beside the door ; he rose and finding the peg loose drove it in again with a mallet —right through the extended hand of the thief, who remained motionless. Then the groom returned to his slumbers and the thief, using his good hand, freed himself and rode away on the horse. He was caught later and given a stiff sentence, a fate deplored by Mrs. Lyttleton, who admired courage and resource even among thieves.

She talked on and on, and the boys listened, forgetful of time. Shadows lay down on the overgrown garden, and the graves under the loquat trees shone in the waning light. Presently her slovenly servant, Jalal, appeared with his prayer mat, which he spread towards the west. They watched him remove his shoes and prostrate himself three times, crying upon Allah, and they knew that all over Amritpore men were praying like this, with their faces towards the setting sun.

When at last the boys had finished their cigarettes they rose, and Mrs. Lyttleton walked with them to the gates. She had apparently forgotten about the parrot, and no one made any allusion to it as they passed the little raw spot in the ground where Arthur lay. When she bade them goodbye she kissed them both lightly, and Macbeth received, as others had received before him, a sense of warmth, an impression that she must, at one time, have been beautiful.

17

THEY RODE to the Fort, and standing beside the sentry-box where last year Jacques had stood with Hardyal, Macbeth stared across the plain and made a sudden exultant gesture of his arms, as though he sought to embrance the landscape and everything it contained. " Funny, when you come to think of it. . . ."

" What's funny ? " Jacques had found a snakeskin and wore it round his neck like a scarf.

" That this should be ours. We won it—just a handful of us against the whole boiling lot. Imagine ! "

Jacques watched the thin, nervous face with its burning eyes. Macbeth's intense possessiveness in such matters always astonished him.

" Perhaps," Jacques suggested slyly, " perhaps some one will come along and take it away again, some day."

" Not now, it's too late and we're too strong." He always used the imperial *we*. " Father says that if they had wanted to a little while ago they could have risen and polished us off. And what could we have done ? "

" Well," persisted Jacques, " what could we do now ? "

" Finish *them* off ! "

" There are still more of them than there are of us."

" But they're not armed as they used to be. Father says we must see that what happened in the Mutiny never happens again." But Macbeth looked as if he would not be very sorry if " it " did happen again, for he was in a warlike mood, and the Fort with its ruins and its reminders had fired his imagination.

They watched goats grazing down in the moat, they listened to the doves, and Jacques felt at peace with himself and with the world. A letter had come to him from Hardyal, yesterday's visit to Mrs. Lyttleton had passed undetected by his family, and last night Aubrey Wall had come back to dinner and had promised to take the boys hunting black buck. That night when his mother came to kiss him good-night Jacques had put his arms around her. " Maman, have the copper boilers been paid for ? "

She stared at him in surprise. " What do you mean, darling ? "

" Boodrie said something about their not being paid for."

She laughed. " Don't you understand that investments like that can't be paid for at once ? They will be, of course, eventually."

He hesitated, then said in a low voice : " Unless the bottom falls out of indigo."

Her surprise gave way to uneasiness. " Where did you hear that, Jacques ? "

" Oh, I don't know. But if that did happen we'd be— we'd be ruined, wouldn't we ? " He'd brooded on it, visualising strange nightmares. Madame St. Remy touched his hair. " Don't you trust me, Jacques ? "

It was his turn to be surprised, and he flushed a little under her pained glance. " Trust you ? Yes, of course. That wasn't what I meant. . . . I meant . . . I wondered . . ."

She bent and kissed him. " I shall be glad when you have grown up, when we can work together, and I can rely on you. That will be my reward."

Her sweetness, her air of strength, restored his sense of security, and it was from this sense that he now felt equal to challenging Macbeth. " I don't believe that there ever will be another Mutiny. They like us too much, they are our friends." He thought of Hardyal and of Ganpat Rai and of the mild, intelligent, friendly men and women he had always known. Dacoities and murders were not uncommon, of course—but they merely helped to make life more exciting and to provide Mrs. Lyttleton with additional wealth of material for her stories. Revolt and mutiny were different things—what had they to do with this sun, with the bleating of the goats under the stunted acacias, with the throbbing sound of the doves ?

Macbeth stretched. " I'm thirsty. Let's go."

Riding home they skirted the village of Ramdatta the moneylender, who saw them and came forth, all smiles and cordiality. " Ah, back from school and filled with learning ! Tell me, Sahib—how many bears did you slay up there in the mountains ? "

" Many, many," replied Jacques. He liked Ramdatta,

who was always jolly and who brought Madame presents every Christmas. " Could we have water ? My friend has a thirst."

" You shall have water and whatever else is mine to give."

He led the way to the courtyard before his house, which was the most imposing in the village ; it was two-storied and leeped in yellow, with a vermilion tiger painted above its arched door. Trees shaded it, and the breeze made a pleasant rustle in the leaves. Buffaloes were milling about in an adjoining pen, and a swarm of children appeared as Ramdatta waved the boys to a string bedstead set under the trees. One of the children was sent in search of the water-carrier, another disappeared into the house and emerged again carrying a brass platter heaped with sweets. While the boys ate the forbidden food and drank the thrice-forbidden, unboiled water, Ramdatta told them about the dacoits who had broken into his house, killed his servant, and robbed him of his valuables. They begged to be allowed to examine the wall, which had been repaired so not a trace of the break remained. One of the dacoits had been captured by the police, and Ramdatta regaled them with a description of how the captors had stripped their victim, placed a large and very active dung-beetle on his bare belly, bound a cloth tightly round it, and waited. Five minutes of activity on the part of the beetle had elicited much valuable information, and the police declared that it was a mere matter of days before they rounded up the remainder of the gang.

The moneylender squatted cross-legged on his string charpoy facing his guests, and told them stories about his early life in Bombay, of the factories and the mills, and the ships which he had seen steaming in and out of the harbour. Friends and relatives appeared and squatted on the ground in an attentive semi-circle before the great man ; someone fetched him his silver-plated water pipe, and one of his children curled like a soft brown puppy against his legs. Sunlight sifting through the leaves touched naked brown bodies, danced off a woman's anklet, shone on a child's shaven skull or on the wet nose of a big black buffalo. There was a continuous murmur of life, heightened by a shrill laugh or a bout of violent coughing. Ramdatta was probably one of the most hated men in his neighbourhood ; there were many who owed him money and the grudge that goes with owing, yet here he sat, the picture of benevolence, varying his tales of sophisticated splendours with nearer and more plausible accounts of ghosts and evil spirits.

When at last the boys rose to go he escorted them to their horses and entrusted Jacques with elaborate greetings for Madame St. Remy. Then he looked keenly at Macbeth. " Come again and visit me—Burra Sahib ! "

" I say, did you notice the ring on his left hand ? " asked Macbeth as they trotted homeward. " It was a ruby, as big as your thumb."

The following day Aubrey Wall took them hunting antelope. They rode out in a cool dawn with Hanif pounding after them on a frowsy pony, his long legs almost touching the ground, a water-bottle strapped to the saddle, a long and murderous knife hanging from his belt. The sky lightened and the plain swam upward from the mists, revealing the land and a little herd of black buck hard as iron against the sky. The creatures saw them and were off at once, bounding into the air like horned gods. The riders raced across the plain with the air whistling in their ears and frightened crows making a din above them. They outflanked the antelope and hid in a gully, their horses hitched out of sight, Hanif passionately nursing his unsheathed knife. Wall brought down a young buck and as it lay kicking in the dust Hanif ran up to it and cut its throat with a loud cry of " Allah Bismillah ! " Blood spouted in a thin fountain, dyeing his arm and his loose white shirt. Then with the dead buck strapped across Hanif's pony and Hanif's song rising and falling, they rode home, warm, tired, friendly.

As they approached Madame's boundary Gisele came out to meet them. She was riding her little half-breed Arab, and her hair was heaped on her shoulders, her face shadowy under the brim of her hat. Wall had been laughing with the others, but when he saw Gisele he fell silent.

The boys rode ahead with Hanif, and Wall reined his horse beside Gisele's. " I wish you had come with us," he said. " We had good sport."

"I don't like to see them killed."

As if by accord, they held their beasts to a walk until the others had disappeared. Wall saw little of Gisele these days, and when they met something intense and unquiet came between them, a self-consciousness which neither could conceal. To the man it seemed as if her beauty had passed beyond the boundaries which divide the mere glow of youth from the beginnings of an exquisite maturity. There were moments when her sudden appearance took his breath away, when it blinded him as though it were a lamp flashed in his eyes. She cast his thoughts, his feelings, into an uproar, although it is not easy to say what those thoughts were, or what the emotion behind them. He was not a man of strong imagination or subtlety ; discontented, unhappy in his exile, he turned with a sense of longing towards the girl whose glow, whose promise, shone against the arid background of a land which he hated.

They rode a little distance without speaking, then she said :

"Do you know that old garden behind the Club ? The one with the pomegranate trees and the Pir's grave ? I'd like to see it, now."

Wall hesitated. "A bit late, isn't it ? "

She gave him a strange, appealing glance, and he managed to smile.

"All right, of course. I'd love to see the garden."

They wheeled and cantered over the unsown fields, skirting the edge of the cantonment itself and approaching the ancient garden by a long circuit. Wall felt a fever rising in his veins as he watched her controlled and charming body riding a little ahead of him. In a little while they were among the tangled pomegranates, and he saw the grave, built of crumbling masonry, with a few sweets placed on it by the faithful as an offering to the forgotten spirit.

Gisele reined her mare. "Our ayah used to bring us here when we were little. I remember I used to steal the sweets ! "

"How wicked of you," said Wall. He dismounted, then went to her side and held out his hands. Gisele freed her feet from the stirrups and slipped lightly into his arms. He held her on his breast and her hair, blown upward by the sudden descent, drifted against his mouth ; he tasted its sweetness and felt, through his jacket, the pressure of her little breasts. When he looked at her he saw that her eyes were closed, that her lips were raised towards his own. The appeal was unmistakable, his own desire no less so. Why not ? he asked himself recklessly. This would not be the first time that he had kissed her, but it might be the last. Yes, he vowed it silently as he bent and pressed his mouth upon hers.

They stood motionless beside the anonymous Pir whose masonry bed the jackals had been undermining. Round them the doves muttered unseen among the pomegranates and a lizard watched them from under a leaf.

" Gisele, Gisele ! "

" Take me away with you, Aubrey."

Incredulous, he lifted his head to stare at her. " Gisele, my darling . . ."

" Yes, take me away. Both of us, you and I . . . somewhere, anywhere."

She clung to him and he held her fast, whispering incoherently :

" I can't . . . how can I ? You're only a child . . . a child, Gisele ! "

" No." Her hands went up and clasped his head, drawing his cheek against hers. " No, I'm not a child, Aubrey. You know I'm not . . . you've known for a whole year that I am not a child."

He led her to the shade beside the tomb, where they sat down ; then he took her in his arms as if she had been a child, trying to assure himself that she was, after all, no more than a child and he a hundred years older. But her hair had settled in a gold cloud about him, her arms clasped him under his jacket and he felt the aroused tumult of her heart against his own.

" Gisele, my dear, let us talk a little."

" Take me away. You could if you wanted to. I'll go with you, anywhere, anywhere."

" But there is your mother, and I . . . and I . . ." He held her as though in defiance of his own reason, his own words. Her warmth flowed into him and he knew that a little more of this and he would be lost.

"Gisele, listen to me. You must be sensible, my darling."

"Then if you won't take me away, love me."

"Ah, I love you."

"No, I mean love me, Aubrey!"

The ants were busy transporting morsels of sugar from the tomb to their own mysterious cities, and there was scarcely a sound except for the doves and the horses grazing nearby. Wall rose at last and drew her to her feet. He passed his hand tremblingly over her hair, then lifted her and set her back in the saddle, standing for a moment with his face buried against the skirt of her habit.

They rode back to Madame's house and Madame watched them from the veranda, her quiet eyes missing nothing in her daughter's face, missing nothing of the man's despair. When he had gone away Madame followed Gisele into her bedroom and helped her to unhook the heavy looped habit. In the adjoining bathroom the ayah was setting out soap and towels and testing the bath water by plunging her wizened arm into it.

Madame took Gisele's face between her hands. "Where did you go, my dear?"

"To the old garden behind the Club."

Gisele's eyes grew deeper, bluer under her mother's scrutiny, and her face was like a saint's face, limpid, expressionless.

"The bath is ready," cried the ayah, jingling all her bracelets.

Gisele put her hands behind her neck and unfastened the hooks which fastened her blouse. Slowly, she began to undress, and Madame picked up the discarded clothes and laid them, one by one, on the foot of the bed.

18

Mrs. Lyttleton listened to the drums. The procession had just passed and she had watched it from her gates, the gilt and paper tazias carried high on men's shoulders, long columns of boys and men beating their breasts and shouting the names of the martyred brothers in a passionate rhythm : " Hasan ! Hosain ! Hasan ! Hosain ! " The festival of Mohorrum always moved her strangely, stirring, as it seemed, the very air to violence. She knew that all over Amritpore the police were anxiously watching the Hindu population. Just let the procession approach too close to a Hindu temple or let a Hindu pipe compete with the Moslem drums, and there was the making of a battle royal. Well, thought Mrs. Lyttleton impatiently, let them have their fight and be done with it. Then she smiled : as though men were ever done with fighting ! Of the twenty-odd wars fought in India by the English she could remember four in which her husband had participated. However, she was convinced that an occasional brisk little war was far healthier than the dry scab of bureaucracy imposed on the raw stuff of passion. And in the end these people know more about self-discipline than we can ever expect to teach them. Let any white man attempt the Fast of Ramadan ! Let him attain—for a day—the contemplative ecstasy of the humblest saddhu ! Mrs. Lyttleton brooded contemp-tuously on the frightened precautions of the local police led by a single harassed Englishman. Mercenaries, all of them. If we are going to be conquerors then let us be con-querors, thought Mrs. Lyttleton, hearing the drums throb-bing in her heart.

She settled down in her accustomed chair with last week's newspapers and a greyhound puppy in her lap. The front page carried a report of a case argued by Ganpat Rai before the High Court, and presently she put the paper down and fell to thinking of the gentle, intelligent barrister and his family. She had gone yesterday to call on Ganpat Rai's mother, and the old lady had entertained her with interminable accounts of the family's history, of pilgrimages and sacrifices, and with new and elaborate plans for the betrothal of Hardyal.

Mrs. Lyttleton had protested, laughing : " Give him time ! He is only fourteen ! "

Vijaya Bhai, squatting cross-legged on her enamelled bedstead, surrounded by sisters and nieces and poor re-lations, shook her earrings in great excitement. " I was betrothed when I was five, my son when he was ten."

Later, when Ganpat Rai walked with her across the

garden to her carriage, he said : " My mother is preparing endless puja for the purification of Hardyal when he returns. To placate her I have gone twice to the temple to offer prayers. I have given a thousand rupees to the family priest, not to mention gifts for sacrifice and for the poor."

Mrs. Lyttleton laughed, remembering his reputation as a hard-headed lawyer, but he went on gloomily : " She is determined that Hardyal must marry as soon as he returns from England."

" It sounds almost as silly as if one were to insist on a marriage for Jacques St. Remy."

He nodded. " I tried to explain to my mother that Hardyal himself may well have different ideas by the time he comes home. Naturally, such reasoning is beyond her."

" You are Hardyal's father," Mrs. Lyttleton reminded him. " It is for you to decide."

He clasped his mild brown hands. " Ah ! But it is not easy. I feel alone in the midst of my own family, for they are all against me. Even my brothers disapprove of my permitting Hardyal so much independence. They will not see that our world is not going to be the same, twenty years from now. I want to free him from the shackles of the past —free him from six thousand years of tradition, so that he may face his future without a burden."

She was touched by his sincerity. " Yes, I can see that it is not easy for you, and that it will not be easy for him."

He responded eagerly to her friendly tone. " You have always been our friend and you love Hardyal. In my position, what would you do ? "

She hesitated, thinking of the women back there in the house, those doting women who clung so frantically to the past ; she had, herself, seen too much to dismiss, lightly, the complexities of such a situation.

She said, at last : " Hardyal seems happy in England. He writes that he has made friends, he likes the life. Why not let him stay there for another year ? It could do no harm and it might well be for the best as far as he is concerned."

" Yes, yes ! As far as he is concerned. That is what matters, is it not ? " His voice trembled and she saw the emotion in his eyes. " Hardyal shall stay in England for another year. I had hoped that you, too, would advise it."

The noise of the drums had retreated and Mrs. Lyttleton was on the point of dropping into a light doze when she heard, in the road beyond the gates, the musical double-note of a carriage bell. She opened her eyes in time to see Madame St. Remy's phaeton pass between the gates and bowl up the weedy driveway.

Mrs. Lyttleton rose, instinctively smoothing her dress and shaking down her numerous bangles and bracelets. Her mind was a riot of conjecture : communication between herself and Madame had been conducted by channels as devious as Mrs. Lyttleton, with a perverse sense of mischief, could possibly devise. For twenty years they had neither spoken nor set foot in each other's house. What, now, could be the purpose of this extraordinary visit ?

The carriage drew up under the porte cochère and Mrs. Lyttleton heard Madame tell the coachman to wait. Then she alighted, gowned in black, her white topi draped in fine crêpe. " Concierge ! " thought Mrs. Lyttleton bitingly.

There was a flush on the faces of both women when they confronted each other across the crumbling furniture. Mrs. Lyttleton spoke first.

" Madame St. Remy, this is a great surprise, a great honour ! "

Madame bowed, then stood with her gloved hands clasping the gold knob of her parasol. Twenty years of hostility divided them : only a triviality could bridge that abyss, and Mrs. Lyttleton supplied it :

" Won't you sit down ? I'd offer you tea, but my servants have gone to the Mohorrum and God knows when they'll come back."

Madame selected the least ramshackle chair and removed her tight kidskin gloves. She missed no detail of her surroundings as she thought with mingled disgust and satisfaction : " Just as shoddy as I expected."

Mrs. Lyttleton settled herself in her chair and arranged her skirts. " You must have just missed the procession. Do you think we shall have the usual row ? "

" If we do," returned Madame stiffly, " it will probably be the fault of the police. They are always looking for trouble, Mohorrum or no Mohorrum."

"Ah yes, *divide et impera*, of course. Is that chair really comfortable? The dogs sleep in it."

Madame's eyes met hers. "Perhaps it would be just as well if I came straight to the point?"

Mrs. Lyttleton shook her head. "I should be most disappointed. I am delighted to see you. I love visitors and I've scarcely set eyes on another woman since Mrs. Brown went back to England."

There was a slight pause. Mrs. Lyttleton thought : She's lost her looks. She used to be very pretty in her sharp little French way. I wonder what in the devil she is after?

Madame was reflecting : She's as dry and yellow as a tarantula. What does Jacques see in her? What did Auguste see?

"Will you have a cigarette?" asked Mrs. Lyttleton, opening the box of Egyptians beside her chair. Madame declined with a stony glance, and Mrs. Lyttleton selected a cigarette for herself, her rings giving off a minor conflagration. No doubt, thought Madame, her lovers kept her in jewels. The vulgarity of it, wearing such things at this hour!

"I came," she began, "to ask whether you would consider selling the doab lands by the river. Perhaps I should have written to you, but I was given to understand that you never answer letters."

"On the contrary, I carry on a voluminous correspondence. For instance, I had—just before you came—just finished writing a long letter to Hardyal. Did you know that his father wants him to go into the Civil Service? My own opinion is that the Army is the place for young men. But then I'm prejudiced, naturally."

"Naturally," agreed Madame. She took a deep breath. "But to return to the matter of the doab. I am anxious to extend my crop next year, and I cannot make plans for hiring additional labour until I know where I stand in regard to acreage."

"You intend to put more land to indigo?" inquired Mrs. Lyttleton with an air of surprise.

"Why not?" Madame's voice was crisp. "Last year was most successful. This year should be even better, in which case I hope very much that I may be able to send my children home next year."

" Home, Madame ? "

" Gisele is eager to enter the convent at Bruges, and Jacques must have a few years of travel before he comes into the factory with me."

" I see that you have many burdens and expenses, Madame."

Their thoughts moved between them, subtle, inimical. Mrs. Lyttleton continued :

" It's funny that you should ask me about the doab. I had a call a few days ago from that rascal Ramdatta. He wanted it himself, to buy or to lease. I have my suspicions about him, however."

" Suspicions ? "

" I don't believe he wants it for himself. He already has more land than he knows what to do with. I think he is acting as go-between for one of his shady friends. He has many ! It may be for one of those big zamindars from Lucknow, and they can easily afford to pay more than they are willing to offer."

Madame stared at her hands. It was at her instigation that Ramdatta had approached Mrs. Lyttleton, on the understanding that the land should be resold or subleased to Madame herself.

Mrs. Lyttleton continued light-heartedly : " He is clever, that Ramdatta. Nevertheless, I told him to go to Jehannum."

" Then," said Madame coldly, " we come back to my question : will you sell to me ? "

Mrs. Lyttleton's eyes were suddenly hard as prisms. " Certainly, Madame—but at a price."

Madame St. Remy named it without hesitation, aware that Ramdatta had offered less.

Mrs. Lyttleton continued to gaze at her. " I was not thinking of money, Madame."

" What ? "

" My price is Jacques."

The name exploded between them like a rocket. Madame flushed.

" What has Jacques to do with this ? "

"Much. Shall we be clear with one another, just for once?"

"Mrs. Lyttleton, I have come to discuss a purely business transaction . . ."

"We shall do so, but let us first discuss something that lies near both our hearts."

Madame relapsed into silence, and Mrs. Lyttleton continued, rather breathlessly : "I am old, Madame St. Remy, and I have not much to lose, now. You know something of my history, and I know something of yours. Whatever I once had and loved, lies buried over there." She nodded towards the garden. "I know you have always disliked me, even hated me, and I can guess why. Slanderous absurdities are bound to accumulate round a woman as unconventional as I, and women as conventional as you are bound to believe them. I don't care. I never have cared, much. And now that I am old I feel that there is very little left that I can lose. However, that little matters to me, considerably." The greyhound puppy returned and clambered into her lap. Madame stared at it fixedly as Mrs. Lyttleton continued : "Madame St. Remy, I love Jacques. I love him as only old and lonely women can love . . ." She laughed faintly. "As they love the promise of eternal life. Can I make you see what I mean? I know what you're thinking, that I'm incorrigible, that I have had lovers and that the taste for love hasn't died in me as it should have died years ago. Well, you're right—it hasn't died. It will die when I die, not before. You must often have asked yourself what your child can see in an old woman like myself . . ah, you're asking it at this moment ! Well, he sees in me the equivalent of what I see in him—qualities which men and women desire in each other—forgiveness, variety, passion, and humour. Those were lessons you scorned to learn. No, please don't go yet. I've been dying to say these things to you . . . hoping for an opportunity which I never dreamed *you* would give me !"

Madame, who had half risen, sank back in her chair. "You are very eloquent," she said dryly. "But I still fail to see what Jacques has to do with the business that has brought me here."

"Then I'll explain. If you will give Jacques permission

D

to visit my house whenever he likes, without hindrance or stealth, I shall sell you that doab at any price you choose to name."

Madame laughed for the first time. "Really, your frankness disconcerts me! You believe, then, that I would accept your offer in exchange for my son's corruption?"

Mrs. Lyttleton was silent, then she smiled. "What a compliment from one woman to another! Somehow I did not expect that from you."

Madame looked at her with detestation. "May I now speak my mind? I too am glad of the opportunity. You and I have misunderstood each other for too long. Years ago, Mrs. Lyttleton, when I came to Amritpore as a bride, young, innocent, and in love with my husband, you lost no time in trying to deprive me of his love. No, please do not interrupt. I was in a strange land, among strange people. I felt desperately alone. Auguste was all I had in the world, all I cared for. *Please* permit me to finish! You have just outlined your philosophy. . . . You love life, you love youth!" Her voice was bleak with horror. "I do not doubt that your friend Aubrey Wall subscribes to the same philosophy. He, too, prefers youth and innocence . . . as though we need to be told what it is you love! You have nourished yourself on other people's jealous misery, other people's love. You won Auguste away from his work, from his home, from his children, from his wife. You taught him to come to you with his difficulties and his disappointments —not to me, his wife! You sympathised with his weakness and condoled with his imaginary sorrows. But in the end what could you give him that I could not? Shall I tell you? It is very simple—every courtesan understands the formula. You provided Auguste with opportunities for vice, and vice, naturally, is not an asset which even libertines knowingly relish in their own wives! But I could forgive him, and you, had it not been for something greater and far more terrible." Her eyes blazed. "There is something neither God nor I will forgive. You destroyed Auguste's faith. Your influence was so strong that even when he was dying he refused the sacraments." Her voice seemed to splinter, to fall everywhere in shrill fragments. Mrs. Lyttleton sat in astounded silence.

Then Madame St. Remy rose, collecting her parasol and gloves. As swiftly as she had lost her self-control she now regained it. "And you have the superlative insolence to demand my son's friendship! Let me tell you, Mrs. Lyttleton, that I would rather have my children dead and buried where such vultures will never dare to search them out!"

Mrs. Lyttleton lifted herself rather stiffly to her feet. She was divided between mirth and fury, but before she could find words to conclude the interview Madame had turned on her once more. "I know very well that Jacques has come to see you during these winter holidays. I have seen that your poison has already started to work in him . . . but he will not come again. He and Gisele are going back to the hills to-morrow."

Mrs. Lyttleton's temper gave way at last. "Well, Madame—allow me at least one claim to mercy. *I* waited until my daughter was dead before I buried her!"

She turned and walked into the house, and long after the carriage had rolled away through the gates she stood alone in her great empty drawing-room, listening to the drums beating in the distance, and to the closer, painful beating of her heart.

19

THE Raja of Jhori, in strawberry-coloured tweeds and bright yellow shoes, greeted Jacques and Macbeth on their return to St. Matthew's.

"Here we are, all together again! Jollee, isn't it?"

"We do not think it is so damned jollee."

"Oh, I say. The same old snobs as of last year, I see."

They gave the unfortunate prince a deadly stare, then went their way.

"I wonder why we don't like him?" Jacques murmured as they strolled across the playground.

"He's a swot, always trying to outdo every one else. It isn't even as though he were a real prince. Government put him on the throne when they found out that the real ruler was a rotter—he kept boys in cages."

" What ? "

Macbeth gave him an amused glance. " Don't you know ? "

" Know what ? "

" Well," Macbeth hesitated, waiting for a little group of third standard infants to kick a football out of range. " Notice young Hicks over there ? Looks like a girl. *He* ought to be in a cage."

Study, prayers, games—the routine caught them up and strove to press and polish them all into the semblance of so many little ciphers, but it remained a semblance. The miracle of personality survived, assertive, defiant. A young Afridi chieftain taking special tutoring from Brother Duane found himself bored, he departed, leaving a note in Pushtu : " Thanks for kindness and patience. My brain wearies, and I go now to avenge the death of my sister's husband. Perhaps I shall return, perhaps not."

He did not return, and spurred by this example young Leggatt, chronically homesick, ran away and was captured at the railway terminal and brought back. For the rest of the year he remained solitary and brooding. Edmonton was caught during a nocturnal visit to the Convent where he had gone to meet young Holtby's sister, and both were expelled amidst a flurry of partisan excitement.

Then one morning in May young Hicks was reported missing, and two days later they found his body lying in ten feet of water near the most sequestered part of the lake. He could not swim and someone said that he had waded beyond his depth, some that he must have fallen from a raft while fishing for minnows . . . others whispered suicide. He was a queer little fellow, not much liked, but his death struck on Jacques' nerves. He had seen death before, down by the ghats in Amritpore, but the death of Indians had not seemed specially significant. But after they had found little Hicks, Jacques could not sleep. He was one of the servers at the Mass for the Dead, and as he knelt beside the coffin and heard the hymns peal over his head, as he watched the priests in their black vestments, a terrible protest swelled in his throat. He felt that he alone challenged God's incomprehensible savagery, that he alone stood up to Heaven with the inaudible question : " How dare you ? " Tears burned his eyes as he listened to the choir, to the indescribable sweetness of boys' voices.

The day after the funeral was Sunday, and as Jacques climbed the hill towards the Macbeths' house he heard a koel whistle in the valley, and the guttural conversation of Bhotiyals driving their sheep towards the plains. He'd passed these cheerful Mongols on the road and they hailed him merrily in a language which he couldn't understand, but which he recognised as being friendly. Their eyes slanted upward at the corners, they wore their long hair braided with coloured wool, and as they disappeared in clouds of dust he could hear them admonishing their sheep with barking noises, like dogs.

The Macbeths' spaniel came wagging to meet him, and a big bearded orderly saluted jocosely as he ran up the veranda steps. The drawing-room seemed deserted, then he saw a figure rise from a chair beside the piano and an unknown voice greeted him : " Are you Jacques ? "

He did not answer at once, but stared through the gloom.

" You must be Jacques," said the voice calmly. " And I am Bertie Wood."

He had known that she was coming, but he had forgotten. He went towards her as she rose—a girl of about his own age, with one of those faces which is more English than anything else about them—a face fashioned out of the alloy of generations, Saxon and Norman tempered by a perverse Mediterranean strain encountered Heaven knows where or when. Bertie's eyes were a light brown like the eyes of an orange cat, her skin but a few shades lighter, her hair a luxuriant black. She was not beautiful nor even pretty, but her face was full of light and movement, her body slight, poised, and eager. But shyness, it seemed, was not part of her accoutrements, for she held out her hand and as Jacques took it she stared at him with a critical thoroughness. " John has done nothing but talk about you since I arrived. I tried to make him describe you to me, but he couldn't." Jacques dropped his hand on the piano keys and struck an inadvertent note. " Well, he described you to me."

" Go on, do tell me ! "

"I don't remember, exactly."

"Did he say he thought I was pretty?"

"Oh no, he didn't say that. Besides, he didn't have to, did he? I've seen your photograph." He picked it up from the piano and examined it, glancing from the pictured face to the living one.

"Well, do you think I'm pretty?"

He put the photograph back in its place. "Well no— not exactly."

She sank on a chair arm, swinging her foot, and he went on quickly:

"All I meant was, you don't look like my sister Gisele."

"Yes, I know all about your sister Gisele, and about your mother, and your servant Hanif, and about Amritpore. John has told me everything. But I wish the dickens . . ." She broke off, and on Jacques there dawned the extraordinary feeling that he had known her all his life. She finished explosively: "I wish the dickens I was lovely . . . really, really lovely!" She stared at him intensely. "You know, *devastating*!"

"Oh, well," he murmured, rather at a loss. There was a brief pause, then he asked: "Does it really matter?"

Bertie sighed deeply. "Before you came I was thinking: how wonderful it would be if, when you entered the room and saw me for the first time, I could just bowl you over. You know, completely bowl you over." When he remained discreetly silent she rose with a sudden, brave air, and taking his arm led him to the big window which gave on a view of the Colonel's rose garden. With her arm linked in Jacques', Bertie gazed at the sparkling hills. "No one ever told me that India could be like this—all light, all green, all sky!"

He listened to her clean accent, so different from the polyglot of St. Matthew's.

She went on: "I'd like to live here for the rest of my life."

"So would I."

"It's a pity that one cannot, isn't it?"

"Why not?"

"Well, eventually one has to go away."

He frowned. "Lots of people stay. Hundreds! They

live here and die here." He thought of Mrs. Lyttleton and of poor little Hicks. Bertie shook her head. " This isn't our country. I haven't been here very long, but I can see that already. And some one was talking about it last night at dinner—Captain Ponsonby, I think. He said something about how essential it is for people to stick to their own culture."

" But," he objected, rather uncertainly, " isn't culture something that is made up of lots of things ? I mean, what is one to do if one *prefers* to live in a place that isn't one's country ? "

She thought this over. " I think that what Captain Ponsonby meant was—that if one stays here too long one loses one's sense of—of identity. That was the word. He said something about people going native."

Jacques nodded. " I wonder if Hardyal will go native in England, if he stays there long enough ? "

" Hardyal ? "

Jacques explained, glad that she showed none of Macbeth's reaction to that cherished name.

" Do you mean to say you have a Hindu friend, really ? A friend like John ? If I'm here next year shall I meet him ? "

Before Jacques could answer, Colonel Macbeth entered the room behind them. " Ah, so you've met ! " He looked from one face to the other.

" Jacques, you don't know it yet but you will before long : this is a most unusual woman."

" I know. She can ride and shoot and sail a boat and stand on her head and talk four languages and see in the dark ! "

Colonel Macbeth laughed. " I see that your cousin John has prepared the ground for you, Bertie, my dear."

She tossed her dark head. " What a liar John is ! Does he still take Cascara when he wants to dodge classes ? "

" So that was it ! "

" He wrote and told me all about it. He was frightfully pleased with himself. And he told me about all the leopards he'd shot. Has he ever killed anything more dangerous than a grasshopper, Uncle Jack ? "

" There is a chance that he may, next week. I've been talking with Lal Singh, my old shikari, and he tells me that

a leopard has been stealing goats from a village not far
away. Would you like to come—and you, Jacques?"

Both replied excitedly that they would, and for Jacques
St. Matthew's had already receded into the distance. Mrs.
Macbeth entered, and now her fluttering delicacy seemed
to clash with Bertie's dark presence. She kissed Jacques,
then asked for her son.

"He's upstairs taking the insides out of beetles," explained Bertie.

"Oh, dear!" Mrs. Macbeth's gaze rested fleetingly
on the girl.

"Bertie, darling, shouldn't you do your hair for lunch?
Do put on a ribbon—the red velvet one."

Jacques' ear caught something a little off-key in her
tone, a sort of exaggerated persuasion, and he wondered
rather innocently why she should suggest an accentuation
of Bertie's charm. He had not failed to observe that charm
was an asset by which the Colonel's lady set great store—
she outshone every woman who came here, outshone, out-
fluttered, out-sang. But he was still too innocent to guess
that youth alone could place Mrs. Macbeth at a disadvantage and that by her peculiar genius she would rise above
even that disadvantage by conniving, in a fraudulent spirit,
at the enchantment of a rival's charm. But if the boy failed
to grasp entirely this little byplay, Bertie did not fail. She
danced out of the room, to return a few minutes later not
only with a bow in her hair but with the hair itself piled
and knotted on top of her head : the transformation made
her at once delectable, at once a rival. Colonel Macbeth
put his arm round her, and at that moment John Macbeth
came into the room behind Captain Ponsonby and two other
officers from the garrison. Macbeth glanced at Bertie, then
gave Jacques a triumphant stare which said as plainly as
words : "Now you see what *I* can produce at a moment's
notice!"

A servant announced lunch, and as they all streamed
into the dining-room Jacques wondered whether he would
not, after all, be a soldier and wear a handsome *putto* coat
with leather buttons when he was not wearing the blue and
gold of his chosen regiment.

20

" WILL YOU," murmured Bertie, " please kill that wasp ? "

It was after lunch and the children lay on the terrace below the house. Bertie had provided herself with a rug and a cushion ; Jacques was propped on his elbow beside her, and Macbeth sprawled at her feet. She had been reading aloud from *Vanity Fair*, but now she lay with the book upside down on her breast, her eyes seeping liquid vistas of sky and leaf. Jacques slew the wasp with his hat, and asked tentatively :

" Do you think we can beat the Boers ? "

He had listened, during lunch, while Colonel Macbeth and his officers discussed the South African War. All were eager to go.

Macbeth repeated slowly : " Beat them ? Of course— eventually."

" But think of Colenso," said Bertie, with a shiver. " And Spion Kop. I wish it would end. I hate it."

Macbeth said abruptly : " I wouldn't mind if Ponsonby went, though."

She smiled faintly, watching Jacques from under her lashes. " Nor would I. It would be nice if he went and the Boers took him prisoner, wouldn't it ? "

There was a long pause, during which each was busy with his own thoughts, then Bertie said : " You know, reading this book makes me think of my governess Fräulein Eberhard. She used to make me read it to her, and she always went to sleep after the first five minutes."

" What happened to her ? " asked Jacques, politely abandoning the Boer War in favour of a more personal topic.

" She died. That's why I'm here—she would never have let me come without her and she wouldn't come herself, so it's just as well that she died."

Bertie reflected without remorse and without rancour on that miraculous deliverance. Like her cousin John, she was an only child, but unlike him she was an orphan whose parents were drowned in a yachting accident on the Norfolk Broads when she was six years old. Bertie spent her childhood with alternate sets of relatives, under the personal care of Fräulein Eberhard—one of those devoted leeches known as a governess-companion. Lying here now and gazing at this Indian sky, Bertie remembered those interminable London winters ; she remembered Fräulein's nocturnal terrors, her fits of crying, her bullying, her passion for taking walks in cemeteries, her jealousy, her moods. Then Fräulein Eberhard died and Bertie, elated by freedom, found herself bored by all her English relatives. They were prigs who looked with a stern eye on her high spirits. She thought yearningly of her favourite uncle and of the happy times which she had spent when the Macbeths were on their rare furloughs in England. Finally she wrote a supplicating letter to Colonel Macbeth, and a month later she was on her way to India.

Now she retraced that journey from Southampton to Bombay—her first voyage, her first great adventure as the watery leagues slid under the ship's keel. She thought of the ocean as a transfusing element which bound India and England together, and this idea grew as she saw the reflections of Bombay breaking on the shallows of the Arabian Sea. The Macbeths had sent their servants to escort her to the hills, and she shared her first-class compartment with two missionary ladies from America. One was middle-aged and nervous and made a great to-do about boiling everything she drank ; the other was young, brisk, and talkative. Bertie soon learned all the details about their home in Iowa and the fact that they were returning to India on the conclusion of what they called their Sabbatical. They were curious about her and looked disapproving when she explained that she had come to India for no better reason than to enjoy herself.

" This is hardly the country for play," observed the elder of the two with a severe glance. " But you will doubtless find that out for yourself after you've spent a summer on the plains."

" I am not going to spend a summer on the plains. I'm going to the hills."

" Even in the hills you will find discomfort," the younger lady informed Bertie with an air, almost, of satisfaction. " One cannot escape it. There are no proper cooking facilities, no fly screens, no refrigeration. To equip our mission we have had to import everything from America."

" Even the simplest things," added the elder lady, not without pride. " There is no question that you English have been very backward about educating the natives. With all these great forests and all the water power, think what could have been done ! "

" Yes, when I think of the settling of our great South-West ! "

Bertie, who felt that her country's shortcoming could hardly be laid at her door, remained silent, watching with covert fascination as the middle-aged lady tied her boot-laces with two little pieces of toilet paper wrapped round her fingers.

" Why do you do that ? " she inquired at last, unable to curb her curiosity.

" One hates the idea of germs." She stared at Bertie. " I trust you brought your Chlorodyne ? "

" I don't play it," replied Bertie politely.

The younger missionary laughed. " It's a medicine, my dear—not a musical instrument. We use it to ward off cholera. Goodness, you *are* ignorant, aren't you ? "

Bertie resented this but felt that she had asked for it, so said nothing more. It was at Benares Station that something happened to disturb her enchantment with the journey. There she saw a tall and dapper Englishman throw a young Indian out of a first-class compartment and get into it himself with his wife, his luggage, and all his dogs. The performance—it was necessarily brief—was watched by an interested but passive audience of natives and Eurasians, and Bertie stared in wonder as the Indian picked up his scattered belongings and walked quietly away to a third-class compartment. A passing guard explained to the missionaries' queries : " Onlee one first-class and that native absolutely refused to give it up. True, he had a ticket, but onlee one first-class available, so what was the Sahib to do ? "

" Why couldn't he share it with the Indian gentle-man ? " demanded the younger lady, who had flushed with indignation. The Eurasian guard looked at her, then shrugged and went his way. He knew from experience that it was impossible to explain some things satisfactorily to American ladies.

As the train drew away from the platform the elder lady murmured :

" Dear me, so distressing . . . that poor Indian."

" But I don't understand ! " exclaimed Bertie. " Why didn't he stand up for his rights ? "

" Perhaps he doesn't have any," suggested the other, in a dry voice.

" But there were all those other Indians standing there —why didn't they go for the Englishmen ? "

The Americans regarded her silently, then the younger one smiled.

" Goodness, you *are* ignorant, aren't you ? "

" I don't see . . ." began Bertie, but the other interrupted, gently enough : " Natives don't strike white men, my dear. Don't forget that ! "

Bertie retired behind *Vanity Fair*, but the scene on Benares platform continued to haunt her. She simply could not understand why the Indian, who looked young and strong, had not defended himself against the uncouth Englishman. She thought of all the men she had known at home and she knew that not one of them would have put up with such treatment. In the first place people did not behave like that unless they were drunk or mad. Yet the Indian had submitted . . . and with this thought there rose an angry contempt for him. She put down her book and glanced once more at the younger of the Americans. " Why do you keep telling me that I'm ignorant ? I don't feel ignorant. I just want to know . . ."

The other hesitated for a moment, then said frankly : " It's not so easy to explain. It's all mixed up with history and with your way of looking at things."

" *Our* way ? "

" The English way, then."

The conversation suddenly embarrassed Bertie, for it was rather like talking about God or about love, or walking about in public showing too much leg. She hesitated, marshalling her thoughts, then decided to come out with them. " I think I know what you mean. We are conquerors, and you don't like the way we behave about it. But after all hasn't every one been conquered at one time or another. The Romans conquered England, and that was very good for us."

The other shrugged. " I suppose it depends on where we decide to stop." When Bertie remained silent, she asked : " Have you ever been to America ? "

Bertie said no, she had not had the pleasure.

" But you remember what happened there, don't you ? We kicked you out. While Warren Hastings was busy saving India for the English, Lord North was losing America."

Bertie felt that something was up to her—though she was not entirely sure just what it was. She asked, in a cool voice :

" What about your own Red Indians ? They can't even vote, can they ? " She had heard this somewhere, and thanked her stars that it now recurred to her memory.

The elder lady interposed with an air of dignity. " That is quite true, my dear. But there are many, many of us in America who lament the tragedy of the American Indian. Life is a very difficult thing . . . a very, very difficult thing." And she gazed steadfastly into space.

Later, when Bertie mentioned this episode to her uncle, he frowned.

" Don't run away with the idea that we are all like that Englishman. I've lived in India for twenty-five years and I've never raised my hand against a native."

" But you have fought them ! " And she examined the little white scar on the back of his hand. He smiled down at her with his gentle eyes. " My dear ! There is a difference, you know. *That* was war."

Now as she lay on the terrace and stared at the immense shadowless sky, England, the American missionaries, Benares Station all seemed very far away, their importance diminishing like a beetle's wing in great tides of sunlit air. She heard the boys discussing the leopard hunt on which they were all going the following week, and she interrupted lazily : " I wish one didn't have to do all this killing."

" You've killed pheasants, yourself," her cousin reminded her.

" I know. It's fun, and that's what makes it so awful."

"Oh well," said Jacques, "think of all the things we eat—the sheep and the chickens and the fish, even the eggs."

"And even a potato must have some feeling," Macbeth went on. "And plums ! How would you like to be a nice ripe plum and have someone come along and take a bite out of you ? "

"And then spit you out because you were full of worms ? " added Jacques.

"And back you go on the rubbish heap, and along comes a hyena and turns you over with his hideous snout . . ."

"Then lifts its head and gives a howl like this : BERTIE ! "

Bertie listened to the echo which pealed away from the nearer hills.

"Now tell me how I'd feel if I were an antelope bounding over the mountains ! "

Macbeth replied crushingly that antelope didn't live on mountains.

"But you could be a wild pig," suggested Jacques.

"Or," said Macbeth, "one of those big black-faced monkeys. *Then* you could have a little black-faced monkey hanging on to you in front. . . ."

Bertie rolled over, burying her face on her arms, and Jacques lay beside her, watching the sunlight play on her hair. It had been a long time since he had felt so happy.

21

"IT'S BEEN ages since I've seen you," said Gisele. She and Jacques sat in the vast cheerless room of the Convent, where the girls were permitted to receive visitors. Portraits of long-departed Mothers and Sisters of the Order stared at them from the walls ; outside, a hot sun beat on the gravel and on the leaves of the horse chestnuts.

Jacques stirred uneasily on the hard slippery chair where he sat facing Gisele. An abyss divided them—she struck him as being even more unapproachable than one of her own beloved martyrs.

"I've meant to come before this, but . . ."

She interrupted coolly : " You haven't really. You know you'd rather see the Macbeths. Isn't that true ? "

He took refuge in defiance. " Yes, it is true ! "

" I'm glad that at least you don't try to lie. I always know when you're lying." When he remained silent she went on : " You're on your way to them now, aren't you ? For the holiday ? "

" Why not ? "

" What will you do when Maman is here ? She'll be here very soon. And when she comes she will want us to be with her. You won't be able, then, to run off to your friends whenever you please."

Jacques felt something white-hot flower in his heart. Why had he come here ? He should have stayed away. Gisele did not love him, she did not really want to see him, and she saw through his brotherly pretence to the sense of guilt which brought him. " Why don't you like the Macbeths ? Why won't you come with me sometimes when I go to see them ? "

" Thank you, I can live without friends."

" But why should you ? "

" Because they take one away from God ! You don't mind being taken away from Him, do you ? You've never been very happy in His presence."

He clenched his hands. " Why do you want to talk about it all the time ? "

" Because you are my brother and because I keep wondering what will become of you. So does Maman wonder."

His heart was pounding angrily. " I don't see why you want to talk about it. I don't see why."

" You could if you tried, but you don't want to try. Oh, it's all very well to love. One should love one's mother, one's family, even one's friends." Her eyes brooded on his face. " I could love just as you do, perhaps even more than you can dream of loving. God doesn't blame us for that, but He cherishes those who renounce love for His sake."

Jacques sat in stony silence, and after a slight pause Gisele went on : " I had a letter from Maman in which she said that she was worried about you. Maman has always told me everything."

Jacques was thinking that he had never really known Gisele, that she could not be his own sister, someone he'd grown up with, someone who used to play with him in the garden at home, who even laughed, sometimes, at the same jokes.

He burst out suddenly : " Can't I have friends ? "

" Why do you care so much whether you have friends or not ? " When he made no answer to this she asked abruptly : " Would you think of marrying someone who was not a Catholic ? "

" I'm not going to marry."

" But would you ? "

He stared stubbornly at the floor.

" You would, of course. You'll let nothing stand in your way."

" Then why do you ask ? "

" I don't really need to ask. I know. I know everything, because Maman told me. She has always told me everything because I am the eldest and there was never any one for her to confide in. I am much closer to Maman than you are, because I have always understood . . ."

He listened, conscious of the growing hysteria in her voice. Gisele was staring at him fixedly. " Maman has always been afraid that what happened to Papa would happen to you."

" What happened to Papa ? "

" He abandoned God. He left the Church and died without taking the sacraments. You didn't know that— Maman didn't want you to know."

" Then it's wicked of you to tell me ! "

She looked at him with eyes that suddenly terrified him. " It was all because of your friend Mrs. Lyttleton. She took Papa away from Maman. She took him away from us, and from God. Maman may have told you certain things about Mrs. Lyttleton, but I don't think she told you that."

" No, she didn't—she didn't, because it isn't true. People don't do such things . . . Mrs. Lyttleton couldn't take Papa away . . . she didn't . . . she wouldn't . . ."

" Why not ? "

" Because . . . because he wouldn't have let her . . . and

because she would never have tried. People don't . . . not grown-up people."

"They do. I know they do."

A shadow passed before the doors and a Nun entered. This was the Mother Superior, a tall, handsome, clear-eyed woman. The children rose as the impressive figure paused before them, its full black skirts falling into still lines like the plaster folds of a statue. "Ah, Gisele! This is your brother." She looked from one face to the other.

"You have a beautiful sister, my dear. We are proud of our Gisele." She touched the girl's cheek with a plump hand. "How nice that you should spend the afternoon together. God bless you."

She swept away, and Jacques saw that his sister's cheek still bore, like a stigma, the pale imprint of the Nun's caress.

Something broke loose inside him. "I hate you," he whispered. "I hate you, Gisele! You spoil everything. . . ."

"I know you hate me, but I don't hate you. I feel sorry for you. I shall pray for you as I pray for Papa, every day and every night."

Jacques made a frantic gesture. "Don't pray for us! I don't care, I tell you—I don't care!"

He seized his hat and with a wild glance at her pale, composed face, ran out of the room, across the sunlit gravel to the road.

The chapel was full of warm, sweet dusk as Jacques went forward and took his place in the confessional. Through the lattice-work screen he could see the red glow of the sanctuary lamp and four candles lighted on the altar. He knelt and crossed himself: "Father, forgive me, for I have sinned!"

In the little window before him he could just see the priest's withered cheek and the grey hairs which grew in his ear. He heard the whispered intercession and a soft creaking of wood as Father Englebert leaned towards him on the other side of the confessional.

"Father, forgive me, for I have sinned!"

His throat, his lips, were dry with a dryness that went all the way down to his entrails, and he could hear the heavy thumping of his own blood. He stared at the little window

which framed the priestly profile, a withered chin supported
on four bent knuckles, and he wondered whether the uproar
in his breast was audible to that attentive listener. He
thought desperately on his sins, but they flew like leaves in
every direction—fragmentary visions and images, small
visceral murmurs drowned in the silencing flood from his
heart. How and where had he sinned ? And what was Sin
—a great Raven hopping through heaven, or all remembered sweetness, all hope, all desire ?

" Father . . ."

" Yes, my child. Go on."

But he couldn't go on, he couldn't even begin, for all
the words he had ever learned blew away when he sought
to clutch them. " I don't know . . . I don't believe . . . I
don't understand ! "

He saw his own father, the portrait in the drawing-
room at Amritpore, the faded brownish portrait which white
ants had eaten, but from which the eyes stared back with
indifference, and he thought : In the cemetery behind
Father Sebastien's church those eyes have melted away.
" There is nothing left, nothing . . . nothing ! " Ice seemed
to trickle down his limbs as he heard himself whispering :
" To think like this is a sin. Nothing is a sin, a sin is nothing . . . nothing . . . nothing . . ."

Father Englebert leaned against the window and·mur-
mured : " You are not prepared, my child. Go now, pre-
pare yourself. Come to me later."

Jacques left the chapel and came into the afternoon
sunlight. Silence swelled and settled on all the half-hearted
activities of a school week-end : he heard the sound of a
piano, someone playing scales over and over again, and the
click of hockey sticks on the playground. The world seemed
to stand away from him, to ignore his existence.

22

A WEEK LATER Jacques arrived at the Macbeths' to find the
household excitedly preparing for the hunting trip which
the Colonel had promised them. Tents and baggage had
already gone and the party were waiting for Jacques to join

them before setting out on the twenty-mile ride to the camping ground. Bertie rushed to meet him. "We were afraid you were not coming after all !" She clutched his arm and he could feel the excitement running through her like a current.

Macbeth sauntered up. "We've got a gun for you. It's gone with the baggage. Father says I can use his."

Mrs. Macbeth appeared with the Colonel and Captain Ponsonby, the latter a slight, dark young man with a silky black moustache. Mrs. Macbeth was all dove-grey with a blue feather in her hat. "I'll take care of Pedro," she declared in her high, birdlike voice. "I shan't let him out of my sight. Poor darling, he'd hate to be left behind, leopards or no leopards."

"Well," said the Colonel, shrugging, "remember what happened to Pongo !"

"And to Dumdum," added Captain Ponsonby darkly. "And to Gypsy !"

Leopards had at one time and another made off with all three dogs. But Mrs. Macbeth refused to be separated from her special pet, a fat breathless spaniel now miraculously in his fifth year.

"Pedro can ride in the dandy with me, and the children will see that he doesn't wander too far when we get there."

Jacques tasted the vagrant thrill which an expedition brings to an unjaded spirit, and he saw that the others shared with him this primitive lust for faring forth, for leaving all that is known and stale and turning one's face in a new direction. Bertie was watching him intently. "Yes," she murmured, pressing his arm. "We're going, Jacques ! We're going to ride all afternoon, lunch under the trees, then there'll be the camp and the coolies' voices coming out of the darkness, and the nighthawk going like this !" She pursed her lips and made the hollow gong-like note of the Himalayan nighthawk as it floats out from a silent valley.

He looked at her curiously. "How do you know it will be like that ?"

"Oh, I know, I know !"

"Come along, every one," cried the Colonel. Mrs. Macbeth was already seated in her dandy with Pedro slavering like a gargoyle on her lap. Four grunting coolies swung the dandy-poles on their shoulders, and their muscular brown legs vanished down the slope among the trees, pursued by the Colonel and Captain Ponsonby. The children mounted their ponies and followed, and after them straggled the grooms and a man with a straw lunch basket balanced on his head.

Their road fell away from the semi-civilisation of Gambul towards the lower hills, and presently they were in the warmer air of cultivated terraces and a village of thatched roofs and bleating goats. They passed a little temple with a red-painted stone beside it, and jostled and were jostled by strings of starved-looking pack ponies coming from the opposite direction. Wizened old women with babies slung in rags on their backs smiled up at Bertie and in passing laid their gnarled hands on her skirts. " *Bhao ! Bhao !* " they cried, and held their babies up to her saddle.

" What do they want ? " asked Bertie, laughing down at the gnomelike faces which laughed back at her.

" They're calling you their sister, and they'd like some money," explained Jacques. " Don't give them any or they'll be all over us."

" Luckily I haven't any," said Bertie, though she hated to refuse.

She and Jacques rode together and at every turn of the road ahead they caught glimpses of their companions—Mrs. Macbeth's parasol bobbing above her white dandy, the Colonel's tall back and the slighter figure of the young officer. Macbeth kept scurrying between one end of the procession and the other, a sort of self-instituted emissary, and presently they realised that he was engaged in a game of his own, a game in which he lorded it over these separate destinies, bringing them under his control, holding them, secretly, in the hollow of his hand.

Bertie laughed suddenly. " It's queer about John. Whenever he is happiest he seems to be most alone. Have you noticed ? "

He had noticed but had not thought of putting it into words.

" Now I," continued the precocious girl, " I am happiest when I am not alone." She glanced at Jacques as their ponies came together in a narrowing of the road. "You know, I'm glad we're friends—you and I and John. Don't you think it's funny, how people come together from the ends of the earth? It's as though a magnet had drawn us together. I've never had friends like this—not ones I wanted and chose for myself." She tossed her fine dark hair. "And yet I've always known what I wanted. It used to make me happy to think about it, but I know now that that was not really happiness."

"Then what was it?" asked Jacques. He did not, as yet, fully understand her, for she seemed older than himself, infinitely more sure of herself. But her exuberance charmed him, he felt himself trembling on the brink of his one great love.

"I think it was my imagination. You know I have a terrific imagination. In England I used to imagine that I was happy. Haven't you, sometimes?"

He thought it over. "No."

She went on dreamily: "I even used to imagine that I was sorry. I hate being sorry. I was, just a bit, when Fräulein died—I mean I was sorry because I knew that I couldn't love her as she wanted to be loved. Once, long ago, I loved someone, really, and that didn't make me sorry. At least not until afterwards." She gave him a brilliant glance. "Would you like to hear about it?"

Jacques suffered from a severe pang of jealousy, but without waiting for his grudging nod, Bertie went on: "It was last summer just before Fräulein died. We were staying in Wales, on the coast. There was a boy there whose father was a fisherman. He was a very nice boy and took me swimming and fishing. Afterwards we used to lie on the rocks and practice staring at the sun to see who could do it longest. He always won. He taught me how to tie knots in ropes and the names of the different fishes. He was much older than I, but very good to me, and I would have liked to stay in Wales and be friends with him for ever."

She fell silent, and Jacques waited, his mind vivid with the visions which she had created in it. Then Bertie continued: "One day Fräulein saw us on the beach. My hair had got wet in the sea and he was holding it for the wind to blow through it. Fräulein didn't like that, and she took me away at once. She took me back to London, but first she said things to both of us in front of each other, and that is something which I shall never forgive Fräulein. Never ! "

Jacques felt that he understood this in the very marrow of his bones.

" She didn't want me to love any one but herself," said Bertie. " And that was something I couldn't help. I'm glad she died. I knew I was going to be glad even before she died."

" Then did you see your friend again ? "

" No. I didn't want to see him again. I didn't even write to him. You see, the things that Fräulein said that time stayed in my mind. I could not forget them, and I was afraid that he could not forget them, either."

" Yes," Jacques murmured slowly, " yes, I know."

Macbeth came tearing back, his horse in a lather. " I say, wouldn't it be fun if we should get a man-eater ! "

Bertie wailed in terror, but Jacques explained that leopards do not attack people. Macbeth gave him a superior glance. " They have been known to. They climb trees after you and even force their way into houses. Oh, not often, of course. But sometimes." And with this contribution to natural history he scampered away at top speed, all hat and horse.

They rode beside a shallow valley under a sky of interminable blue ; from a sunlit terrace a black partridge called as it had called to Marco Polo : " *Shir dharam ke shakrak !* " (" I have milk and honey ! ") Then they began to climb and sprays of yellow dogwood brushed their hats as the ponies snorted and toiled up a slippery pine-spilled slope. Hills rising on either side flung heavy shadows on their road and the harsh cadenza of the partridge died behind them. The road widened and slipped out of sight round the edge of a gorge which seemed to open on nothing but an ocean of sky. Bertie suddenly reined in her pony and sat motionless, staring at a jagged rampart of quartz and cobalt which cut the world in half.

Jacques, reining his pony to a halt beside hers, said softly :

" Tibet."

23

THE TENTS were pitched in a semi-circular glade with a fragment of the snows before and a densely wooded slope behind. Underbrush had been cleared and a shelter of boughs erected for horses and men. As the frail blue evening spiralled into darkness a bonfire sprang up in the centre of the semi-circle and a charcoal brazier glittered in the dark triangle of the cook's tent. Here on this pin-point of the continent the nomadic English once more found home. But it was not enough, for like their poet who held eternity in an hour, their consciousness streamed towards the outer fringes of the firelight and embraced the brown hillmen who squatted there smoking their *chelums* and spitting on the stones.

The Macbeths and their guests sat round a table improvised out of a packing-case, and in the fire-glow and the flicker of a smoky lantern they ate their tinned sardines and heard their own voices disperse in the starry air. When dinner was finished Lal Singh the old tracker squatted beside Colonel Macbeth, and they discussed plans for the next day's shoot. Lal Singh was tall and spare with a greenish beard and the bright, eternally youthful eyes of the hunter. " I have arranged with the head man of a village not far from here to tie out a young goat. Tomorrow he will bring me word of the kill."

" Must it be killed ? " inquired Bertie plaintively.

The Colonel laughed, and Captain Ponsonby smiled, tilting back his camp chair. In the firelight their faces and hands shone like gold, their gestures were like abrupt portents flung upon the screen of darkness. Jacques, coming suddenly from his tent, saw Captain Ponsonby's hand lightly brush Mrs. Macbeth's, saw their fingers twine and cling. The furtive intimacy sent a pang through him ; he hesitated, then took his place between Bertie and Macbeth.

Bertie whispered : " This is just as I said it would be. Listen ! "

He listened, and heard the nighthawk strike its copper notes, two high and two low, and as though in answer to a signal the fire fell together in a burst of sparks which perished, in their turn, under the full avalanche of night.

Long after Macbeth had tumbled into sleep on the cot next
to his own, Jacques lay awake, attentive to the Indian
darkness where there is no such thing as silence—only a
subtle shift of key and volume dividing the sound of night
from the noise of day. Man is against nature, his thought
is death to everything else that dares to move. Perhaps the
child half-way between animal and man felt this without
the necessity of words as, propped on his elbow, he stared
through the opening of the tent across miles of starlit foliage
to the pointed and luminous snows. And as he felt the other
world stretch and stir around him he shared with nocturnal
creatures an awareness of night and its meaning, for as
human consciousness retreats the wilderness revives : it
opens its golden eye, sets its soft black paw on the expectant
stone. To be an animal is to be a thing as it is, not something inscribed in meaning, but a form without future, a
palpitating and singular heart.

Jacques fell asleep and slid gently on to his pillow, the
faint light touching his head and lying on his closed eyes.
The shriek which woke him awoke, with its shrill stroke of
terror, the whole camp. A little clot of humanity leaped
and gesticulated, crying vengeance against the intruder who
had outraged their temporary innocence. Every one collected outside the Colonel's tent, and into their midst stalked
Lal Singh, to appropriate and to magnify his moment.
" A leopard has taken the Memsahib's dog ! "

It was true, Pedro had vanished. Leaving the foot of his
mistress's bed he had paddled forth to investigate the midnight stones, and in a single weighted flash his pampered
little spirit had bubbled into red silence in the gully behind
the camp. Now all the whistling and crying in the world
would not bring him wagging out of the darkness.

" By Jove ! " exclaimed Captain Ponsonby, rushing out
of his tent in pyjamas. " I thought the tribesmen had
risen ! "

His glance sought Pedro's mistress, who sat weeping on
the edge of her bed, with Bertie beside her. The Colonel
stalked outside to quell a babble of grooms and coolies, then
he addressed Lal Singh. " You're quite sure it was a
leopard ? "

" The dog is dead, Sahib. Not a hundred yards away.

I ran at once to see, and the leopard, hearing me, dropped the body and made off. But he will come back. We must, at once, build a *machan*." And he vanished into the shadows, trailed by two shivering hillmen carrying axes.

The Colonel looked at his wife. " Poor darling ! But you know Pedro always was a fool. . . ."

" I should have chained him ! "

Bertie shuddered. " It must have been awfully sudden. He couldn't have suffered."

" How do you know ? " demanded Macbeth. In the feeble lantern light his face was white and drawn. " That scream . . . of course he suffered ! "

" Oh, don't ! " wailed Mrs. Macbeth. " Don't, don't ! "

Colonel Macbeth broke in decisively : " We had better toss up for the first shot. Anybody got a rupee ? "

" You needn't bother about me," said Bertie. " I'm not going to sit up for the thing. Wild horses wouldn't make me."

" Then it's between us four. All right, Ponsonby ? "

The coin spun upwards and fell on the Colonel's outstretched palm.

" I'm with you, Bertie," said the Captain. He sat down beside her and lighted a cigarette.

The Colonel looked at the two boys. " All right, Jacques ? "

" Heads," said Jacques, his voice sounding odd in his own ears.

" Heads it is. Now it's between you and John."

" Heads," said Jacques again, presentiment gripping him.

The coin described its broken arc and landed once more on the Colonel's hand. He smiled at Jacques. " You win ! "

Jacques watched the colour flow slowly back into Macbeth's face, and he thought with a queer, inward thrill : " *He* was frightened too ! "

Colonel Macbeth picked up a rifle which stood at the foot of his own cot, and Jacques watched stiffly as the brass cartridges slid into the breech. " It's a bit long for you, but I think you can handle it. Better cock one barrel at a time. You may only need one unless you just wound him, in

which case try and get in the second shot as fast as you can.
Aim for the shoulder, or just a fraction behind the shoulder,
unless you're sure of a good head shot." He peered into the
boy's face. " What's up, old chap ? You're trembling."

" Excitement," murmured Captain Ponsonby, who had
been watching Jacques steadily.

Jacques took the rifle. " I . . ." He broke off, meeting
the Colonel's cool blue eyes. " Shall we go ? "

They were preceded by a coolie carrying a lantern
which shed its silly little varnish on the nearer leaves and
the big pale boulders of the gully. They found Pedro lying
on the stones ; his throat was torn open and his tongue
hung horribly from a corner of his mouth. Colonel Macbeth
whispered sharply : " Don't touch him. We want to leave
as little scent as possible. Ah, they've got the *machan* ready.
Good work, Lal Singh ! "

The *machan* comprised two short planks lashed between
the branches of a tough little oak which leaned out towards
the gully about twenty feet above Pedro's body. Lal Singh
had contrived a screen of boughs which made a perfect
eyrie for the hunter, and into this Jacques was pushed and
hoisted, with a handful of extra cartridges and a few final
instructions. " Don't move. Keep your fingers off the
hammer until you're ready. The moon may come up before
he decides to return. Now, good luck ! "

They left him there and he watched the lantern dance
away among the trees and vanish with their voices and the
sound of their cautious feet. With their going the night
surged upon him like a tide ; he was alone with the bleed-
ing corpse below him and murder stalking among the
shadows. He was alone, and in a little while the camp,
which he could not see, settled into indifferent silence. They
had cut him adrift from their warmth and the comfort of
their bodies, they had abandoned him utterly.

A breath of wind rustled the stiff leaves of the oak in
which he sat and he felt the sweat steal down his face, felt
it wet the palms of his hands, gripping the rifle barrel. The
unrelenting steel thrust against his flesh. Use me, it said,
for that is what I mean, that is what I am. Holding his
breath, he practised drawing back the hammers, then re-
leasing them, feeling their sinewy strain against the ball of

his thumb. All I have to do is to pull the triggers and the
hills will rock in uproar and every living thing go to earth.
Well, why not ? Tell them that I aimed at a shadow or at
a flitting owl, and let them laugh. Then he saw Colonel
Macbeth's offended eyes and behind those eyes a succession
of others, the eyes of men who abhor a coward. And yet,
he thought, I am not really a coward, not really afraid.
But to be alone, to be left out, to be abandoned. . . . How
far away the morning seemed !

One of his feet went to sleep and he stared earnestly at
the sky, which seemed to change as the moon thrust invisibly
past a barrier of hills. The silence had become a tensile
web which stifled him. Pedro lay limply dark on the lighter
stones, he might have been a stone, a furred stone from
which the blood escaped with a lively logic. I wonder,
thought Jacques, what is fear ? Is it mauling, uproar,
struggle, pain ? And he remembered Pedro's dying shriek.

He clutched the rifle, reminding himself that its de-
structive force was a matter dependent on his own will.
God of death, he sat waiting to destroy, and the terror of
the destroyer fluttered in his body. All that was demanded
of him was that he press the curled metal tooth under his
hand and shattering death would cleanse the darkness
before him. Out of man's brain had come this miracle,
this beautiful little shining capsule which injects death into
life's unsuspecting body. He was trembling, then his trembling ceased as he heard the sound for which he'd waited—
the tiny creak of a dry leaf. It was as though the earth had
drawn a faint extra breath, and this breath stirred the hairs
along the back of his neck. There was no further sound,
but a stone which had been dark now appeared light, and
another which had been light concealed itself. Just as when,
an hour ago, he had known that he was about to win the
toss, he now knew that his presence was detected, that he
was being pondered and judged, his fate meditated by a
stealthy and humid god.

Silence crouched in the slow fire of the rising moon as
Jacques, beside himself with terror, reached forward to
tear away the screen of leaves before him ; a twig brushed
against the triggers and he caught in his left hand the full
roar of the exploding charge.

PART TWO

24

STRIKING eastward across Ceylon the monsoon burst and divided like a pair of arms, one arm clasping the peninsula to the west and the other to the east, and in this cataclysmic weather men pondered their fields and returned thanks to God for the blessed reprieve of rain. Weather, they would have you know, was invented by God for men alone : it starts or stunts their crops, stalls a war, incites cholera, or allays, for a spell, the sprue. When weather misbehaves, men read in its defection a retribution for their wrongdoing ; no wonder that, in gratitude for these tons of liquid, humanity returns thanks in appropriate fashion. It harnesses up a flowery cart and submits its body to the grinding wheels, it plunges into a river formed of Divine sweat, and remembers that when Juggernaut appeared in the guise of man he caused the prosaic nim tree to put forth champak flowers. If there were no weather there would be no God ; He'd diminish, attenuated to a philosophical concept, or relapse into memory until the day when nature decided upon a further outrage against the human race. As Aubrey Wall drove towards Mrs. Lyttleton's house where he was to dine for the last time, he watched rain drench the road and knew that everywhere humble people were praising the Lord as they paddled through the downpour, guiding it in crude channels to every plot and *bigha* of soil. But he was incapable of sharing in the jubilation of these god-infested folk—their joys and their griefs were on too vast a scale for his participation.

He drove between the sandstone pillars of Mrs. Lyttleton's compound and drew up under the porch. The garden, stimulated to undreamed-of luxuriance, spewed forth frogs and fragrance and an occasional cobra. Only round the graves under the loquat trees was there any semblance of order.

His groom led the tonga away towards the stables, and

Wall went up the steps to greet his old friend. She took his hand and stared into his face. " I can't believe that this is the last time I shall see you."

" I am only going on furlough, you know ! "

They sat as usual on the veranda under the stuffed heads. Wall poured himself a brandy from the decanters which waited beside his chair, and played with a glass eye which had popped out from a mouldering socket above him.

" Well," murmured Mrs. Lyttleton, the sense of parting hanging over her like a cloud. " Can it be two years since we said good-bye to Hardyal and you longed to go with him ? "

" Two years ! Hardyal and I will probably pass each other in the Mediterranean."

They were silent, their thoughts branching at this point. For Aubrey Wall these two years were memorable less as sequences in time than as accidents which bore little relation to his past but which must in some indefinable way colour, or discolour, his future. For Mrs. Lyttleton they were the final wave of the last century, carrying her forward and depositing her neatly within the boundary of the twentieth. She congratulated herself on a sense of achievement, for just as everything in her experience retained its vivid aura, so for her, now, did time retain it. Each year that she survived assumed the character of a personal possession, to be cherished as in the past she had cherished intenser pleasures.

To her companion she presently remarked that the years were like journeys which seemed shorter between certain points than between others, but for this phenomenon she held the human moon entirely responsible. " After our forties time picks up speed and we know where we're headed, and that, my friend, is the age of resignation."

" Resignation ? To what—the end ? "

" Oh no, I am not at all sure that there is an end."

" Then to what else is one resigned ? "

" Well, let's say to the consolatory rôle of the by-stander."

He laughed. " You—a bystander ! You will always be instrumental."

She gave him a grateful smile. " After all, I'm long past seventy."

" Yet you are still not sure that there is an end. That sounds like a Hindu."

" I am one at heart."

" God forbid ! "

" Ah, but just consider the mercies of a rebirth."

" Not for me, thanks. One life is enough."

She gave him an acute glance, appropriating in all their details changes which the years had wrought in him. Not that she had ever thought him distinguished, but he interested her now as he had not interested her before. One life, he'd just said, was enough. Might it not perhaps have been almost too much ? She knew that in every life there comes a sort of *crise*, after which anything is possible. Where and when had his *crise* occurred ? He had never struck her as being specially inflammable, yet she was sure that something must have ignited him : something still smouldered there within a feverish glow.

She murmured : " Perhaps for you England will constitute a rebirth."

Two years ago—even a year ago—he would have kindled at the prospect, to-day he shrugged.

" Oh, perhaps."

" But you are glad to be going ? "

" I suppose so."

" And you will come back to India ? "

" It's my bread and butter, you know."

" What a dull way of looking at it ! " She laughed, then said gravely : " I shall miss you, Aubrey. One by one my friends are disappearing."

He gave her a gentle and understanding glance. " You're thinking of Jacques St. Remy. But it's your own fault, you know. If you were a more forgiving woman . . ."

She interrupted with an angry flash of her diamonds. " Yes, yes, if I were more forgiving I would be less lonely ! But after all, if one cannot forget one cannot forgive, no matter how cleverly one pretends. I have pretended, often, in love—but never in hate."

He shrugged. " Feuds bore me."

" Yet they can be a means of preserving contact," she

reminded him, with an incorrigible laugh. After a brief silence, he said :

" Well, at any rate, you will soon have Hardyal, with whom you have no feud. Be good to him, won't you ? Keep him up to the mark. They lose it . . . so easily."

She did not need to be reminded what it was that " they " lost so easily, for she was familiar with his ideas on the subject. Wall went on : " Yes, I think . . . perhaps . . . to get away will be a sort of rebirth. I'm tired." He broke off, then finished on a note of temper : " I'm fed up ! "

This was obvious, but Mrs. Lyttleton had heard too many rumours about him to venture even a discreet inquiry, so she changed the subject by inquiring after the health of friends on whom she knew he had been paying farewell calls.

" I saw Father Sebastien, who gave me his blessing." Wall smiled wryly. " The good man seemed to think I needed it. When I called on Madame St. Remy, she gave me *durwaza bund*." He used the uncompromising Hindustani term for the English Not at Home.

" And the children, what news of them ? "

Wall hesitated, staring at the glass eye which lay in his palm.

" Well, Father Sebastien informed me that Gisele is happily established in her Belgian cloister."

" Ah ! They would have seen to that."

" Perhaps she saw to it herself."

" That child ? Hardly."

" They sometimes marry, don't they, at her age ? " His flippant tone surprised her and she replied : " I thought you felt as I did, that Gisele's decision was a tragic one."

He tossed the glass eye in the air and caught it again. " Oh tragedy, tragedy ! That's an overworked horse."

Mrs. Lyttleton shook her head. " I had a glimpse of her last year. I have never seen a more beautiful girl."

Wall drained his brandy. " I have, though I must confess . . . somewhat duskier, somewhat muskier ! "

The words, the tone, troubled Mrs. Lyttleton. She hesitated, then asked for Jacques.

" Father Sebastien said that this was his last year at St. Matthew's. Do you think they'll make a monk out of him ? "

She frowned. " To be fair, I don't think they ever intended that."

" If not, it is only because Madame has other plans." The glass eye slipped from his fingers and fell in a corner, where it lay balefully glaring. " She will bring him back to Amritpore and set him to work in her factory, which he loathes. In due time she'll import a meek little wife for him from her so-aristocratic France. Oh, I think we can rest assured that Madame will attend to everything."

Mrs. Lyttleton looked at him curiously. " I sometimes think that you must dislike Madame almost as much as I do."

" If I do, it is because she frightens me, rather."

She laughed at that. " Frightens you ? She doesn't frighten me."

" Well, she frightened Gisele, and she has tried, I imagine, to frighten the boy."

" By the exercise of power ? " Mrs. Lyttleton nodded slowly. " I see. But after all, they are her children, and I suppose that in a sense she redeems herself by her love for them. I don't see, though, why she should frighten you."

" Perhaps because I realise that she can have no redeeming love for me ! "

" Well, neither can she have any conceivable power over you," objected Mrs. Lyttleton.

" Nevertheless, the spectacle of any one exercising tyrannical power over others is revolting, don't you agree ? Especially in women."

" Why especially in women ? "

He brooded for a minute. " Perhaps because women are not, as a rule, subject to the same discipline as ourselves. Power doesn't go to a woman's head as it goes to a man's —it goes straight to her emotions."

" What you are trying to say is that power doesn't make for greatness in women as it very often does in men ? "

" For intellectual greatness, no. They usually end up by becoming victims." Mrs. Lyttleton, remembering some of the stories which she had heard of his brutality to his servants, wondered silently whether he, too, had not fallen victim to his own power.

She gave him a keen glance. "However, you don't deny that Madame St. Remy is intelligent."

He looked suddenly bored. "Oh, intelligent—yes."

"I don't know whether you meant to, but you have given me a distinct impression that you regard her as a thoroughly immoral woman."

"I never said so."

"Tyrannical power," Mrs. Lyttleton repeated slowly, "unredeemed by intellectual greatness . . ."

"Oh, that!"

"Yes, that." She watched him pour himself another brandy. "And what's more, I agree with you."

There was a brief pause, then she wondered aloud : "Do you think that Jacques will stand up?"

"I can't see that it signifies."

"It will signify for him, if not for us. I know you've accused me of reading too much importance into minor matters, but I think that Jacques' struggle is important, though he himself is hardly aware of it, as yet. Whenever I see youth break with the past I know that the future will feel the shock."

He smiled sceptically, but she went on : "I cannot help wondering about these children. It might have been a different story if they all stayed in their own country, but in India they—like you and I—will be on trial."

"On trial?"

"Lately I have felt more and more this sense of being on trial—not only that we are being judged for our short-comings as rulers, but for our capacities as human beings."

Wall frowned, but she went on quickly : "You have always seen the natives as a mass, with an occasional shining example of loyalty, and that is how you judge them. But doesn't it ever strike you as odd how well we've suc-ceeded in elevating the natives' loyalty to a major virtue?"

"What's so odd about it?"

"That we should appraise the loyalty purely from the point of view of its relation to our own good."

Wall disliked the turn which the conversation had taken. He enjoyed Mrs. Lyttleton's wit and her malice just so long as she confined herself to more or less airy and per-sonal affairs, but he had a horror of the controversial soul-

E

searching to which she seemed increasingly given. By
cutting herself away from most of her own people she had
come to question and to criticise them more and more from
the Indian standpoint—a dangerous and a futile attitude.
The General's widow was a relic of days when it was still
possible for Indian and Englishman to meet on an autocratic footing. She had more than once laughingly described
herself as the last of the English Begums, and declared that
had she not had the luck to live in Victoria's time she
would have chosen that of Queen Elizabeth, thus unconsciously, perhaps, identifying herself with an age of imperial
and matriarchal vitality. What she seemed unable or unwilling to grasp was the fact that those reigns were over and
done with : there was a brand-new spirit in the air. Aubrey
Wall, for one, felt out of step with this new spirit ; lately
he'd begun to question whether he should ever have left
England, to wonder whether his was an organism which
survives transplanting. The question remained unanswered, for what would have been his chances in England,
where every one jostled every one else and where the possession of brains—when not allied to birth and money—
was considered an unfair advantage ? You were invited to
take them elsewhere and to be careful how you used them.
Naturally it never occurred to Wall to question this state
of affairs—he was essentially English, with a dyed-in-the-
wool attitude towards social inequalities. But personal
frustration and bitterness found their inevitable release in
contempt and dislike of exile, and the land of the exile.
In India he'd found a poverty so deplorable that millions
sipped life rather than lived it—and he saw them tamely
submitting to their fate. Wherever an oasis occurred the
starving hordes closed in and the oasis diminished. The
white man created his own oasis, ruthlessly aware that he
must, while his conscience-stricken mind bore the notion
of an inherent superiority, the myth of the self-anointed.

Mrs. Lyttleton's problem had been simpler, for she had
accepted exile with an aristocratic philosophy and the
knowledge that one undertook a voyage round the Cape of
Good Hope once in a lifetime. She had come to India with
her mind made up and she had never unmade it ; but for
Aubrey Wall the psychic grudge of separation was kept

alive by periodic leaves spent in England. Not India, but England was his home; he could not forget that, he did not want to forget it. And what after all did Mrs. Lyttleton know of *his* India, the new India with its developing social consciousness? What did she know of the official India composed of time-servers, petty subordinates, cravens, conspirators, and sycophants? For five years he had had to do with Indians and although he'd liked several, even loved a few, the feeling was never deeper than a sentiment which they shared with his horses and his dogs. Even in the self-effacement of debauchery he was bitterly conscious of the difference between himself and them, for the dark skin was aromatic with it.

25

As NIGHT fell the rain paused then stopped, and out from the obscurity burst the frogs' voices. Aubrey Wall could imagine the countless pallid throats swelling in chorus, and a sense of suffocation came upon him: there seemed no respite from the country's fecundity, no crevice which did not house some musician-snout, some fixed eye, some coiled spring of venom, or a fistful of feathers cheeping with lust. He conjured up visions of home, of England's antique serenity, and the effort brought him to the brink of revelation. He no longer felt alone and spectral but part of the solid structure of a tried and rational whole. Another second and the mystery of his own plight would have ended, he would understand all things—then Mrs. Lyttleton broke the spell:

"Where is that boy with the lamps?"

A deliquescent light which bathed the garden stopped short at the veranda steps. "Jalal!" screamed Mrs. Lyttleton in the sudden fury of autocracy neglected. "*Butti jalao!*" ("Light the lamps!")

There was no answer except from the frogs, who renewed their chorus.

She peered at Wall through the gloom. "I'm so sorry. He thought we were talking, so decided not to interrupt us. But the lights, the lights! It's getting as dark as pitch."

"No doubt Jalal will come in his own good time."

"I shall dock his pay !"

"You won't. You know you won't. You have never punished him and that's what's the trouble with him. It's what's the trouble with all of them !"

She realised that her guest was somewhat drunk. "I'll go and find Jalal," she murmured placatingly. "I won't be a moment."

But Wall rose suddenly. "I'll go. I know my way."

There was something menacing about him, and she demurred : "I wish you would let me, Aubrey."

"Don't worry, I'll find him."

Mrs. Lyttleton suffered from the sudden helpless fear which assails old people, for she had caught the note of temper in his voice and she knew that tone, having heard it often enough in her long life.

"Aubrey . . ."

But he walked across the veranda and disappeared into the darkened drawing-room. She heard his feet on the matting, heard him bump into a chair, then she guessed that he had entered the dining-room beyond. Darkness swallowed him as it had swallowed everything in the great empty house ; only in the garden did forms remain and retain their meaning. She fumbled for her cigarettes, assuring herself that she was a fool to be anxious on Jalal's account. Either he was drunk in some remote nook, or wide awake to see the Sahib coming and to make his escape, for Wall's temper was a byword among the servants of Amritpore.

Wall felt his way through the dark rooms to the veranda where dishes were washed and lamps trimmed. Beyond it stretched an untidy compound and a line of servants' quarters, where a light or two glimmered. At sight of them his formless anger flared into rage. He had always detested Mrs. Lyttleton's servants, who epitomised—for him—everything that was typical in the native character : inertia, instability, opportunism, filth. He'd settle them !

He started across the veranda and immediately fell over a large bundle which lay in the shadow of a meat safe. The bundle was Jalal, snoring in the deep oblivion of his favourite drug. Wall, in falling, cracked his elbow on a corner of the meat safe and a white heat exploded inside him. Pulling himself together he kicked the supine figure twice, with the precise weighted kick of an athlete. Jalal groaned and rolled sluggishly on his side ; he did not waken but lay snoring on a changed note, with his knees drawn up like a trussed fowl.

Wall turned away and shouted into the gloom for his syce to fetch the tonga, and when a faint answering shout reached him, he made his way back to the front veranda. " I found your faithful servant, but he is so stuffed with *bhang* that I doubt very much whether you will get any dinner, or any breakfast for that matter."

" Did you try to wake him ? "

" I gave him a couple of kicks, but he merely snored."

" You kicked him ! "

" Not hard enough, apparently."

They heard the jingle of harness and watched the soft beam from the carriage lamps bloom on the puddles. Mrs. Lyttleton felt sad that they should part on such an ugly note, but Wall was silent, staring into the darkness where rain was beginning to fall again. He had a sudden strange feeling about the rain, a personal feeling, as he thought of it falling all over north-western India, swelling the rivers and the reservoirs, rushing along his canals into the great retaining tanks, and spilling over into the arid, wasted land. The violence of a few minutes ago had calmed him, his blood flowed cool in his veins, he was conscious of a revived sense of generosity and well-being.

The tonga drove up under the porch and his coachman leaped out and ran to the horses' heads. Mrs. Lyttleton put out her hand and said in a firm voice: " Well, Aubrey ! "

He took the dry, wrinkled fingers. " Au revoir, Laura."

" Yes," she murmured. " Au revoir."

26

" COME IN, come in ! " cried Ganpat Rai, catching sight of his visitor behind the bamboo screen. " Come in, Abdul Salim ! "

" I see you are busy. I can wait."

"Wait, then, in the drawing-room. I shall join you in a moment."

Salim retired, stepping cautiously among an array of shoes outside Ganpat Rai's study. Within, clients were squatting on the floor round the barrister's English desk, and Salim could hear their droning voices punctuated by the nasal interruptions of Ganpat Rai's clerk taking down depositions. Salim knew that study, its bookcases stacked with works on jurisprudence, its walls hung with engravings of famous English judges and lawyers. All the paraphernalia of success was here, paraphernalia so dear to the eyes of harassed miscreants out on bail.

As he loitered on the veranda Salim watched servants hoist the curtains on the tennis court ; rain had soaked them and they travelled stiffly on their pulleys. Nearby, a gardener was clipping a hedge, another raking the gravel.

Salim reflected grimly on his own house, a stone's throw from the bazaar, a house with no garden, no tennis court, and no punkah in the hot weather ; he thought of the drab and dusty compound invaded by cats and pi-dogs and smells. From the study behind came a nasal whine : "Wherefore your humble servant petitioneth . . ."

He wandered down the veranda to the drawing-room with its muddle of English and native furnishings, a muddle for which he had no particular fondness since he'd become a convert to the new school of Swadeshi and would not permit foreign things in his house. Here were altogether too many brass and teakwood tables, cane settees, a Chippendale mirror. There were too many photographs in ornamental frames—photographs of Hardyal taken during the successive stages of his sojourn in England. Hardyal standing before a low stone house in the uncertain English sunlight ; Hardyal on horseback with a row of little willows behind him ; Hardyal taller, stronger, in flannels and the striped cap of his school. Hardyal, every inch the pukka sahib ! Then, as he examined a recent portrait of Ganpat Rai in the black gown, curled wig and notched collar of the High Court, something hot and unhappy flowed upward from his heart. It was not that he grudged his friend his success, yet how resist a pang of envy ? True, a diploma from the Moslem College at Aligarh and an M.A. from

Calcutta University were not to be despised, but they were
not Balliol and the Inner Temple. Salim thought again of
his own sons, young men with superior ambitions occupy-
ing inferior government positions. Where was the money
to come from, or the opportunity for that matter, in a land
where the English and their toadies had cornered all the
jobs? As the Mohammedan brooded on his pet grudge he
paused before the mirror and examined his features :
bearded, black-eyed, the hair under his fez streaked with
grey. He knew himself to be equal if not superior to many
of his friends, yet nothing in his life gave evidence of this
fact. He was poor, his house was shabby, himself and his
sons frustrated at every turn. Salim's forefathers had been
officers in the court of the last Mughal, something which
he found impossible to forget and painful to remember.
Pride sustained him, pride which fed on a temper which
in its turn sucked the bitter core of resentment.

He turned impatiently to a bookcase filled with history
and biography, with the novels of Thackeray and Dickens
and Balzac, and Dante's *Vita Nuova*, which last the white
ants seemed to prefer beyond all others. Too many books,
Salim decided, sliding one back into its place. Men can
glut themselves on learning and remain chained.

Ganpat Rai appeared in the door behind him. " Which
do you prefer, the garden or the house? Both are
yours."

The garden was damp and full of ants ; Salim preferred
the house. Free from European eyes, they sat on cushions
on the floor and a servant brought them *pan supari* and
cigarettes.

Salim said : " I came to thank you for sending me the
Khwaja case, though I hoped you would have come in on
it with me."

" What need ? You have far greater skill than I in
handling these police prosecutions."

" You mean I understand their methods ! Well, I fancy
I left the Assistant Magistrate with very much the same
impression." He stroked his beard with a studied air of
triumph. He had enjoyed too few in his time, and this one
had been exceptionally sweet—while it lasted.

" That was a witty remark of yours to the sub-inspector,"

said Ganpat Rai. " ' Wherever your exalted footsteps have fallen, there has an informer been born ' ! "

Both men laughed, reliving the splendid moment of the policeman's discomfiture. They were in native dress and their postures were characteristic : the Hindu all repose, the Mohammedan austere and intense. The latter's air of triumph waned a little as he asked, presently : " I take it you have not heard that judgment was delivered yesterday on the Khwaja case ? "

" I have heard nothing."

" Well, it is true that I made them squirm—I made them squirm ! But in his summing up that *badzat* Jones chose to indulge in sarcasm at my expense. ' Mr. Abdul Salim,' said he "—and here the Mohammedan veered into a passable Oxford drawl—" ' Mr. Abdul Salim has seen fit to inject political considerations into this case, consider-ations which are bewildering, to say the least of it, and to say the worst—irrelevant ' ! "

" Ah ! " an expression of keen disappointment passed over Ganpat Rai's face. " Case dismissed ? No ! "

" Case dismissed."

There was a disturbance in the veranda and they watched a mob of clients drift down the steps and cross the drive towards the gates. The light changed subtly, a ser-vant came in and rolled up the screens. When he had gone Ganpat Rai inquired gently : " You attribute the judg-ment not to your own but to Jones's political bias ? "

" Isn't it obvious ? "

To the Hindu what was obvious was his friend's readi-ness to seize upon what, in this case, was not obvious at all. Salim shrugged with affected unconcern. " What matter ? Jones is an ignoramus. He has fallen under the spell of his snobbish friends."

Ganpat Rai nodded soothingly. " Perhaps he will be transferred."

" Would that God might transfer every mother's son of them to Jehannum ! "

The other smiled. " To make room for another Mah-mud of Ghazni ? " He alluded to the first great Moham-medan conqueror of India. Salim shrugged. " Why not ? " When his friend remained silent the Mohammedan burst out : " Allah ! How tired I am of them all ! You do not see it, you do not feel it ! But we are like sheep, we are slaves, for ever obeying, salaaming, fawning ! "

" Let us be honest, you do not fawn—neither do I."

" I would be naught but honest. Let us all be honest, then, and force honesty upon them. Let us share in such honesty as would make the affair of 1857 look like a garden party ! "

" No, my friend, no."

" Why not ? That is the sort of honesty they best understand. It is something we all share, for blood draws men together."

" Yes, blood draws men together, yet everywhere else in the natural world extinction comes from ripeness, dropping heavy with life."

" You speak as if we were rotten apples ! "

" And what are we but rotten flesh ? "

He sat sad-eyed like one of his own Bhakti saints, for he knew very well that in Amritpore there were many, Hindus and Mohammedans, who shared Salim's feelings ; men with grievances festering like bamboo slivers in their flesh, honest men with the everlasting dream flowing in their veins.

Salim regained his composure. " We see things differently. I have not your forbearance, for I cannot believe that in life changes occur of themselves. Nothing comes of itself but sickness."

They were silent, their thoughts running close but divided. In character and in mentality both were diametrically opposed ; both knew this and had ceased to resent it, yet much as they had learned to understand each other, psychologically they remained unreconciled. Like cloth which has been deeply dyed their separate traditions clung to them : to the militant unswerving Moslem and the speculative, peace-loving Hindu.

Ganpat Rai offered his friend another cigarette and attempted, with a lawyer's skill, to divert the conversation into less stormy channels. Had Salim heard the story of Ramdatta's attempt to bribe the new Superintendent of Police ? The moneylender had sent an emissary with an offering of mangoes, several of which had been cunningly

opened and gold coins inserted in place of the big centre
seed. But it seemed that the Englishman had received some
warning of what to expect : a humorist in his way, he received Ramdatta's gift with a great show of geniality,
admired the mangoes, then regretfully explained that he
was himself unable to eat the fruit, which gave him diar-
rhœa. However, since it was out of the question to return
such a gift he would presume to share credit with Ramdatta in an act of grace ; and sending a constable to round
up a group of itinerant beggars, the policeman distributed
the fruit amongst them. The story diverted Salim, who
hated the moneylender only a little less than he hated the
English. And speaking of Ramdatta—had Ganpat Rai
heard the rumour of Madame's indebtedness to the moneylender ? This was mere gossip, but plausible enough. The
world, always excepting poor Madame, knew that indigo
was done for, yet last year she had put another three
hundred acres to the crop while her foreman openly stated
that they could no longer dispose of what they had on
hand.

Ganpat Rai looked grave. " So she is borrowing from
that *gid* ? " (Vulture.)

" Birds of a feather ! " said Salim. " Let her ruin herself. If it were not indigo it would be something else. The
country is a treasure house for these people. And by the
way, I met your friend Wall's successor the other day."

" How did he impress you ? ".

" You should know by now that your English friends
do not impress me—they depress me." He gave the other
a sidelong glance. " Since we gossip, what do you happen
to know about the strange death of Mrs. Lyttleton's servant, Jalal ? "

" Nothing stranger than that he died of a fall."

" I heard whispers that he was beaten to death."

" By Mrs. Lyttleton ? " And Ganpat Rai laughed.

" Feroze the assistant surgeon is my cousin, as you
know. He was present at the autopsy and he tells me that
Jalal's spleen was ruptured by what looked like a sharp
blow. Feroze assured me that it could not possibly have
been self-inflicted."

Ganpat Rai gazed at his friend. " I know Jalal was a

co-religionist of yours.   Can that be the reason for this
morbid concern ? "

"It doesn't happen to be the reason.   But mysteries
amuse me, especially when they implicate the English.   I'm
not suggesting that Mrs. Lyttleton was responsible or
even that she knows how it happened.   However, there are
certain points which intrigue me : Jalal was a stupid
fellow, he had no enemies, nor was he athletically given to
rushing about inviting physical injury.   And Feroze tells
me emphatically that the spleen was ruptured.   He
has seen malarial spleens in people who have been beaten or
kicked."

Ganpat Rai frowned.   "I fail to see just what it is you
are driving at."

Salim lighted another cigarette.   "The local authorities
have made their customary efficient investigation, and their
verdict is death due to accidental causes.   Jalal was only a
poor servant and there were no witnesses.   However, I
have gone to the trouble to make a few inquiries on my own
account.   The results turn out to be rather interesting.   The
gardener, the scullion, the sweeper all assure me that Jalal
was far too lethargic to have become involved in a brawl.
He had not left the premises for several days nor had his
friends visited him during that time.   Yet according to
Feroze death must have followed almost immediately after
the blow."

"Truly, a mystery ! "   Ganpat Rai spoke sarcastically,
but he felt a sudden uneasiness.   Salim was no fool and his
little discoveries were often of a disquieting nature.

"Another thing," continued the Mohammedan.   "The
night they found Jalal dead in Mrs. Lyttleton's house, your
friend Aubrey Wall was there.   It was the evening before
he left Amritpore for Calcutta."

He had the Hindu's attention now, all of it.   "Why on
earth should Wall's presence have any bearing on Jalal's
death ? "

Salim hesitated for a moment, then spoke with bitterness : "I know that Wall is your friend, that you like him
greatly.   Perhaps I should not speak of him to you.   But we
all share the same idea of justice, do we not ?   You and I,
Wall himself.   No, listen . . ." he put out a hand as the other

seemed about to interrupt. " He is your friend, but he was never mine. Nor was he ever friendly to many whom he knew as well as he knew you, and who might be said to have as much claim as you on his kindness. He disliked me, and for good reason—I disliked him. Perhaps for that reason I am better informed of his character than you could be, for I have kept a little dossier on him ever since he came to Amritpore."

" You spied on him ? " The Hindu's voice was suddenly hard.

" It was not necessary to spy. The English rarely descend to concealment—they are above that sort of thing. But I must say I think Wall was more indiscreet than most men. For instance, he had prostitutes brought into his house."

" An indiscretion even in a lonely bachelor, I grant you ! " And Ganpat Rai laughed, not very happily.

" Did you not know that he was diseased ? "

" That I will not believe ! "

" Come now, as a man of the world . . ."

Ganpat Rai interrupted in a troubled voice : " I speak as a man of the world."

" Don't worry. It will all be charged up to our account." He was back on his favourite ground and Ganpat Rai listened in despair. " Not enough white women to go around so we must take what we can get—black, brown, or tea-coloured. This beastly country, don't you know, quite unfit for white men."

" Oh hush ! " Ganpat Rai implored. He rose and walked to the door, peered out, then came back. " Abdul Salim, sometimes I think you are quite mad. I cannot understand your feelings, I cannot ! "

The Mohammedan looked at him sombrely. " You mean you *will* not. You love these people," he said in a heavy voice. " I wonder why ? I have tried to see them through your eyes, but I cannot. You say you do not understand my feelings, but there are many who do. There are more and more, every day, who feel as I feel."

" Do not misunderstand me ! I do not scorn your feelings—there is much in you that I admire and respect. But when you tell me that I love the English, you are right. We shall be governed by someone—by Hindus or Moslems or by the English. What does it matter?"

"Nevertheless the English do not love you, Ganpat Rai."

"You are mistaken. They have proved it."

Salim shook his head. There was, suddenly, something prophetic about him, an ominous dignity. "No, they do not love you. They do not love any of us. They have done us too much wrong ever to be able to love us. It is easier for us to love them, for us to forgive them." He gazed at his friend. "Beaten people have but two alternatives to humiliation—they can hate or they can love."

"I do not consider myself a beaten person!"

"That is because you have chosen one alternative."

Ganpat Rai was about to break into a sharp rejoinder, then the spirit went out of him and he sighed. "Perhaps you are right. You are very subtle. But there is nothing very subtle about affection and gratitude. Aubrey Wall is my friend and I have eaten his salt. For two years his family have befriended my son. I cannot—I will not listen to you."

"Then I shall say no more about his personal life. Let us confine ourselves to his public actions. You know that he was given to thrashing his servants on the slightest provocation? On the night of Jalal's death he drove to Mrs. Lyttleton's and sent his syce to the stables while he talked with Mrs. Lyttleton on the front veranda. Later, the syce was summoned to bring the tonga to the front of the house, and he tells me that Wall shouted to him from the back veranda—from the very place where Jalal was later found dead."

"And it is on the strength of these flimsy details that you try to build a case against Wall? Remember, you have yet to show cause."

As the Hindu took up the cudgels, Salim smoked with an enigmatic air.

"Let us for a moment," said Ganpat Rai, "ignore the all-important why and wherefore and stick to your story of circumstantial evidence. I am, as you know, familiar with the general plan of Mrs. Lyttleton's house. The distance which separates the front from the back veranda is roughly a hundred feet. There are no doors, not even curtains in between, merely open arches. On your own showing there

were but two people present on that evening, Wall and
Mrs. Lyttleton.   Presumably, there was not much noise
going on.   Had Wall for any reason whatsoever attacked
Jalal, there must surely have been a scuffle, an outcry. Do
you imagine that Mrs. Lyttleton would have allowed any
one to lay a hand on her servant ?   She told me herself
what occurred that evening.   Wall had come to dine with
her, but Jalal never appeared and she was obliged to let
her guest depart supperless.   When he'd gone she found
Jalal on the back veranda, fast asleep, as she thought. She
summoned a scullion and between them they tried to rouse
Jalal, but on taking his pulse Mrs. Lyttleton realised that
something was wrong.   She sent for the doctor, who pronounced the man dead.   The autopsy revealed that he was
saturated with opium, and they arrived at the perfectly
justifiable conclusion that in his drugged state he'd walked
into some sharp object like the corner of a table or a packing-
case, and had driven it into his stomach, which in its relaxed condition put up no resistance to the blow.   There
never was any question of foul play.   Why should there
be ? "   He stared at his companion.   " Come now, confess
that you are by nature suspicious !   Any excuse to pin guilt
on your bugbears, the English ! "   And he laughed, laying
his hand on Salim's knee.   But the Mohammedan sneered.
" After all, you are staking your argument entirely on the
word of Mrs. Lyttleton."

" I would stake my life on her word."

The unconventional statement, intended merely to
clinch the argument, induced a curious effect in the speaker ;
for as he uttered the words they seemed to release a shock
of intense, spontaneous joy which illumined him through
and through.   He would stake his life on her word !   How
pure and how simple the truth, yet how overwhelming !
He could not, now, have borne to hear a word spoken
against her, so he rose, saying firmly :   " Come, let us go
into the garden."

Salim responded, less to the command than to the tone,
for he sensed the emotion which inspired it, and it was
always easier for him to respond to emotion than to cold
logic.   They went out and the scent of damp earth rose
against their faces, refreshing them.   As they strolled be-

tween glossy hedges their separate suspicions and rivalries dissolved and they fell into easy talk of local affairs, of their work, of their families. In a little while Salim asked for news of Hardyal, and Ganpat Rai took a letter from his pocket and handed it to him. Salim read it, smiling.

" What a beautiful hand ! And how splendid it will be to have him back." This was brought out fully and generously, and Ganpat Rai's eyes filled with tears. " Yes, I shall be glad to have him back. I have missed him."

They came to the end of their path and saw before them a sort of arbour whose walls were screens of the same blue stuff which served as backstops on the tennis court. From behind this screen came a sound of women's voices and the music of a sitar. Salim knew that purdah was a source of irritation to Ganpat Rai, who would have preferred his sisters and aunts to come into the open like white women ; but at first sound of those voices the Mohammedan averted his eyes, striving also to avert his ears. His own feelings on this subject were contradictory ; he saw himself as a modern man opposed to iron tradition, resenting the tyranny yet psychologically incapable of resisting it.

He said, slowly : " Hardyal will miss his grandmother."

" Yes." And Ganpat Rai thought of the old woman who had died six months ago. She had always declared that she would not see her grandson again, and in grief and remorse Ganpat Rai had performed *shradda* for her ; he touched her forehead with the sacred mud of the river and walked seven times round her pyre with a blazing torch. Through the night and all through the next day the pyre burned, fed with oil and sandalwood.

Love, Mrs. Lyttleton had assured him, transcends ceremonies and systems ; love makes memory intelligible, love is what we must remember.

" I wonder . . ." mused Salim, and hesitated.

" Yes ? "

" I wonder what changes we shall find in Hardyal."

" I too wonder," said Ganpat Rai, and he saw form in the air before him the young, unforgotten face of his son.

27

IT WAS on the day of the Coconut Festival, when men celebrate the abatement of the monsoon, that Hardyal landed at Bombay. No one met him, and for a little while he felt solitary and elated as he stood on the Apollo Bunda among a mob of tongues and races and stared at the ship which had brought him home. Passengers were still disembarking in tenders rowed by blue-trousered Lascars ; the ship itself stood at a distance, its reflections breaking and mending on the dirty sea. Wondering whether he dreamed, Hardyal now concentrated on this hour of his return and on all the small events to which it seemed intimately related. Already the *City of Sparta* whose throbbing existence he had shared for the past four weeks seemed about to dissolve in its own reflections, a creature casting off its robes one by one and with them, particle by particle, its flesh and its bone.

Some of the passengers whom he had known on the boat passed him with absent-minded greetings and were immediately lost in the crowd. He remembered how well he had seemed to know them : the jolly Scotch engineer, the dour captain, the genial doctor with his bright red moustache, the Civil Servant and his family from Agra, and two young officers back from leave in Ireland. These had been his familiars, and it was with a mixture of joy and melancholy that Hardyal watched them disappear, the same feeling which had moved him when he said good-bye to his English school, to Miss Bella and Miss Margaret Wall, to the receding English shore ; a feeling of sweetness, of resignation. Something of himself stayed with them, for had they not looked in his eyes and touched his hand and uttered his name ? But now, with a single breath, India drew these last friends into her body, and only he—being Hardyal—stayed aloof.

Tall, slender, dressed in English clothes, he passed for a sunburned English boy as he stood there in the gale of voices and a rich profusion of smells. Wherever he turned he encountered the expressive stares of the East, where curiosity is a legitimate function of human intelligence.

Touts and pedlars whined their enticements in his ear,
Parsee gentlemen wearing shiny black hats stalked past,
bent on large affairs, and Hardyal's glance was caught by
the vision of a Parsee lady in a sari the colour of a canary's
wing.

Presently, not aware himself that his movements had
adjusted themselves to the tempo of his own land—a tempo
which even in emergencies remains the tempo of leisure—
Hardyal turned to make inquiries about his luggage, and
found himself gazing into the eyes of his father's servant,
Krishna. They regarded each other silently, each marking
the passage of time whose tiny signals were more visible in
the boy than in the man. Krishna clasped his hands with
thumbs against his breast in the characteristic Hindu salu-
tation, which does not rely on contact or garrulity. It was
two years since Hardyal had seen a man weep for joy, and
the sight of Krishna's tears loosed a responsive emotion in
his own breast. " Ah, Krishnaji ! "

" My lord ! "

" But where is Bapu, why did he not come to meet me ? "

" He could not come, but he has sent these letters."
And Krishna combed his numerous shawls for the letters
which he'd brought. One was from Jacques St. Remy,
the other from Ganpat Rai explaining that he had been
detained by an important case, so sent Krishna instead.
Money was enclosed and instructions for their journey to
Amritpore. While Hardyal read his father's letter and
listened to Krishna's welcoming monologue he felt the
pressure of an immense and increasing familiarity. It was
in the air about him, in his ears and in his nostrils, but some
instinct urged him to fend it off, to preserve a little longer
the consciousness of his own unique identity and of the
other men and other places. It was in this instinctive clinging to a mood that, after slight hesitation, he put Jacques'
unopened letter in his pocket and said to the servant :
" Let us go."

They completed arrangements for the disposal of
Hardyal's luggage, then elbowed their way through a storm
of humanity to the street beyond the Bunda, where Krishna
had a hired landau waiting. The coachman in a dirty pink
turban saluted Hardyal with a flourish of his whip.

" Whither, Sahib ? "

Sudden and irrepressible gaiety poured through Hardyal.
" I care not ! Just drive. Drive until I tell you to stop."
He sat back on the lumpy cushions and sniffed the water-
proof lining of the hood which sheltered himself and Krishna
from a blaze of the afternoon sun. The landau wheeled
away from the pier and headed towards the city where the
tops of trees moved against a chaotic design of walls, arches
and domes. Hardyal had glimpses of the sea, of the outline
of the Malabar Hills, and the sepia-tinted earth of Bombay.
And while Krishna talked of home and of family affairs
Hardyal engaged in the secret task of reviving much that
had lain dormant in his memory. How often he'd dreamed
of this homecoming ! But now the dream itself claimed
him, the dream contained him as a detail in its complex
pattern ; he no longer controlled it nor could he escape it.

Great streets opened before him as the landau threaded
between other carriages, between ekkas and bullock carts
and bicycles. He smelled the fading freshness of the sea as
it lost itself in the city's spicy breath and knew that at last
he'd reached a stage in his life when to look back is to count
experience as golden. A youth with long black hair and
an hibiscus flower tucked behind one ear pedalled beside
the carriage, eyeing him with eyes like a dove's and crying
in birdlike tones. Krishna spat an imprecation and the
male Apsaras, losing heart, veered off down a side street.
" Everywhere one finds them," murmured the servant
philosophically. " Tell me, didst thou not also find them
in Belait ? "

Hardyal considered, then smiled. " There also, but they
did not wear hibiscus flowers in their ears."

" Where then did they wear them ? " inquired the
coachman, genially flicking a passing bullock with his
whip.

The landau moved northward through the sprawling
Crawford Market, where Hardyal suddenly ordered the
coachman to stop, that Krishna might buy *pan supari*.
Leaning on his elbow, he watched the shopman pick a wet
green leaf from a square of folded linen, smear the leaf with
lime and betel-nut and press it in a triangle to fit the human
mouth. The taste of *pan* on his tongue brought a sort of

intoxication to Hardyal ; he chewed, while every pore in his body exclaimed in delight. The coachman volunteered over his shoulder : " The Sahib-log who come to Bombay for the first time ask always to be taken to see the Towers of Silence on Malabar Hill."

Krishna interposed quickly : " That is no place to celebrate a homecoming ! Let us wait and go instead to the Coconut Festival, down by the sea."

Hardyal cried : " We have time for both. I would like to see the Towers of Silence."

Krishna looked glum, he was a good Hindu and the funeral customs of other people did not interest him ; but this was his young master's first day at home and he did not have the heart to demur. As they drove towards the outskirts of the city, past the great balconied houses of Bombay's Parsee merchants, Hardyal was thinking of a day in Sussex when, over the breakfast table, he listened to Aubrey Wall's sister argue about the Towers of Silence.

" It is where they keep the outcastes," insisted Miss Margaret, always the more forceful and the less accurate of the two. " I ought to know because I was reading about it just the other day."

" But Aubrey *told* me that the Towers are where they put their dead," Miss Bella had contradicted her sister with a flatness which for forty years had availed nothing. Both ladies then appealed to Hardyal : " Am I not right ? " And he answered gravely : " When I am in Bombay I shall go myself and see, and I will write and tell you."

Rain had beautified those strange gardens on Malabar Hill, where the Parsee *dhakmas* rise under a massed shade of trees. As the landau stopped, Hardyal got out, noticing everywhere the droppings of the vultures. Several of these feathered monsters stalked about in the sun, their wings drooping, an air about them that was not all bird. He examined the low roofless towers where the Parsees bring their dead for these birds to translate into eternity, and something of his young optimism faded when, continuing his glance upward, he saw in the soft blue sky a ceaseless wheeling flight of wings silvered a little by the sun.

" Yes," observed a voice in English, close beside him. " Barbarous, I call it ! "

The speaker, a sallow man in shabby clothes and a stained yellow topi, appeared suddenly from behind a bed of canna lilies. Hardyal, who in his dealings with Englishmen had acquired something of their reserve, smiled noncommittally. The other smiled back, revealing a row of bad teeth. " Two thousand years of Christianity, two hundred years of civilised rule—and look at them ! "

Which does he mean, wondered Hardyal—his teeth, the vultures, or the Towers ? The other elucidated by a wave of his arm. " I must say, I'm disappointed. First time I've been in Bombay and I paid a gharry-wallah two dibs to drive me here, expecting that I'd see at least one corpse. But no ! We're not even allowed to go into the bloody things."

" I don't think I'd care to," said Hardyal. His voice caught the other's attention and he turned upon Hardyal an eye as seedy as everything else about him. " Oh, you wouldn't, wouldn't you ? " The eye narrowed, concentrated, " I say, are you English or what ? "

The boy, always disconcerted by bad manners, remained silent and after further point-blank staring the stranger shrugged. " Of course, I see ! One of our young rajas. You do look so damnably English in that get-up, I must say."

Some imp of mischief entered Hardyal, who presented himself briefly as the Raj Kunwar of Amritpore. The other frowned. " Amritpore ? Can't say that I've ever heard of it. One of those little up-country States, I suppose. Does your Highness happen to know the Raja of Jhori ? He is, I should say, about your age."

" Afraid I don't."

" He has a salute of eleven guns. And your Highness ? "

" But seven," murmured Hardyal modestly.

" Ah ! Well, I'm Jhori's secretary. That is, I am his Secretary's secretary. My name is Smythe." He spelled it. " My young Raja is visiting relatives not far from here and I got a few days' leave in order to see Bombay. Must say I'm disappointed. Not a patch on Calcutta, especially the statues. Do you know the Octerlony statue in Calcutta ? "

" I don't think I remember it."

" One of my uncles served with Colonel Octerlony in

the Gurkha War. I myself was born in Bihar, but my family goes all the way back to the time of John Company."

Hardyal listened politely, repelled though he was by the man's spurious inflection and by his manner, at once intimate and arrogant. He recognised the native-born white, poor, thwarted, full of weird conceits and fantastic aspirations, and suddenly he felt sorry that he had embarked on this silly masquerade. He listened guiltily while Mr. Smythe jabbered on : " What a piece of luck to have met your Highness ! You see, my gharry-wallah ran away because I refused to pay him three rupees instead of the two which we'd agreed on at the start. These damned natives . . ." He checked himself. " I hope you'll let me cadge a lift back to the city ? "

Hardyal had no desire to share his privacy with the under-secretary to the Raja of Jhori, but he could hardly refuse. It became evident that Mr. Smythe had no intention of letting him out of sight. He took Hardyal's arm and, talking in the jocular tone of an old and experienced mind to a young and inferior one, conducted him on a tour of the gardens. They admired the flowers and studied the architecture of the Towers from every angle, while Mr. Smythe enlarged in scornful amusement on the funeral customs of the Parsees. " Your Hindu custom of cremation is, I must say, practically civilised. The next best thing to burial as we practise it. Give me the good old ground every time, worms and all ! Imagine exposing the body of someone you loved to these carrion-eaters ! "

Hardyal, who had been imagining exactly that, stood quite still and stared at the grass and pebbles at his feet. He suffered a sort of seizure to which he was occasionally subject, when it seemed that everything that he had ever known, and a premonition of things not yet experienced, flowed with a bitter flavour into his mouth.

Mr. Smythe was tugging at his elbow. " What about the Coconut Festival ? Does your Highness intend to see it this evening ? "

The spell was broken and Hardyal raised his eyes. " The Coconut Festival ? "

" They all gather on the beach and chuck coconuts into the sea as offerings to—who is it, Varuna ? " He nudged

the boy's arm and winked with inexpressible lewdness.
" Afterwards there are places I could take you . . ."

" My train leaves at midnight."

" Oh, you'll have time. I'd be glad to go with you to
the Festival, if I could be of any assistance."

Hardyal's brown eyes met his at last. " I must tell you,
sir . . . I'm not really the Raj Kunwar of Amritpore."

" Eh ? " He reddened.

" I'm not a prince at all. I was just joking."

" The devil you were ! " He dropped Hardyal's arm.

" I do beg your pardon, sir." It was the English school-
boy who spoke, but Smythe's bewilderment hardened into
anger. " Damned cheeky even for a native, aren't you ?
Or is it part of your education ? "

This was brought out in the sudden temper of an up-
start deprived of all his little props, and for a moment
Hardyal was afraid that the man would strike him. But
the threat passed. Smythe glared, then shrugged. " Well,
you can jolly well give me a lift back to the city, just the
same."

They returned to the landau, where Smythe stared at
Krishna.

" There is room on the box beside the driver."

The servant hesitated and glanced at his master; for
a second the air seemed to stretch and to become brittle
with tension, then Hardyal nodded, " Do so, my brother."

Krishna got out of the landau and climbed up beside
the coachman, whose sophisticated features had assumed a
sudden blandness.   While Mr. Smythe arranged himself
over the greater part of the seat under the hood, Hardyal
perched on the smaller one facing him. Access to authority
exerted a soothing effect upon Mr. Smythe's feelings ; he
produced a cheroot, and leaning well back propped his feet
on the seat beside Hardyal. The landau swung down the
hill and under the big gates, then turned towards the city.
Hardyal, to avoid meeting the eyes of his fellow passenger,
watched the shadows of the vultures making arabesques on
the red, sunlit earth.

28

PRIDE's natural reluctance to concede its hurt prevented Hardyal from brooding too long on that little adventure on Malabar Hill, and Mr. Smythe dropped out of his life on the instant that the landau deposited him, with his topi and his cheroot, on the outskirts of the Crawford Market. There, with a perfunctory nod, he vanished into the heaving mass of India just as earlier in the day Hardyal's fellow passengers had vanished. The encounter was trivial, but it left a faint troubled stir, a tiny whirlpool which required a larger disturbance for its eventual stilling. So it was with a conscious resolve to put Mr. Smythe in his proper place among the insignificant items of experience that Hardyal decided to attend the Coconut Festival in Hindu dress, a yearning which he had not felt this morning as he stood on the Apollo Bunda and struggled to preserve the unique sense of his own identity—not as Englishman or as Hindu, but simply as Hardyal.

Accompanied by Krishna he sauntered among the native shops, and bought a white dhoti, a muslin shirt with silver studs, a flowered waistcoat, a cap of Kotah cloth, and sandals which rasped his feet after two years of English wool and leather. Krishna had hired a room in the respectable Hindu quarter and here Hardyal bathed and changed his clothes. As he assumed the friendly garments his limbs seemed to take on independent life ; memory gave a little stir, and he remembered an afternoon in Amritpore when he and Jacques St. Remy had exchanged their clothing and presented themselves before his father's guests. He stood motionless on the mud floor of the hired room, watching Krishna fold the discarded garments and lay them on a string charpoy. A grey lizard crawled on the wall and from a mitred niche beside the window a crude and glossy picture of Varuna stared back at him— Varuna, god of the elements, his eyes beaming fire, his hair streaming like a hatch of serpents.

Krishna said : " Here is the letter, which you did not open."

It was Jacques' letter, but a childish instinct to postpone

pleasure moved Hardyal to put the envelope back in his pocket. " I shall save it to read on the train."

They had commanded their original charioteer to drive them to the shore, and it was dusk when they stepped into the tremors and the marigold smells of a little street where lamps were glimmering behind ironwork grilles and bamboo blinds. The landau picked its way southward this time, skirting the docks and warehouses and the pointing fingers of mills. Swarms of people were pushing in the same direction and progress was slow, with a great commotion of tikka-gharries, carriage bells, bicycles, the cries of touts and vendors and sporadic yells which splintered against the brusque commands of city policemen. Hardyal gazed at the lights of Bombay. The city had ignited in a fine transparence of balconies and cupolas, in spidery lattice-work and the stern flat line of rooftops all laced together in a web of glittering telegraph wires. As the city glowed with a sustained and intense preoccupation Hardyal felt that it was solitary and complete, and that the millions who lived in it were the fleshy pores through which it drew its enormous breath.

The coachman drove through by-streets and disgraceful slums in whose sudden convulsive darkness and rancid odours Hardyal's throat seemed to close up. Beggars and lepers seeped from black crannies and staggered, whining, beside the wheels ; children with old miserly faces capered in thin slivers of light, crying for pennies. Shutters creaked, spit flew, and a conglomeration of mangy cats, descending from nowhere, struck the cobbles and exploded like firecrackers, shooting off into the hideous night. Hardyal held his nose and cried : " Why must you bring us by this route ? "

" Why not ? It's a short cut, isn't it ? "

But he whipped his browbeaten horse to a sprightlier gait, almost mowing down a knobby, noseless Something upon whose half-human face the carriage lamp flung its single revealing ray.

At last they were free of the slums and on the road towards the sea, with the celebrating crowd billowing round them like foam. A drum rattled and a man's voice soared into the serene, expressionless sky. Hardyal had never seen the Coconut Festival. He thought : " I must write about this to Miss Bella and Miss Margaret." And he started composing a long letter to his friends, including them in to-night's magic, conversing with them in small, lordly, expository gestures, his eyes aglow with generous light.

Then the carriage lurched and slowed to a crawl as it ran abreast a perfect avalanche of humanity. Hardyal stood up, clinging to the little rail behind the driver's seat. Below were the shore and the sea quivering in leagues of moonlight which broke into shadows amongst the moving crowd. Driving through the city he had forgotten the moon, but he saw it now as it hung in the sky between himself and Arabia ; its cool radiance flowed over his hand, twinkled on the drop at the end of Krishna's nose, and lingered for a second on the scrofulous ear of their tired horse.

They ordered the coachman to wait for them on this spot, for they must get back to the city in time to catch their train, and Krishna followed Hardyal down the sands into the crowd which ebbed and flowed like the sea itself, a tide of dark limbs and glistening heads and sudden apparitional faces. Hardyal struggled to the water's edge and stood there with the sea nibbling his feet, where moonlight slid like mercury over a surface littered with bobbing coconuts ; Krishna brought him one and Hardyal flung it with all his force, a prayer going out with it from his heart, a voiceless prayer which he left to the god to interpret as he would. Half a day had passed since he stepped ashore on the Apollo Bunda and sent a final glance at the ship which had brought him home, but he felt that he was not the Hardyal who had gone away, nor was he, quite, the Hardyal who had come back. Broodingly, he slipped two fingers of his right hand into his shirt and felt, under his nails, the delicate hairs on his breast, the steady beating of his heart. Beside him moaned and swayed a thousand other bodies like his own ; they brushed against him, he smelled their human sweat, he felt their life. A woman laughed and the sound trembled in his ear with the articulateness of a song, but when he turned to look for her he faced a thousand eyes and lost her voice in a hoarse murmur

of invocation from uncounted lips. Then something cool
and white struck his thigh and fell to the ground, and as he
stooped to pick up a garland of flowers their scent rushed
through his body, thrilling him. He held the garland and
cast about for the owner, but no one approached to claim
it. Men brushed past, and a little group of children, as
brown as coconuts and as bare, dashed under his arm
towards the sea, in whose smallest wave they skipped with
tiny splashes and infinitesimal cries.

Hardyal caressed his flowers and smiled to himself. He
no longer thought of writing to his friends of this adventure,
for he no longer saw them as essential to his mood. In a
passion of joy and reverence he stooped and laid his garland on the sea, watching it as minute by minute the
accepting tide bore it away.

Hardyal read Jacques' letter as the train carried him
northward through the night, towards Nasik and Khandwa,
on towards the goldfields of Indore. Folded in a Scotch
travelling rug whose fringes tickled his chin, he swayed
luxuriously with the train's motion while on the next berth
Krishna slept rolled up in blankets like a corpse, his snores
drowned in the humming wheels.

" In ten days," wrote Jacques, " you will be back in
India ! Now that you are on your way home I find it hard
to write because when I start to think about things they
suddenly become not so very much. This is one reason why
I've never got a great deal out of books : words make time
seem all queer and wrong, for when you are alive everything that happens takes a proper length of time—minutes,
hours, days. And in two years so many things have happened—things I can put into a few sentences.   Last
spring Macbeth's mother ran away with Captain Ponsonby. No one speaks of it now, except Bertie. She's told
me a lot. Macbeth was awfully cut up, but the Colonel
behaved very quietly.   He always behaves quietly and
sometimes you wonder whether he notices anything except
his garden and his soldiers. I like him because I can never
forget the night when I was hurt and he lifted me down
from the tree and bent over me, telling me over and over
that I was all right, that there was nothing to be afraid of.

So, you can see it is not really surprising that he should have behaved like a gentleman when Mrs. Macbeth ran off with Ponsonby. Bertie is living in Gambul with the Macbeths. It's queer, you know, the feeling that Mrs. Macbeth is still with us. I feel that she might walk into the room at any moment, and I know that Macbeth feels it too—more than any of us. He hangs around looking as if that was what he was waiting for.

"Mr. Wall must be nearing England now. And you won't see Gisele. Have I told you that this is my last year at St. Matthew's? I shan't sit for the Cambridge exams—what would be the use? Maman says I know enough as it is, so after this year I shall be in Amritpore learning about the factory. Father Sebastien will go on giving me Maths and Latin, and I suppose I can get the rest out of reading.

"Here is a story which Hanif has just told me. Mrs. Lyttleton's servant died a few days ago, and Hanif says that a devil entered into him and killed him, and that now he haunts Mrs. Lyttleton's house. Hanif won't walk past the gates after dark, though he is very brave in broad daylight!

"I keep wondering what you will think of Bertie Wood. I must tell you, in strictest confidence, that I am going to marry her eventually, perhaps in two or three years. No one knows of this, not even Maman, but Bertie and I have decided.

"The rains have broken and this evening there is a sunset which makes everything look like a lighted room. There is so much to tell you, so much to ask you—I can't believe that we shall be seeing each other soon . . . soon! Well, *mon chère* !"

Hardyal finished the letter and lay for some minutes with the loose pages on his breast, feeling the urgent rhythm of the wheels as they rushed through the darkness. Then he rose and pushed the baize cover over the ceiling light, plunging the compartment into gloom, and at once the sound of the wheels turned into a song which Krishna had taught him when he was a little boy :

"Eke eke anna,
Doh doh pisa !

> Teen teen pisa,
> Doh doh anna ! "

He fell asleep with the childish refrain running through his head.

29

ONE afternoon, three months after Hardyal's return to Amritpore, Madame St. Remy sat on the same veranda where she had sat with Father Sebastien on the afternoon of Jacques' fourteenth birthday.   Time had wrought no striking change upon Madame, for whom shocks and mutations were always of an interior order.   Her features, more sculptural than pictorial, concentrated vitality in her brown eyes, which missed nothing except that which the brain behind them had never cared to recognise.   Mrs. Lyttleton often asserted that Madame had inherited the instincts of a French *concierge*, but the charge was hardly just ; Madame had cultivated stoicism as an attribute of good breeding, she had, through sheer will-power, acquired much of the literary lumber of aristocracy—lumber which Mrs. Lyttleton had long since cheerfully thrown overboard.   Madame's metamorphosis might have been complete but for her secretiveness, that hallmark of *banias* the world over.   However, she never lacked force, a fact which Mrs. Lyttleton was to discover too late when Madame intervened between herself and Jacques.

Madame might well preen herself on having scored, for there was no doubt that Jacques' affection for his old friend had been effectively nipped in the bud.   Madame had indeed won that round as in the past she had won others, yet when she paused to ponder on her victories her reflections were followed by others of a less triumphal nature. There had, of course, been a succession of rounds, and even if she were not prepared to admit defeat in all of them, she could not in any honesty claim unconditional surrenders. Madame St. Remy was always most candid with herself when she was least observed as she happened to be at this moment, alone on her veranda overlooking the rose garden and the trees which massed their airy green between her and the flat brown plain. She had need of candour, since for the past two hours she'd engaged in a process of recapitulation—mental, spiritual and financial. The materials for this process were spread before her on a table : letters, account books, bills of sale, receipts, beside a black-and-gold japanned box with an intricate lock which only she knew how to open. It was a marvellous box, composed of drawers and compartments and hiding-places, every one of which contained something that with the years had become as native to it as a seed is to its fruit. Locks of the children's hair tied with wisps of silk, a gold crucifix worn by Auguste St. Remy when he was a child, a locket with portraits of Amélia and Auguste at the time of their engagement, and a pair of diminutive enamelled foxes which Auguste had given his bride on her nineteenth birthday. For years Jacques and Gisele had coveted these foxes, but Madame explained sternly that they were not toys.

To the St. Remy children these reminders of their own and their parents' past were the most fascinating things in the box, but it contained other reminders which they had never been permitted to see, and it was upon these that Madame had brooded with a sombre and unrewarding candour for the past two hours. Stacked in the largest compartment between locks of Gisele's hair and a package of her husband's letters lay several sheets of thin native paper covered with spidery Hindi, each bearing a three-anna stamp and flowing signatures. These were notes of hand to the credit of Ramdatta the moneylender, and a simple sum in arithmetic had started the pin-wheel of speculation spinning in Madame's head. Meshing with all its neighbouring wheels it wove an inevitable sequence of doubt, conjecture and frustration, though nothing of all this was visible in her expression. Perhaps she realised that she faced ruin, but to fuss was not in her nature. Let the world make its own discoveries, she would rest upon her faith, which had carried her over every natural and artificial obstacle planted in her way by luck or by design. Nor was hers a blind faith ; rather, like her intelligence, it was an intense and narrow one. Whenever she thought of the past she managed to revive the peculiar thrill of the self-righteous who glory in defeat, attributing it—as in her case—to the machinations of the Devil or of the English, both of whom she would have missed badly, since between them they kept her faculties alert and her faith radiant.

For Madame St. Remy there never could be any acknowledgment of paradox, a concept which she feared was already exerting its heretical fascination upon the mind of her son. It was becoming increasingly difficult for her to guess what went on in Jacques' thoughts. How strange that Gisele's beauty and sensibility—and by these Madame meant Gisele's sex—should have posed a comparatively simple problem. Gisele was provided for, she was even provided against. Gisele was beyond all question safe. But Jacques was a different story, and at this point Madame's reflections changed ; she seemed to exude shadow, making her body a separate world, a separate climate almost. She suffered from the assault of a memory which occurred to her often when she found herself alone, as now, the empty garden before her and at her back the empty house.

Her servants were in their own quarters, Jacques had gone with Macbeth and Bertie to visit Hardyal, and it was with a sense of desolation that she found herself not only remembering, but intensely and actually reviving that day, two years ago, when she received Colonel Macbeth's telegram informing her of Jacques' accident.

Accompanied by Hanif she arrived at the Macbeths' house and they had taken her to see Jacques where he lay on the Colonel's bed, in that dressing-room which smelled of Pinaud's Brilliantine and boot polish. The Macbeths left her at the door, but Hanif followed her in and crouched at Jacques' feet, clasping them in his slender brown hands, weeping over them.

Madame drew a chair towards the bed and sat down, bending towards her son. His left arm lay across his breast under the sheet. His eyes, wide and steady, stared at her from the white pillows.

She whispered : " Don't talk. Lie very still until you are well again."

" But there is something I want to tell you."

" I know everything."

" I want to tell you myself." He gazed at her with his young lion eyes. " They had to cut off my hand at the wrist." He said it in a cool, measured voice and she guessed that he must have lain here practising how to say it. She caught her breath. " Yes, I was afraid . . ."

" The regimental surgeon did it. But it was Colonel Macbeth who saved me. He lifted me down from the tree and put a tight thing round my arm. He helped the dandy-coolies carry me back to Gambul. He and Bertie and Macbeth . . . and all the time when I felt I was going . . . you know, Maman ? going . . . they held on to me as if they knew, as if they understood that I felt I was going."

" Don't talk," whispered Madame between dry lips. " My darling, don't talk."

" I want to. I must. You see, it wasn't any one's fault. It wasn't *their* fault. Maman, you must promise me . . ."

She strove, vainly, to read the question in his eyes. " Promise me . . ."

" We will talk to-morrow, Jacques. Now close your eyes. I am here. I shall stay beside you until you sleep."

Dinner was brought to her on a tray, and when at last the boy fell asleep she went downstairs to the strange, lamplit room were the Macbeth family awaited her. John Macbeth had disappeared, but Bertie stayed, curled like a tawny cat on the window-seat. Madame, with something of the air of a somnambulist, allowed her hand to be taken, and accepted the chair which the Colonel brought forward. Mrs. Macbeth expressed her concern in faint, incoherent murmurs, then relapsed into unhappy silence, but the Colonel faced Madame, fixing her with his pale, luminous eyes.

" Nothing," he declared, " nothing could have upset me more than this, not even if it had happened to my own son."

Madame St. Remy returned his gaze expressionlessly. " But it did not happen to your son, sir. It happened to mine."

Seated beside the piano in a little pool of light, Mrs. Macbeth stared at her hands, but the Colonel continued to withstand the icy shock of his visitor's gaze. " At least, we know now that Jacques will recover. He is young and strong. We must thank God for that."

"I shall never cease to thank God, but you, I think, have additional need to thank him." After a brief pause, she went on : "Jacques was in your care. Now I realise that it might have been better had I acted on my first impulse, which was certainly not one of blind confidence."

"Then what was your impulse, Madame ? " inquired the soldier, gently.

"My first impulse was to forbid Jacques spending his holidays away from the authorities whom I had entrusted with his safety."

Mrs. Macbeth glanced up in distress, but it was Bertie who interposed in a high, excited voice : "Good heavens ! You couldn't leave him stuck in that horrible school all the time, could you ? "

It was always difficult for Madame to lose her temper in English, and to have lost it in French would have made the situation ridiculous, since she was quite sure that these barbarians spoke nothing except their own language. Ignoring Bertie, she said swiftly : "Of course I realise that the English have odd notions in regard to the training of their children, ideas of nobility and courage, virtues which you exact from mere infants. I suppose this is admirable. It is, no doubt, one reason for your great success as colonisers."

The Colonel twisted his moustache. "Well, upon my word, don't you know . . ."

"*Enfin*, Monsieur, not being English myself I have less exalted ideas. I do not believe in throwing my children to lions and panthers. I do not believe in compelling them to sit in trees with loaded guns, and in leaving them there for hours until they go insane with fright ! "

Colonel Macbeth took a short step in one direction, changed his mind and came back. "By jove, I never thought about it in quite that light. You see, it was all a matter of luck."

"Luck ? "

"*Qui porte bonheur !* " He smiled with an air of relief, as though he was sure that this succinct phrase must clear away all misunderstanding.

" Jacques, you see, won the toss."

She smiled bitterly. " You are wrong. He lost ! "

" Oh no, he didn't ! " As she spoke, Bertie crossed the room and took her uncle's arm. " And if you were to ask Jacques, Madame, he would tell you, himself, that he won."

Madame seemed to notice her for the first time ; as a matter of fact she had met them all several hours ago but then she was conscious of little except of her son. Now, as the mist of terror and anxiety began to lift, she saw these cold-blooded English in the baleful light in which she had always judged them. Their composure, their acceptance of irresponsibility as something which involved no more than a stroke of " luck " or a point in sportsmanship, roused the dormant hatred in her breast. They were in league, as usual ; they stuck by each other even when they were in the wrong—perhaps never so loyally as when they were wrong ! They forgot their differences and pooled their strength against the stranger, for this, too, was part of their code. And as she glanced from one face to another, Madame felt grateful to a chance to speak her mind—her poor, distraught mind.

She addressed herself to Bertie. " I do not need to ask Jacques anything, Mademoiselle. I have seen him, and that is enough. I have seen that he lost the toss, as you call it, and that he has permanently lost the use of his hand as a consequence. I am not interested in the details of how or why such a thing should have been allowed to happen. Do you not understand that this has made him a cripple for life ? "

They winced, and the tiny convulsion drew all three faces into a single momentary likeness. Then Bertie's eyes filled with tears.

" Do you think that we need to be reminded ? Do you think that after seeing him lying there . . . after watching him fight to keep alive, to do more than just that . . . to be a man about it . . ." She ignored a warning pressure of the Colonel's arm. " We are not trying to dodge responsibility, as you seem to think. But it was up to each of us, that night. It was just as much up to Jacques."

Madame stared at her. " I am afraid that I do not understand you, my child."

F

" But what is it that's so difficult to understand ? Jacques did what any of us would have done. He couldn't back out of it, could he ? "

" Had you been my child I should never have permitted you to get into such a dilemma."

" You couldn't have stopped me ! "

Madame smiled. " I could, and would, have stopped Jacques."

They exchanged a long, hard look, then Bertie asked : " Would you have tried ? " She did not wait for an answer. " Because if you had, it would have been very unfair to him."

Madame shrugged. " Possibly."

Bertie flushed. " You would have made him look like a coward when he was trying his hardest not to be one. What's more, I don't think that he'd have let you."

The Colonel put his arm round her shoulders. " My dear Bertie, we mustn't forget that Madame has been through a frightful ordeal." He looked, now, as though he were going through one himself. Of them all only Mrs. Macbeth seemed exempt from suffering. Since she could not escape the embarrassment of this scene she divorced herself from it by retreating into a sort of trance.

Madame was silent for a minute, then she shrugged with an air of resignation. " For years I have lived among you people, but I confess that I have never understood you. I don't think that I shall ever understand you. Perhaps no one will understand you. Others will hate you and resent you, some may even try to ape you, but they will never understand you. For myself, I simply do not know what to make of you. You are—what shall I say ? " She spread her hand despairingly. " *Impossible !* "

They accepted this in silence, unprotestingly, with a sort of meditative gallantry that poor Madame recognised as one of the most *impossible* traits in their benighted racial character. The silence continued, it threatened to last for ever, and she realised that this was part of an unrehearsed collusion—she was to be permitted the full, triumphal satisfaction of the Last Word.

Conscious, suddenly, of her own fatigue, she rose, distributed fragmentary bows, and went out of the room. But

in the dimly lighted hall she paused a moment to get herself in hand before going upstairs to Jacques. She stood in
an angle of the staircase, her dark dress merging with the
heavy shadow which fell about her. From here she had a
partial view of the room which she'd just left, and of
the tableau now being enacted there in the golden lamp-
light. Mrs. Macbeth was not visible but the Colonel's
figure was amply framed, his arm still round his niece's
shoulder. Madame heard his deep indistinguishable murmur, followed by Bertie's voice as clear as a bell : " I
hate her ! She's going to try and take Jacques away from
us, you'll see."

There were further murmurs from the Colonel, then
Bertie's voice again : " It *is* our business. I'll fight her if
you won't. John and I will fight her together. We'll fight
her—tooth and nail ! "

Madame turned away, stepping from the shadow
towards the foot of the stairs, and she saw then that she was
not alone, that John Macbeth leaned against the newel-
post facing her, racing past her towards the open doors of
the drawing-room. From his expression Madame guessed
that he'd heard what Bertie said and that he had caught
her, herself, in the intolerable rôle of eavesdropper. As she
prepared to pass him their eyes met, and she thought
bitterly : " Yes, they're in league, all of them, even the
children ! "

Her sense of desolation increased as she mounted the
stairs and found Hanif squatting like a watchful genie outside Jacques' door. He rose, reassuringly strong and familiar
in his elegant garments, and Madame waited a moment
to get her breath. " Does he sleep ? " she asked at last, and
raised her hand to her own tired eyes.

" He sleeps," the young man replied softly. " He woke
but once, thinking you were near, and he asked something
of you."

Madame stared at her servant. " He asked something ?
What was it ? "

Hanif's eyes gleamed darkly in his smooth brown face.
" Perhaps he was not entirely awake, but it seemed to me
that he begged a promise of you."

She waited, and the deferential voice continued : " Have

I liberty to speak ? You are my father and my mother, else
how should I dare ? "

Madame drew a deep breath. " Oh, go on, go on ! "

" Then you must know that he has set his heart on
these friends. Do not take him away from them, for if he
should come to believe that you intend to take him away,
he may lose heart . . . and he must not lose heart ! "

Madame hesitated, a strange emotion leaping and dying
within her. Hanif waited, his hands clasped before him,
his eyes lowered. Then with a curious little sigh Madame
put her hand on the door and walked past him into her
son's room.

30

A FLOCK of crows alighted among the trees and their uncouth din roused Madame from her reverie. Imperceptibly,
the tragic concentration dissolved in her features, and her
thoughts retired into a privacy as inviolable as the secret
compartments of the japanned box. If she had gained
nothing by this short spell of retrospection neither had she
surrendered anything ; so long as she alone knew where
and how she stood in her devious relationships, they must
endure. Other people's minds might be as enigmatic as her
own and behind the humdrum exchange of everyday life
all sorts of conspiracies might be brewing, but these were
dangers on which she dared not brood. As for Ramdatta
. . . reaching forward with her finger-nail, she snapped the
hinged lid on the compartment which contained the *hundies*,
knowing well enough that so long as she continued to owe
him money he would continue to advance her more. The
end remained hidden, as it should, according to God's will.

She heard a step on the gravel and presently Hanif
appeared, sauntering among her roses. He did not see her
at once, and as she watched him move like some painted
and fastidious bird among the flowers Madame experienced
the peculiar emotion which this young servant alone had
power to evoke in her. It was, perhaps, less an emotion
than a sort of vicarious thrill which other people derived
from plays, from music, from books or from conversation.

His loyalty touched her, his peccadilloes were an endless source of astonishment to her impeccable soul. She knew that he lied to her, that he stole tea and sugar from her godowns, that he helped himself to her perfume. He was a spendthrift, a gambler, with a weakness for fine clothes and loose women—vices which Madame would never have tolerated in a white man, nor dreamed of forgiving in any one related to herself. But Hanif was her periscope into another world ; because he was not her son she had never suffered for him, she had never troubled to change him, to correct him, to dull him. Nor, strangely, had she thought to convert him or to use her influence towards his conversion. He stood, for her, in the light of some rare and costly animal, absolved from Christian retribution as he remained, inevitably, exempt from Christian salvation.

It was something of the same feeling that she extended to Hardyal, even to Ganpat Rai, for although she would vehemently have denied prejudice in the matter of race or of colour, her sense of racial identity as something foreordained was so deeply ingrained as to have become practically unconscious. Unlike Aubrey Wall and Mrs. Lyttleton who acknowledged the dilemma and hated it, unlike Father Sebastien who, in his own way, laboured to mitigate it, Madame never even paused to question its existence. She was simply not interested in natives as human beings and for this reason they had never posed a problem to her intelligence nor offered a challenge to her conscience. This, in fact, was the secret of her acceptance of Hardyal as Jacques' friend—she was no more capable of jealousy on Hardyal's account than she was capable of it on Hanif's. Throughout her life she remained supremely unaware of this contradiction, and she would have been scandalised had any one ventured to bring it to her attention. Her feeling towards Hanif had been intensified and somewhat complicated by that evening in Gambul when he begged her not to take Jacques away from the Macbeths. That appeal, which she had ignored but not neglected, recurred to Madame for days afterwards. She knew that she could never have brought herself to examine, let alone grant, such a plea had it been made by one of the Macbeths. Consciously or not, she was girded for that battle which Bertie

Wood had declared as being joined—tooth and nail, and
to the bitter end. Strange that it should devolve on Hanif
to come forward with an alternative, one by which Madame
stood to lose nothing, nothing whatsoever of her dignity,
her pride, her possessiveness. Jacques' life was what
counted, and Jacques' life was what Hanif held up to her,
not as a threat but as a reward. If God had saved Jacques
then Hanif had saved Madame, and in her silent decision
to ignore Bertie's challenge—for the time being—Madame
was hardly likely to forget Hanif or to consider him the
less because of his deft and innocent intervention.

Now as she watched him, resplendent in Baluchi trousers
and a green velvet waistcoat, a velvet cap tilted to one side
of his pomaded head, Madame smiled with a rare spontaneity. Dawdling among the roses, he caught sight of her
from under his long lashes and at once a not too subtle
change came over him. He twisted a long stem topped with
a half-blown rose from its circling leaves and carried it,
swooningly, to his nose. He hummed a song and moved
with languorous grace towards the veranda.

Madame addressed him. " I did not raise those flowers
to be plucked by you and distributed amongst the bazaars,
my friend ! "

He mounted the veranda steps and laid the rose alongside the japanned box and the marbled account books.
" The Fair is soon, and I must have new trousers." He
glanced with abhorrence at his pantaloons. " If I am to
escort the children I cannot go dressed in these rags."

She surveyed him critically. " When you escort my son
you will wear your livery."

He smiled ravishingly. " That still leaves the problem
of trousers, and of shoes. Two weeks ago I saw a pair—
blue leather worked in gold. Unfortunately I had bestowed
my last pice on a beggar, else I might have persuaded the
skinflint of a *mochi* to let me have the shoes on a small down-
payment."

Madame clasped her hands and rested her chin on
them. " You shall have the shoes. Tell me, where did the
children ride yesterday ? "

" To the Fort, as usual. It was hot. Allah, how I suffered ! "

His manner had not changed but she saw at once that she could get little out of him. While his personal loyalty to her remained unswerving, she knew that with him Jacques came first ; the knowledge both pleased and angered her.

" Well, what did they talk about ? " she demanded bluntly, and he lowered his limpid gaze to the floor. " They conversed in English, naturally, so how would I understand what they said ? "

" You understand very well when you are not supposed to. Now tell me, were you present when Macbeth sahib fell from his horse. He assured me it was nothing, yet his knees were badly cut."

Hanif made a bland gesture with pale, upturned palms. " Ah, that Macbeth ! Difficult to tell which is rider and which is horse. He jumped the ditch beyond the canal and his horse came down, but when it stood up again Macbeth was still in the saddle."

" I have given you authority to prevent such reckless-ness. Why do you not control them ? "

" Macbeth is the reckless one. He has a devil, which drives him."

" Devil or no devil, I want no accidents while they are my guests."

Hanif put his head on one side and gazed at her. " There will be no accidents—on that I pledge my life. But the shoes ? "

Madame opened the box and took a little chamois-leather bag, from which she extracted two rupees. " These come out of your wages, remember." She inclined her head slightly as he took the money and salaamed her deeply with both hands. Then she glanced at the little gold watch pinned to her blouse. " It is late. The children should be returning."

Hanif tucked the coins in his waistcoat pocket. " You know what happens when they get among those Hindus. It is all jabber, jabber and eat, eat."

Madame heard, far away, the sound of Father Sebas-tien's church bell and knew that he was preparing for Benediction. She had hoped that Jacques might return in time to accompany her ; his laxity in these matters was getting more pronounced, but some obscure fear prevented her from acknowledging it, even to herself. Ever since his accident she had been aware of a new strength growing in him, as though the lopped branch of his hand had sent the vitality back into his spirit, steeling it.

Once more she glanced at her watch. " We will wait half an hour. Then you shall go and bring them home."

31

WHILE Madame St. Remy was poring over the contents of her despatch case, Bertie Wood sat rather shyly among the ladies of Ganpat Rai's household in their zenana at the rear of the house. It was here they spent their days, when they did not prefer the arbour at the end of the garden. The zenana itself, comprising several large rooms and the inevitable veranda, opened on a courtyard with high walls and rows of custard-apple trees. In its centre was a goldfish pond and a plot of grass on which grazed a tame antelope, its wicked horns capped with brass, a silver bell ringing at its throat. Suspended from the veranda ceiling was a large basket-work cage filled with *lals*, tiny coloured birds whose ceaseless fluttering and twittering transformed the upper air into a world of their own. Babies wearing silver amulets, and little else, stumbled or crawled everywhere, or finger in mouth, stood staring with kohl-painted eyes at the stranger. The ladies—there must have been twenty of them—crouched on rugs or perched cross-legged on enamelled charpoys, a silver anklet or be-ringed toe peeping under the deckled edges of their *saries*. The atmosphere, new to Bertie, seemed redolent of a femininity which tinkled, rustled, whispered and giggled in a continuous minor orchestration, fanned by the breeze which moved from the courtyard into the house and emerged again, freighted with odours of sweet oil, warm flesh and tinselled gauze. The air kept rising against Bertie's face, strangely disturbing and exciting her as she sat in the main chamber on a chair especially provided for her. She felt the women's liquid gaze cover every detail of her own person. Some returned her frank smile, others, overcome by shyness, turned aside their varnished heads and gave little deprecating tugs to their veils. They had, of course, seen other white women, but Bertie was the youngest ever to visit them and perhaps for that reason they vested her with additional glamour. Her Hindustani was still shaky but she ventured a few remarks which was received with instantaneous, charming attention. How unlike us, she reflected, ruefully remembering her own and her cousins' squeals of mirth when foreigners mauled the Queen's English.

But for Bertie, creature of the open air, the zenana was like walking straight into a dream. Draperies and screens fell behind her, shadows grew like forests in every corner and from their gloom demure figures emerged to greet her, their little narrow hands touching vermilion-starred foreheads. She had a confused impression of flashing glass and metal, of fire spurting from the centre of priceless jewels, and of the concentrated gaze of these denizens of a culture six thousand years old. Ganpat Rai had explained to her that Hindu women borrowed the custom of purdah from their Mohammedan conquerors. " Before that time they were as free as you," he told her, sadly. " Now they shrink from a freedom that is always within their grasp."

It was several minutes before Bertie could reconcile Ganpat Rai's female establishment with the rest of his household, with the barrister himself and with his charming son. Now she found herself surrounded by a palpitating community of aunts and great-aunts, cousins and the wives and sisters of cousins. She allowed herself to be touched, to be gazed upon, to be addressed in exquisite Hindi to which she made overloud and inadequate replies. Ganpat Rai's aunt, a blue-eyed woman from Kashmir, who spoke a little English and understood more, touched Bertie's skirt and exclaimed : " Pure wool, yes ! "

When Bertie nodded and smiled the others exploded in little cries of admiration and wonder. The aunt's blue eyes lingered on Bertie's face. " Husband ? Marry ? Engage ? "

" I'm afraid I'm too young yet."

The aunt smiled, and corresponding smiles flowered everywhere.

" Too young ? I was married when I was twelve. My

daughters are all married. The youngest, fifteen, has her first child."

"I think perhaps we are rather backward about such things," Bertie ventured, and assisted her meaning with vague explanatory gestures.

The statement was received by a musical clashing of bangles and bracelets. Mirana Bhai nodded approval. "I've been told that in past times in Belait it used to be with you as it has always been with us, folks married young and lived long. But no matter how long one may live, time is too short. I have ten children," she added complacently, "ten children and eighteen grandchildren."

There was a further outburst of trills from the gauzy audience, and the aunt shifted her *pan* to the other cheek. "I suspect that in your country you waste much time. The best years are the years of our youth, yet I am told that among you many wait until middle-age, even until old age, before they take husbands. Many, I hear, never marry at all."

A moan of compassion and bewilderment eddied through the room as Bertie assented to this melancholy fact. Mirana Bhai looked at her keenly. "But you have a young, strong body and beautiful breasts. What is it you wait for?"

Taken aback by the directness of the question and the frankness of the admiration, Bertie coloured up ; then half-laughing, she attempted an explanation while the others listened, fixing her with tender and inquiring glances. Mirana Bhai shook her head. "Nay, I have heard that white women set great store by something they call their independence. My nephew has explained this term to me, but I still have difficulty understanding it. For if women will not bear children they must assume some other responsibility. Would they be teachers and servants rather than mothers?"

Her sari, slipping from her head, revealed a coiffure varnished smooth with coconut oil, tasselled with bright threads which, passing behind her ears, supported clusters of heavy silver earrings. She went on with an air of authority. "As for us, we perform our duties better if we are not distracted by matters which, in the end, cannot have any great importance. I understand these things, for I have heard much about them. We are born with bodies, with wombs, and nothing can ever change their meaning. Now, tell me, little one, wilt thou, also, wait until thou art an old back-toothed hag before thou bearest a child ? "

Bertie laughed. " I don't know, I hope not ! " But she felt a heat in her face and an unexpected sting of tears in her eyes. In the brief ensuing pause she thought, confusedly : " They live for this—for their dark, inscrutable men and their fruitlike children, for this hushed, dim existence. . . ."

Mirana Bhai rose suddenly. " Now we shall have *tee*. Do you like hulwa ? Do you like batasas ? "

Jacques had warned her not to refuse the hospitality with which she was bound to be showered, and for some time she'd been aware of mysterious preparations going on in the background. Now, as Mirana Bhai clapped her hands, various curtains shuddered and parted, and three female servants appeared carrying vast platters of food. There was tea in a massive china teapot, there were English biscuits, sardines, and bowls of Hindu sweets strewn with almonds, and glimmering with silver foil which melted when she helped herself.

Bertie ate without self-consciousness ; she was still young enough for food to constitute a vital if not an æsthetic pleasure. And presently as they watched her and urged her to try this dish and that, the women relaxed and settled into unconstrained postures, as though they had but waited for a signal, a spontaneous acceptance of friendship. Now the true significance of hospitality dawned on Bertie ; it was an intimacy, a sacrament almost.

The ladies all began to talk at once, teasing each other, shooting bold little questions at her, examining with passionate interest her net stockings and the French lace on her petticoat. They cried " Aré ! " and " Wah wah ! " at her feeble attempts at wit, and when, finally, she relapsed with a groan, declaring that she could not possibly eat another morsel, they fell upon her with outcries and urgent recommendations that she swallow just one more trifle of this or another fragment of that. " I cannot ! " she protested, despairingly. " I simply can't ! "

Nature, coming to the rescue, supplied the essential note of sincerity and she gave a loud hiccup. It was the magic sign, one which she would never have known how to render unaided. The platters were borne away to be distributed among the hand-maidens, and Mirana Bhai produced a box of Egyptian cigarettes given her by Mrs. Lyttleton.

The conversation continued for some time, but for Bertie the air seemed to thicken, and she gazed longingly at the little courtyard where the antelope tossed its head and charged a blowing leaf. She felt suddenly sated, as much with food as with the overladen atmosphere, but she knew that she must stay the appropriate length of time, for to do otherwise would constitute an unpardonable breach of etiquette. So she stayed, nodding and smiling, answering interminable questions and offering fragmentary observations while minute by minute her attention strayed from her surroundings to the mysteries which bounded them. Then, as the sense of intimacy which had first kindled in her began to wane, it struck her that these voices lacked a dissonance to which her ears were accustomed and for which she now listened with increasing nervous impatience. This, she felt, was the conversation of caged beings, the conversation of the little *lals* whose ceaseless flutterings and chirpings provided a diminuendo to a theme perversely tuned to the minor key. When at last she rose to take her leave the ladies rose too in a great upsurge of gauze and tinsel, a climax of tinkling anklets and bracelets dying away on long-drawn sighs of farewell.

Mirana Bhai put her arm around Bertie. " Come, you may pass through the courtyard into the garden, and join your friends."

In the veranda Bertie paused to admire the *lals*. " Isn't it a pity to keep them shut up like that ? " she inquired, for something to say.

Mirana Bhai smiled. " Look again. You see, there are no doors. They are free to come and go as they wish." She put out her hand and a crimson tuft of feathers the size of a thimble alighted on her finger.

" See, he knows me ! Sometimes he takes sugar from my lips. There now ; fly, little one, fly ! "

The bird left her finger and fluttered back to join its companions in their cage. Mirana turned, smiling, to Bertie. " There are many of them loose outdoors, but these know each other. They are happier, living together like this."

As they walked across the courtyard to a heavy door set in the wall among the custard-apple trees, Bertie wondered whether Minana Bhai's comment was intended as an observation, or as an intimation.

32

WHEN the zenana gate closed behind her Bertie found herself standing in an unfamiliar corner of Ganpat Rai's garden, where she could see the river coiling between muddy shores and the sun poised on the edge of a plain already swathed in bluish haze. This, she had been told, was the Hour of Cowdust when cattle wander back to their pens, and smoke from cooking fires rises above mud roofs under the mango trees. She stood with her hard, clear little mind at a loss to understand the sudden pain which touched her heart. From the day of her arrival in India there had been recurrences of this mood ; a breath of wind could inspire it, a flash of colour, a voice singing.

Across the river a light glimmered, a dog howled on the long-drawn immemorial note of village dogs ; in the courtyard she heard a child's fretful whimper and pictured the small face turned expectantly to its mother's round, brown breast.

The Hour of Cowdust when men and beasts turn their faces towards some fragment of earth known to them for a thousand years ! Behind her in the zenana life persisted unchanged, a humid existence from which she was excluded, and the thought left her feeling vaguely homesick. Then three figures appeared in the path before her : Hardyal, Jacques, and her cousin. They were in tennis flannels, and as she walked towards them Bertie felt the tension increasing within her, felt an indefinable urge towards tears. But by now the light was going fast and no one noticed her strange distress.

"You've been ages," exclaimed Jacques. "Hanif has come to fetch us home."

He stood with his left hand thrust into his pocket, a posture which had become habitual. Hardyal said: "Father thought you must have decided to adopt *purdah nashin* yourself, Bertie!"

"Did I stay too long?"

"Oh no. My aunts will be very pleased. They will pester you to come again, to come often."

"What was it like?" asked Macbeth. "Did they wear those nosebag things they wear travelling?"

"They were all very kind, but I ate far, far too much."

Eager to take Jacques' arm, she took Hardyal's instead, missing Macbeth's swift, disapproving glance. As they moved up the path between the glossy hedges, Jacques asked: "Would you like to live like that, Bertie?"

Hardyal answered for her, forcibly: "I hope not! Father and I disapprove of purdah, but my aunts have always lived like that and nothing will persuade them to change, though many of their more enlightened friends have given it up. Abdul Salim says that only a revolution will shatter our customs, and his!"

"Would Salim like to start a revolution?" asked Macbeth. He lopped off a budding gardenia with his racquet.

"I think he was just talking," said Hardyal. He stooped and retrieved the flower, handing it to Bertie. The smell of the bruised petals caught her throat, and feeling her hand tremble Hardyal glanced at her curiously. "Did the tea party make you ill, Bertie?"

She shook her head, and anxious to distract attention from herself, inquired what Abdul Salim meant when he spoke of revolution.

"Well, he has all manner of ideas." Hardyal hesitated. "He believes that a country as ancient and hidebound as ours must have what he calls an internal revolution. It is the only way to break down our absurd religious tyrannies and to bring enlightenment."

"He sounds like a cut-throat," observed Macbeth scornfully. "If he were in the Army and talked like that he'd be jolly well shot."

" But he is not in the Army," returned Hardyal, quietly.
" And I am fond of him. He is our good friend."

" But do you agree with him ? " asked Bertie. Hardyal
fascinated her ; seeing him for the first time through
Jacques' eyes she had quickly learned to accept him on his
own merits. Macbeth had put up a more determined
struggle against the same attraction, and although he had
never surrendered as Bertie had, to the young Indian's
charming and gentle spirit, he had succumbed to admiration for his skill at games.

" Not a bit like a native," Macbeth wrote to his father
a few days after meeting Hardyal, and this accolade was
to place Hardyal in that peculiar category of beings isolated
much as a collector's specimen is isolated, from its own
and from every other genus.

" Do I agree with Salim ? " Hardyal considered
Bertie's question. " Perhaps, though I don't like his idea
of violence."

" Violence, violence ! What is this talk of violence ? "
Ganpat Rai emerged suddenly out of the gloom. " What
are you young conspirators talking about ? "

" Hardyal thinks that your ladies need a revolution to
bring them out of purdah," exclaimed Bertie. She liked to
watch this father and son together ; there was something
rare, something subtle and alive in their relationship.

" Perhaps Hardyal is right," observed Ganpat Rai,
lightly. " But if we wait for revolution I fear my aunts and
sisters will not be here to reap the benefits. Tell me, Bertie,
how does purdah affect you ? "

" They all seem very comfortable and happy."

" But you would not change places with them ? "

" Change places ? That is hardly possible, is it ? One
can go forwards, but can one go back ? "

He peered at her keenly. " Perhaps if you were to come
more often to see my aunts and sisters you would inspire
them with healthier ideas."

She hesitated. " They are happy, and that is the main
thing."

" Is it the main thing ? " He shook his head. " Come,
be frank. Purdah is an anachronism. Salim, good Moslem
though he is, agrees with me on that—but like myself, he

feels helpless to do anything about it. Indian women have
far greater power than is generally believed—their fate is
largely their own fault. But if I could bring my ladies into
closer communion with you, with Madame St. Remy and
with Mrs. Lyttleton, perhaps something would come of it.
We all learn from one another."

" But suppose your ladies should succeed in persuading
us ? " asked Bertie, laughing. Standing beside her, Jacques
felt flowing between them a warm and intoxicating
current.

Then Hanif's voice reached them from the gates. " For
the love of heaven ! Am I to wait here all night ? "

As they rode home through the dusk Bertie listened to
Hanif's singing ; he sang always of love unrequited, despairing wails bursting from him and dying in the darkness.
Macbeth, unconsciously affected by the song, hummed
under his breath while his hunter's eye explored the shadows
for a glimpse of some passing hare or fox. And when Jacques'
hand discovered hers Bertie felt her blood swarm towards
him, and wished that this ride might last forever. She
dreaded the evening which she knew must follow the pattern
of other evenings passed under Madame's roof ; she dreaded
the elaborate formulæ, the mistrust and concealment which
for the past two years had characterised her relations with
Jacques' mother. Although pretence was unnatural to
Bertie she sometimes wondered whether it were not, after
all, second nature to Madame.

This evening the conversation struck her as being more
than ever forced and irrelevant, for although Madame and
Father Sebastien talked, in French, of matters dealing with
the church and the factory, she felt that both adults were
secretly far more preoccupied with conjectures about herself and the boys.

When dinner was finished they all gathered in the
drawing-room, where the boys played chess, and if Bertie
had doubted the importance of her own presence here she
might have derived a sort of amusement from the situation,
for it was obvious that with one exception, all were em-
barrassingly conscious of one another. Like creatures in a
wood, half fearful and half curious, they awaited only the

crackle of a twig to freeze into immobility or dive into silence.

The exception was Macbeth. Crouched over the chess-board, his features drawn in characteristic lines of concen-tration, he remained as he was to remain for much of his life, oblivious to everything which lay beyond the circle of his own interest. This was the most childlike, the most touching of all his traits, and in this room, on this evening, he constituted, all by himself, a sort of caduceus, a touch-stone, for to look at him and to be reminded of him was in a sense to acquire reassurance.

But later that night when they had all retired, Bertie found it impossible to sleep. She lay in Gisele's bed in the room which used to be Gisele's, where everything re-mained just as its owner had left it ; her prie-dieu stood in one corner under a portrait of the Sacred Heart, and on the dressing-table were her comb and brush with a few golden hairs still tangled in them. The Dutch doors were open and Bertie watched the stars blaze through the pale cloud of her mosquito net. Though she'd bathed before going to bed she could still smell on her hands the tincture of attar, and her brain was filled with fragments and echoes of the afternoon's adventure.

When a breath of wind rattled the loose hinge of the door she sat up, remembering the noise which the wind had made among the oak leaves on the night when Jacques was hurt and she stood in the gully watching her uncle lift the unconscious body down from its tree. It had made her think of the Crucifixion ; it had shaken her, changed her. She longed now for the assurance of joy ; she could not bear the thought that people come into one's life and endear themselves, only to vanish. Nor could she yet be-lieve that indifference resembles death, that it sometimes supplants death. Did those women in the zenana under-stand these things better ? Did Mirana Bhai, in the satu-rated wisdom of her kind, realise that life is frightful, impossible to endure alone ? And can that be the reason why we turn to the humid warmth of corners and convents and zenanas, even to the balm of death, so we may forget for a little while how lonely we are ?

This thought had occurred to Bertie on a morning when

John Macbeth came into her room at Gambul and drew aside the curtains at her window. Standing with his back to her he said : " Listen to the partridge, Bertie ! "

" *Shir dharam ke shakrak !* " cried the black partridge from its terrace below the garden. " *Shir dharam ke shakrak !* "

" Do you know what it's saying ? " Bertie asked her cousin. He turned, his face working painfully.

" Yes, it's saying that Mother has gone away with Captain Ponsonby."

This had been Bertie's first glimpse of the human creature as a victim, and the vision stirred a pity which, in her impetuous judgment, passed for love. What was she to say when, later, her uncle came to her with his new, tightened smile, and murmured : " Don't *you* desert us, Bertie."

What was she to say or do but what she did—fling her arms round him and cry in passionate assurance : " Oh, as if I could ! "

So, where her aunt had succumbed to the occasion Bertie rose to it, rose on a generous scale which they, bruised and inarticulate, accepted as wounded men accept a crutch or a cup of water.

But as for Bertie, pity had broken away from her like an untamed pet ; it eluded her until, at last, she could pursue it no further, and it was at this point, almost a year after her aunt's elopement, that she realised her own exhaustion, a sort of weakness as though she'd risen from an artificially induced fever. Now she longed for food that was not medicine and for emotion that was not pity. Perhaps it was inevitable that she should turn to Jacques, to find in him what had been there from the day of their first encounter in Gambul. He restored something of the exuberance which she expended on others, he gave back in richer measure echoes for which she provided the evocative note.

At midnight the wind drifted against her curtains and she opened her eyes, seeing Jacques standing beside her bed. For a moment she lay wondering whether this were not a continuing figment of her dream, but then he knelt, pressing his face against the net, and when she put out her hand she felt the thrust of his nose, his breath warm against her fingers.

" Bertie, did I wake you ? "

He loosened the curtains and crept in, head and shoulders first, until he perched on the edge of the bed. " I couldn't sleep," he whispered. " I kept wondering what happened to upset you at Ganpat Rai's."

" To upset me ? " She dropped her hand on his bare feet, strong and slender on the sheet beside her. " What do you mean ? "

" Oh, I don't know. I thought you seemed upset."

" I was," she admitted. " A little. It was because of the *lals*, I think."

" The *lals* ? "

" Those silly little birds all hopping about outside their cage, trying to get in."

He had caught the contagion from her heart, and laughed breathlessly.

" I can't imagine why they should have upset you."

He leaned across her body, supporting himself on his elbow, his crippled hand hidden among the bedclothes. " They were only birds, Bertie . . . Mirana's tame birds."

She stared at his face poised above her own, and something whispered to her that this was how one really studies, really understands, the fascination of the human face. He put his hand on her head in a trembling caress. " Bertie . . . how silly . . ."

" I know I'm silly, and it wasn't only because of the birds. All those women made me wonder . . . Jacques . . . why are lives so different ? Why are we all so separated from one another ? "

Both talked to gain time, to delay for a second the cataclysm which they felt closing upon them, but their youth, the weight of the smoky night and the flight of stars beyond the net conspired against coherence and pathetically acquired restraints. Their breath mingled, their lashes brushed each other's cheeks ; they smelled like daffodils, faintly rank, as their virginal limbs sought and discovered each other in the darkness. Then Jacques drew the mosquito curtains and, blindly turning, felt under his good hand the hard globe of her breast, and against his face the en-

veloping richness of her hair.   They lay for a long time
silent and motionless, almost dead with terror.

33

HARDYAL, playing the piano with concentration, did not
hear Abdul Salim until he had crossed the drawing-room
and presented himself suddenly at the boy's elbow.   There
he stood smiling down at the absorbed young face until
Hardyal suddenly dropped his hands from the keys and
swung round on the piano stool.   " Ah, Salim Sahib !   I
did not hear you come in."

" I told Krishna not to announce me.   I heard you
playing and I could not forbear to listen."   His brilliant,
restless glance appraised the new upright piano.   " Have I
seen this before ? "

" Father sent for it, from Calcutta."

Salim examined his young friend with a fresh curiosity.
No one had told him that Ganpat Rai's son had brought
home such expensive attainments.   A year ago he would
have resented the discovery, a few months ago he could not
have refrained from gibes, but since Hardyal's return they
had seen much of each other, and each recognised the other's
sincerity.   Now it pleased Salim that his friend's son should
possess European accomplishments, for not only did it
place Hardyal on a footing with his English friends, in
Salim's estimation it placed him on an even higher level,
for while to the English these gifts came as a matter of
course, to an Indian they were prizes won only by painful
struggles against long odds—or so he liked to believe.

" I came to inquire whether you would drive with me
to the village where I have business.   It is early and we
would be gone one or two hours."

Hardyal was flattered by the invitation, but when he
made as if to rise Abdul Salim waved him back and sank,
himself, into a nearby chair.

" Play again what you have just played.   I should like
to watch you."

Hardyal turned to the keyboard.   His playing was
amateur but he possessed a sure touch and a particular

feeling for this music, which appealed to something complex and inarticulate in his nature. Aubrey Wall's sisters had taught him the piano, but what he had learned was largely of his own choice—a little English ballad, a Mozart sonata, Handel's Largo, a Brahams waltz. He had memorised them with the boyish hope of impressing his father and his aunts. Ever since the arrival of the piano a few days ago he had been unable to tear himself away from it, recapturing moods and visions which he'd left behind in England. His nature, emotionally rich, had developed fresh complexities under the reserve which two years of English life had taught him. But when he read poetry or listened to music the reserve crumbled and outward expression became one with inward dreams and desires. Now as he played, once more, the Mozart sonata, his face and manner assumed a sort of raptness; watching him, Salim thought : " He has taken in, through his pores, the best that they have to give. What will he do with it ? "

Hardyal finished playing and turned once more, smiling as Salim clapped his hands. " Even in my ignorance I know that that was beautiful ! "

" It is my European side," said Hardyal, pleased by the compliment. " You know, I wish more of us understood these things."

The Mohammedan lighted a cigarette. " I agree. We should develop our own art." He blew smoke through his nose. " We are a huge land with a diverse culture, like Russia. But look at us ! " He gestured somewhat theatrically. " Where is our music ? Where our painting, our literature ? Oh yes, we have our mosques and our temples and our palaces. We have our Ramayana, our Bhagavad-Gita, our Koran. But Allah ! When my friends come to me with their boastings of Hindu and Moslem attainments, what do I say ? I am cruel. You, I remind them, have been stopped short in your cultural development long before the time of Asoka. But Europe has never even paused. I fling Shakespeare in their teeth. I fling Racine and Molière. I fling Chaucer, Spenser, Dryden, Pope. I fling Voltaire and Hugo. I fling Wagner. But it is all wasted. Most of the poor devils cannot even read English, let alone French or German. We are subjugated and poverty-stricken, so how should we expect a high degree of artistic development which is, itself, the result of ages of prosperous civilisation ? "

While Salim talked with the fluency of a man who has thoroughly rehearsed his part and who believes in it, Hardyal listened. He could not resist a glow of pride in the thought that he had been singled out to be this man's confidant and friend. Ganpat Rai had cautioned him against taking these radical conversationalists too seriously, but although Hardyal listened respectfully to his father's warnings he could not agree with him on this score, certainly not on Salim's score, for he felt, instinctively, the man's sincerity and passionate conviction. Salim could not be lightly dismissed by friends or enemies, simply because as a fearless man he posed a special problem. It was this quality of fearlessness which attracted Hardyal. He had met courage in the English, oh, many times ! But in them it had become a national trait, an abstraction, almost. Fearlessness as an inherent attribute was something he had not yet learned to appraise, not even in his father, whom he loved with an intimate, sensual love. During Hardyal's childhood Salim had loomed as a somewhat forbidding figure, all black beard and flashing teeth, one of many men who came and went in his father's professional life, yet one who in the child's eyes moved always with a special distinction. Now he realised that Salim lacked what musicians call *pitch*—he was quite unable to inject the tame note into any social gathering ; instead, he disrupted accepted themes, threw every one off key, and struck a dissonant chord in every breast. But it was not until they met again after two years that the boy experienced that shock of recognition, that pang, with which a sensitive mind receives its friend.

Never a creature of repose, the Mohammedan suddenly sprang to his feet. " Come, let us go before your father returns from the courts. He might object to your being seen in my company."

" What ? "

" Well, I happen to be *persona non grata* with the authorities, and Ganpat Rai is very much in the opposite case."

Hardyal protested. " Abdul Salim, you should not say such things ! You are our friend, we are yours."

The tall, testy Mohammedan hesitated, then shrugged. "One cannot help one's moments of doubt. But forgive me!".

A dog-cart, old and shabby, with an uncurried pony between the shafts, waited in the driveway. They got in and Salim picked up the reins. "My cousin Feroze lent me this trap, in your honour. Ordinarily I hire an ekka. This vehicle belonged to your friend Aubrey Wall, and Feroze bought it from Wall when he auctioned off his things before going back to England."

They wheeled between the gates and Salim glanced at his young companion. "You must miss Wall. He was quite a friend, was he not?"

"I never felt that I knew him very well, but I have always looked upon him as one of my very best friends."

"His family were kind to you in England, then?"

"Yes . . . they treated me like a son or a nephew."

"And you had no unfortunate experiences with the English?"

Hardyal hesitated, frowning. "A few, perhaps. But they do not count." He was sorry that Salim should have asked the question, for it stirred a train of recollections . . . small slights and insignificant occasions among his schoolmates and others; the occasions had been few as he said, and they did not really count. Nevertheless he was sorry that Salim should have asked the question.

They drove towards the river and after a brief silence Salim murmured: "This question of friendship . . . it can be tragic, don't you agree?"

"Tragic?" Hardyal repeated the word gingerly.

"Ah, how young you are!" It came on a sigh, impatient, envious. "You love your friends Macbeth and Jacques—even the girl, Miss Wood."

Hardyal watched the flies which clustered round the pony's ears.

"Tell me," said Salim abruptly, "do you find yourself attracted to her?"

"To whom?" He slightly averted his head.

"To Miss Wood, to Bertie. I confess she appeals to me."

"I am fond of her."

"But you do not desire her?"

The boy hesitated, not from embarrassment, for in matters of sex his thought was free from romantic taints, but for subtler reasons. He was not in love with Bertie, no ; but he remembered that on the evening of the purdah party when she came out from the zenana she had taken his arm, and he had experienced a sudden warmth in his veins and had spent much of the night thinking of her. Now he tried to find words that would once and for all excise the doubts in Salim's mind and in his own. " I do not, I never have desired her."

" Because you think that Jacques does ? "

" Simply because she does not attract me."

And having said it, he was comforted, feeling it to be true. The older man nodded. " I am glad, otherwise it might have made for great unhappiness."

Hardyal laughed suddenly. " I have loved only one white woman—Mrs. Lyttleton ! "

Salim thrust out his beard in an angry *moue*. " Ah yes, I know. Well, so far as love is concerned she is too old to be dangerous. Nevertheless I do not trust her."

The boy turned to stare at him. " You do not trust Mrs. Lyttleton ? "

" Do not forget that she is English."

" Ah, Salimji ! . . . That is not fair of you."

" Fair, fair ! " He exploded. " What has reason to do with fairness ? What sort of logic is it that holds up an individual virtue as being synonymous with a whole race ? She and Wall—they are the same *jat*. They stick together, I tell you—they stick together ! "

Viciously, he slapped the reins on the pony's matted back.

" But," objected Hardyal, timid yet compelled by loyalty to speak out, " but do you not find the admirable in them, that they do stick together ? " He added slyly, " And would it not be better for us if *we* stuck together ? "

" Yes, yes, it would be better for us, but it would be worse for them—oh, far, far worse ! "

Hardyal remained silent ; Salim's ferocity sometimes confused him. Now he thought of Mrs. Lyttleton, who had welcomed him home with tears, clasping him in her arms, making him think of his own grandmother.

Salim glanced at the boy, and moved by a generosity that came as naturally to him as passion, he laid his hand on Hardyal's knee.

"Come, you and I will not quarrel. Life is short. These things will all resolve themselves."

As they skirted the bazaar with its beggars and its monkeys and drove on a narrow rutted road towards the canal, Hardyal sniffed the dusty air and watched a tide of green parrots tilt, shrieking, across the sky. He never felt, as he knew Jacques felt, and as Macbeth felt, any particular sense of intimacy or ownership in the countryside, and lately he had begun to question this lack in himself. He loved his home, his father and his family with an intense and personal love which stopped short with its immediate object ; but beyond that, life and land seemed huge and shapeless and impersonal, matters for wonder, but not for curiosity or love.

Salim was explaining the purpose of their ride ; they were going to the village of Ramdatta the moneylender where he expected to meet two men who had offered to stand as sureties for his client Ganga Singh, at that moment lodged in Amritpore's new red-brick jail. Once the sureties had been found and their pledge accepted by the magistrate, Ganga Singh would be bound over to be of good behaviour, and released.

"The men are caste-fellows of my client, but they are likewise Ramdatta's tenants, and the police have been at some pains to make it difficult for us to obtain sureties anywhere. You know how our lathi-wielders batten on convictions ! "

"But what about the Superintendent, Crichton ? " Hardyal remembered the able, red-faced Scot.

"Oh, Crichton is all right," Salim's tone was grudging. "But even he cannot know all that goes on. If he did he'd be obliged to suspend half his police force ! "

The village appeared under its umbrella of trees ; a white temple and raised water tank gleamed in the sunlight, shadows striped the walls and the threshing floors and danced on the flat roofs. As Salim drove up, a whole battalion of dogs rushed forth barking and snapping at the pony's legs. Salim, who generated temper while he talked, rose from his seat and laid about him with the carriage whip. The dogs fled howling, and Hardyal saw a figure appear in an opening of the low mud wall which bounded the village. Although they had not met for some time he recognised Ramdatta the moneylender. Ramdatta wore a voluminous dhoti, his head and body were bare, glistening with coconut oil. He was accompanied by a little group of men and boys and as Salim, still brandishing the whip, pulled his frightened pony to a halt, Ramdatta hailed him. " Ah, my friends ! I apologise for these curs."

He came forward, smiling, and Hardyal wondered as he had often wondered in the past, why so many people detested this man. Ramdatta's good-nature never faltered ; his person reminded Hardyal of some rich and succulent sweet.

Without waiting for Salim's reply, the moneylender turned to Hardyal. "On my word, this is twofold honour ! Come, both of you—come to my house. I have fruits and tobacco and my sons shall wait on us."

At sight of the man, a sort of vibration had set up in Abdul Salim. He put the whip back in its socket but kept the reins in his hands. His eyes, like two vivid and fiery stones, stared down at Ramdatta.

" We are pushed for time. Tell me, Protector of the Poor, how is your servant ? "

" Which servant ? I have many."

" I refer to one whose head I broke when I threw him out of my brother-in-law's house."

Ramdatta pondered, then slapped his thigh, laughing. " That numbskull, Govind ! It was not with my permission that he went to collect interest on your brother-in-law's debt, my friend ! Govind has an officious temper. You would have done me a service had you finished him completely."

" It will be a pleasure, at any time," rejoined Salim.

There was a brief pause, charged on all sides with a sort of passionate attention. Then Salim said : "I have an appointment with two men of your village—Ram Prasad and Munnu Singh. Would you of your kindness tell me where I might find them ? "

Ramdatta, his strong legs planted in the stance of meditation, his brown arms folded across his hairless breast, put his head to one side and frowned. " Ram Prasad ? Munnu Singh ? You expected to meet them here ? "

" That was our arrangement. If you would send a boy to fetch them . . ."

A voice interrupted from the group behind Ramdatta. " They are not here. Ram Prasad went to Lucknow for the funeral of his wife's mother, and Munnu has gone away to the hills."

Hardyal felt that the air around him gathered suspense ; he had not looked for it, he had not expected it. Intent on the scene, on the village which nested among the trees, on the figure of the priest whose orange robe shone like a flame against the temple wall, he was prepared only for one of those long, boring conversations by means of which most grown-up people waste their time. But now, sitting beside Salim on the narrow leather seat, he felt the air grow still and tight. It was Salim who shattered the silence : " You must be mistaken, brother. Ram Prasad sent me word that he would meet me here this very noon. Had he changed his plans I would have been the first to know."

Ramdatta turned masterfully to the little crew behind him. " I have, myself, been absent for a day or two. Are you sure that Ram Prasad and Munnu are not here ? Go, my son," he addressed a small boy. " Go to Munnu's house and find out."

The boy, who had been standing on one leg like a stork, shook down the other and squirmed deferentially. " My lord, I myself saw Munnu depart. He rode away in the same cart with Ram Prasad, late yesterday evening."

Salim burst out in a sudden terrific laugh. " Nay then, do not put yourselves to any further trouble. I see that others have been here before me. . . . Mighty ones, walking on their flat feet and shaking the gold fringes on their turbans. The very thud of their big toes can slay a man's mother-in-law and raise a fever in the lungs of a. prize-fighter like Munnu Singh, making it imperative that he depart into the hills. Wah ! What heroes ! Allah, no— what gods ! "

Under this pelting sarcasm the little crowd swayed and

fell back ; but Ramdatta remained, his sandalled feet firmly planted in the dust, one hand resting on his hip, the other hanging at his side.   His face, smooth, with full lips and mocking eyes, reflected an imperturbable composure.   " If you would honour me by setting forth in my village we might discuss, in peace and amity, the strange disappearance of your friends.   Had I known that you were coming I would have used what influence I have to delay them.   Nay, I would have insisted that they wait until you had concluded your business with them.   However, who is this Ram Prasad ?   Who is Munnu Singh ? "   He snapped his plump fingers disdainfully.   " Unreliable souls from their birth ?   But there are other men of worth and good will, as you will doubtless find, for Abdul Salim, as I well know, is a lawyer of stupendous talents.   Come, my friends—Come, Hardyal.   Wah !   Thou hast grown."

Hardyal listened, hypnotised by a voice which oozed rather than spoke.   Glancing at Salim he had a glimpse of a single blazing eye ;   Salim's fingers gripped the reins as though he were in the act of strangling something.   " You are most hospitable, Maharaj," said the Mohammedan. " But then, why should that surprise one to whom your name has long been a byword for charity ?   One who dispenses golden mangoes to the poor, and before whose august face the police bow down like grass in the wind ? Hardly a man breathes but to pray for your long life and continued health.   May you live to conceal many gold mohurs inside mangoes and melons, and may the echoes ring with the guffaws of your brothers, the English.   But come, this is not a farewell.   You and I occupy a restricted area upon the earth—too restricted, alas, to allow for fat ! We shall meet again, without doubt."

The moneylender shrugged a glossy shoulder, and replied, mockingly :

" Salute your client for me.   I am told that in the jail yard there is a mango tree whose fruit is always sour ! "

Salim, suddenly jerking the off rein, pulled the trap round so that it brought him several feet closer to the moneylender, and leaning forward he spat over the wheel into the dust at Ramdatta's feet.   At this insult a small boy, popping out from behind his elders, flung a stone at the pony, which promptly whirled about and bolted. Salim swore, plied the whip and hauled on the reins in a paroxysm of fury ; thanks to some miracle they regained the road where, after a final defiant buck, their pony lapsed into its habitual decorous gait.

In a voice gone suddenly flat and ominous Salim declared : " I should have killed the fat swine."

They were nearing the canal locks where Aubrey Wall and Father Sebastien used to fish for crocodiles. Hardyal saw one of the cold beasts slumbering at the water's edge, while Pity-to-do-its stepped like privileged spirits beside its motionless jaws.

" Yes, I should have killed him. Do you know what would have happened had I stuck a knife in his soft brown belly ? It would have spewed forth a gutful of rupees, annas, and pice ! "

Hardyal stirred uneasily. " Yet he does not look to me like a bad man."

Salim seemed not to hear. He laid the reins on the pony's back and lighted a cigarette. " In my grandfather's time we threw our enemies to the elephants. Once, when even I was a boy, I saw a big durbar elephant kill its mahout. It caught the man as he was about to mount and drew him slowly, slowly down, then knelt on him. It knelt on his head, on his belly, his genitals, and all its weight and all its hatred were in its crushing knees. Then it lowered its forehead, all painted for ceremony, and set it squarely on the man's body and flattened him out like a taxidermist's hide. Never have I seen a job of death better done."

Behind them a cloud of dust rose and settled, and before their eyes stretched the level fields, a young green the colour of evening skies.

34

EVEN in the resplendent days of her youth Mrs. Lyttleton was not famous for displays of public spirit, nor was she given to excesses of neatness and order. It came, therefore, as something of a shock to her rag-tag and bobtail crew of servants when, a day before the opening of the Agricultural

Fair, she suddenly commanded them to set to and clean
up her garden. It was a jungle, no less, but it had been a
jungle for more than thirty years, and the fact had never
weighed very heavily on her spirits. In fact she had taken
a rather perverse pleasure in the contrast afforded by her
own compound and those of her more conventional neighbours. That she should out of a clear sky elect to bring
order out of chaos stupefied her ancient gardener, who had
scarcely lifted a finger since the death of his master, the
General.

"Truly, she has lost her mind," declared the old man
to his colleagues in the servants' quarters. "For a month,
now, one dare not cross her path. She is bewitched, or the
food no longer sits well on her stomach."

"It has nothing to do with the food," replied the cook,
grinding the day's supply of spices on his basalt grindstone.
"I, too, have watched her closely. One day she appears
to be her old self, praising my kedgeree, asking for gossip.
Then without warning this silence descends on her and she
shrinks in her chair like a sick child. Or she will suddenly
turn on me and curse me for a down-at-heel wastrel!
However," he shrugged, "as I have said before, I have my
own ideas on the mystery."

"I also," observed the syce thoughtfully. "It all dates
from the death of Jalal."

The cook lowered his eyes. "I am not one to spread or
to listen to rumours."

"She grieves for him," said the syce. "That, I believe,
is at the bottom of it. She has a heart of sugar."

"And a tongue steeped in acid," mumbled the gardener. "Where am I to procure labour for this task? I
shall have to hire half-wits and paralytics not already
engaged by the Fair Committee. If they cut down the
wrong tree or uproot the wrong vine, who will be to
blame?"

In spite of the mali's misgivings a platoon of coolies
presently descended on the garden, and with their arrival
a general exodus took place as multitudes of rats, snakes,
lizards and toads debouched into the road and into adjacent
compounds. The hoopoes, used to strutting unmolested
near the graves under the loquat tree, suddenly fled. Blue-

jays flew, chattering angrily, with the parrots and the seven sisters, and the garden's aromatic breath dispersed on the winter air as Mrs. Lyttleton, smoking her Egyptian cigarettes, supervised the exhumation from her chair on the veranda.

Madness, grumbled the gardener, untangling himself from a rose tree which he'd planted heaven knew how many years before ; now its hooked talons ripped the flesh from his legs. The lilies had rotted, the orange trees and the limes were dead, but a laburnum twisted to a travesty of itself bore amidst its yellow flowers the wreath of cuckoo-lantana and the wild palm. To the gardener this rifling of time's palette was a sacrilege, no less ; since neglect had claimed the garden, spirits dwelt here, good and evil forgathered to compare notes ; to let in the sunlight was once more to separate the two and to invite retribution from both.

" Fool ! " cried Mrs. Lyttleton, rattling her bracelets. " What spirits there are crawl on their bellies and carry poison in their fangs. Others hop on two legs and keep me awake all night with their infernal croakings. Chop down the cactus ! Pull up the vines, uncover the roses and the sandstone basin of the lotus pond, and the old paths where I used to walk. They must still be there. Stones do not walk away of themselves, do they ? Have I kept you in food and blankets fifty years for nothing ? "

By the end of the second day the garden had exchanged its crazy charm for complete confusion. Whole patches were whittled down to raw soil flanked by mounds of decaying vegetation. Weeds, rain and drought had usurped every vestige of an original architecture, and of the lotus pond all that survived was a blackened pit which oozed delegations of pale, nameless worms.

As Mrs. Lyttleton roamed among the clearings her dogs followed her, stepping gingerly as if the denuded earth hurt their feet, pausing to sniff an alien stone or to examine some naked stump or to retreat, growling, from the edge of the lotus pond. They sought, unfailingly, to keep their mistress's petticoats between themselves and the spectral air of these unfamiliar vistas.

On the third day it rained slightly, big drops pocking

the dust and stirring a troubled breath from the bruised weeds. Mrs. Lyttleton watched her coolies as one by one they wrapped their rags over their heads and retired to await a clearing sky. Then she summoned her gardener and as abruptly as she had ordered the assault upon the garden she now ordered him to cease. " I was a fool," she said in a tired voice. " A fool, to imagine that we could bring it back as it used to be."

He stood before her on legs as bowed and knotted as an old acacia.

" I do not understand. Are we to wait until the rain has ceased ? "

" Tell them to cart away the rubbish and dismiss them."

He shook his shrivelled head. " I am too old, now, to relish such jokes."

" It is no joke. I wish the garden to be left as it is."

When he turned away she called him back and said gently : " Pardon me for having spoken roughly to thee. I also am old, but I had no cause to upbraid thee."

She had always been a generous mistress, but this was going far, even for her. He fell at her feet, crying : " You are my father and my mother ! How can there be talk of forgiveness between us ? "

When he'd gone at last she stood motionless, gazing at her ravaged garden, watching the rain fall in delicate spears from a sky that was still partly blue above the trees. " What a fool I am," she mused, striving by the admission to allay a far deeper disquiet. " What a fool ! "

A bicycle bell chimed down the road and she saw Hardyal pedal between the gates, saw him swerve wildly to avoid the rubbish which littered the driveway. He propped his machine against the veranda steps and came running up, breathless, to greet her. " Heavens ! What have you been doing ? "

He stared at the garden, then at her, his eyes big with inquiry. Mrs. Lyttleton lighted a cigarette. " I have been playing the snob, Hardyal . . . attempting, at my time of life, to impress my neighbours ! " And she laughed on a stilted note.

Hardyal dropped into a chair and clasped his hands between his knees.

She went on in an affected voice : " Amritpore will be filled with distinguished visitors for the Fair, and it suddenly occurred to me that I had no wish to pose as an exhibit on their agenda . . . the Old Woman who lives in a Jungle, don't you know ? "

He stared at her uncomprehendingly, and she went on : " So I decided to astound them all by putting my house in order. I thought that it might impress them as a sign of my regenerated soul. They would wonder whether perhaps, after all, they had not been mistaken in me ? Perhaps I was really quite all right in spite of my eccentricities. Perhaps they would now accept me as one of their own *jat*."

It was a weird and uncharacteristic speech and the boy continued to gaze at her with unfathomable eyes. Then he asked : " Who do you mean by *they* ? "

" Oh, Mr. Crichton and Mr. Swan, Mr. and Mrs. Burrows, and . . . good lord, yes ! Madame St. Remy, Father Sebastien and his Christians, Macbeth, Miss Wood, Jacques ! "

His lashes fell slowly, then he raised them in a fierce, direct look.

" So for that you have spoiled your garden ? "

" I meant only to restore it."

He turned once more to survey the ruins. " I feel that I have never been here before ! "

" Ah, but you have been here before, Hardyal."

" I know, I know. . . ." Suddenly he seemed on the verge of tears, and she said quickly : " Never mind, my dear, it will grow again. Everything turns to jungle sooner or later."

Hardyal shook his head. " It was lovely as it used to be. I loved it. I remember when Jacques and I used to come here and play among the bushes. It seemed like our own, and now it's gone."

" It will come back," she insisted, troubled by his emotion. " Give it one monsoon and it will come back."

But he was inconsolable. " No, it won't come back."

She thought silently : He is right, he sees something that I have not wanted to see : it won't come back, no monsoon will ever bring back his innocent and imaginative love for it.

G

After a brief pause she remarked with a false air of gaiety : " You came in time to cheer me, for I was beginning to feel neglected." Inwardly she thought, bitterly : There I go, making a bid for pity ! She pulled herself together and reached for her cigarettes. " Remind me to give you a box of these for Mirana Bhai."

His face cleared. " And that reminds me why I am here. Mirana has sent you a present, too." He reached in a pocket and fished out a little heart-shaped box of brass and enamel, intricately chased.

Mrs. Lyttleton took it, exclaiming : " But I know this box ! It is one in which Mirana keeps her betel-nut. Surely she cannot intend it for me ? "

" You know she would be hurt if you were to refuse it."

Mrs. Lyttleton guessed that there was something special in the nature and the manner of this offering. The chill which had touched her heart a little while ago touched it again. She met Hardyal's eyes, and he nodded, smiling faintly. " Yes, Mirana thinks that you have neglected her lately. The box is a reminder . . . a token . . ."

" I have not been very well. Will you tell her that I shall see her very soon, and that I shall reserve my gratitude until I can thank her myself ? "

" Father, too, has missed you. You know he has a conspiracy in mind. He believes that if only he can persuade English ladies to visit our house constantly they will fire my aunts with an ambition to come out from purdah. Already they ask Father to buy them stockings like Bertie's, and a piano like mine. But while Father plots from outside, Mirana Bhai plots from within ! "

Mrs. Lyttleton laughed. " Which do you think will win ? "

" I don't know. Abdul Salim insists that persuasion is a waste of time. He believes that such matters should not be left to individuals but should be decided politically." The last word was brought out with a hesitant, conscious pride, and she looked at him keenly.

" Salim said that ? He is quite a friend of yours, then ? "

" He has always been our friend."

" Yet I know that your father does not wholly approve of him."

" Oh, Father does not share many of Salim's views, but he admires him, as I do also."

She glanced away from his young, serious face. " I know Salim only slightly. He is an avowed seditionist."

Hardyal rose eagerly in his friend's defence and she listened, troubled by his loyalty. It troubled her that she was unable to share his enthusiasm as she had shared others. The truth was, she did not like Abdul Salim ; she had never found him sympathetic, and she mistrusted his truculence. She was more weary of violence and of violent characters than she would have believed possible a year ago, even a few months ago. Time compresses events into narrow channels, decisions are precipitated in seconds, even in split-seconds. I'm old, she reflected, bleakly. Old . . .

Now as she listened to Hardyal speak of his Moslem friend she remembered what Aubrey Wall had once said to her : " Hold on to Hardyal ! Keep him up to the mark, won't you ? They lose it so easily."

She wished that it was not Aubrey Wall who had said that ; she wished that she could forget Wall ; but he, too, had forced a decision whose consequences were still in the making. And while Hardyal talked with affection and admiration of his Mohammedan friend Mrs. Lyttleton studied the boy's face and reflected on all that she knew about him, all that she had thought and hoped for him, remembering him as a brown seraph with silver *kurras* on his wrists, and his disconcerting infant's gaze. Hardyal was inextricably part of her love for the country as he was in a sense part of her love for Jacques. She had lost Jacques : was she, now, to lose Hardyal ? She saw him suddenly beset by new forces—forces inimical to her philosophy, her experience. She caught the virile note in his voice when he said : " It is nice to be treated as an equal by a man like Salim. Father and I talk, but we seem never to disagree about anything ! "

Mrs. Lyttleton imagined the nature of conversations which must give rise to such disagreements. Here, then, was an allegiance which had already claimed him. Would there be others, infections and contagions of whose exact scope she could never hope to learn ? The thought startled her with its intimation of the distance that separated her

sphere from his. She might guess at the forces which con-
ditioned Jacques' life or John Macbeth's, but in Hardyal's
case she remained in the dark ! She felt suddenly the need
to make some possessive gesture without which everything
that had happened until now would become meaningless.
She, who had always insisted that she knew where she
stood and, by that token, to a large measure, where others
stood, she, who had kept her spirit free, submitted at last,
reluctantly enough, to the necessities of that freedom, to
its inexorable paradox. She felt that she must exert herself
to hold Hardyal up to that mark which not only Aubrey
Wall and herself, but which his own father had set for him,
the mark which, should he miss it, or abjure it, would
result in incalculable dismay. But the moment was too
portentous, too delicately in balance, its springs still too
deeply hidden for her to dare risk anything but subtlety.
Whatever her gesture, it must be equal in portent, equal in
delicacy, its springs as carefully concealed as the fear which
prompted it.

She said presently, with an air of lightness : " Of course
you know that Salim loathes us ? "

The boy hesitated, frowning. " Salim is a very honest
man. He knows that like others he is bound by silly customs and prejudices against which he alone can do little.
That is why he always insists that great changes must be
enforced by law rather than by personal whims. He hates
the English because he thinks that they are immoral."

Mrs. Lyttleton gasped slightly. " Oh, he does, does
he ? And he'd enforce his own brand of morality by throwing his enemies to the elephants, as his forefathers used to
do ? "

The boy smiled.

" That's only his way of talking. Father says that
Salim's bark is much worse than his bite."

" I must say that I don't personally fancy either."

Hardyal remembered the Mohammedan's judgment of
Mrs. Lyttleton. Young and generous himself, he was filled
with a desire to have everything straight between his friends.
It was towards this end that he'd conspired with Jacques
for Macbeth's good graces ; he had compelled Macbeth
to accept him, just as in England he'd compelled others.

You have but to loom a little larger, a little deeper, in all
your capacities, for people to lose their differences in you.
This belief had gradually assumed the proportions of a
characteristic in Hardyal, whose Hindu nature was learning the subtlest lesson of the Christian, at a point where both
were nearest each other, at the point where they had first
diverged.

He said gently : " If you and Salim were really to know
each other, you could not help liking each other."

She was touched by his artlessness. Tenderness rein-
forced her resolve to hold on to him, and the resolve re-
kindled her spirit. There had been a time when she felt
equal to everything, when she had in fact proved herself
equal to a great deal. This was such a time, and her eyes
shone with the realisation.

" Well, I shall take your word for Salim, my dear boy.
Why don't you bring him to call on me one of these days ? "

The degree to which she found herself equal revealed
itself to her conscience, which did not flinch before Hardyal's
responsive pleasure.   " Do you mean that, honestly,
honestly ? "

" Honestly ! " She went on quickly: " And now
since we are on the subject of friendship, what do you hear
from your friends the Walls ? "

His radiance faded somewhat. " I have had only one
letter from Miss Bella, nothing from Mr. Wall."

It was her moment, and she rose. " I have heard from
Aubrey, and there is a letter I'd like to read you, from
him."

When she had disappeared into the house Hardyal
turned with a deliberate exercise of will to confront the
desolate garden. All through the conversation he'd kept
his back towards it, but now it recurred like an unhappy
dream. He was horrified at sight of the raw branches and
castrated soil, at the defeated look of familiar old trees and
the rags of creepers which still clung to them. Whatever
was creative in Hardyal sprang from a submerged religious
source, from an almost superstitious dread of destruction.
He remembered his first fox-hunt in England, and the
unuttered and unutterable sensation which filled him when
the Master had " blooded " him with the raw stump of the

fox's brush. He had in that instant resurrected the creature's agony, while his intelligence insisted that this feeling was irrelevant and sentimental, that in the civilised world death and desecration had a waning importance. But the confusion could still take him unawares, as it had taken him at first sight of Jacques Remy's mutilated hand, as it took him now at sight of Mrs. Lyttleton's mutilated garden.

It was with a sigh of relief that he greeted her when she reappeared carrying a bundle of letters. Like most old women, she could never bring herself to destroy letters. Now she paused, staring at him in surprise. " Hardyal, what is it ? You look frightened."

He laughed, turning aside. " I was afraid that there might be *bhuts* in the garden."

She laughed, too. " You're too old, now, to see *bhuts*. Sit down and let me read you Aubrey's letter."

He sat at a little distance from her, gazing eagerly at the bundle which she untied and spread on the wicker table before her. She skimmed through one and then another, and he had no means of reading the expression which increasingly tightened the corners of her mouth, which seemed to cause a sort of shrinking in all her features, as if a drop of acid had fallen somewhere within their calm and familiar mask.

" Ah," she said at last. " Here it is."

She did not, however, begin to read it at once. Instead, she read the first page to herself, then the second, and it was only when she was half-way down the third that she glanced up and said : " This is the part that will interest you . . ." She began to read in a clear, almost a ringing voice : " When you see Hardyal give him my love and tell him I think of him often and look forward to the day when we shall meet again. I have heard nothing but good reports of him from my sisters, who miss him badly, as do most of his friends here. Every one has been charmed by his manners and his spirit. I have always believed, myself, that he was one of our best, like his father. We need more like them, for they are the stuff and the hope of the future. Perhaps I shall see Hardyal when he comes back to England, or at any rate, surely when I come back to India."

She read a few more sentences, picking them out from

the body of the letter, then folded it and replaced it in its envelope, which she laid on the table among the others. " I thought you ought to hear that, Hardyal."

He was glad to have heard it. An extraordinary elation filled him as he listened, a sense of pride, affection, and justification. Naturally modest, flattery tasted to him like a sip of forbidden wine—and it went to his head. Watching his face Mrs. Lyttleton saw that she had indeed achieved a victory : for the moment at any rate she and Aubrey Wall had caught up with, had perhaps even passed, Abdul Salim. Yet while she talked, putting little touches and flourishes to the victorious moment, laying the ground for its further development, her heart grew heavier and heavier. If only it had not been through Aubrey Wall that she should have recaptured Hardyal ! If it could have been through Jacques or John Macbeth—through any one else ! The thought of Wall bit into her soul, poisoning it, numbing it, so that presently Hardyal saw that she wore an expression of extraordinary fatigue. He'd been on the verge of asking her to let him see the letter, even of asking whether he might take it home with him to show his father and Abdul Salim. He'd known Aubrey Wall to be friendly, but he had experienced the man's reserve, and the tone of this letter surprised him—it profoundly stirred him. He was too shy to suggest that Mrs. Lyttleton read it again, and while he hesitated he became obsessed by an almost mystical longing to possess the letter, to make a talisman of it. But he sat quietly, with his eyes fixed on the grey envelope where it lay on the table between the cigarettes and a folded newspaper, a few feet away from him. If only she would read his mind and offer it herself, saying : " Ah, Hardyal ! This really belongs to you, for in a sense it was written to you. Won't you take it and keep it ? "

The request trembled on his lips, he longed to speak out, but with every second the words became more difficult to utter : he was too shy, insistence would have seemed immodest and conceited—worse, she might chaff him ! Indecision paralysed his tongue, and he finally rose.

" I must go now. I will tell Mirana Bhai that you will come soon to see her."

Mrs. Lyttleton rose too, putting her hand on his shoul-

der. He felt her slight weight lean on him, felt her strange
tiredness when she murmured : " Yes, soon, very soon."

He went down the steps and picked up his bicycle, and
as he threaded his way down the littered driveway he kept
thinking of Wall's letter, thinking of it with a passion which,
as a child, he used to feel towards certain objects and certain people, vesting them with an impossible value. When
finally he reached the gates he knew that he could go no
further, for his legs had become dead weights, all the purpose accumulated in his shoulders and his arms. He swung
the handle-bars round and once more faced the tall, dark
arches of the veranda. He'd go back, he would ask Mrs.
Lyttleton outright whether she would give him the letter to
keep. She would give it to him, of this he had no doubt.
She would understand, as in the past she had never failed
to understand, everything ! He dismounted by the steps,
but the veranda was empty. He called her name, softly at
first, then a little louder, but when his voice died away on
the unresponsive silence he thought : " She has gone to
the bathroom."

He hesitated, while from their places on the wall the
stuffed heads brooded upon him, and past him on the
garden, where the rain had ended in a burst of saffron light.
Then Hardyal turned to the wicker table where the letters
still lay ; he had no difficulty in picking out the one which
she had read to him, and he trembled slightly, not from
doubt or fear but from the excitement of doing something
which he had never thought of doing before. He picked
up the letter and for a full minute stood motionless, waiting
for Mrs. Lyttleton to appear in the dim and silent doorway.
She did not appear, and the house stood before him, echo-
less and wrapped in shadow. He tucked the letter into his
breast pocket and went down the steps to his bicycle. No
one had seen him come back ; no one, now, saw him go.

35

He did not read the letter at once ; he did not, as a matter
of fact, read it for several days. It remained untouched in
his pocket and the thought of it lay in his consciousness like

a dry shard, slowly, mysteriously germinating an independent life. While his memory retained the gist of what Mrs. Lyttleton had read to him, Hardyal could not have explained the instinct—it was obscure enough to be called instinct—which prevented his satisfying himself of its contents, once and for all. Perhaps he felt that to do so would disrupt the charm and break the spell, and he was still of an age and of a kind which more than half-believes in spells.

As the days passed he found himself thinking long and intently about Aubrey Wall, a man like a hundred other Englishmen yet one who by virtue of a certain sensitivity, a certain force, has been saved from the category of " type ". And that particular virtue, as Hardyal realised, was what he now sought to recover—that singularity, that difference. Because Wall had expressed a special liking for him, Hardyal felt bound to uncover an equivalent feeling for Wall—a feeling which had not hitherto distinguished their relationship. He set himself to recall all the things that Aubrey Wall used to do and say, his likes and his dislikes, his kindnesses, his explosions of temper, every manifestation of a character with which he'd at one time been familiar. Yet, in the end, what did it amount to, that familiarity, that understanding ? Nothing more than a handful of ashes which a fire leaves below the ghats when wood and oil have done their work. Nevertheless, there must have been something that he'd missed until this moment ; some current, some depth which he'd been too young or too careless to fathom. Wall had liked him, had liked him more than he'd known how to express, more than he could bring himself to reveal except through the medium of letters ! How queer the English were ! Only an Englishman could have written a drama like King Lear, and built a tragedy on the inanity of a single tongue-tied maiden !

But Aubrey Wall had been instrumental in Hardyal's destiny ; that was an unforgettable fact, one which made them in a sense belong to each other, an exchange like the clasp of hands or the mingling of a glance. For Hardyal, the Oriental, intimacy carried a profound responsibility, and he began to reflect with remorse on his own possible shortcomings.

" Aubrey was reserved and rather cold, giving little of

himself even to his sisters. And now I discover, in that in-
expressive spirit, this small flame of warmth and affection
for me. And I, what did I give in return? Nothing! I
took him for granted, I was even a little bit afraid of him.
I must have let him down a hundred times without knowing it. I must have hurt him, disappointed him, puzzled
him by neglecting to let him see that I understood."

At this point in his broodings Hardyal suffered from a
stab of memory. He had a vision of Malabar Hill and of
the shabby Englishman he had encountered there beside
the Parsee *dhakmas* under the trees. He remembered the
man's face, the dingy freckles and seedy eye, the whole
offensive personality, and he was shaken by fear lest something in his own behaviour might at one time or another
have given Wall to reflect, with a fatal shrug : " Damned
cheeky, even for a native ! " But not once in the days which
followed his visit to Mrs. Lyttleton did Hardyal suffer from
a twinge of conscience in having taken the letter itself. He
was convinced that it belonged to him in the first place ;
his intention had been innocent—the act could not be less
so ! And when, a few days afterwards, he saw Mrs. Lyttleton again—this time when she came to call on his aunt
Mirana Bhai—he ran out to greet her and to help her
alight from her carriage. She put her hand on his shoulder,
and he knew at once that she had not missed the letter.
From this knowledge there budded instantly the conviction
that she knew he had taken it, that she had intended all
along that he should take it, and therefore found it super-
fluous to remark on its disappearance. This sort of rational-
isation could not, perhaps, have occurred in the minds of
either Jacques St. Remy or of John Macbeth, for in both
the sense of guilt would have been inevitable, followed by
a breakdown into contrition and a final confessing. But in
Hardyal the whole thing originated in a completely different
point of view, the Oriental view which sticks to essentials
and which regards most Occidental ideals as hypocrisy or
convention. Two years in England had not taught Hardyal
to demur in such matters when his emotions were deeply
involved, nor had his own sense of honour suffered by contrast.

When Mrs. Lyttleton emerged from the ladies' quarters

and asked him to play for her he whirled gaily on the piano
stool and asked :

" What would you like to hear ? "

Anything, she assured him, would please her. She sat
on the chair where Abdul Salim had sat, and as she watched
Hardyal she became aware, once more, of the man growing
within him, visible in the thickening muscles of his neck,
in the strength of the profile where a short strong nose
jutted above sensuous lips. He wore half-native dress, a
dhoti with an English jacket ; the folds of the dhoti slipping
to one side revealed a leg which swelled in a single sinewy
curve from calf to ankle, ending in a well-shaped dark foot
cased in a rope sandal. Mrs. Lyttleton was no great admirer
of Oriental beauty ; instinctively she, like others, sought
what was foreign in Hardyal—sought the impress of her
own country and her own standards. She thought she saw
it in his eyes when he glanced up at her, and in his quick
and fluent hands.

He finished at last, and turned, dropping his hands on
his knees.

She applauded with the characteristic native exclamation : " Wah, wah ! It makes me homesick for the past, to
see a man play the piano. I never have understood why
music, any music, can make one vaguely unhappy."

He walked with her to the door of the drawing-room.
" I don't feel like that at all. I like to play, I have all kinds
of fancies and visions—visions of fountains and of clouds,
of strange birds flying through purple light, and sometimes
I see a temple where the sun falls like an offering of little
coins on Shiva's body, and thousands of tiny bells speak
with separate tongues, announcing the arrival of Kali ! "

She turned to gaze at him. " That comes from your
heart, doesn't it ? "

" From my heart ? Yes, and from my mind also."

A little while after she had driven away in her ancient
carriage Abdul Salim and Ganpat Rai appeared riding in
a hired ekka, and as it drew up before the veranda steps
Salim leaped out, laughing and offering his hand to help
his friend alight.

" Ah, Hardyal ! Your father condescended to accept a
lift in my humble equipage ! It is, I believe, many years

since he has so far demeaned himself. But after all, isn't the true measure of a man's greatness his willingness to descend to the level of obscure friends ? You," he waved imperiously at the ekka-wallah. " Withdraw a little distance and wait for me."

The ekka creaked away, and they turned to the drawing-room where all three cast themselves on cushions upon the floor, and Krishna brought them the usual offerings of *pan* and cigarettes. Hardyal saw at once that both men were in good spirits. Ganpat Rai had just won a case, and his satisfaction expressed itself in numerous small gestures of affection towards his son and his guest, while his kind, shrewd face beamed with content. Salim was exuberant, for he, too, had passed a successful morning in court, where he had finally obtained the release of his client Ganga Singh.

Hardyal sat facing the two men with his arms clasping his knees. As any well-bred boy must, he listened more than he spoke, and felt himself secreting a special delight in his father's success and his friend's good humour.

Ganpat Rai slapped Salim lightly on the shoulder. " You know, you ought to write a treatise on Section 110 of the Criminal Procedure Code. You have made it your special study, and by publishing it you would be doing us all a great service. I would find a publisher for you, in Calcutta or in Bombay. Easily." He blew an elegant spiral of smoke.

Salim folded his white-pantalooned legs under him ; the silk tassel of his fez swayed slightly above his right eye. " You believe that any publisher would glance twice at what an obscure up-country pleader has to say ? "

" Pooh ! You are full of false modesty. Any publisher would seize on what you have to say, for you write well—yes, exceedingly well."

Salim inhaled luxuriously, his black eyes softer, kinder than Hardyal had ever seen them. " The Subordinate Police would not like to read what I would like to write ! " He laughed. " Crichton would not like it, the Inspector General would not like it ! And for that reason . . . who knows ? Yes, yes—for that very reason perhaps I shall write a treatise on Section 110 of the Indian Criminal Procedure Code."

Ganpat Rai smiled. " It would be a relief to me to know that you were devoting your talents to such an end. Writing would be a worthy substitute for indiscreet speech and misdirected energy. Yes, it would be a service to the country and a great load off my mind."

An air of fraternal well-being coursed between them. For Hardyal, the moment seemed complete ; he related it to a sensation which he sometimes experienced, half-way between the allurement of a dream and the languor which washes gently against the shore of consciousness. He felt drowsy with happiness.

Ganpat Rai turned once more to Salim. " My aunt has been in consultation with Mrs. Lyttleton on the problem of selecting a wife for our young friend here." He glanced shyly at his son. " They have found one at last. She is fat beyond belief, pock-marked, and with defective vision. But she is of good family and some wealth. Tell me, son, did Mrs. Lyttleton use her good offices to persuade you ? "

" Mrs. Lyttleton is my friend. She would not stoop to such a low trick."

" Yes, yes, we all know how you feel towards Mrs. Lyttleton ! " And Salim shook his head, the black silk tassel waving wildly.

Hardyal laughed. " I repeat, I do not intend to marry until I am so old that I have need to lean on a woman."

Salim could not refrain from making a rather crude little joke, and all three laughed. Then Hardyal repeated, firmly : " I will do as other civilised men do, marry whom and when I please."

" Then you will fare better than many of us," said Salim. " Perhaps even better than some of our rulers. I have just seen the wife of the Deputy Commissioner. I could not be sure, at first sight, that she was a woman. She looked like a giraffe, with enormous teeth. Were I her husband I should be terrified to sleep with her for fear she might become hungry in the night and mistake me for a cabbage. By the way, what *do* giraffes live on ? "

" Their husbands, like every one else," replied Ganpat Rai gravely. He glanced at his son. " By the way, your friend Miss Wood has made a great impression on Mirana. She is now determined to find a husband for Bertie, too.

Truly, the thought of marriage is a plague with these women."

"Hardyal assures me that as far as Miss Wood is concerned, he has no designs," Salim observed. "Personally, I think he errs in taste. She is admirable in many ways, though I do not approve of her wanton manners."

Ganpat Rai said quietly :

"Hardyal has too much sense to let himself be attracted towards white women."

"Ah, but there are always the landlady's daughters, and one is not obliged to marry them," replied Salim with his incorrigible sarcasm. "When they meet what in England they call a black man, they jump to the conclusion that he must be a prince or a nawab. Then, when he brings them back to India—wah ! They find that he is nothing more than some nondescript pleader like myself or a starveling medical student like Feroze. Also, it transpires that we have seraglios filled with beauties of our own preferred blackness, so the washed-out little landlady's daughter pines away with T.B. or else we seal her up in a cupboard, or stake her out on the plains for red ants to devour."

He finished this flight of fancy on a burst of laughter, echoed by Hardyal. Ganpat Rai shook his head. "Nevertheless, I hope that when Hardyal marries he will find one who will be a companion as well as a wife."

"Talk with the old ones, sleep with the young," Salim admonished the young man, with mock gravity. "But come ! I feel in the mood for music ! Play for us, child. Play for us as you would play for two angelic females who recline here upon our pillows, their hips swelling like the Himalayas, their breasts like melons ! "

Hardyal was laughing helplessly. "I have played enough for one day. I was playing for Mrs. Lyttleton just before you arrived."

"Ah ! " his good humour died like a flame. "So you play for your English friends, but not for us ? "

Ganpat Rai met his son's eyes. "Play, Hardyal. We are weary. We have worked all day."

Hardyal rose at once and went to the piano. Behind him he heard Salim's voice : "I confess I was taken aback by her affability when we met on the road a little while ago.

She greeted me as though we were old friends, a courtesy which I do not recall ever receiving at her hands."

"She is a woman of rare sensibility," said Ganpat Rai.

"She also is somewhat mad," returned the Mohammedan, shrugging. "They tell me that she has completely destroyed her garden, that she has cut down her choicest trees and ploughed up her rosebeds. They say it is because she desires to make the place uninhabitable for ghosts."

Hardyal turned on the piano stool. "Ghosts!"

"For the particular ghost of Jalal, her servant—who died under mysterious circumstances."

"What circumstances?"

Salim started to speak, but Ganpat Rai interposed almost roughly:

"I beg of you, my friend!" He turned imperatively to his son: "Play for us, Hardyal."

Hardyal struck the opening measure of a waltz, but there were now no visions of flying clouds, no sound of bells speaking each with a separate tongue, no thought of the sun caressing Shiva's prostrate form nor lighting with its vibrant fire the hair of the goddess Kali. He played, thinking of Mrs. Lyttleton's garden as he had last seen it, full of melancholy and confusion, haunted by a discontented spirit whose face remained hidden from him.

When he had finished both men clapped and asked for more.

"What would you like?" he asked Salim. "The piece which I played for you the other day?"

The Mohammedan seemed oddly to have regained his humour. "I care not! It all sounds alike to me—a beautiful noise."

Hardyal played on, though spontaneity had died within him.

"Wah, wah!" exclaimed Salim, when at last he finished and rose from the piano stool. "That was beautiful, it was impressive." But he looked bored and did not ask for more. Hardyal left the piano and came back to his cushion. As he sat down he felt his father's presence beside him, felt it as warm and as powerful as the attraction between lovers, and although their glances did not meet nor their bodies touch, he knew that Ganpat Rai had read his heart.

Presently Salim began to talk of the Fair which opened
on the following week, of the merchants whom he'd seen
streaming into Amritpore from outlying districts, and of all
the small and fascinating squabbles and intrigues without
which no communal event can be considered complete.
Hardyal only half-listened. He stretched himself on the
floor and clasped his hands on his breast, staring at the
ceiling where the wasps were building their little nests of
mud. He heard, flowing round his head, the voices of his
father and of his friend, and he began to think of the Fair
where he would buy gifts for Jacques and for Macbeth and
Bertie. He would spend all the money he had, he would
spare no expense, and he would watch their faces as they
uncovered his gifts from their wrappings and turned to him
with astonishment and delight. He shut his eyes, and his
face had the passive sweetness of one who dreams.

36

JACQUES sat in his mother's white-washed office at the
indigo factory, and laboriously copied four columns of
figures from one ledger to another. He hated every stroke
of the ink-caked pen which reminded him of St. Matthew's
and of a sedentary existence which he'd hoped that he had
put behind him forever. He was aware too that this was
wasted labour, a form of penance, a calculated attempt to
divert his energies into a routine which they were expected
to pursue for the rest of his life. On this score he was not
in the least deceived ; he knew that the hours spent in this
cool white room were hours which in the end must amount
to little or nothing, since these ledgers had long since been
audited and put away for future reference. He was not
permitted to examine the later accounts, kept under lock
and key in his mother's safe.

To-day, if Jacques submitted to boredom it was simply
because he felt the necessity of making some return to
Madame for favours received, favours which she had con-
ferred with tact, even with grace. The truth was that
Madame had truly endeavoured to live up to the letter of
her agreement with Hanif, tacit though that agreement

had been. She had not tried to come between her son and his friends as once she had come between him and Mrs. Lyttleton. The visible cost of this self-effacement was not lost on Jacques, and to preserve its grace he felt that he must somehow prevent its deterioration into mere bribery. Therefore he would accept with gratitude whatever margin of liberty and privacy she accorded him, and he would take care to make a scrupulous accounting of it—scrupulous to a degree which Madame might never suspect. Jacques had no intention of becoming a party to further schemes and arrangements; certainly, now he had no intention of becoming a victim.

Madame had explained that when he mastered the complexities of book-keeping and management it would be his privilege to preside over the future prosperity of the factory, but that time was not yet, for it could scarcely be said that he had until now displayed any notable talent for such responsibility. He had not actually displayed a talent for much of anything beyond the companionship of his friends, for long rides across the plains hunting blackbuck or stalking crocodiles on the river bank, and for occasional inexplicable lapses into what Madame impatiently described as *ennui*.

On the table before him, a table on whose surface uncounted generations of white ants had traced their muddy dynasties, Jacques noticed a sample cake of *leel*, the finished product of the factory done up in thin yellow paper. It made him think of Bertie; he remembered the first time that he'd taken her on a tour of the factory and she held a square of this substance in her hand, examining it with the childish curiosity which she brought to everything new and unexplored. She'd remarked then that the little cake of indigo reminded her of the sky above Gambul that first year when she came out from England. The oblong of powdery blue shaped like a tessera revived, she said, all her first impressions, her first enthusiasm for a new land. But she was unable to find the word, or the symbol, which might preserve for herself and for Jacques the past and the present, and which might project them, together, into the future.

Now as he played with the fragment of indigo Jacques

thought, not of mountain skies, that saturated distance upon which the clouds moved with vast invisible intention, but of the thing itself, the residium of seed and soil and moisture, of thought and idea, deed and ambition, all concentrated in a cube of colour so intense that it burned in the mind long after the eye had discarded it. He thought of men hunting gold and diamonds, mining for coal, killing for fur and ivory ; seeking, seeking everywhere, indefatigably, feverishly—the precious thing, the precious word, the precious experience.

He sighed and stirred as he became aware of a pair of dark eyes watching him from across the room where Boodrie the foreman sat at another desk, beside a large tin clock which ticked like some ferocious insect. " I have been observing," said Boodrie, severely. " I would bet that you have not performed one stroke of work for the past five minutes."

" I finished what you gave me to do, twenty minutes ago."

" That is so ? Why, then, did you not tell me ? You will have to learn initiative. There is always something more to do, in this life."

Jacques yawned, for he wasted little ceremony on the poor Eurasian, whom he had always disliked. He'd learned that an occasional overture served only to dislodge an avalanche of attentions, half servile and half insolent, in keeping with everything else about the man. Boodrie was half-and-half, black-and-white, a zebra personality. When unobserved he slid into the path of least resistance and went native with a vengeance, but on public occasions he remained offensively, pervasively *white*, an ubiquitous reminder of man's sexual democracy, despised by the natives and deplored by the whites.

" It will shortly be time and you may proceed to join with your friends. Where, exactly, do you propose to conduct your amusements, if I might presume to ask ? "

" Ask, and ye shall receive," murmured Jacques indifferently.

Boodrie lighted a cigar which Father Sebastien had given him that morning. " You know, you are occasionally exceedingly bad-tempered. I think you have learned such

from your friend Macbeth.   I do not like that Macbeth.
He is a snob and cheeky even when he does not open his
mouth.   How in the world either of you ever got through
St. Matthew's I fail to comprehend."

"We cheated."

"Oh my !   You are also getting to be a great liar.   It
is not funny to lie.   And that reminds me, we have not had
the honour of your assistance at Mass or at Benediction
for I don't know how long."

Jacques was drawing a caricature of the foreman's
profile on a corner of the ledger.   He replied :   "I have
become a free-thinker."

"That is purest heresy.   What if Father should hear
you, or Madame ? "

"Why don't you tell them ?   It's part of your job,
isn't it ? "

"You do not believe that I am a pure common or
garden sneak ! "

Boodrie's eyes had filled with slow, greasy tears.   When
Jacques remained silent he retreated into a silence of his
own and pretended to busy himself with his account books.
In his heart he wished that he possessed the arrogance of
this white man's son.   He wished that he cared as little of
hisab kitab, for all the sweat and tedium, the thankless ex-
penditure of mind and energy on the mere necessity of
earning a living.   He envied this boy his pale skin and curl-
ing, light brown hair, his clear features, his clear eyes, his
clear soul ;   envied him, in fact, every item of spiritual and
physical good fortune.   It must be wonderful, thought
Boodrie, whose mother was a low-caste Hindu and his
father a low-class white—it must be wonderful to be wholly,
wholesomely Some One.   And for a single bitter moment
he longed for a state of mind, a state of being, which might
make such bitterness unnecessary.

Jacques, conscious of something unusual in the other's
long silence, glanced up to encounter tear-filled eyes.   His
own cheek flushed slightly.

"Oh, good heavens !   Must you *blub* ? "

Boodrie produced a handkerchief and blew his nose.
"You have fractured my feelings."

"Well, I didn't mean to."

" You always treat me as though I was dirt."

" I don't."

" All the time you are nicer to the coolies than you are to me. You treat Hanif as though he were your brother, and he is altogether a native. Hardyal also. But, as for me . . ."

He began to snivel.

" Oh, good heavens ! " Jacques whirled angrily on his office chair, glaring at the floor, secretly ashamed of himself. Boodrie watched him covertly. " I do only my duty, as I am bound to do. Madame has told me that I must make you attend to your work. How can I help it if she and Father Sebastien are worried about you ? I am not the only one who notices how you have changed." His glance crept, in unwilling fascination, to the boy's crippled hand which rested on the open ledger. " Changed in many ways. You do not, for instance, go to church as you should, as you always used to."

" Shut up, will you ? "

" It is a serious matter ! Can you blame us because we care ? Can you ? It is only because we love you."

" I don't wish to be loved by you or any one ! " Jacques burst out in fury.

" You cannot prevent people from loving you if they want to. Even I love you. I have watched you grow up, you and Gisele. You never watched *me*. Oh, no ; after all, who am I that you should bother your heads about me ? But you cannot prevent my looking upon you as though I were one of your family. Gisele has been saved . . . yes saved ! But you, you make me think of your father, Monsieur Auguste." He drivelled away into murmurs and Jacques rose, slamming the ledgers. Words crowded to his lips, but he did not utter them. In a flash of discernment he realised that this relatively insignificant scene held a far deeper importance, that it had been brought about less by Boodrie's lacerated feelings than by Boodrie's fortuitous use of those feelings. I am on trial, thought Jacques. I am being watched and tested, and for a price, no doubt. To-day it is a cigar, to-morrow some other form of *baksheesh*. Anger died and a rather cruel amusement took its place. He rose and picked up his hat. " Eleven o'clock ! " As he passed the Eurasian's chair he paused and said in Hindustani : " Brother, your cigar has gone out."

Outside, the air was clear, with a sparkle of dust and a noise of crows in the trees. A water-carrier was sprinkling the ground nearby, and his water-skin made a pleasant gurgling as he hitched it on his shoulder, tendrils of water sprayed from the pale arc of his hand. Jacques' bad temper vanished ; even the subdued hum of the factory possessed a charm, now that he was leaving it for a little while. Poor Boodrie ! He permitted himself the luxury of pity, but it could not survive in the rush of relief and expectation. As he crossed the compound towards the gates, coolies shuffled past, some bare-footed, others in heavy shoes, making for the vats and the boiler rooms. They salaamed him, some with smiles, others with a dim, primordial gaze. The bare bodies of these last ones, the Haburas, had a dusty bloom on their thick sweatless skins ; the others shone like copper, muscled like Greeks. The rags of all were splashed with the separate shades of dye, olive and ochre which had eaten into the cloth, and the feet and hands of some were steeped in brilliance as though they served still another god in their endless calendar of deities, a god who demanded pigment as offering and who made return in those varying towers of silver coin at the month's end.

The big Sikh policemen who squatted in the shade, smoking and throwing dice, rose lazily as Jacques approached. They greeted him with jocular salutes, and he read the liking in their eyes.

" Thy friend waits," said one, nodding towards the gates where Hardyal sat on his bay mare, holding Jacques' horse by its bridle. Strolling towards him Jacques thought : " There is a difference nowadays in the way they greet me." He knew why, and he knew that they knew, a fact which would have disturbed him in his own people. But it did not trouble him in Hanif, in Gisele's old ayah, in these policemen, and in Hardyal. In its celebration of concupiscence the East retains its respect for a man's personal privacy. Jacques knew that his was safe in the keeping of his Indian friend and his Indian servants. Coming out of Bertie's room at dawn he had met the ayah, a woman who had served his mother for thirty years, who had scolded

and spoiled him from babyhood. Now she stood aside and
drew her veil over her eyes as he passed. Hanif looked at
him as he might have looked at a brother. " You are a
man," said Hanif's black glance, and his voice, when he
spoke of other matters, had a little ring of possessive pride
in his master's coming of age. This was an accolade, silent,
tacit, but Jacques felt a tingle in his veins and springing in
his feet.

Hardyal walked the horses to meet him. " I brought
Robin because I thought it would save time. Bertie and
Macbeth are to meet us at the Fort."

They trotted through the gates, the horses sidling and
prancing as the white road opened before them. Hardyal
was in high spirits and talked of plans for the next day,
when they would all attend the opening of the Fair and
return, afterwards, to his father's house for a grand repast.
" All manner of people have been invited, Hindus and
Moslems, the Collector and his wife, Mr. Crichton and his
guests. My aunts have been cooking, cooking, cooking for
days.· The place smells like a *barwarchikhana* ! "

Jacques thought of those mounds of food, of platters
of rice cooked with raisins and saffron, of vegetable curry,
of chutneys and sauces, sweets, pastries, syrups, spices ;
of all the gorging and belching, the happy surfeit. He
adored native meals and always ate until—as Hardyal said
—the grease stood out all over him like a fried cake.

" Do you think Bertie will enjoy it ? " inquired Hardyal,
anxiously.

" Of course—why not ? "

" I just wondered."

Hardyal could not have explained this sudden anxiety
on Bertie's account, for, ever since Abdul Salim's ill-con-
sidered remarks, his attitude towards her had suffered a
faint, indefinable change. Now when he found himself in
her company he experienced a sense of loss ; he found it
difficult to meet her gaze, and shrank from her friendly
touch. All this pained him and he longed to make amends
to her and in a sense through her to Jacques. Hardyal had
accepted Bertie as, in England, he'd accepted other girls,
and as they had apparently accepted him. His response
had been friendly, merry, even sexless. But Salim's jesting

observations had transformed this innocence to something
which at times amounted to an aversion. Confused by his
own reactions, Hardyal was at infinite pains to conceal
them, but they escaped from him disguised as small erratic
gestures and exaggerated concern for the comfort and
happiness of his friends. It was, in other words, another
facet of his new attitude towards Aubrey Wall. It sprang
from anxiety, from a passionate desire to meet and to
measure up their undeclared opinion of himself.

As they rode under the portcullis Jacques and Hardyal
fell silent, for they were never quite able to resist their own
sensations as they emerged from under the shadowy arch
into the arc of walled sunlight. The silence which awaited
them here seemed sudden and premeditated, an invisible
retirement took place, and their flesh tingled under a close
and imagined scrutiny. Ruins are more than history ; like
shells they belong to a huge oceanic process. Stranded, the
life in them falls dormant but it does not die, it persists in
our idea of it. At any moment this suspense might give
way and an invisible barrier release the pent-up years.
The boys rode into the courtyard and dismounted,
hitching their horses to the same gnarled acacia where they
had once hitched their own and Gisele's ponies. Bertie and
Macbeth were nowhere to be seen, there was scarcely a
sound except the plaintive crying of the doves. Then
Jacques saw their wicker lunch-basket perched on a rampart beside a sentry-box, and beside it, like a flag, Bertie's
long blue veil which she had unpinned from her hat as a
signal.
"They've gone down the river," said Jacques. "Let's
climb up and have a look."
They strolled across the courtyard and climbed the
ruined stair to the rampart, and standing beside the little
sentry-box shaped like a medieval helmet, they stared
across the plain towards the river. It glittered flat and
straight like everything in the landscape. Tiny creatures
moved under their gaze : a pair of bullocks so white they
shone like mica, threads of water fed by wells into little
channels, men and women patching the channels and
guiding the precious trickles to the yearning soil.

Hardyal stretched, feeling the sun hot on his back. "There they are!" He pointed, and Jacques saw the riders, small and active in the distance.

"Let's go and meet them," he suggested, but Hardyal shook his head.

"You go, I'll wait for you here."

He watched Jacques ride under the portcullis and disappear, and as the silence rose about him once more he was half-tempted to follow. Instead, he seated himself resolutely beside the sentry-box to wait for Jacques' appearance beyond the farther reaches of the moat. Macbeth and Bertie had vanished in some fold of the land, the sun, signalling the river, drew a single answering flash, and a multitude of crows clamoured above a dead something half a mile away. Above the crows wheeled the kites, their shrill whistles falling through the void, and above them circled the vultures.

Jacques appeared, galloping, but it seemed no more than a second before he, too, had become a detail in the intricate pattern of the plain. Then an unaccountable loneliness descended on Hardyal. The scene, as familiar to him as a room at home, stretched now in an alien light. It was too vast, too impersonal—his eye could contain it, but it could not contain him—he felt lost within it. He turned away to look down at the courtyard where his mare stood quietly in the shade of the acacia, but beyond her placid, insentient form rose a series of broken doors and the arches of what used to be officers' quarters and shelters for horses and men. In the piercing light these dim unexplored interiors grew shadows, and as he gazed they deepened and darkened and generated within themselves other shadows; these seemed to stir, to move beyond the penumbra, to press against it as a hand might press, or a shoulder, in the movement of figures which pass secretly behind a heavy curtain. What if that curtain should suddenly part and all the dead, with all their unfulfilment, come trooping out towards him?

Hardyal's nerves trembled in a sort of arterial protest against the developing magic. He rose, crossing his arms on his breast in the unconsciously pathetic attitude of a man about to be shot; and he felt under his fingers the firm edges of Aubrey Wall's letter in his pocket. The contact restored, in a flash, the known and ordinary world. He sat down again and took out the letter, surprised by its thickness until he remembered that when Mrs. Lyttleton read it she had skipped much. Now he would read it all, read it from the beginning, and so recapture each coveted phrase, and thrill again, without shame, to the praise.

Wall wrote a small but clear hand and for several minutes Hardyal read with a purely visual sense, scarcely grasping the full import of the words. The letter was more than a month old, postmarked from Bognor, in Sussex, and he was sure he knew the room in which it had been written, and the view, from a window, of the lazy sea beyond.

" My dear Laura,

" Your letter has reached me and if I did not answer at once it was because I wanted to give myself time to understand, to reconstruct the situation which you have put before me. But perhaps you yourself have not waited, perhaps you have already taken the course which indignation would prompt you to take, in which case this letter must prove wholly irrelevant. However, I have a feeling that you will wait for my answer, for—shall I call it my confession ?—which is likewise my defence; that is if, in accord with your rather incoherent insistence, I am at least entitled to a defence. How fantastic this sounds here, in these surroundings, in this unbelievably tender England where, although doubt and horror exist, they wear a recognisable face. You voiced the hope, once, that in England I might find a rebirth. You guessed, apparently, that I stood in need of one, and you were right. Can you blame me now if I hesitate to exchange the mercy of that rebirth for the damnation of exposure by law and the inevitable end of all my hopes ? Perhaps I am mistaken, but can you blame me for placing my own fate on a level somewhat higher than your servant Jalal's ? And if I choose, as I do choose, to put my fate in your hands, I do so with a conscious pride in its value, and because I believe in your judgment. Of your mercy I know nothing, as yet. I can only trust you, as I would trust you had you been my mother."

Hardyal came to the end of the page and looked up. Far across the plain he could see his friends converging on each other ; in a few minutes they would meet, and turn to ride back to the Fort. He wondered whether they saw him up here beside the sentry-box, a living speck among the dun-coloured ruins. Then he returned with a growing heaviness to Wall's letter.

" I have been thinking and trying to remember. You tell me that your servant Jalal is dead and that I killed him. You make the picture very clear, for you write with such bitterness and anger that I wonder you have kept this knowledge to yourself, that you have not carried it to the authorities."

Hardyal stopped short. " No ! " he gasped. " Oh, no, no, no ! "
A butterfly hovering near him was not alarmed ; it settled on a stone and spread wings the colour of butter-cups.
" No, oh, no—no ! " repeated Hardyal wildly. But it was impossible, now, to leave it at that. He felt compelled towards a final, frightful discovery. The letter continued :

" Has it occurred to you to question your own reasons for such a delay ? You must know that you've not exactly strengthened your position, for by hesitating, by waiting, you, in a sense, condone if you do not connive at the whole predicament. I know you to be a fearless woman ; I know that once you have made up your mind you will act, heed-less of consequences to yourself or to me. Yet the fact re-mains that three months have passed since Jalal's death and you have not acted. Why not ? Can it be that in spite of our conventional morality you and I share something more profound, a kinship which, in our precarious mo-ments, we dare not deny ? You've asked me for an ac-counting, for an explanation of what you describe as my unspeakable act on that last evening of my visit to you. You remind me that when I returned to the veranda after having gone in search of Jalal I callously remarked that I had twice kicked him while he slept. Well, my answer, if not my explanation, is that the act was neither unspeakable nor inexplicable : with no desire to extenuate the circumstances, I must make them clear to you, as they are, at this moment, clear to me.

" It was raining that evening. I had come from Father Sebastien's and you greeted me, as usual, on your veranda. We talked, and I poured myself several brandy pegs from your decanters. We talked of the St. Remys and of Hardyal and of the future, we talked of India as though the country were something we held in our hands, pliable, intimate. I drank a good deal of brandy, and I remember feeling that much of what happened to me while I lived in India had the character of a drunken dream. I have always felt, while there, as if I were contained in a dream, and that is the extent of my feeling towards the damned country, the total of—what shall I call it ?—*my committedness*. And here I must mention something which you do not know and which I, myself, don't yet really understand. I was unhappy. I had been unhappy for a couple of years ; the reason for that unhappiness won't interest you, since it has ceased entirely to interest me. It is not important now but it was important then. Brandy helped me as it has helped many men, it helped to put the world in a light which made existence just a shade or two more endurable.

" Well, on that evening you called for your servant and he did not appear. I went in search of him and found him asleep in the darkness of the back veranda. I say I found him—but as a matter of fact I stumbled over him, and it seemed to me that the insensible clod lying there at my feet symbolised India, drugged and snoring, wrapped up in its own idea of itself, unimpressionable, indifferent to everything else. I saw this as one sometimes sees a single monstrous detail in a landscape or in a crowd. And I lashed out with the instinct to destroy whatever it was that I had seen—a fragment of something unclean, sub-human, parasitical. Well, then—I killed Jalal, and perhaps by doing so I have killed myself. I have no remorse, I have no emotion, I have hardly any feeling for Jalal. I cannot even now remember what he looked like, although I know that he did exist.

" Can I make you see, Laura, that I am not afraid of

the consequences of this action : I just cannot bring myself to believe that I have done another human being out of his life. There is, in me, something which makes it impossible to ' believe ' in Indians. You have assured me fiercely that they are human beings, but I have known horses and dogs almost as human, and I have loved them better. You will resent this, you will hate me for saying it, but let me say it, for I must. I do not believe in Indians, I do not hold with the sentimentality of treating dark people as one treats even the lowest, the humblest white. I do not believe that there will ever be equality of race—why should there be when there is not equality between one white man and another ? Our Christian teaching and humanitarian policy have between them made a mess of our honesty. We simply do not begin to understand Indians. They never will approximate our civilisation, even our individual accomplishment. If they should do so, so much the worse for us : it will be from imitation, and it will be of the worst kind of imitation. Oh, I know what you'll say to all this—I can hear you saying it : We all sprang from the same root, originally. Possibly. But *we* have gone a long way from there, and *they* have not. They are where we started from and there they will stick. For every Ganpat Rai and Hardyal there are a thousand—no, ten thousand Jalals. Whatever good has come to them has come from us, and what have they given ? Rather, what have they to give ? They have tried to adopt our ideas, even our ideals ; above all, this very justice before which they would be the first to summon me. They know their own inadequacy and they hate us because they know we know it. There is in every one of them an ember of hatred ; blow on it and it will make our feeling towards them appear as a smile of mercy by comparison. And in the end they will turn against us, yes even our charming Hardyal will turn against us, the enlightened Ganpat Rai himself will turn against us. When one lives amongst them one makes the best of them, for not to do so would be stupid. But between them and ourselves there can be only one relationship, the relationship of our mastery over them."

There were a few additional sentences but Hardyal did

not read them. Before him, the plain reeled in a glare devoid of shade or boundary, an abyss of light. From it emerged three figures which cantered towards him, waving, but he made no attempt to respond. He rose, staggering a little, and stumbled down the steps to his horse, clambering into his saddle like a wounded man. The mare bore him under the portcullis and her hooves struck a hollow note from the bridge above the moat, where the little doves were crying ceaselessly. When, a few minutes later, Jacques with Bertie and Macbeth rode into the Fort, they shouted and looked for him in vain.

37

A CLOUD of dust hung over Amritpore. For two days people had been streaming towards the Fair grounds which lay just outside the cantonment. They came in ekkas, in bullock carts, in carriages, in fine fast dog-carts. A few rode bicycles, but most of them trudged on foot, carrying bundles on their heads, babies on their hips, and leading tottering infants by the hand. They brought their dogs and their grandmothers, even their great-grandmothers, and invalids who flatly refused to be left behind. All were dressed in their best, all wore the expectant smiles of incorrigible celebrants in this land of festival. There was not one who did not intend to buy something, there was not one who did not come with a whole-hearted determination to enjoy the occasion to the utmost.

There would be buying and selling, looking and longing, wanting and going without. There would be cheating, beating, exchange and assignation, sighing, lying, intrigue. For this was more than a fair where the industrious and the virtuous brought their wares and inducements ; there would be more to marvel at than the largest turnip and the fastest gelding in a hundred miles ; the whitest bullock, the smallest dog, the maddest saddhu, and the Government Agricultural Station's most successful experiment with artificial fertilizer. Besides these things there would be countless others, things as yet unseen, even undreamed of, by villagers who worshipped a pot-bellied god named

Ganesh, and who marked progress by the simple revolutions of an ancient wooden wheel. There would—above all things—there would be people, hundreds of people, for this was a *mela*, a coming together of all one's fellows. It was not necessary to be Hindu or Moslem, Christian or hedonist, black, yellow or brown : for full enjoyment one had merely to want to be here.

The authorities had taken precaution—riots have a way of breaking out—but in this crowd there seemed to move a deep, sweet current of good-nature. Their gods, looking down on them, must have observed that mass itself possesses an incipient order, every individual stirred by a private design, intent upon his own discovery. The women's kirtles swayed above silver anklets, and a touch of gold or silver on a humble *sari* added its pennyworth to the pounds of tinkle and glitter. Bare feet trod the dust as their owners carried new shoes strung on sticks over their shoulders, to save wood or leather for the proper moment of ceremony. They tramped in the soft dust and left the hard middle for wheeled craft which rattled and creaked at a speed somewhat beyond that of the traditional snail's pace. The purse-proud swept by with a flurry of bells and swaying curtains, drawn by ponies with beads round their necks, driven by conceited servants. Ramdatta the moneylender rode in his own ekka, one with a black-and-gold canopy, under which he sat in splendour, his stout legs gleaming with oil, his muslin cap encrusted with pearls.

At night the outskirts of the Fair grounds had twinkled with the fires of those who arrived early. All ages and all castes converged upon the flat shadeless plain which the Municipality had bedecked with beds of drooping petunias and blatant canna lilies. The booths with concrete floors and tin roofs were gaudy with paper streamers and banners of every description, and here the visiting merchants made themselves at home. They had come from the great cities of Allahabad and Lucknow and Benares, from Agra and Fyzabad and Barielly. Some still worked feverishly among their boxes and bundles and bales, putting temporary quarters in as seductive an order as their calculating imaginations could devise. Others, earlier birds, squatted portly and expectant, marking down the nearest rival and the likeliest prey.

There were shoe-sellers and cloth-merchants, gold- and silver-smiths, purveyors of brass and enamel and cane-work, of toys made from painted clay, and little boxes which fitted into one another and ended in one so minute it had to be picked out with a pin. There were furred animals made from the pelts of real beasts—camels and leopards and tigers. There were jewellers with their wares, real and fake, blazing under keen and wary eyes. Beside these sat the workers of marble and inlay, and next to them the makers of clothing in every colour and of every design, the corners of their stalls hung with great fans of plumed grass dyed and embroidered like the tails of peacocks. Scattered among them were the sellers of food, where sunlight danced off enormous, plated cauldrons and vast platters stacked with intricately shaped breads and pastries and sweets. Here the flies and the wasps collected in swarms, and women waved palm-leaf fans with brown, languid arms strapped to the elbows in silver and coloured glass. Their new *saries*, slipping from their pomaded heads, revealed tassels of bright silk, and the ears of some of these women were torn in strips from the weight of silver earrings. All displayed the gay red or yellow tikka between their brows, and the hands and the gestures of almost every one were beautiful, like the hands of dancers, like the posturing of a perpetual creative impulse.

The stalls were arranged in two rows that faced each other across a baked expanse which had been watered and swept and rolled flat by the Municipal servants. Alleys and byways opened off the main channel and here were the side-shows, little tents of canvas or matting ; within lurked the fortune-tellers and exhibitionists (these with one eye on the quality and probable tastes of their clients, the other on the police). This was a happy-hunting-ground of jugglers and the trainers of parrots and monkeys. There was even a tiny circus which comprised a single haggard tiger and a small old elephant whose only role seemed to be the feat of balancing himself—with every indication of reluctance— on a board laid across the belly of a fat man. The fat man was depicted on a poster outside the marquee ; he was almost as big as the elephant and easily twice as strong, with blazing eyes and bulging arms crossed on enormous feminine breasts.

Children were almost as ubiquitous as the flies and wasps ; they hung round the side-shows and the sweet-stalls while their elders roamed among more serious attractions.

The Fair opened in the morning with a formal address by the Collector. It was the usual speech, delivered first in beautiful precise English and then in beautiful sonorous Hindustani by a dried-up little Englishman wearing a morning coat and striped trousers, a large pipe-clayed topi, and a *har* of jewelled tinsel round his neck. Behind him on the dais stood his orderly supporting a large red umbrella, and on a semi-circle of hard varnished chairs were his wife, their friends, and a sprinkling of local and visiting dignitaries, waving away the flies and trying to look interested in what the Collector had to say.

To the unjaded sensibility there are two pronounced elements in a native crowd—noise and smell. These break upon one's awareness as unfamiliar music breaks for the first time on uneducated ears—disturbingly, even frighteningly. The police had been to some trouble to exclude professional beggars and the prowling bazaar dogs, but no sooner had the crowd thickened into its fullness than every beggar, every leper, every cripple and every pariah for miles reappeared as if they had been squeezed from the pores of the earth. The noise, like the dust and the smell, seemed more substance than sound, it lay within, round, and about, pricked by sudden dissonant notes which rose straight up like the thrust of a sword—the scream of a stallion in the stables set up by Pathan horse-dealers, the clear singing of a bugle from the police station a quarter of a mile away, the shriek of a baby with colic ; and under these combined noises the beating of the eternal drums, the little tinpot drum of the professional singer, and the cavernous throbbing of a drum from a Sikh regimental band.

38

It was afternoon and the dust, the heat and the smell were at their height when Jacques drove to the fair with Bertie and Macbeth, Hanif riding as usual beside the driver. Madame St. Remy had said that she might join them later when the air cooled a little. Crowds annoyed her and noise always gave her a headache.

Hanif, wearing brand new finery from the crown of his cap to the fantastically curled toes of his shoes, twisted in his seat to smile at the young people. " Does my appearance reflect glory upon the household ? "

" You are dazzling," Jacques assured him. " Simply dazzling."

The driver flourished his whip. "Ah me, the wenching in store ! "

" Nay," protested Hanif gaily. " Not for me, not this afternoon. Have I not instructions not to let these un-trustworthy ones out of sight ? "

" We also have instructions not to let you out of our sight. Maman has no desire to pay compensation to out-raged husbands."

The driver chuckled. " Ah, if there be talk of outrage . . ."

Hanif gave his elbow a jolt. " Fie ! "

They drove under the shisham avenue and out on the hard white road. Bertie slipped her hand through Jacques' arm. " I adore fairs ! "

" Let's hope there'll be some good side-shows," said Macbeth. " I want to see the two-headed man and the six-legged sheep."

" No side-shows," said Hanif firmly. " I have express orders to that effect."

" You know you like them as well as we do ! "

" Nevertheless I have my orders."

" Nevertheless you will take ours."

" Or shall we tell Rahat Ali where you were last night ? "

" I do not know any one named Rahat Ali."

" But you do know Mrs. Rahat Ali ! "

The driver laughed, and Macbeth grinned. " Why

H

don't we tell all the men where Hanif is when *they're* away from home ? "

Hanif was quite unabashed by these jokes. He adored attention.

" Such talk ! If the Memsahib should only hear."

They drove smartly along the road, passing small companies of late-comers, when Hanif exchanged taunts with the men and brilliant glances with the girls. He had produced a large pink rose from somewhere in the folds of his clothing, and now tucked it behind one ear. Jacques stared at the bobbing flower. " That is Maman's new Queen Victoria rose—you picked the only flower on it ! "

Hanif replied without turning his head. " Pruning brings strength to the roots, so the *mali* tells me."

They drove between tall plaster gateposts which marked the main entrance to the grounds, and were immediately engulfed in the crowd. The driver plied his whip and the crowd made way for the carriage and its freight of white folk guarded by supercilious servants. Jacques looked everywhere for Hardyal. Ever since yesterday when he had ridden to the Fort and not found his friend, Jacques had been puzzled and anxious. There seemed no explanation for Hardyal's disappearance, and it was not in his nature to indulge in moods or in silly jokes.

Later that afternoon Jacques had ridden over to Ganpat Rai's house, but Hardyal was not at home, nor was his father. A servant assured Jacques that his young master was well and that all was tranquil in the house. Jacques left a message and rode away, more bewildered than anxious, but reassured by thoughts of the next day, for Hardyal would be at the Fair—had they not talked of it and looked forward to it, together ?

Inside the Fair grounds they dismissed the carriage and, accompanied by Hanif, plunged into the crowd. Bertie clung to Jacques' arm ; once, finding her crushed against him in an amalgam of hot and happy strangers, he turned and kissed her. She whispered : " I would like to buy you something beautiful and expensive ! "

They were beside the gayest and richest stall, surrounded by people who pushed and shoved in their anxiety to see everything at once. The box wallah who squatted among his wares saw the young white folk and waved invitingly. " What will Your Magnificence have ? Name it . . . name your wish. Behold, ten yards of gold tissue with birds of Paradise flying upon it. Two rupees per yard. For others, rupees three—but because you are young I make it only two. Nay, reflect : two rupees for thread which is pure gold, and birds . . ."

" Which are *not* birds of Paradise," Macbeth broke in, coldly. " Who ever saw a bird of Paradise with a short tail ? "

The cloth merchant, a genial man from Benares, and used to the ways of Englishmen, gave the boy a friendly smile. " Others I might deceive, but thee—never ! Well, these are even better than birds of Paradise. They are earthly birds, my lord ; they live among the passion-flower trees of Assam, and are rare indeed, else surely you would have seen them. I doubt not that you miss nothing—nothing, indeed."

Bertie stared at the glowing silks, at the bales and bundles and bolts of brocade and cotton amongst which the merchant sat like some queer persuasive deity. He had already taken up his steel measuring staff and was peeling off yards of material, his practical hands unwinding the heavy bolt and stripping it in loose, glistening lengths.

" Nay," cried Jacques. " We never said we wanted it. Do we, Bertie ? "

She wanted it, she wanted everything in the shop. The richness, the peculiar odour of native cloth spun or woven by clever fingers in close spice-tinctured interiors fascinated her. It was unlike the characterless product of machines, it had substance, and a life of its own. The merchant glanced at her and smiled. " I have others. I have shawls from Kashmir, muslin from Dacca, silk from Kotah. I have *saries* with a hand's breadth of silver for selvedge and others which I sell by weight for the metal in them. Which does the lady prefer ? Point out the bale. This one ? That ? Or here . . . this, which only maharanies and princes can afford to buy. Look ! " He rose and taking the loose end of a bolt drew it out to his own height, standing to one side and shaking the stuff gently as a dancer might, so it gathered the light and broke in constellations of fire and colour.

" How much ? " asked Bertie.

He stared at the material draped on his arm as a man might stare at his beloved, and for a moment he made no answer. When he did, it was in a soft, almost an indifferent voice : " How much ? How should I say ? This is not for ordinary folk. It is for those who never need to ask how much ! "

" Cheek ! " exclaimed Macbeth. " We don't want your old cloth. Besides, I don't believe that is real gold and silver any more than that those birds are birds of Paradise. Come on, Bertie."

They strolled away, followed by Hanif. The rose had wilted and one by one the petals fell on his shoulder.

Jacques was looking everywhere for Hardyal.

" Perhaps he is here and we just haven't run into him," suggested Macbeth.

" I would have seen him. We never miss each other."

" Oh, look out ! " gasped Bertie, and sprang aside as a naked, legless man strapped to a board on four wheels, using his hands as fulcrums, skittered past them like some monstrous beetle.

Then the crowd parted and Mr. Crichton the Superintendent of Police strode forward, followed by a little company of constables. Crichton was big and burly. He paused to exchange greetings with the children, then went his way, his men pattering after him. The crowd closed in again like the sea in the wake of a ship, and Jacques felt Bertie's hand tremble a little on his arm. She smiled faintly when he glanced at her. " I wish he'd stay ! "

" Mr. Crichton ! Why ? "

She was unable or unwilling to explain that she found something reassuring at sight of the big Englishman, and later in the presence of the Collector himself. She felt that both officials would not be indifferent to her presence in this upheaval of a diverse and, to her, vaguely inimical humanity. It was a new feeling, one which disturbed her by its unheralded arrival.

Macbeth sauntered beside her with his hands in his pockets. He was secretly debating what to buy for his mother, wondering how he might accomplish the transaction in private. The thought of his mother was a constant ache, a spot of decay in his healthy youth. It made him shy and sometimes cruel, it tended, year after year, to add salt rather than sweet to his nature.

Jacques was thinking: "Hardyal, Hardyal! Where *is* Hardyal?"

Bertie noticed his disquiet and for the first time she experienced the cramping pangs of jealousy. "Why worry about Hardyal? He'll turn up. Perhaps he doesn't want to come, after all. Perhaps he's gone off somewhere with his Mohammedan friends."

"Rot."

"Well, I do think it was funny his running away as he did, yesterday."

"Something must have happened."

"He's only a native, after all."

Jacques stopped dead and stared at her. "What did you say?"

She saw the temper in his eyes. "Oh, Jacques, I'm sorry! I didn't man to say it. I shall never say it again."

Hanif and Macbeth had fallen behind, but now they came up and Macbeth said: "I just saw that barrister chap, Salim. He's over there with his friends."

"Is Hardyal with them?"

"I didn't see Hardyal." He added impatiently: "Look here, I'm not going to hang round waiting for Hardyal. Let him hunt for us. I want to see the side-shows."

Hanif attempted a firm stand. "No side-shows! I was given express orders . . ."

They ignored him, and with a sigh that was part despair and part relief, he followed them down one of the noisome alleys where drums rattled and barkers chanted inducements through their noses.

Hanif managed to steer them past the Two-headed Baby, the Siamese Twins, a group of Hermaphrodites and the Six-legged Sheep. They selected a tent dovoted to the antics of trained animals. As the children entered with their retainer, the little crowd inside the tent fell back, and the owner greeted them with a burst of nasal chanting while his assistant beat a feverish tattoo on the drum. Hanif spoke swiftly to the master of ceremonies: "No indecencies, please. These are exalted persons."

The young people stood near the entrance where the air was somewhat less murky, and stared in fascination at a little group of monkeys dressed in kirtles and quilted jackets. There was also a parrot, whose duty it was to walk up to a tiny cannon, seize the lanyard, and make the gun go off. The master of ceremonies addressed the parrot in loud encouraging tones and gave it a poke with his wand. There was something indescribably lewd in the bird's eye as it tilted its head and sidled forth. It seized the lanyard in its beak, braced its little grey feet, and pulled. The cannon went off with quite a respectable plop and a smell of gunpowder, while the crowd clapped and exclaimed : " Wah wah ! "

Bertie gazed at the talented bird with some pity. " Poor thing ! It has hardly any feathers."

" Make him do it again," commanded Macbeth, infatuated.

The owner adjured the parrot and his assistant rattled the drum in a fresh overture. The bird's bleached lid slid upward, then suddenly lowered, revealing a bright gold orb. It sidled up to the cannon once more, then in a sudden access of temperament it dropped the lanyard and stood with a stubborn air, sealing up its eyes. The master chanted, commanded, cajoled, the assistant thumped his drum, but the moody creature refused to budge.

" The monkeys," cried Macbeth. " Let's have the monkeys ! "

Hanif gazed doubtfully at the monkeys, but their owner seemed to have them well under control. He dismissed the parrot and picked up the leading-strings of his monkey troupe. The drum rattled and a horrid little dog dashed into the arena. One of the monkeys sprang on his back, another climbed up behind him, and they raced in circles while the others looked on, their depraved little faces and listless gestures reminiscent, for all the world, of a troupe of passée prima donnas. The dog act came to an end and was followed by a dance, by handsprings and tumblings, amidst the plaudits of the crowd. In a little while it was the parrot's turn again and the monkeys retired to their corner to misbehave in a bored fashion among themselves.

" Come ! " cried Hanif, with authority. " It is finished.
Let us go."

They flung a few coins to the master of ceremonies and
made their way out into the wider if not fresher air of the
alley. Once in the crowd, Macbeth slipped away from his
friends and singled out a jeweller from Agra, a little pale
man with a cast in one eye and the still, sweet smile of a
child. He sat alone behind his show-case of jewels, and
catching sight of the English boy, saluted him with a deferential air.

" I don't want anything," said Macbeth, flushing, fearful lest one of his friends find him here. " That is, I'm not
sure. What've you got ? "

The man studied his client with a single keen glance.

" Everything," he sighed. " Everything ! What does
the Sahib desire ? What I have not I can procure, no
matter the price, no matter the gem."

His serious manner reassured Macbeth, who had
dreaded an outburst of chaff. The man leaned forward and
unlatched a flat case, felt among the contents, and picked
out a single fat uncut stone. " Take this in your hand. No,
don't be shy—take it."

Macbeth took the strange stone, which felt like a piece
of butter, but it did not melt in the warmth of his fingers,
rather it seemed to thicken and to increase. He stared at it,
rubbing it with the ball of his thumb, and an indefinable
pleasure passed from the stone into his flesh. He looked at
the owner. " That's funny stuff, what is it ? "

" White jade. But you do not want that. Try this."

It was an amber necklace smooth and slippery as a live
serpent, but the weight and colour did not appeal to Macbeth. " No, something small, something bright."

" Something for your sister ? " suggested the jeweller
in his soft voice. Macbeth shook his head. He was intent
on an amethyst brooch shaped like a butterfly.

" For thy mother, then ? "

The boy's head jerked upward and he gave the man a
suspicious stare.

" It is none of your business for whom. Let me see that
one, that purple thing."

The jeweller handed it over. " Seventy-five rupees. It

has seed-pearls for its eyes, and is, as you see, cunningly mounted in gold."

"Seventy-five rupees!" He handed it back precipitately, staring with increasing indecision at the glittering wealth before him. He had no idea of the value of precious stones, no idea what he should pay for the smallest piece of silver or the smallest garnet. But his mother had loved jewellery and now he remembered her as she had appeared on that last evening before she left him. She came into his room to say good-night, and she wore a white dress, with her favourite earrings.

He saw the jeweller's eye fixed upon him. "Have you any emeralds?"

The man's expression did not alter. "Emeralds? Assuredly, I have emeralds."

He plunged his hand into the confusion of treasures and found one, a ring with a square stone set in silver. Macbeth took it, his heart beating painfully. How beautiful it was, how green and bright, and how terribly it reminded him of her! He saw her now as she stood before the looking-glass in his room, adjusting the fine fish-hook which fastened the emerald to the lobe of her pretty ear, turning her golden head sideways to smile at him as if he, too, were a lover.

Macbeth was not aware that he was under the steady scrutiny of one besides the jeweller. A little distance off at the next booth Ramdatta the moneylender waited for one of his relatives to conclude some transaction. He'd seen Macbeth approach the jeweller and he had not missed a word that passed between them.

Macbeth, drawing his breath, held up the ring and looked its owner in the eye. "How much?"

"You are young to be buying emeralds, and the fact makes me hesitate."

Macbeth frowned. To him an emerald was an emerald, no more and no less. He said in a strained voice: "I may not be able to pay you in full, but if you will take part of the price I will give you a chit for the remainder. I will give you references. My father is Colonel Macbeth, and I have friends in Amritpore."

The man interrupted with a wave of his hand. "Could

I live a day without trusting my clients ? And shall I presume to demand references from the son of a Colonel Sahib ? " He lowered his voice confidentially : " What can you pay me on account ? Perhaps if I cannot sell you that very stone I may have one a trifle smaller, for less."

" I'll give you fifty rupees," said Macbeth at once. He had been saving his pocket-money for months in anticipation of his mother's birthday.

The man leaned back with an air of profound deliberation. " Fifty rupees . . . fifty . . ."

Macbeth turned the ring in his hand, making it catch the light. Then a shadow fell across the show-case and he looked up to find Ramdatta standing beside him. The moneylender smiled. " You remember me, Sahib ? "

Macbeth remembered him. He felt at once, in the air which surrounded this man, the warmth of a particular, protective vitality. Gently, with an exquisite gesture of respect, Ramdatta took the ring from him and held it to the light, turning it in his plump fingers in a way which even Macbeth realised must be the way of the true connoisseur. Ramdatta's hand was full of knowledge, one felt that his flesh, like a tuning-fork, rang truth from the prized object. The jeweller sat motionless, his smile vanished behind the set mask of his face.

" Fifty rupees for an emerald, an emerald the size of this, an emerald of the first water ! "

Macbeth looked at him eagerly. " That's just on account. What do you think it's worth ? "

" That is not easy to say at first glance," returned Ramdatta. He had not so much as glanced at the jeweller. Suddenly fumbling at his breast, he found a chain to which was attached a little silver toothpick. So swiftly that Macbeth hardly followed the movement, Ramdatta bent back the tiny claws which held the stone, picked the emerald out with his nail, and scratched away the square of green paper which was pasted on it. The " emerald," a piece of ordinary glass, lay wanly on his palm.

As Macbeth turned on the jeweller Ramdatta laid a restraining hand on the boy's shoulder. " Do not curse him, Sahib. He shall make redress."

The jeweller burst into violent explanations, but Ram-

datta silenced him with a look. " Do you wish to attract
the attention of the police ? "

The man relapsed into growls, his one good eye burning
like a spent match. The moneylender turned to Macbeth.
" Let us select a stone for you. What do you say to a pearl ?
See, here is one. A real pearl."

The owner of the real pearl craned forward in anguish,
but Ramdatta waved him aside. " Or, failing pearls, here
are some little rubies. Like drops of blood pricked from
a woman's finger ! Do you fancy rubies ? "

Macbeth saw that he stood in the centre of a minor
clash of personalities ; with every second Ramdatta seemed
to increase in stature, an imposing tower of flesh and authority.

" Moonstones are not considered precious, but they have
beauty. What do you say to a double string of moonstones
with earrings to match ? "

Macbeth peered at the nearest case and his glance fell
on the little amethyst butterfly. " There, that. I like that.
Are they real stones ? "

Ramdatta signalled the jeweller.   " The amethyst
butterfly," he commanded sonorously.   " That with the
seed-pearls. What is the matter with thee ? Hast thou a
stroke ? "

" I will not sell," replied the other, sullenly. " I am not
obliged to sell. Go elsewhere for thy gems."

" And send the police for thine ? "

Speechless, the man lifted the cover of the jewel case
and extracted the amethyst butterfly.

Macbeth felt an intense amusement. " Yes, I like this.
Is it real ? "

" It is real," said Ramdatta, who had given the thing
a single cursory glance. " Men do not waste such work-
manship on an unreal stone. But amethyst ! Is there not
something else you would prefer ? What of the sapphire
there in the corner, next the gold earrings ? "

" Nay ! " wailed the jeweller despairingly. " That is
a true sapphire ! I have but three."

" What, only three ? But these others . . ." He shrugged
and turned to Macbeth. " Take the amethyst if it pleases
you. Pay this blackguard five rupees."

" Five rupees ! My God ! Five ? It's worth ten times five."

" Since when have amethysts and emeralds been the same price ? " Ramdatta's big face glistened with benevolence. " Before the city magistrate your fine would be ten times ten, with ten years in jail. Come, be sensible if you cannot be honest. The amethyst goes to the young Sahib for rupees five, cash. Give him the money, Sahib, and take your jewel."

39

DUSK was falling when Ganpat Rai's guests assembled in the garden. The light still lingered in the sky and on the river, and great cranes were flying homeward two by two, their harsh cries falling towards the submerging plain as regiments of flying-foxes emerged to feast in the nearer branches. Servants had sprinkled the drive and the garden paths and strung paper lanterns among the trees, where they glowed like fruit, already attracting big soft-winged moths. One by one carriages and bicycles wheeled through the gates, delivered their passengers, and were taken away to the rear of the house. Tables had been set on the lawn between the tennis court and the arbour where Hardyal's female relatives listened and peeped excitedly between their shielding curtains. Here, later, they would receive the visiting ladies, Indian and English.

The Collector and his wife had arrived, and in honour of this official presence Ganpat Rai was wearing European clothes, a jasmin in his buttonhole. It surprised him when, at the last minute, his son appeared in native dress.

" I feel more comfortable in these," explained Hardyal. Puzzled by the boy's manner, Ganpat Rai put a hand on his shoulder.

" You are not ill, my son ? "

" Ill ? " He stood, gazing heavily at his sandalled feet.

" All yesterday you hardly spoke and to-day you did not want to go to the Fair. Naturally, I wondered."

Neither was given to prying, and when Hardyal answered : " It is nothing," the father let him go, deciding to postpone inquiries until later.

Hardyal went down the steps, making his way between groups of friends towards the St. Remy phaeton which had just swung between the gates.

"We missed you!" cried Jacques.

"I was so sorry. I was detained."

The formal word astonished them. "*Detained?*"

"First you run away from the Fort, then you don't turn up at the Fair."

"Beast!"

"We missed you . . . we missed you!"

For a moment he said nothing, his expression that of a deaf man to whom meaning comes one beat after the sound of words. Then he repeated in a detached voice: "I was detained."

He stood before them, slender, white-clad, and it was Jacques who first felt the difference in him. It was more than a difference of dress and of manner, for these had not troubled him before. He felt, now, a creeping chill. When at last Hardyal lifted his dark gaze and their eyes met, Jacques knew that something had gone wrong.

Hardyal said: "I think that perhaps I had a touch of the sun yesterday. That is why I went away."

"You might have waited. We couldn't have missed you by more than a few minutes!" Bertie sounded friendly enough, but she, too, had read something in the air. She read it, not in Hardyal but in Jacques. Were they, then, so close that they could commune without speech? She felt again the swift clutch of jealousy, and turned away, followed by her cousin.

A cloud of voices, Indian and English, drifted among the flowers and the darkening hedges; they seemed to continue in a humming monotone among the glowing Chinese lanterns.

For a moment neither boy spoke, then Jacques said: "Hardyal . . ."

Hardyal lifted his hand, and said softly, in Hindustani: "Do not let us talk now. Perhaps, later."

More guests were arriving, and hearing his name called, Hardyal went away to join Abdul Salim and a group of young Mohammedans who wore the black coat, white trousers and red fez of Aligarh College.

Jacques felt vaguely sick as he used to when he was a child and something frightened him. He realised that the sensation had been gathering might ever since yesterday, when the morning's pleasure had been spoiled by Hardyal's disappearance from the Fort. All afternoon at the Fair he waited with an increasing nervous impatience for this moment when they were sure to meet in Hardyal's own house . . . when surely the air would be cleared, for the simplest explanation must clear it. Then : " I was detained ! " The stilted sentence was more confusing than no explanation at all. Jacques kicked the gravel, and felt a hand laid on his arm. He turned to find Mrs. Lyttleton standing beside him. " More than ever, you remind me of Auguste ! "

He stood rooted. It was a long time since they had spoken, and the years had crowded out his old affection and cast it into a half-shamed memory. Her gave her a troubled smile, saying nothing.

" I won't keep you," she said in a tart voice. " I know your mother is here and that she would object to my speaking with you . . . that is, beyond the bounds of common politeness. Or would she resent even so little ? "

Her irony had a stab to it and he winced. She released him with a harsh little laugh. " I am glad that you look like Auguste, though I had hoped you would show a sterner spirit. You will certainly have need of it, my dear."

Jacques felt completely miserable. Somewhere behind a storm of conflicting thoughts shone the remembrance of all his previous anticipations. Youth, when it does not live completely in the present, looks forward. Now it seemed as if everything he loved was twisting into deformity under his eyes. As a child he had acquired perceptions natural to animals, but which in men are considered psychic. He knew that the change which he now observed in his old friend owed less to time itself than to some other cause : it was as though age, bored with stepping softly, had made a sudden pounce. He had never thought of her as being old, as being cruel, or even unkind. He had never thought that she could change. But now her head trembled in the pathetic vertigo of age, her eyes had lost their humour, her movements had the groping hesitancy of blind people. It shocked him, he felt the crumbling away of some structure within himself. What had happened to her, to himself, to Hardyal ? What were the forces at work behind the familiar everyday world ?

They stood together, the boy and the old woman, watching a crowd of figures move singly and in pairs, listening to civilised accents speaking together under the Chinese lanterns which glowed with an intensity they lost when one looked up at the deepening sky.

Mrs. Lyttleton asked querulously : " Where is he ? "

" Where is who ? "

" Hardyal, of course. I must see him. I must talk to him."

Her voice cracked, and Jacques winced. Then he forced himself to look at her directly. Was he seeing her for the first time, this wrinkled, yellow, shivering old woman who was also perhaps somewhat mad, as many described her who had never known her ?

He asked gently : " Shall I find Hardyal for you ? "

" Ah, you would welcome the excuse to escape, wouldn't you ? "

His lips trembled. " No, I . . ."

She interrupted with extraordinary bitterness. " Don't lie to me. I'm sick of lies. It's a lying world . . . even children . . . lying, stealing ! "

He felt a little thrill of aversion. " Won't you let me fetch you a chair ? "

" One must dissociate oneself from liars and cowards. But the world is full of them. They are all murderers . . . murderers, I tell you ! " She peered at him from under her hat. " You too, you too ! "

" Please ! Take my arm. Let me fetch you a chair, and some ginger beer ! "

She gave a shrill cackle of laughter. " Ginger beer ! Yes, do. Find me some ginger beer. It is exactly what I need, exactly ! "

Horrified, Jacques slipped away in search of a servant. Everywhere, people were sitting at little tables, eating, drinking, talking. Individual had gravitated to individual, group to group. Propinquity, sympathy, drew them together. Macbeth and Bertie were laughing with a young

Englishman, the guest of one of Amritpore's officials.
Madame St. Remy sipped tea with Father Sebastien and
the English doctor. The Collector had removed his white
helmet and his tinsel *har* and was smoking a cigarette,
surrounded by barristers and lesser fry. He was apparently
telling a funny story, for bursts of laughter and a great
slapping of thighs and shoulders indicated both sincere
and sycophantic appreciation. Many of the ladies had disappeared into the arbour, from whose discreetly drawn
curtains there escaped an occasional peal of laughter and
crisp, English voices.

Jacques watched Ganpat Rai move from group to
group ; he had the air of a proud, wise, and happy man.
Every one, reflected Jacques . . . every one is happy except
Mrs. Lyttleton and Hardyal and I. Once or twice when
he passed Bertie he had a feeling that she deliberately
averted her glance. He saw Hardyal in the distance—
always in the distance !

Standing for a moment near Abdul Salim, Jacques
could not help overhearing the Mohammedan's emphatic
speech : " Crichton is not here. I doubt whether we shall
see him this evening. There was some sort of a row at the
Fair grounds. I didn't see it, but Feroze told me. I met
Feroze on his way to the hospital. It seems there was a
beating or something . . . and our friend Ramdatta was
involved. Feroze could tell me only the little he had learned
for himself. The story is, Ramdatta tried to cheat some poor
devil of a jeweller out of a gem. There was an argument,
and as Ramdatta was leaving the grounds sticks and *kanker*
were thrown, and several people were hurt. Oh, no, Ramdatta was not hurt. He never is ! From all accounts the
police arrived just in time to check the makings of a nice
little riot. Naturally, Crichton cannot very well leave in
the middle of a riot ! "

A group of musicians appeared and spread their mats
a little distance from the guests. Glad of a diversion,
Jacques wandered towards them. The ripple of a *zitar* and
the soft growl of rice-bowl drums brushed against the subdued hum of voices and clatter of plates and knives. A
young man sitting cross-legged between the *zitar* player
and the drums sang in a high minor key and his voice,

soaring above all the other voices, had the special sweetness
of an awakened bird.

A man standing near Jacques spoke to another in a low
tone :

" You heard Salim ? It is true. I was near the south
gate and I saw it happen. Ramdatta drove past in his ekka
and a man tried to jump on the wheel and drag him out.
Others closed in. I saw one throw a large stone. It was the
signal—you know how these things happen ! I removed
myself. It seemed unwise to linger."

Afraid that they might suspect him of eavesdropping,
Jacques moved away. Now he noticed that a sort of segre-
gation was slowly taking place ; Hindus had gathered in a
loosely knit group under the trees, while the red fezzes and
astrakhan caps of the Mohammedan contingent seemed to
gravitate towards a summer-house beyond the tennis courts.
Between these recognisable islands flowed the other guests,
a few English and Eurasian, servants preoccupied with their
duties, and those perennially unattached characters who
seem always to wait for some signal before deciding where
it is they belong, if they belong anywhere.

A clatter of dishes and the hum of voices rose into the
darkening air which, as it darkened, struck chords of light
from the doors and windows of the house. The Chinese
lanterns bloomed golden among leaves which took on
sharpness like details etched in iron, round whose stillness
the white moths came and went. Beyond the garden the
plain fell away into a dark blue haze and the cooling air
captured all the essence of evening, distilling it in keener
breaths of wood-smoke and of flesh trying hard to be discreet, to remain immune to its own secret agitation. The
closer all these diverse elements were drawn together, the
nearer they approached towards ultimate unity, the more
urgent became their unconscious resistance. It seemed as
if some perverse and original memory asserted itself to remind them that moths are moths and bats are bats, that
the devoted cranes which desert their crimson pools at
sunset obey a wisdom which has determined to put more
than space—to put form and substance—between life and
life. The closer these people came to resembling one another
the more strenuously they strove to separate. Only in the

orgasm of love or of death could they ever forget their identity, and between themselves and this forgetfulness they had raised their fantastic barriers.

40

HARDYAL had seen Mrs. Lyttleton ; he had, as a matter of fact, waited intently for her arrival. He saw her approach Jacques and watched them as they talked together ; then Jacques went away and for several minutes she stood there alone, staring at the crowd. A servant brought her something on a tray, but she waved him aside and walked slowly across the lawn towards the tables, and he lost sight of her.

> Down by the river
> When at night on the pyre of sleep
> You burn with decreasing fire
> And the very sky melts towards you
> With longing, with longing,
> Love with his hand shall part the sacred water
> And revive you with showers from his hair.

Hardyal listened as the song threaded its nasal syllables between drum and *zitar*. He did not linger more than a few minutes with any group of friends, but moved quietly from one to another, keeping a little space around himself. His mind ached from the chimera of a recurring, feverish dream in which the unbelievable sentences from Wall's letter alternately blazed and faded. Other words, other voices detached themselves from figures which moved round him in the gloom. He heard Abdul Salim wondering aloud whether Mrs. Lyttleton and Madame St. Remy would come to blows here in Ganpat Rai's charming garden. A friend hushed him, and they disappeared among the shadows. Another voice spoke suddenly, with nervous emphasis : "I trust Crichton. He has tact and force—a good man in a situation. I think perhaps the story may be exaggerated, for had any one been hurt we must have learned of it by now."

Hardyal stood in the golden light of a lantern and

watched the musicians. They sang on, indifferent to the
crowd to whom they sang.

> Love with his hand shall part the sacred water
> And revive you with showers from his hair !

He heard Macbeth explaining impatiently to Bertie :
" Moths *don't* love the flame ! The light cramps the muscles
of their eyes and blinds them. . . ."

Then he saw Mrs. Lyttleton coming towards him where
he stood apart under the trees. He waited until he was
sure that she had recognised him, then stepped forward
to meet her.

" Hardyal ! I have looked everywhere for you."

" I have been here."

" But you never even came to greet me ! "

" I am sorry. There are so many guests, some who do
not know me as you do, and whose feelings would be hurt
were I to neglect them."

She stood in the frail light of a paper lantern, peering
at him.

" Are you trying to hurt my feelings, Hardyal ? "

" How should I ? " His heart was beating strangely, as
though he had taken an anæsthetic.

She shuddered. " Don't . . . don't prevaricate ! Don't
lie . . . I can't bear it. I won't bear it ! " She went on
harshly : " You have avoided me and now you make
excuses. Why ? You never used to."

He turned aside and found a chair, which he carried
forward and set down for her. She sank into it and he saw
her hands move tremblingly on her old silk parasol. " Hardyal . . . what has happened to every one ? They are all
changed . . . all, all, are changed ! "

He stood beside her, his face half hidden in the gloom
of the leaves, the folds of his white dhoti shining like the
sculptured folds of a marble robe. They were alone except
for the musicians who sat a few yards away. The song had
ended but the *zitar* sent an occasional melancholy note into
the darkness, and the drummer's pliant hands stirred a
murmur from his drums.

" Answer me, Hardyal ! "

"I do not yet know what it is you wish me to say."

She cried brokenly : "Tell me the truth !"

He bowed slightly, his brown hands clasped before him.

"I have lost Aubrey Wall's letter. Hardyal, did you take it ?"

"Yes."

The sigh which escaped her was half groan and she lifted one hand shakily to her eyes. "You took it ! You of all people, you !"

"You read it to me, do you remember ? You read me things out of it. Things about myself and my father. Do you remember ?" He had himself in hand now, and the words came readily enough, though his heart still beat painfully. "It pleased me to hear those things. They made me feel proud and happy."

She dropped her hand from her eyes and her frail old body seemed to gather itself together in a frenzy of protest. "But the letter, the letter ! Don't you know that you should never read people's letters ? It's most dishonourable. You didn't read it, did you ?"

"Yes, I read it."

"Oh, no, no !"

"All of it."

Silence fell heavily and at that instant it touched, or seemed to touch, the entire garden and all the preoccupied people in it. Hardyal heard the moths whispering round the nearest paper lantern, he saw their eyes glow like rubies in the dark.

When Mrs. Lyttleton spoke at last her voice had regained something of its old acerbity. "I might have believed it of any one else, but not of you."

"Was it so wrong ? I did not mean to be dishonourable. I meant only to keep the letter a little while because of the things that were in it. Like—like a tikka."

"What do you mean ?"

"A charm, a touchstone. It had made me so happy and so proud to think that there were people who felt . . . happy and proud on my account. Then I discovered that I was wrong . . . that everything was wrong, that the letter . . . the letter was a lie."

"And you read it, you read it ! You know, now, every-

thing that was in it.   How many people have you told?
How far have you broadcast that horror ? "

He was silent, listening to Ganpat Rai bid the Collector
and his lady good-night.

" I suppose you have told your father and all your
friends, and that untrustworthy Salim !   By this time, it
must be all over the bazaar."

He moved, putting his hand inside his shirt and bringing
out the letter, which he laid gently in her lap.   " I have
told no one.   I have said nothing.   There is the letter."

As her fingers closed upon it all her rings glittered like
water.

" What good to return it to me now ?   You know what
happened, and no doubt it is a mere matter of time before
the whole world knows ! "

" I have told no one.   No one has seen the letter, no one
except you and me."

" You expect me to believe you ? "   Then when he
remained silent she cried again :   " Why did you ?   How
could you ?   I should have destroyed it, but I was confused.
I thought I should keep it as a sort of—a sort of threat over
Aubrey.   I didn't know what to do . . . I don't now know
what to do."

" Nor do I."

A carriage bell twanged, a pair of yellow lamps disappeared between the gate-posts as another pair appeared.

" You read it to me yourself," said Hardyal in a low
voice.   " But what I do not understand is, why the things
that you read to me were not in the letter."

She made a despairing gesture.   " Oh, I was a fool . . .
a sentimental fool ?   I wanted to spite Aubrey Wall . . . to
use the evil he had done, and to make some good come of
it.   It was perverse of me . . . it was wicked, stupid of me !
But I didn't think."

" Then when you read me those things, those things
which made me feel proud and happy . . . tell me now,
were they there, or perhaps in another letter ?   Or did you
make them up ? "

" Yes," she replied coldly.   " I made them up.   With
his beastly words under my eyes, I made up the things that
I said to you.   It pleased me to do so."

" But why ? " His voice was suddenly desolate, and the sound of it went straight to her heart. She lifted her hand and took his, drawing him down on the grass beside her. " Oh, Hardyal, what have we done, between us ? "

She laid her hand on his rich, dark hair. " I hate Aubrey Wall. I hate everything he stands for, everything he is ! But I know that hate is not the answer. I have behaved like an idiotic, romantic old woman, simply because I wanted to make amends to you . . . to you and to others, for another's brutality. I was confused. I felt old and powerless, yet I could not escape the responsibility which he had thrust on me. I have been too long out of step with my own kind, who think me mad and disloyal. And I even tried to retrace my steps, to conciliate them by showing that I cared what they thought. I wanted to put some tiny fragment of the world to rights, starting with my own garden ! " He felt her fingers tremble on his head. " What a fool ! "

He sat like a stone, not moving an eyelash when a big sphinx moth darted out from the shadows and hung on electric wings beside his cheek.

" Ah, Hardyal ! This damnable violence in men ! Why, why ? "

" I don't know."

" But what are we to do ? Jalal is dead, and Aubrey . . . what can it prove, now, to betray him ? "

" Betray ? "

" A friend, a countryman—and he couldn't have known what he was doing. I hate him. I detest him. He has destroyed the last few years of peace left to me. But what am I to do ? What am I to do, now ? "

She leaned towards him, the old woman towards the young boy, who turned his head aside as though he heard another voice.

" Who am I, to tell you what you should do ? "

" But if you were I, Hardyal ? "

" What could I do, even then ? And he didn't like me. He said I . . . was not to be trusted."

Mrs. Lyttleton was trembling violently. " Oh, that letter, that letter ! "

" I do not know, now, whether I should even trust

myself. He did not trust any of us. He said that we would turn against him in the end. But he didn't wait, did he ? "

" Wait ? Wait for what ? "

" For the end, for the proof. He liked horses and dogs better. They were more human, he said."

" Oh, don't, don't ! "

" I wish I understood. You see, I don't really understand at all."

" Ah, Hardyal, do not think of it. There are others who are not like Aubrey Wall. You have known many ! There is Jacques, there is myself. We love you . . . yes, yes, we love you ! Do not turn away from us, forgive us, Hardyal ! "

He sat without speaking, and she went on eagerly : " See, I shall destroy the letter. I shall burn it, and when it has vanished, everything it contained will have vanished. To tell any one, to make it public . . . what would it bring except more misery ? "

" You need never fear that I will speak of it. Do you think that I would dream of hurting my father, or others, as I have been hurt ? "

Her shame was complete and for a moment she was unable to speak, feeling age sweep upon her in a deafening wave. Then Abdul Salim's voice boomed through the darkness. " Hardyal, where are you, my child ? "

" Help me," murmured Mrs. Lyttleton, and put out her hand in a blind gesture. He rose, drawing her gently to her feet. She felt light and dry, like last year's leaf, as he led her back to the other guests.

41

A CANOPY of firelit dusk hung above the Fair grounds as night brought an accentuation of gaiety and excitement. Booths twinkled in the glow of charags and lanterns, drums throbbed, pipes shrilled, colour melted into colour or flared in strokes of crimson or gold as the darkness beat towards the edges of light, spilled, and receded.

A file of red-turbaned police arrived to relieve their fellows ; their shoes clumped noisily and the brass knobs of their *lathies* gleamed like wands of ceremony. The afternoon's disturbance had scarcely affected the general turmoil of gaiety and good humour. Fewer than fifty people had seen the scuffle, the volley of stones and the broken head of one of the participants. Mr. Crichton congratulated himself and his men on averting a row of far more serious proportions, and after posting guards and increasing his normal contingent, he went home to bathe and to dine.

The cause of the outbreak was still more or less of a mystery. Crichton had listened to contradictory accounts : one had it that Ramdatta used his whip on a group which attempted to bar his passage through the south gate. A one-eyed vendor of jewels was seen egging on the stone-throwers. Mohammedans joined in, singling out their ancient enemies, and the police arrived in time to break up the party. But the man with the cracked head would probably die, for Feroze, the assistant surgeon, held out little hope. Should he die, the news must somehow be kept quiet until the Fair was over and the crowds safely dispersed. Crichton had no intention of permitting communal violence to mar the success of the Agricultural Fair.

Hanif had missed the fight, but as he moved among the crowd rumours of it filtered through to him, a word here, a whisper there. Two little Hindu boys capered up to him, making insulting gestures. A big Punjabi spat in the dust and shook his fist, for a piece of *kankar* had caught him in the eye. But the mass remained unaffected, and like a rock at high tide that single moment of bloodshed sank under a preoccupied human sea.

Hanif had decked his ear with a fresher rose ; now he made his way past the food stalls, past the humid byways and the strong-smelling purlieus given over to prize-winning goats and the rampant stallions of the Pathans. The young man's expensive elegance excited an occasional smile or a bawdy quip, and he retaliated in kind. The night was his, he breathed its exhilaration and felt its invitation in his warm and gentle blood. The pearls in his new cap and the intricate pattern of his new shoes filled him with satisfaction. He laid his hand on the silk of his waistcoat and played with the silver chain and the links which fastened his shirt. His own beauty, his own youth went to his head :

he turned his face to the smoky sky and flung his song to the stars.

"Wah!" exclaimed a fellow Moslem at his elbow. "Congratulations—but must you tell the world?"

They laughed together, then Hanif glided unobtrusively down an alley which branched away from the main body of the grounds. Here were the sellers of birds, a little arena where the grey partridges fought each other, and a thousand caged canaries contributing their silly din to the general uproar.

Hanif headed towards a *chhatri* at the end of the lane, pushed aside the heavy plaited screen, and went in.

"You are late," came the inevitable tender reproach, and he felt the cold caress of her glass bracelets against his neck.

"I had duties, but they are finished."

Inside the *chhatri* the floor was freshly leeped and immaculate; there were no windows, and charags burned at the corners. The outside world beat against this impermanent abode which housed everything that is permanent in human life. She was a girl of perhaps thirteen, still fresh and firm, her hair threaded with jasmin, her round arms laden with glass. Hanif carried her to a heap of coloured quilts in a corner of the room, then came back and stooping, blew out the charags. He was quite sure that he was in love, and the knowledge made his knees tremble as he groped his way back to the bed. He was always sure that he was in love, and the knowledge always made his knees tremble.

More than an hour later he stepped forth into the pulsing air, and the tireless voices of the birds rose about him. He bought a cigarette made of black, sticky native tobacco, set his cap at an angle, and sauntered towards the nearest gate and a short-cut across the fields towards the road. Once or twice he stopped to smile and to raise his left wrist upon which he'd managed to squeeze a single glass bangle. Remembering her little hands, he laughed huskily, his blood and brain filled with drowsy sweetness. Well, there was to-morrow. He must invent a sick friend.

As he walked away from the Fair grounds the noise fell behind him in a soft roar from which smaller, keener sounds escaped like raindrops stroking the leaves closest to

one in a storm. People passed him, coming and going. A
bullock cart creaked its wooden wheels, a boy on a bicycle
veered by with an important shrilling of a nickel bell. An
old man loped past, riding a bedraggled horse.

As Hanif reached the road he met the little orchestra
which had played for Ganpat Rai's guests. The singer
strolled happily in the dust and his song caught Hanif's ear
as they passed each other :

> " And the very sky melts towards you
>   With longing, with longing . . ."

The voice dimmed and died, but Hanif hummed the verse,
as he walked, smoking his cigarette, alone now on the white
road. It was half an hour's walk from here to the cantonment and the gates and gardens of Madame's neighbours.
He was in no hurry, for the night smelled delicious in his
nostrils and the cigarette had a special savour.

A tiny eye of light flickered in the darkness and as he
approached he saw it was the ember of a fire, beside a cart
drawn by two bullocks. From behind the cart stepped a
little group of men. They hailed him :

" Where goest thou ? "

He answered them gaily, but as he prepared to pass
they strung out across the road, barring his path. He saw
now that they were Hindus ; he saw also that something
was amiss, and his mind worked fast.

" Do you spend the night beside the road, my brothers ? "
he inquired in friendly accents. No one replied and for a
moment they confronted him in a silence whose menace
was unmistakable. He loosened his feet in his shoes, preparing to kick them off at a second's notice and to make
a run for it.

One of the men spoke up at last : " What business is
it of yours where we spend the night ? Who are you, a
police spy ? "

" I am the servant of a great lady. Make way ! "

Another laughed. " The servant of a great lady, dressed
up like a pimp ! "

" Where is thy badge, thy livery ? "

" Perhaps he is wearing it," suggested a third, and they

laughed, a sound unpleasantly devoid of mirth. Hanif glance round him out of the corner of his eye. On either side of the road were a few trees, and beyond them the open fields. Once in the fields the darkness might hide him. Silently, he cursed the glittering whiteness of his new pantaloons.

A voice burst from the gloom : " I would swear this one was amongst them ! "

" Amongst whom ? I have been to the Fair with my friends and masters."

" And know you that my brother is dead ? He died an hour ago at the Government dispensary. That dog of a Mohammedan doctor killed him."

" And it was you threw the stone ! "

Hanif stood his ground. " I know nothing of all this. I have never seen your brother, nor you. Now let me pass."

But they were keyed up and half frantic with passion ; and they had waited some time for their revenge. What did it matter whether this lad had been present at the beating, or whether he had not ? A Mohammedan had thrown the stone, and here was a Mohammedan, defying them. He was one and they were many. They moved nearer and Hanif began to back, but he kept his head, sure that could he but get a good start he would outstrip them.

" Fools ! " he cried, his voice firm and strong. " I have never set eyes on you, your brother or your uncles ! Lay a hand on me and you will live to regret it."

His young voice stayed them for a moment. Then one spoke on a changed note. " Perhaps he tells the truth. We don't punish innocent men."

There was a slight, enigmatic pause, then the same voice addressed Hanif. " Go, then. Go your way, but hurry before we change our minds."

Hanif threw away his cigarette and stepped forward. His heart was beating faster than he liked, but he was no coward. The men parted as he strode towards them and he saw that they all carried sticks, and one of them a heavy brass *lotah* or drinking vessel bought, no doubt, that very day at the Fair. He walked past them with a resolute step, and they let him go. Then they closed in behind him, and he who carried the *lotah* whirled it suddenly and sent it flying through the air. It caught Hanif between the shoulders, making him stumble. A short heavy stick flew between his legs and he fell face down on the road. They were upon him in a minute, and he gathered himself together with his head in his arms and his knees drawn against his stomach, bracing his muscles against the rain of kicks and blows. They tore his shirt from him and his trousers and beat him until the breath sagged in his chest and his head lolled helplessly in the dust. Then they withdrew a little and provided themselves with stones. Forming a semi-circle about him, and leaving room so they would not hit one another by mistake, they threw stones, every sort and weight of stone they could lay hands on. And while they worked they made short grunting sounds, the spittle running from their mouths. No one spoke—the only noise was the grunting and the soft thud of stones striking Hanif. At last one man, the tallest, moved away to the edge of the road and returned with a boulder. He straddled Hanif's body, lifted the boulder, and let it fall squarely on the glossy head. An hour passed before they were finished with him, and when at last they moved away, staggering a little from their orgy, all that was recognisable of Hanif under his coverlet of stones and rubble was one hand, darkly articulated against the white dust.

PART THREE

42

BERTIE WOOD, coming out of the house one hot July afternoon, found her uncle standing in rapt contemplation of
a new flower-bed on the eastern edge of the terrace. When
she approached and linked her arm in his, he murmured :
" Cottage tulips, I think. They flower early."

" I still don't see, if you are going to retire next year,
why you should bother to plant them."

He was silent for a minute, and she examined his profile
which in this diamond light had the character of rock, and
much of its changelessness. It was always difficult for her
to guess what her uncle was thinking ; his gentleness never
failed to surprise her, well though she knew it. But she had
learned that professional soldiers sometimes possess a peculiar simplicity and a tenderness often lacking in subtler men.
Colonel Macbeth had remarked on this trait in his com-
rades but he seemed unaware, or unimpressed, by the same
quality in himself. His love for flowers, for animals, for
women, was entirely without affectation. It seemed at
times as though consecration to the doom of war had bred
in him and in his kind a wistful hunger for everything
ephemeral in life. He had no talent for tortured intellec-
tuality, no time for doubt and very little for hate. Because
he had never spoken of it, because she never would know
his thoughts or his feelings when his wife deserted him,
Bertie never ceased to wonder about her uncle. He had
killed men and men had tried to kill him, yet here he stood,
pulling the ends of his grey moustache, meditating on the
virtues and disadvantages of an experiment in cottage
tulips.

He repeated her question with an air of surprise. " Why
should I bother to plant them ? Why not ? "

" They'll be wasted if you sell the house."

" Oh, I don't think so." He straightened his great
height and stared at the house which had been his home

for thirty years. It never occurred to him that he would not leave it, in the end, for a remote and less familiar England.

Bertie said slowly : " I hate to think of your selling it. Must you ? "

" Well, I can't afford to keep the place for John. A colonel's pension is hardly a fortune, and I intend to live at home when I retire."

" If there isn't a war," she reminded him, frowning.

" If there isn't a war."

They turned and began to saunter up and down the terrace before the house, Bertie's arm linked in her uncle's, their feet keeping step. " If there isn't a war," he repeated. " If Grey can persuade them all to meet and talk it over."

" You don't really think there will be a war, do you ? "

He hesitated, then removed his hat and struck with it, lightly, at a flock of brown spaniels which emerged from the house to greet them.

" Yes, I think there will be war, and soon."

" Yet you want to plant all those tulips, and you talk about retiring and living in England."

" Life goes on, doesn't it ? One can't very well stop in the middle."

" But what makes you think there is going to be a war ? "

He shrugged. " I'm a soldier. I've been a soldier all my life. War is in the air. My men feel it. I can see it in their eyes."

She drew him to a halt and turned to stare at him. " Do you mean it ? You've never said this before."

" One hates to put some things into words. But there is a stir . . . a stir."

They resumed their walk, and she burst out suddenly : " Life goes on ! It's been going on, everywhere, for years and years ! And all the time there is always some one calmly plotting a war ! Isn't it funny ? "

He glanced at her with his pale, gentle eyes. " It is funny, you know. Awfully ! "

They came to the end of the terrace, then turned and walked slowly back. Bertie said : " If there should be a war, do you think that John will try and transfer from the Police into the Army ? "

"Why should he? He will have his work cut out for him here. The Police in India are every bit as important as the Army. More so now than ever, with these Swaraj-wallahs on the rampage. There was a speech in yesterday's *Pioneer*, by Gokhale. I do not intend to read it."

She kicked the gravel. "Just the same, I'm glad that if war should come, the people I love won't be in it. Jacques because of his hand, John because he will have to stay in India, and you . . ." she pressed his arm, "you because you are an old Methuselah."

He smiled faintly. "Women have no shame."

"You mean we don't always pretend to be heroic."

"On the contrary, you never stop pretending all sorts of things until you're faced with a moral issue. Then you behave realistically."

"Well, I certainly don't pretend to like the idea of war."

He laughed. "As long as you don't make a scene, I shall forgive you anything." He tilted her face towards his. "Do you know, I never believed that you'd grow into a lovely woman. Do you remember how you used to want to be told that you were lovely? You are. Is Jacques responsible?"

Her animation gave way to brooding. "Jacques! You said just now that life went on, but it seems to me that only situations go on. On and on! It seems to me that the situations which I found here when I first arrived have never really been resolved. We've all changed, grown older—but how far are we from where we started? It frightens me to think about it. Nothing seems to happen, nothing."

He looked away. "Next year you and Jacques will be married, and you'll find, then, that life has taken a turn. Hold on to your vision of the future, my darling."

"Oh, the future, the future!" Her voice sounded brittle. "These delays . . . sometimes I think that time can strangle everything just by itself."

Impatience had become increasingly a characteristic with Bertie, though she seemed unconscious of this. Eager-ness, anticipation were transmuted to a nervous craning, and an indifference towards all that was not immediate.

Colonel Macbeth knew that she was thinking of Jacques, of their long engagement, of all the obstacles which necessity had set in their path. Both lovers were beginning to show the strain of a difficult and too delicate relationship, both seemed more and more obsessed by their difficulties than by their passion.

He reminded her, tenderly : " You will see him very soon. Perhaps there'll be a letter from him, to-day."

" I'm going down to the post office now. Uncle Jack . . ." She stared at him rather shamefacedly. " I never used to be a coward . . . I don't want to sound like one now, but you know . . ."

" I know. Sometimes it's rather beastly, isn't it, just to be young ? "

Every afternoon from her window Bertie watched for the mail-carrier on his way up from the railway terminus thirty miles below. He was always heralded by a jingle of bells on a short iron spear, and she had learned to catch the first sound of those bells while the man was still out of sight. Presently he would appear on the semi-circle of road across the lake, a dirty mail sack on his back, its leather strap supported on his brows, his unbelievably thin and wiry legs covering the miles up hill and down at an undeviating trot.

Bertie had been on her way to the post office when she met her uncle in the garden. Now she left him and walked down the hill to the Mall, past the European shops and the band-stand to the stuffy little post office. There she waited in a white heat of impatience while native clerks squatted on the cement floor and sorted the letters into tidy heaps. They were supervised by the postmaster who wore European clothes offset by a filthy cap and a Kashmir shawl draped across his consumptive chest. Bertie spied Jacques' writing among all the others being pawed over by dilatory black fingers.

" There it is in the grey envelope."

" It is not yet stamped," objected the postmaster, and spat blood into a brass spittoon.

" Never mind the stamp."

" But that is strictly against regulations ! "

They could not live without their regulations. Temper flared in Bertie : " Hand it over, Babuji."

" Oh, very well," murmured the postmaster resignedly. He took the letter, fumbled about for the date seal and pressed it with artistic deliberation on the envelope. It passed through several pairs of hands into her own, and the additional delay fed her impatience. My God, what sloths ! How slow life was, how incredibly careless and indifferent these minute processes of civilisation ! Anything might have happened to Jacques, he might be dead or become cold towards her, he might this very second be on his way from Amritpore to Gambul, and she torn with suspense while these leisurely apes mooned about with their miserable official scruples. Damn them, damn all natives.

The afternoon was hot and still and when she came to a turn in the path she stopped and leaned against a wall where bunches of pink sorrel grew among the rocks. It was along this path that Jacques St. Remy had come a long time ago on his first visit to the Macbeths. It was down this path that Captain Ponsonby had ridden away with Mrs. Macbeth.

Bertie, trembling with the almost painful happiness which Jacques' letters always brought her, opened the envelope and took out the thin grey sheets. Her joy receded slowly, giving way to a stupefaction of despair ; the blood seemed to drift from her face to her feet, leaving her cold in the clear blaze of sunlight. She stood with the letter in her hand while the words repeated themselves over and over in her mind : Jacques is not coming, Jacques is not coming !

A sailboat stood motionless on the indigo blue of the lake. Round her the cicadas droned, the oak leaves rattled, a spider the size of her hand clambered from branch to branch, spreading its net for little birds. She thought dimly : Inanimate forms survive, while round them the whole performance of life falls and rises. One is always alone, always, always.

When she got back to the house her uncle had disappeared. Slowly, she made her way upstairs to her cousin's bedroom. Macbeth lay thin and narrow in the light of an open window, and for a moment she thought he must be sound asleep. But when she hesitated on the threshold he spoke without moving his head. "That you, old girl?"

Bertie came in and sat on the edge of his bed, taking his hand. She said, mechanically: "The fever's broken, hasn't it?"

"I think so. But I've had the damnedest dreams."

"Dreams?"

"You know the kind one has when one has fever—huge landscapes and very small people. The feeling of unimportance."

"Dreams," she repeated sombrely. "I think that I prefer them, sometimes, to reality."

He opened his eyes. "Anything up?"

Bertie was holding back her tears, but they filled her voice. "Jacques writes that he is not coming to Gambul, after all. Madame St. Remy has broken her leg."

"Oh, the dickens! No!"

"Yes," said Bertie. Then, explosively: "I wish she were a centipede and would break all her legs!"

Macbeth clasped his fingers tightly round hers, but said nothing. He watched her, seeing her as he often saw her after a pause in their communion, seeing her as something fresh and strong and desirable, all of a colour, everything he knew and understood.

As for Bertie, she had not yet learned to see him as man sprung clear of his boyhood. Her love for Jacques had kept the world at a distance, it had kept other men at a distance. Little by little now the world and its occupants were beginning to intrude upon and to challenge her indifference.

She said suddenly: "Do you mind if I talk? I'll burst if I don't."

"Fire away."

"Madame is going to be my mother-in-law, and I know I ought to be feeling sorry for her this very minute. But what's the use of pretending? To say that I love her would be a lie. To love her at all would be fantastic. Whenever anything happens to her, whether it is good or bad, comes between Jacques and me."

"Perhaps later, when she is well again . . ."

"She'll take jolly good care not to get well in a hurry.

I

She'll keep him down there among her coolies and her
half-castes. I know."

"Not if he makes up his own mind."

"He's had *years* to make up his mind."

They avoided each other's glance, then Macbeth said
gently : "It's just as rough on him, you know. Don't forget
that."

"Oh, heavens, forget? Oh, damn her, damn her
soul !"

Bertie sprang up and walked to the window and he
watched her as she stood there crying to herself. His fever
had gone, leaving him clear and composed, even his love
for her a special and clairvoyant thing.

He said softly : "Bertie, fetch me a cigarette, will
you ?"

She came back to the bed and found his silver case,
lighting a cigarette for him and one for herself. He said :
"After all, there is only this summer. You'll see him in
Amritpore, and next year you'll be married."

"Will we ? That's what we've all supposed. Madame
gave her gracious consent. Oh, that graciousness ! Like
a thin Persian cat. She knows I don't trust her, that I never
have trusted her. Not from the day when Jacques was hurt
and she came up here to this very house and tried to take
him away from us. She knew then that she was in for a
fight. We have seen through each other from the very
beginning, like two women in love with the same man."

"Oh, look here !"

"Yes, and we've played the game that women in love
always play, pretending to be friends, trying to buy each
other off with bribes and hypocrisy."

He was silent, strangely disturbed by her excitement.

"Nothing, no one, was ever to be allowed to stand in
her way. Not even Gisele, her own daughter. Gisele was
beautiful, Gisele was a problem, perhaps even a rival !
And if she permitted Gisele happiness she could hardly
deny it to Jacques, could she ? So Gisele was stuffed away
in some convent, and Jacques . . ."

He stirred uneasily. "My dear, your imagination . . ."

"Oh, don't be silly !"

Both were silent, while she struggled to get herself under

control. Presently she went on : "Madame has no intention that Jacques and I should marry. She is very clever. She is making time work for her. And with every year, with every month, with every week, she comes closer to winning."

"She can't win."

"Do you know why I went to England last year? It wasn't just to buy my trousseau. It was because I was frightened."

Again, he took her hand. "Frightened of what, Bertie?"

"You know perfectly well of what ! I was frightened because I thought if we went on seeing each other I might have a baby."

Their hands lay together numbly on the blanket. He said in a thick voice : "Well, if you had, it would have pretty well settled everything, wouldn't it?"

"It might have settled everything except for Madame's cleverness." He looked at her questioningly, and Bertie went on with a rush :

"She saw what troubled me, she knew that being young, being decent, I was bound to be frightened. She knew that I'd have to go away, that I'd have to put space as well as time between Jacques and myself."

He pressed her hand. "Bertie, why worry now? You're going to marry him. Never mind the past, never mind the present. Think of the future. Think of the future, Bertie !"

"That's what Uncle Jack said. Think of the future ! But when have I had a chance to think of anything else?"

She got up again and began to walk round the room and he followed her with an aching glance, noticing her strong, lithe movements, the despairing pride in her carriage.

"You see, John, the trouble is that Madame loves Jacques. Mothers must love their sons. It is absolutely right and natural and nice. The greater her love for him the more praiseworthy every one thinks it. The trouble with me is that I love him too. The greater and more unbearable my love, the more praiseworthy. But do you know, I sometimes catch myself wondering whether there is really much difference between Madame and myself?"

"Rot."

" Is it ? " She came and stood beside him, looking down at him wistfully. " I wish I could be as sure as you seem to be. I can't be sure of anything any more. I don't want to hurt Jacques. We have never hurt each other, at any rate not intentionally. Yet how am I going to endure seeing him put his mother before me ? You know, it's because of what happened to her once. Her husband was unfaithful to her, with, of all people, Mrs. Lyttleton."

" It's what they say, and it's ancient history, rather, isn't it ? "

" It's what Madame believes, and she doesn't regard it as ancient history. Jacques is determined that she shan't be hurt again. That's why he goes on making concessions, why he goes on putting off our marriage, why, in the end, he will be forced to hurt me rather than hurt her."

Macbeth drew a long breath. " You talk as if all this were final, but you do intend to marry him, don't you, after all ? "

She brooded on his face. " After all ? After we've finished caring about each other ? Madame will certainly have won then, won't she ? "

There was a long silence. A dog scratched himself on the gravel outside ; far away in the barracks a bugle sang and sang, its music breaking against their thoughts. Then Macbeth changed the conversation to a less painful subject. " What were you and Dad talking about a little while ago ? I could hear you as you walked outside."

" We were talking about war."

He raised his brows, and she repeated : " War." But she was not interested in war. Obsession with her own problems made everything else insignificant. Let the world cut its own throat. People were beastly, really. Beastly.

Macbeth said : " The Germans ? "

" I suppose so, and the French."

" And us."

" I don't see why."

" Well, can you see a war without us ? "

Bertie sighed, coming to the surface for air. " Oh, why not ? "

" We couldn't keep out. Any one else might, but we couldn't. Old Grey can try and try but he can't stop it."

" He's a peaceful man. He loves birds."

" He can't stop it. Think of the German Navy ! "

" But after all, Queen Victoria was the Kaiser's grandmother."

" He hates us just the same. They all hate us." He pondered the fact, dispassionately. " When you stop to think of it, the Germans are really unspeakable parvenues."

She made a gesture of impatience. " How silly it all is, how childish ! "

He shook his head. " War isn't childish. It's very grown up. It's the most grown-up thing we ever do."

She stared at him with sudden attention. " If it should come, will you try to get into the Army ? "

He moved restively. " I'd like to, but Dad thinks I ought to stay here, in the Police. We are probably in for trouble, war or no war."

She smiled sceptically. " Another Mutiny ? "

" Lord no, the Army is loyal. All it needs is someone to fight against. The Police are trustworthy. But there are lots of others. . . . Men like Tilak. But he's in the Andamans. I wish all the others were. You simply can't trust these educated natives . . . they're bent on making trouble. If the Army goes abroad the Police will have to take over its job." He frowned. " Things have started, as a matter of fact. Have you heard of a man called Jagnath Singh ? "

Bertie shook her head. " I can never remember one from another."

" He's one of the political leaders in my district. Personally, I rather like him. Impersonally, I think he ought to be shot."

" Perhaps you'll get a chance to shoot him," Bertie suggested. Something in the recesses of her mind gave a little twist of pain. Could she have brought herself to say such a thing a few years ago ?

Macbeth went on : " You must remember Abdul Salim, Hardyal's friend ? "

" What about Salim ? "

" He's a great admirer of Jagnath's. Between them they're spreading the gospel of Non-co-operation far and wide. My district borders on Amritpore, so I have a dossier on Mr. Salim. He has been busy organising the ryots to

strike against paying their rents. Not very successfully;
so far it's a pretty minor affair, but it could easily spread.
You know how these things do spread in India. Like fire
carried by the wind. They are all so emotional, and so
poor that the silliest promise inflames them. Jagnath Singh
and Abdul Salim are both clever, tenacious men, and they
are only two of God knows how many more. If war should
break out they'll think it a God-given opportunity to make
things hot for us. And that's where the Police come in."

She said slowly : " And Hardyal, what about him ? "

" Oh, Hardyal is all right."

" You really trust him ? "

" Trust Hardyal ? Good God, why not ? "

" He, too, is Salim's friend."

" But we mustn't forget that he is also Jacques' friend,
and ours."

She shook her head, flushing a little. " I don't know.
I feel that Hardyal has changed from the time when we
first knew him. Why did he never go back to England ?
Imagine, when he had the chance, when his father wished
it, he preferred to tutor with some obscure Eurasian pro-
fessor, and chose Calcutta University instead of Oxford.
There are other things about him that I don't quite understand. . . . I can't even tell you what they are. But I'm
conscious, whenever I see him, of a . . . of a . . ."

" Yes ? " He was looking at her attentively.

" A coldness."

" You mean, towards you especially ? "

She hesitated. " Yes, I suppose so."

Macbeth was silent for a moment, then he said gently :
" There is something you must bear in mind. You are an
Englishwoman and Hardyal is an Indian. No matter how
warm his friendship for you, there must always be a barrier, and he understands that. He can't do anything about
it, even if he should want to."

She brushed this aside impatiently. " Men stick together. You have loyalties which we women can never
quite understand."

" Perhaps we are not as possessive as you are."

The remark, coming from him, surprised her. Once
more she sank down on the bed beside him. " I don't know.

It's only when one feels one cannot have something that one becomes possessive. Strong people are hardly ever possessive, are they? I wonder whether my love for Jacques isn't based on the suspicion that I don't really possess him. No one will possess him, not even his mother."

He clasped her hand. "Jacques is awfully decent. Really too decent."

"Can one be too decent?"

"I think so. Father is. Jacques . . . Hardyal."

She withdrew her hand. "I don't share your view of Hardyal. I used to. I don't now."

"Aren't you, perhaps, a bit jealous of Jacques' friendship for him?"

For a moment she looked as though she might burst into violent denials, then she shrugged. "Oh, I'm sick of pretending! I suppose I am jealous of everything that concerns Jacques. Everything, every one!"

He nodded. "I understand. But you know, a chap like Jacques is a sort of accident in society. I've often thought of it. You wonder and wonder how they happen, why they are born into the same circumstances as the rest of us, and in our time. They are really not one of us, at all. They don't seem to need us as we need them."

She looked at him strangely. "I wonder! I wonder whether Jacques' whole nature isn't on a different plane from ours. Whether, because his need, like his generosity, is much deeper than ours, he has put a curb on himself, knowing that he can never receive a quarter of what he gives."

Macbeth accepted this without comment and for a long time the cousins remained silent. But their faces wore happier expressions, they felt drawn towards each other, warmed and comforted by this exchange of confidence.

43

As THE August sun forced its way through a bank of cloud above Amritpore, it sucked a scalding breath from the sodden plains. The river, like a gorged yellow serpent, crept past fields and jetties, swallowing funeral pyres and more than one unwary life. A few birds fluttered, a crocodile rose from the flood, bellowed its hellish message, and sank. A man standing on the ramparts of the Fort would have seen spread beneath and around him, a brown pastiche slowly giving way to tides of delicate, timid green.

But to-day rain and sun had made a yellow puddle of the factory yard where the nim trees laid their fragile shadows. The noise of the factory was on a diminished scale, for half the vats remained unused and two of the great boilers had been sealed off. Beyond, the compound acres which in the past grew indigo were now reverting gradually to millet and pulse. Familiar, discarded forms revived and moved with a tentative air.

Jacques St. Remy, strolling between the empty vats, wondered why he was not depressed by this atmosphere of desuetude. But he found a strange charm in the muted sound of the place, in the phases of dye which peeled away from the vat walls and lay like petals on the bottom, where a lizard blinked in a morsel of shade. The boiler rooms had a different smell; there the machines were shedding their scale, an invisible principle converting them to another fate. In the midst of life we are in death : he had never thought of the words as possessing a coherent meaning but now he felt that he understood them for the first time. The energy of death embraced this cold plaster and inert metal while the energy of life throbbed ceaselessly in a farther corner of the plant. He picked up a crumb of dye and threw it at the lizard, which lifted its head and steered away like a tiny battleship battling an invisible sea.

Jacques left the vats and walked slowly towards his office. A few coolies eating their noon meal under the trees turned modestly aside when they saw him. A factory policeman squatting near the well put down the vernacular paper which he'd been reading, and rose, saluting with a listless air. Heat like a steaming lid hung above these human heads, and Jacques felt it pressing on his shoulders as though it sought to crush him to the ground.

He stepped from the glare into his office and found Boodrie collapsed across a desk. The man lifted a pallid face, locks of grey hair falling over his eyes. " I am com-

pletely done up. The assistant surgeon says I am coming
down with dysentery if I do not look out."

Jacques regarded him critically. "You do look seedy,
I must say. Take a week off, old man."

The Eurasian gave a feeble laugh. "A week off!"

"Why not? There's not much going on just now."

Boodrie pulled himself together and wiped his face on
his sleeve.

"The minute your back is turned, or my back, wah!"
The native exclamation escaped him before he could check
it. "The bloody coolies go to sleep or they steal something."

Jacques took off his hat. His drill suit clung to him like
a second skin; he felt light and transparent, but well
enough. These unrelenting summers had accentuated his
remarkable looks, which reminded Boodrie, suddenly, of
a little picture he had of the youthful St. Anthony of Padua.
It struck Boodrie as extremely unfair that any one should
retain youth and resemble St. Anthony when he, himself,
felt old, ugly, and ill.

He said querulously : "I should go to the hills."

Jacques was looking among the letters and papers on
his desk, hoping to find a letter from Bertie. "Yes, you
should. Why don't you?"

"And who will pay, may I ask?"

"Oh, Lord! Put it on the factory account and stop
grousing."

"The factory account? Oh, my! And the factory will
pay with what—with cowries? With *kankar*?"

Jacques sat down and lighted a cigarette. He felt the
sweat slip down his body, leaving a chill. The indefatigable
white ants had built a new set of tunnels under the edge of
his desk and he held a match against the little mud structure, baking it until it crumbled and the disgusting little
occupants tumbled out. "No letters have come for me, I
suppose?"

"Nothing from Miss Wood, if that's what you mean.
She is too busy enjoying herself in Gambul, no doubt. Ha
ha!"

Jacques looked at him. "Trot along home, why don't
you?"

Boodrie's eyes glittered with fever. "I have been

thinking and thinking. This war ought to help us. It is
bound to bring back indigo. All German due-stuffs will be
cut off. What a chance ; my God, what a chance ! "

Jacques smiled. "An irony, isn't it ? When we need
new boilers, new linings for the vats—for all the vats. New
pressure-gauges, new this, new that, new everything. But
you know, when something has started to die you can't
bring it back."

"Bosh ! " retorted the Eurasian angrily. " What has
started to die ? We have the factory. All we need is money."
He stared at the young man, who sprawled in his chair
across the room. "Twenty-five thousand rupees would
make all the difference. When I was in Calcutta two weeks
ago every one said that this was our great chance. You
will make lakhs, they told me, lakhs ! "

A yellow wasp floated into the room and attempted to
settle on his face. He brushed it away violently. " Lakhs ! "
He continued to stare at Jacques. " Why in God's name
do you not ask your friends ? "

" Ask my friends for what ? "

" For a loan. There is Ganpat Rai and Colonel Macbeth. They love you. There is Miss Wood. She has money
of her own. Not one of them would refuse you."

Jacques watched the stricken wasp crawl along the
matting. He said slowly : " No, not one of them would
refuse me."

" Then why do you waste time like this ? Why . . . why
. . . when you could do something . . ."

Jacques remained silent, and Boodrie gestured despairingly. " I do not understand you. I have never understood
you. You do not care about anything. You do not go to
church. You do not go to confession. You are utterly without ambition and responsibility. Everything is going to pot
and there you sit smoking cigarettes ! "

Jacques said nothing, but he was thinking : The poor
blighter has hit on the truth : everything is going to pot
and here I sit smoking cigarettes.

He thought of the disused vats and the rusting machines,
objects used and forgotten, ancient ideas, lost battles.
Catastrophe's perverse beauty obsessed him as he remembered the breaking of the monsoon in Gambul, the splitting

crash of lightning as it struck a tree, the look of a hillside
as it careered downward into the lake. Then he thought of
the ghats by the river where once he and Hardyal had seen
a body rear up and confront them from its convulsion of
flame. And now, now the war ! There was a secret here,
a fascination in the paroxysm of death.

Boodrie's voice interrupted his thoughts. " You should
go and see Ramdatta the moneylender."

" Why Ramdatta ? "

" You should speak with him." Boodrie played with
pencils on the desk. " He would be flattered if you were
to stop and see him some day when you are riding past his
village."

" Why should I bother to flatter Ramdatta ? "

Boodrie dropped the pencils in agitation. " Ramdatta
is influential. Should we ever find ourselves in a fix, he
might be useful. It is just as well to keep in with him. And
you do not keep in by hobnobbing with others such as that
scoundrel Abdul Salim."

Jacques was amused. " What on earth have you got
against Salim ? "

" I have nothing against him, personally. But Government has. You know that he has been making trouble
among Ramdatta's tenants ? "

" I can't see that it has anything to do with you or me."

" Sometimes you talk like a fool. If Ramdatta's people
won't pay him, well then . . . what is he to do, pray ? "

" Oh, pray away—don't ask me ! "

" But it is very important to ask you. We are all in the
same boat with men like Ramdatta."

Jacques shrugged. " I think you need a pill or something. Why don't you go home and take one ? Take
several."

When the Eurasian had gone, muttering and mysterious,
Jacques tried to concentrate on his work, but it was too
hot and his thoughts kept breaking away. He was consumed
with unrest and uneasiness. War ! For three weeks Europe
had been at war. The Germans were sweeping everything
before them—and here he sat smoking cigarettes ! He laid
his useless left arm on the table and stared at the smooth,
blunt stump of flesh. He was young, and the thought of

war filled him with inexpressible emotion. But what could he do? What was he good for? All yesterday afternoon he had sat and listened while his mother and Father Sebastien discussed the war. The Germans were in Belgium, headed towards the Channel ports. Madame thought of Gisele in her convent at Bruges. " *Impossible !* " she exclaimed, while the impossible was taking place before her. " *Impossible !* "

War was ridiculous. This one must surely end before it had really got under way. Who cared about Servia? Who, really, cared about anything enough to go to war for it? This was a typical Prussian gesture. Bismarck was dead and there was not another man in Germany equal to the task of winning such a war. The Kaiser's generals would betray him. The French army was invincible. The English would never permit the situation to pass out of their control. The Pope himself would intervene and the whole Catholic world rise against this affront to the peace of God.

But Liége had fallen, and in Father Sebastien's little church the candles burned for the succour of France and for the souls of those already dead. As far as they were concerned, certainly, the war was over almost as soon as it had begun, and for those who had loved them hope itself was over. But the little dark-faced Christians lifted their chi-chi voices and their prayers to mingle with the chirrup of squirrels and the echo-less voice of the brain-fever bird.

War !

Outside Madame's house the pipul leaves rustled in the hot air and shutters of heat stirred the parched flowers. It was difficult for Jacques to believe that the world was not moribund under this siege, that it was not here in its entirety—naked, sweating, burning in its native fevers.

War !

He thought of Bertie. It was ten days since she had written and her last letter had seemed to him cold and detached. She wrote about the war, about impersonal things. He knew she was bitterly hurt and angry that he had not gone to Gambul, but he had counted on her forgiveness and understanding. Now he thought : She does understand, but she won't forgive. She wants to hurt me, to force me. His love had become a perpetual ache, a chronic longing compounded of desire and the instinct towards inviting and inflicting injury. Well, if she would not write, then neither would he. Let her suffer too, let her wonder what had happened to him, let her wake up in the night and lie sleepless, twisting under the hot sheets, limbs and brain on fire with memory.

Now as he sat before his desk in the white-washed office he brooded over the past. There seemed to be an incredible aura of innocence and serenity about those days which war had thrust into a distance as a storm sometimes thrusts a fragment of landscape, and one sees it shining beyond one's reach. Those days in Gambul when they walked or rode together along the narrow mountain roads. Nights when the moonlight seemed to inclose them in its special substance as they lay on the terrace below the Macbeths' house and listened to the nighthawk sound its copper gong in the valley. Her body lying beside him took on something of the moon's pallor as it stirred, cool and fragrant, under his touch.

He relived that last year of her absence in England ; it had been a strange experience during which both contrived, somehow, to banish the actual for the future, and to exist in a state of physical suspense which had held them both in an identical mood. But this exaltation, in the end, proved unequal before the breathless hour of the reunion. Separation had bred desperation, it fed their appetite but not their love. The truth was, something was dying within them ; they were obsessed by unconfessed fears, and stared blindly towards a hope which was gradually becoming dull and inadequate.

Jacques decided that concentration on mundane affairs was beyond him. He flung the papers into a drawer and left the office. Outside, the heat fell upon him like a tiger, and he gasped. The thought of home was repugnant, for there as everywhere, life had passed into a coma. Across the sea a world was splitting apart, but in Amritpore the brown horde drowsed, starved, scratched itself, shrugged. In the developing struggle, what could there be for them ? They breathed as best they might under an accumulation of years which had no memory, no clangour, no echo.

Their own past had been lost to them—and it was left to strangers, to intruders, to revive it.

Jacques craved the company of youth, the feeling of the storm just as when he was a child he longed to run out into the downpour and the lightning. A servant brought his bicycle and he rode through the gates towards Hardyal's house. The roads were still deserted, since several hours must pass before Amritpore came to life in the cool of the evening. As he approached the gates of Mrs. Lyttleton's house he slowed, more than half tempted to go in and call on his old friend. They met rarely and had little to say to each other. Jacques knew that her mind was failing and the knowledge hurt him, for when they did meet the mists before her lightened and lifted and he encountered the old, clear, familiar glance. What, he wondered, would she have to say about this war, she who had lived through so many? He wheeled in an indecisive circle before the sandstone pillars, then continued on his way. What Mrs. Lyttleton or any one else had to say about the war could make no difference. War had come. No one had been able to stop it, no one!

He pedalled unhurriedly under the shadow of the mango trees which bordered the road, and presently found himself near the spot where Hanif had been killed. Beyond the trees lay the soggy fields where a few big blue buffaloes were grazing. Jacques dismounted and laid his machine against a pile of *kankar* beside the road. It was here, on this spot, that the police had found Hanif's body. Madame St. Remy bought the plot of ground nearby, and there they buried him. Now Jacques walked to the grave to make sure that the rain and the jackals had not been at work. The simple white-limed surface bore Hanif's name and his age, and under these a single word : *Khatm*, which is the Moslem *Finis*.

44

JACQUES found his friends gathered as usual in Ganpat Rai's drawing-room. They sat or reclined among a welter of cushions and goat-hair rugs, under a frilled punkah which barely stirred the warm, spicy air. Besides himself there were several visitors, two young Mohammedans and a trio of Hardyal's cousins. When Jacques was announced they rose, and he had an impression of embarrassment swiftly dissimulated, as though a conversation had been abruptly nipped in the bud.

Ganpat Rai, clothed in a thin dhoti and holding a palm-leaf fan, put his arm around Jacques' shoulder. " Do you know Mr. Mahmud Ali and Mr. Hosain ? You have, I think, met our cousins."

The young men exchanged salutes. " Sit," Ganpat Rai commanded them, genially. " It is only our young friend, Jacques."

Hardyal patted a cushion beside him. " Tell us what you think of the war. Will the Germans reach Paris ? "

" Will they take the Channel ports ? "

" Ah, if they do—England is lost ! "

" Shall we have conscription in India ? "

" If so, I shall most certainly resist."

" Ha ! Easy for you to talk so big just now, Sheo Dyal ! But when the time comes we shall do as we are told, just as usual."

" Yes, like Salim's cousin Dr. Feroze."

" Feroze was not told to do anything—he went of his own free will."

" Salim says he always was a lickboot of the Government."

" My brother Shaukat is no lickboot, but he too has gone into the Army."

" However, Jacques, here, will not have to go. You are lucky, Jacques ! "

" Am I ? " He lowered himself on a cushion between Hardyal and one of the young Mohammedans. He liked to sit on the floor, a posture which makes formality difficult. " I'm glad someone thinks so."

Hardyal repeated impatiently : " Tell us ! Tell us what you have heard about the war ! "

" You know as much about it as I do."

" How can that be, Sahib ? We are told little or nothing."

The speaker was Mahmud Ali, a teacher in Amritpore's

High School. Ganpat Rai looked at him. " Come now,
Mahmud ! You read the papers, do you not ? For myself
I refuse to worry too much about the war at this early date.
We must not forget the French Army. But Jacques, my
poor boy ! It is your France that is overrun. Ah, how it
must feel to be a Frenchman ! " His eyes were moist, and
the young men lowered theirs out of deference. This
emotional coming-to-the-point would have been impossible
among Englishmen, but among these Indians it seemed
natural enough, since with them sympathy, pity, curiosity
are not ingredients to be deliberately excluded from conversation.

Jacques shrugged. " Good Lord, what difference does
it make whether one is French or what ? In the end, we're
all human."

Hosain said quickly : " Yet if India were invaded the
English would fight only to preserve their own skins. The
rest of us would have to shift for ourselves."

" Assuming you would not fight for yourselves," observed Jacques, coolly. He spoke, not from any honest
objection to Hosain's remark, but from an instinctive dislike
of the young man, whose appearance was unprepossessing
and who never failed to inject the note of grievance.

Ganpat Rai interposed : " What, after all, is the question ? Men are right or they are wrong. It is essential that
we choose our own side and stick to it."

" That would be easy were the issues clear," said Hardyal in a low voice. " I admit that for myself they are not
so clear."

" They are clear to me," returned his father, giving
him a troubled glance. " Surely you and I know where we
stand ? "

There was a brief silence, and Jacques wondered
whether this had been the point under discussion when he
entered. Mahmud Ali now cleared his throat. " But do
we stand, sir ? Sometimes it seems to me that we spend
much of our time in crawling."

A murmur, half protest and half approval, greeted this
remark. Ganpat Rai made a gesture of impatience. " Why
must you young men always exaggerate ? Why must you,
in particular, exaggerate the wrong things ? What is im-

portant to-day is the scope and the significance of this war. We stand in as grave peril as the rest of the world. On that we are agreed, are we not ? "

" *Be shak !* " came the swift Urdu response in one voice. The young Hindus stared anxiously at their host, but said nothing. Ganpat Rai went on : " It is important that we see, or try to see, what it is that we all want. For myself I have found that what men want, what they think, and what they do, remain for the most part widely separated things."

" Nevertheless, they work together towards an end," said Hardyal.

These discussions always interested Jacques. He knew that they originated in a deep inner discontent from which few of his Indian friends seemed immune. Yet it seemed to him that when men argued politically what emerged was their smallness, their egocentricity, their pitiable assumption of clairvoyance. With Indians a sort of hysteria was added to all this, making it difficult to debate with them without at the same time wounding their susceptibilities and exciting their passionate resentment. Would Hardyal, he wondered, escape the infection ? Jacques met Ganpat Rai's glance and read the same question in his kind, expressive eyes. He's seen it coming, too, thought Jacques, and suffered a pang of love and fear for his friend, as he would have suffered had someone told him that Hardyal was doomed to an incurable disease.

Ganpat Rai turned to Mahmud Ali.

" Now tell me, Mahmud, do you and Hardyal desire the same things ? "

" Certainly, certainly we do ! What else ? We want only our rights."

" That is most original. I live in your world. What is available to me, is, surely, available to you ? "

" Oh, sir ! How can you say so ? I am not even able to procure for myself a university education."

" And how many Englishmen or Frenchmen do you imagine enjoy that advantage ? "

Hardyal answered for his friend : " If all may not, then Mahmud is still right ! "

" Also it is well known that under English rule Brahmins get all the good jobs," complained Mr. Hosain, with dreadful tactlessness. Every one laughed, and Mahmud Ali gave his co-religionist a sarcastic glance.

Ganpat Rai pursued his advantage. "We always get back to the beginning, do we not? Hosain would substitute Islam for England and call that a fair solution."

"Why not?" muttered Hosain. "Islam has a better right than some others."

"That also I have heard. If one listens long enough one hears always the same things."

"But that is because there is no change, no reform, no justice!" Hosain was becoming excited. "One of our leaders has said that if we Moslems are not careful we shall become like the Jews, a religion without a country."

"You more resemble the Catholics," observed Ganpat Rai, slyly, "with your vicar in Turkey."

There was a scandalised pause, but they were too young and too much in awe of his age and superior wisdom to do more than step gingerly aside from the dynamite which he proffered. Then Mahmud Ali began humbly: "Myself, I cannot be altogether sure of these matters, but Salim says . . ."

"What says Salim?"

A shadow moved behind the screen and the tall bearded Pleader came in. He had kicked off his shoes in the veranda, now he stooped and laid a hand on Ganpat Rai's shoulder. "Do you, my friend, permit these whippersnappers to discuss their betters?"

The barrister reached up and pulled the big man down on a cushion beside him. "They quote you as an oracle."

"Hardyal, my child, a cigarette!"

He folded his legs under him and his bare, strong toes stuck out on either side. Ganpat Rai watched him closely as he lighted the cigarette. "Tell me, from where have you come?"

"From the Collector Sahib's."

"Ah, I thought so!"

"But you are not surprised? Why should you be? This is not the first time I have been summoned to such a conference."

Jacques felt the gathering tension. It was Mahmud Ali who spoke first : " Did he threaten you ? "

They leaned forward, their eyes stony. But Salim laughed. " How little you understand these people ! He offered me a cigar. Allah, how it burned my unsuspecting tongue."

" But what happened ? " demanded Hardyal impatiently. " Tell us what he said. Speak frankly, we are all friends here."

Salim glanced at Jacques, then shrugged. " What does it matter who hears ? There were Government chuprassies listening at every door. Well, the Collector was affable, even friendly. You know how disarming they can be when they are sure neither of themselves nor of you. We talked of this and that. He spoke of the increasing seriousness of the war. It would, he declared, be prolonged, for the Germans were proving themselves far more formidable than any one had dreamed. Had they not been preparing for this for the past twenty years ? Their frank boasting had thrown dust in the eyes of the world. Ah, yes, it looked serious, most serious. On this point the Collector and I agreed, *ad nauseam*. From there he went on to emphasise the necessity of free men sticking together, but I thought it best to let the injunction pass, for the moment. He dwelt at some length on the loyal support which the Government was receiving from the public, and how charmingly he alluded to the patriotism of my cousin Feroze, now with a regiment of Punjabies, and also of your brother Shaukat, training at Nasik ! When an Englishman desires to flatter you the process is so delicate, so subtle, that you are in gravest danger of not discovering what has befallen your virtue until nine months afterwards ! "

They met this with laughter, Jacques joining with them. Then Hardyal asked : " But where did all this lead you, Sahib ? "

" Well, it led me charmingly to believe that for the first time in my humble career I have attained a certain eminence in the eyes of high officialdom. I, a mere Pleader in the district court ; poor, practically unknown beyond the limits of my native town ! It seems that I now constitute something of a splinter in the august flesh of the Raj. I ventured to point out the absurdity of my position *vis-a-vis* his own. After all, I reminded him, my personal history during the past few years could scarcely be described as lurid. I have lost a good half of my practice—clients do not incline naturally to one who stands in doubtful odour with the authorities. My touts report a distinct falling away in all quarters. In order to live I have had to sell some of my belongings. Several of my close friends have dropped me. True, I have made others, I have even accumulated what in a larger arena might be described as a political following. But Allah ! What can the sum total of these activities amount to in an insignificant segment of Empire such as Amritpore ? "

His sarcasm stirred the uneasy silence. No one seemed to know what to say next, and it was Ganpat Rai who made the first move, his profound gaze challenging the other's. " In the end, did you part friends ? "

Salim did not reply at once, but when he did it was with electrifying passion. " Friends ! He offered me his hand, there in the open door of his office, before the eyes of his servants ! And I, too late I recognised the manœuvre designed to put me in the position of a fellow sportsman pledged not to deliver a foul blow. My God ! These English."

" And you, did you take his hand ? "

" Why not ? I am an Oriental. These gestures mean nothing."

" Why did you not oppose him frankly ? "

" Because I am not an Englishman."

The barrister slammed his palm-leaf fan on his knees. " Bah, how you quibble ! "

Salim spoke on a quieter note. " I do not believe that what is in store for the world is just another game of football on a universal scale, nor do I hold that political immorality can be palmed off on us disguised as political necessity. We are not fools. ' Stand beside us in our hour of need,' cry our masters, ' and when the common danger is past you shall have your reward ! ' But I would ask our Collectors and Policemen, our Lat Sahibs, this question : ' Why can you not bring yourselves to forget the military rebellion of 1857, and in order to enable us to stand beside you, and beside each other, make colonels and generals out of our sepoys, and train them in the use of heavy artillery and the complexities of modern warfare? If death is the final equality between men, then we must first learn to live together.'"

"Bravo!" exclaimed Ganpat Rai, sarcastic in his turn. "Why did you not visit this eloquence upon the Collector when you had the opportunity?"

"I do not choose to waste my eloquence on dunderheads."

Ganpat Rai made a wild gesture of the fan. "You are utterly without judgment."

The other's temper rose once more like wine to the surface, and a responsive tremor went through the listeners. "I tell you, the Raj will use this war as an excuse for thrusting us back from where we started. It will appeal to our patriotism, even to our venality, in face of a common enemy. Time enough, says the Raj—time enough after the battle has been won. And it will make the same vague promises which have not changed for the past sixty years. The Raj will remain sole judge of the ripeness of time. The Raj will decide when, if ever, adult human beings are to emerge from kindergarten."

"But can you honestly hold that the intrigues and squabbles of a handful of illiterate ryots are reason for inciting to unrest, to violence even, at such a time?"

Salim looked at him. "Why not? Does the Raj give a damn about the ryots? It is far too busy fighting its war abroad and supporting its moneylenders at home, to worry about the ryots. If this is not the time to force the issue, then there never will be a time. Not for us. For the Raj, yes. For the Raj, endless time. Listen, in Ahmedabad, Mohandas Gandhi is actually recruiting for the Government! Everywhere men who should have learned their lesson succumb like fish to the same rotten bait. The time to strike is now, when the iron is hot. Else we shall wake up to find it cold and heavy on our wrists and ankles."

Ganpat Rai replied sombrely: "Men are going to die like flies before this war is finished. There is going to be violence enough for the most bloodthirsty amongst us."

Salim's hands closed into fists as they rested on his knees.

"You have surrendered to the virus of the West, my friend. It has made you sentimental."

The young men held their breath for as long as the silence lasted, then Ganpat Rai turned and laid his hand across Salim's shoulder. He said gently : "You and I disagree, as always, but do not let us quarrel. There are others . . . leave it to them. This is my house and you are my friend—for me, that is sufficient."

It looked for a moment as though the fiery Mohammedan would resist this appeal, but Hardyal came to the rescue.

"It is sufficient for all of us that you remain friends ! As for me, I am stiff from long sitting." He turned to Jacques. "It is cooler outside, now. Shall we walk ? "

They rose and Hardyal smiled at his friends. "There are matters I wish to discuss with Jacques. We shall return very soon."

45

HEAT rose from the ground and crawled towards them from every side as they strolled past the zenana gate to the end of the garden. A flock of mynas twittered beside a flooded tank and there was a hint of freshness in the air, but Jacques felt the sweat start out on him at every step. He was glad, however, to escape from the argument, which had become oppressive.

Hardyal had brought a palm-leaf fan which he waved before them as they walked, Jacques in his crumpled drill suit, Hardyal in a loose muslin shirt and dhoti. Where the garden ended on a slight eminence they could see the river changing colour with the changing light. Clouds were heaped in an ornate mass whose edges glowed with subdued fire.

The young men said little until they reached the boundary of the garden, where under a row of eucalyptus trees they found a stone bench and sat down. The panorama before them contained little that seemed important ; they watched an umbrella supported on two naked brown legs bob along a soggy road, and two humped grey bullocks dragging a *ruth*. Life was everywhere, but it remained concealed, muted, awaiting a signal to declare itself in the sudden spark of village hearths and the homeward flight of birds.

Hardyal said at last : " You must not misunderstand Abdul Salim."

" On the contrary, I understand him very well."

" If what he said to-day were to reach the ears of a Government official . . ."

" You mean through me ? Surely you know me better ! "

" Forgive me. The war has made us all unsure of ourselves, and of one another."

Both were silent, then Hardyal asked: " You like Salim ? "

" You always ask me that and I always reply : Yes, I like him. What is more, I admire him, though I fear he will not get very far."

" Because he is too outspoken ? "

Jacques nodded, then he said : " In a way I envy him. There is always something thrilling about a man who will not back down."

" I like to hear you say it. People do not, as a rule, admire Salim. His brand of courage makes demands on them—it makes them uncomfortable."

Jacques pondered. " He is revolutionary, of course, and that is unique in India."

" Yet I sometimes think that he is not wholly aware of his own tendency. Revolt is instinctive with him."

" Yet he remains a good Moslem."

" Well, liberal compromise doesn't offer much scope to the Moslems, does it ? Salim realises that. He realises that they are still stuck with their limitations."

" Like the Brahmins."

" And the Catholics."

" Not to mention the Jews ! "

Both smiled, feeling the air clear between them. Jacques shook his head. " Damn it, I wish I had it in me to be a political animal ! " Hardyal gave him an affectionate look. " Sometimes your incapacity for faith troubles me. Then again, I seem to understand a little. You are essentially Gallic, and they were the first to ripen."

" And will be the first to rot."

" That I did not say. Certainly they are proving themselves vigorously now. You say you do not believe, that you are not ' political ', yet if you were able, you would fight ? "

" Of course."

" Then I do not understand."

" One hates to be left out."

Both were conscious of a difference between them, a difference not in love or in sympathy, but in passion. Jacques tried to explain :

" It's like having one brick after another knocked away from under you. Hanif's death did not help . . . I have thought and thought about that death, its stupidity, its waste. Then, when I listen to your father and Salim argue . . ."

Hardyal interrupted quickly : " Ah, Hanif's death was cruel, but it was in the nature of an accident."

" Was it ? He was murdered. Behind it all lies the intention. If I could ever bring myself to believe that the intention stems from men's essential sanity, their morality . . ." He shrugged and laid his crippled arm on his knee. " Was this an accident ? Here again, I find myself wondering. I was up in that tree. I felt deserted, friendless, as poor Hanif must have felt."

Hardyal ceased waving the palm-leaf fan ; he rested his head on his hand, gazing sideways at his friend. Jacques went on meditatively :

" I remember distinctly how it felt to be left in that tree all by myself. I thought the leopard was stalking me. Pretty soon I was sure. And I was so bloody frightened. . . ." He drew a sharp breath, then laughed. " Anyhow, the damned rifle went off. I don't know, I wouldn't swear, now, that I pulled the trigger in order to break the suspense and release myself, or whether it happened of itself."

" And you think that what you call your faith has suffered a similar fate ? "

" Doesn't it happen, more or less, to almost every one ? "

Hardyal nodded broodingly. " For me, too, there was a leopard . . . but it came out of the sunlight, like a friend."

Jacques waited for the confidence, but Hardyal said no more. They watched the clouds build and rebuild vast citadels of light and purple, a single shaft striking the distant line of the canal. Hardyal broke the silence at last : " However, I did not bring you here to talk of Abdul Salim or of the past, but to tell you that I am to be married very soon."

Jacques' surprise crept upon him by degrees. " Married ? Good Lord, you've never so much as hinted . . ."

" I thought it better not to speak until I had made up my mind. Now I am sure. Father is pleased, and so are my aunts."

Jacques stared at him. " I don't quite know what to say. If you're happy, then so am I."

Hardyal held the fan before him as though it were a book. " It is something I should have done long ago, but then I was filled with different ideas and aspirations. She is a splendid girl. Our families have known each other for many years."

" Are you in love with her ? "

The other waited a moment, then smiled. " They are strictly orthodox, so naturally I have not set eyes on her nor she on me."

" Oh, good Lord ! "

Hardyal laughed. " What does it matter ? This question of love . . . you know that in India romance does not enjoy the exaggerated importance it does elsewhere."

Jacques hated the false note. " I don't understand ! When we used to discuss these things you agreed that a strong mutual attraction was the best basis for marriage, no matter what happened afterwards."

Hardyal continued to study the fan. Something of its blankness was reflected in his face. " Perhaps the attraction will follow on marriage. It is a safer bet."

Jacques said bitterly : " You sound as if you'd succumbed to the domination of all your aunts ! "

" It is not easy, at a moment's notice, to throw aside the traditions of many thousands of years."

Jacques made a gesture of hopelessness. " A moment's notice ! What people ! Politically, spiritually, you are a match for the world. Socially, you stagger along under the abracadabra of centuries. Hardyal, be honest, tell me . . ."

The other turned a face that was full of emotion. " Yes, I can tell you, but I can tell no one else—not my father, not Salim. You insist that you do not believe in much of anything, but in love you must believe. That is something which has not died in you, as I sometimes think it has died in me. Tell me, now, where in my society shall I find, for instance, a woman like your Bertie ? There are some, of course, but I know none. I do not look for equality and companionship among the women from whom I must choose. Try to understand ! I must marry. I have tried the other thing, for sex becomes a problem only when one tries to live without it. I have responsibilities towards my family. But I am not in love, how can I say that I shall ever be in love ? It is a state of mind, a condition which depends on many other things."

Jacques was moved by his friend's emotion. " On what other things ? "

Hardyal seemed to grope for words ; they came at last, breathlessly :

" It depends on everything that goes to make up a society. You are right when you say that politically and spiritually we can be a match for the world, and you are also right when you remind me that we stagger under the abracadabra of centuries. This has made us sensual rather than passionate, mystical rather than rational. But isn't that bound to happen when the form of a society is stronger than its individuals ? There are times when life seems clear and good, other times when I wonder whether it is not a colossal blunder from beginning to end ! "

Jacques was struck, as he had been struck before, by something that almost invariably occurred when he talked with Indians : they seldom failed to relate their personal problems with larger, indeed with universal considerations, and he wondered whether this were not the inevitable concomitant of a country ruled by outsiders. He found himself at a disadvantage, and, unable to think of anything omniscient, or even comforting, he reverted to the familiar note. " Well, so we are both to be married. Do you think our wives will like each other ? "

Hardyal's features cleared slowly of their strange discontent. He smiled, but said nothing, and in a little while they heard, in the garden behind them, the voices of the other guests. "Jacques ! Hardyal ! Where are you ? "

" It is almost cool enough for a game, if Hardyal will lend me his tennis shoes."

" How provident of you always to forget to bring your own ! "

" Why should I bother when my cousin has fourteen pairs, all of which fit me to perfection ? "

46

ONE AFTERNOON in mid-September Ramdatta the money-lender lay on a string cot under his favourite tree. The air was warm and moist, but a light breeze stirred the mango leaves. Beside Ramdatta's cot squatted a little company of his neighbours ; a Kyeth, or scribe, perched on a camp stool, reading aloud from a pink-tinted vernacular newspaper. He was reading about the European war and the others listened as only natives can listen to the printed word : they listened with an entire concentration of their bodies. Ramdatta's youngest son, a boy of ten, stood behind his father, fanning him with a wand of plumed grass.

The Kyeth's sing-song voice mingled with a creak of well-wheels and the sound of water gushing from its big leather sack. Sundry tinklings and jinglings escaped from the arched door of the house, figures appeared and vanished with a twinkle of feet and a flash of anklets. Nearby, strutted Ramdatta's tame peacock, spreading its tail in a patch of sun. Village life established its peculiar fabric of sound which scarcely varied from day to day or from evening to evening ; an attentive ear would have picked up the running-stitch of birds and squirrels, the steady champing of cattle chewing dry cornstalks in their pens behind their owners' houses, and the soft, incessant crying of a sick child. From fields beyond the village a voice rose high and keen above all the others : " Oh, Allah Din ! Allah Din, oh ! " But the Gift of Heaven, whoever he was, chose to make no reply. The voice wailed on plaintively, then gave up.

"The English ships *Aboukir*, *Hogue* and *Crecy* have been sunk by the Germans," read the Kyeth, and a stir went round the listeners.

"Tobah," exclaimed one, and turned aside to spit.

Ramdatta snapped his plump fingers. "That is nothing. We have many ships, all of them superior. When I was at Bombay in the old days I saw them—like great birds they were, resting on the water. There is no cause for anxiety. We have many, many more, all bigger and better than the Germans'."

The Kyeth waited respectfully for his master to finish, then went on reading. Ramdatta's son, bored, changed the wand from one hand to the other and watched a pair of razor-horned lizards manœuvring for battle on a nearby branch. The sun, slipping west of the village, laid its patina on mud walls covered with little pancakes of cow dung, each with its imprint of a hand. An emaciated cur nursing a row of puppies dragged herself to her feet and wandered away, panting, pursued by her insatiable brood. Tired of watching the lizards, Ramdatta's son transferred his attention to an ant-hill near his feet. He gave it a poke with his toe and watched the startled inhabitants scurry about, clinging tenaciously to their bundles.

"Art thou asleep, my son?" asked Ramdatta softly, and the boy, swallowing his yawns, fanned with renewed vigour.

The moneylender was recovering from an attack of fever which still lingered in his bones; but except for a slight dullness of his eye and a peeling of the lips he showed little sign of illness. The brown flesh grew as firm and as glossy as ever on his big frame, his shaven head shone like a bullet. Hieratic, impressive, he reclined among his cushions, attended by his son, admired by the sycophants who crouched round him.

Jacques St. Remy, riding in through an opening in the village wall, saw this tableau set against the white wall of the house where a rampant tiger had been freshly painted in vermilion. The sound of hooves struck on Ramdatta's ear and he sat up, spilling his shawls and waving the Kyeth into silence. "Behold, a Sahib comes to visit me! Depart, all of you. Send one to take the Sahib's horse."

Jacques dismounted and surrendered his beast to a servant who came running. Ramdatta's coterie melted away but the boy remained, staring shyly as the young man approached. "Hallo, Ramdatta! I come, bringing you quinine."

The moneylender rose and salaamed. There was scarcely a change in his expression, but he was well aware of the many curious and admiring eyes that watched from shadowy doorways; there was something imposing, even noble, in his bearing as he greeted his visitor.

"Huzoor, this is an honour." He turned to his son. "Go and tell them to fetch the chair—the European chair. Hurry!"

The boy scampered off and Jacques gazed quizzically at the moneylender.

"Boodrie gave me to understand that you were practically at death's door!"

"These *Keranies* always exaggerate. They must, to make up for their own lack."

The boy reappeared, proudly ushering two men who staggered under a huge chintz-upholstered chair which they set down a little distance from Ramdatta's cot. This chair was the pride of his heart; he had sent for it several years before, from Bombay, and it was produced only on state occasions. Jacques, assuming a fitting air of dignity, lowered himself into the ample seat and crossed his legs. He wondered a little at all this ceremony. Boodrie, with an air of excitement, bordering on panic, had passed on Ramdatta's invitation, adding the mysterious injunction that Madame was on no account to be told.

"He is a sick man, or he would have come himself to see you."

Jacques, enjoying an afternoon's canter across the plain, saw no reason why he should not drop in on the moneylender. The man had always exercised a sort of fascination over him in spite of the loathing in which he was generally held in Amritpore. Now, as the young man lighted a cigarette Ramdatta returned to his cot, on which he sat cross-legged, the shawls draped over his shoulders. His little son was dismissed and departed, dragging his feet, glancing back at the pale young Sahib who smiled after him. White men were certainly not rare in the village, but Jacques' beauty affected Indians even more profoundly than it did his own kind.

Ramdatta said presently : " It is considerate of you to accept the invitation of a sick and ageing man, Sahib."

Jacques lighted a cigarette and smiled. He knew better than to congratulate his host on his recovery or to compliment him on his appearance, for to do either would have been a breach of etiquette and a direct provocation to the Evil Eye.

Ramdatta crossed his sleek arms on the folds of his shawl.

" I have grave responsibilities and it is sometimes a relief to speak of them to an intelligent and well-informed person. My sons are all devoted and good, but quite without worldly knowledge or ambition. That seems to be the fate of fathers like myself. By our own labours we deprive our children of an essential initiative."

" You can always cut them off with a pice," suggested Jacques, slyly.

The other smiled. " They would straightway become beggars, or worse. No, there is no solution to the problem. One must accept it." His glance slid off Jacques to the ground. " One learns to accept much. There are, however, men who abjure the doctrine of resignation. They believe that by a mere wave of the hand they can move mountains."

Jacques waited, silently enjoying the situation and the taste of his cigarette. He was filled with happiness, because Bertie had written with a renewed passion and yearning, and her letter had fired him with responsive ardour. The reassuring effect of love was to put a distance between himself and his immediate surroundings ; he felt immune from all their uncertainties.

Ramdatta heaved a sigh. " Madame is indeed fortunate in her possession of a son such as you. You have but to marry and produce sons of your own, and you will complete her happiness."

The peacock reappeared. Sumptuous, arrogant, it put its head on one side and listened, aware, as all pampered creatures are, of an alien presence.

Ramdatta went on conversationally : " I have heard

that in the holy book of the Christians it is written that when a child is born he comes into the world with his hands empty, and empty-handed leaves it. But we put it differently : we say that a child comes into the world with hands closed, clutching all his hopes and all his gifts. It is when he dies that he goes forth empty-handed."

Jacques said : "I think I like your version better."

"One must use one's gifts while one has life. One can but conduct oneself according to the potentialities one brings with one from the past creation. Not to do so would be sinful. Nevertheless, I have not found it easy, for the world is full of envious men."

Jacques, realising at once that the conversation had arrived at a crucial stage, schooled his features to a cautious impassivity.

"You and I, Sahib, are in the same case. We were born into a category of men who, to survive, must work, and who by working cannot help but accumulate fortunes which rouse the jealousy and greed even of our friends. But that is the way of the world, is it not ? Even on isolated and forgotten islands there are some who have and some who have not."

"And there are likewise those of whom it is said that there shall be taken from them even that which they have not," observed Jacques with an absent-minded air.

The moneylender gave him a keen glance. "Ah ! That I had not heard, but I believe it."

"However, there are scholars who insist that the statement applies not to worldly wealth but to the attribute of wisdom," Jacques finished, gravely.

A golden smile spread over Ramdatta's features. "Would that you were my son ! There is none other with whom I can converse in such a vein. My family are dunces, my friends liars and worse."

"God forbid ! "

"Nay, it is true." He leaned forward, fixing Jacques with an eye that was suddenly as cold and steady as a cobra's. "But perhaps I am luckier than you, after all, for I at least am not deceived."

Jacques lighted another cigarette as Ramdatta straightened up and stared round him. The courtyard was

empty, the arched door under its vermilion tiger framed
only a bluish, smoky interior.

"Draw your chair closer, Sahib, that we may not have
to raise our voices."

"Must we be so mysterious?"

Ramdatta arranged his plump, well-shaped legs under
him.

"There is no mystery, except perhaps where you are
concerned. Innocence is often a shield in one's childhood, but in men it is folly. I asked you to come here so
that I might, with your permission, exercise for a little while
the prerogatives of a father and extend to you a word of
warning and advice."

The young man shrugged resignedly. "Well?"

"Let us not beat about the bush. You are a friend of
Ganpat Rai's son Hardyal. Ganpat Rai I have always
admired. Hardyal also. But men change with the times,
and time has most strangely changed Hardyal. No, do not
be offended if I venture to suggest that in Hardyal's case
the change has not been for the best."

"The suggestion offends me, nevertheless."

"Would that I could withdraw it! But Hardyal has
fallen into the wrong hands. He is seen everywhere with
Abdul Salim, and Salim, as you know, or should know, is
under police surveillance."

Jacques felt a stab of anxiety. "Since when?"

"For months past. It is no secret—Salim himself knows
it. But he is a fanatic, and nothing short of a jail sentence
will cure him."

Jacques started angrily. "He is, I believe, fully entitled
to his convictions!"

"Ah, Sahib! You talk like a child. What are Salim's
convictions? He is an obstructionist. Sooner or later the
Government will lose patience and clap him into jail, but
in the meantime he is at large, he is vocal and popular, and
becomes increasingly so. Young men like Hardyal are
attracted by his teaching because it is novel. But Salim
will end by carrying all his friends off to jail with him."

"And what, exactly, is this teaching to which you so
violently object?" Jacques spoke sarcastically, in an
attempt to cover his real concern.

The moneylender shrugged. " You must have heard as much about it as any one, for you see him often. You meet at the house of Ganpat Rai, and Hardyal himself carries Salim's words of wisdom into your home, does he not ? They use your friendship as a blind. Nay ! Do not lose your temper with me, Sahib. I speak for your own good. Salim has been warned repeatedly by the Collector himself. Yet he continues to hold meetings in his house, he even addresses public gatherings on the Maidan and in the bazaar. He has toured the Province with that notorious agitator Jagnath Singh. Well, I say let him risk his own neck if he so desires—who cares ? But what right has he to involve young, idealistic, and inexperienced men like Hardyal in these criminal activities ? "

" You use strong language, my friend ! "

" I have strong feelings. You must forgive me, Sahib— I speak for us all."

" Speak for yourself, if you must. I fail to see where I come in."

Stillness descended on Ramdatta, then he made a strange gesture of his hands, bringing the palms together in an attitude of prayer, and letting them fall in his lap. " Well, then, Sahib—hear me out. Two days ago Abdul Salim was at the village of my brother-in-law. He collected the people around him and outlined to them a plan for the non-payment of their rents and taxes. In my brother-in-law's village, and indeed in my own, there are a certain number of Moslems. They are shiftless, in debt almost to a man, yet they kick and scream against paying interest. Why ? Because to charge or to pay interest is contrary to their religious code. Every Hindu pays his interest, or at least accepts the responsibility even when he is unable to meet it. Well, Abdul Salim has exploited this situation to such an extent that he has succeeded in rousing, everywhere, something approaching organised revolt in the villages. The Police are worried, so are the district magistrates. Salim is poisoning the public mind against the landlords and even against the Sircar. He has succeeded so well that many Hindus have banded with Moslems in a flat refusal to meet their obligations or to work them off in labour. In some cases they have resisted lawful attempts

K

at eviction or confiscation. And do you know what Salim tells these people ? He tells them that before the English came the land was free, tilled and tended in common. But, says Salim, the conquering English, finding no documents or proofs of ownership, parcelled out the land as they pleased and distributed it amongst their favourite Zamindars, who hold it in perpetual ownership. It is easy, is it not, Sahib, to guess the effect of such talk on unlettered peasants ? But what Salim is unable to explain is this : If the peasants will not pay their dues to the Zamindars, how are the Zamindars to pay the yearly revenues to the Government ? If we moneylenders cannot collect our legal rate of interest, on what basis are we to continue making loans ? "

While he talked the sweat had started out afresh on Ramdatta's flesh and his eyes began to glow with fever. Jacques had listened attentively, less to the man's complaint, the sense of which caused him no great surprise, than to a special subterranean quality in his voice. It was a quality which he was sure had not been there earlier in the conversation, one which seemed to develop gradually like a fissure under the fluent speech. His own thoughts hidden under an air of judicious consideration, Jacques smoked in silence, turning over the possible significance of that odd, unfamiliar note. It came to him suddenly that what he'd caught was the note of fear. It is not a human note, for like a child's cry of pain or a lover's unintelligible mutter it lies quite outside the subtle inclosure of language. Jacques had heard that note before : hearing it now he was moved to a curious excitement, a sense almost of revulsion.

Ramdatta was afraid. Afraid of Abdul Salim, afraid of Hardyal ! Ramdatta the Great, the omnipotent Ramdatta, friend of the Police, privileged crony of officialdom, sumptuous, engaging old sophisticate . . . there he sat, secretly frightened out of his clever wits ! To Hardyal, Jacques had observed that there is always something thrilling about a man who will not back down. The thought recurred to him now as he saw the moneylender for the first time as more than a familiar figure, more even than a symbol : saw him as that opponent against whom Abdul Salim would not, would positively never, back down.

Ramdatta broke the silence which had followed his last question.

" So now perhaps you can see, Sahib, what I mean when I insist that I speak for all of us, for you as well as for myself."

" You mean to say that you think we're all in the same boat ? "

" Can you doubt it ? "

" And that Salim may attempt to capsize the whole bloody *sub cheez* ? "

" It is no joking matter, Sahib."

" For you, no—I can see that. But what I still fail to see is where Madame and I—where I specially—come into the picture, or shall we stick to the simile of the boat ? "

Ramdatta gazed at him thoughtfully. " You believe that Abdul Salim would not dare to encroach on your preserves ? Does the thought reassure you ? "

Jacques laughed. " Good Lord, man ! I feel under no compulsion to strike attitudes."

" You may find yourself compelled to strike an attitude, sooner or later."

" Against my friends ? " Jacques leaned forward in the chair of state. " Would you like to hear the truth as far as I'm concerned, Ramdatta ? If my mother's half-starved coolies decided to burn down the factory to-morrow, I wouldn't lift a finger to stop them."

The other smiled faintly. " So Boodrie has informed me many times." He hesitated, the smile melting into the corners of his full, childish mouth. " I was a coolie once, in Bombay. I sweated. I starved. But I survived. It was an instructive experience, one well calculated to cure a man of any illusions he may have cherished about his fellows. I have learned that there are but few complete human beings in society, Sahib. The rest are cattle."

The smile had vanished and from the rich brown oval of his face his eyes gazed piercingly at Jacques. " That is my attitude, if you wish to call it one. And I repeat, Sahib, that sooner or later you will yourself be forced to assume an attitude which, in the nature of things, must be opposed to such men as Abdul Salim and Hardyal."

" In the nature of what things, Ramdatta ? "

" You are not really obtuse, Sahib."

" I do but ask enlightenment."

Ramdatta hesitated, then he said slowly :

" It distresses me that I should be the instrument of
your enlightenment. I do not hope to be forgiven, but I
have no alternative."

Jacques cried impatiently, " Must we talk riddles all
afternoon ? "

Ramdatta made no answer. He rose from the cot and
reaching under it pulled out a highly decorated tin box
fastened with a brass padlock. From somewhere in the
folds of his clothing he produced a bunch of keys. Jacques
watched him unlock the box and lay back the lid ; he was
reminded of his mother's japanned dispatch case with all
its little compartments, the locks of hair, the letters, the
pair of tiny enamelled foxes.

Ramdatta groped among the contents of his box and
lifted out a large package covered in oilskin and tied with
black tape. This he opened and after a glance at the
contents, laid them on Jacques' lap.

" Read them, Sahib. Take your time. There is no
hurry."

He retired to his cot, folding his legs under him, clasping his shawl across his breast. Shade lay heavy on the
ground and there was a pleasant smell of cooking in the
air. The peacock, struck by an athletic notion, shot suddenly upward and alighted on a neighbouring roof, where
it perched motionless as the light died slowly, reluctantly,
on its jewelled breast.

47

An hour later as Jacques rode away from the village he met
the returning herds driven by children whose shrill voices
pierced the dusty haze. Smoke hung in the air, life seemed
to concentrate once more on the few hours of daylight
which promised change and refreshment. As Jacques
pulled his horse from the path of wet black snouts and tossing horns, the herdsman—a child of perhaps six or seven—
smiled up at him and cried : " Salaam, Maharaj ! "

The title struck ironically on Jacques' ears. The child himself could scarcely have understood its meaning, yet he lisped it out in mimicry of his elders. Jacques pictured the infant's panic were he to pause and explain, in grown-up language, that he was no longer a Maharaj, that in fact, possessing nothing, he had become nobody. The knowledge brought a curious elation ; he tried to capture it, to pin it down, but it eluded capture and he remembered how once as a boy he'd broken a clinical thermometer and the mercury, running loose between his fingers, had fascinated him by its silvery substance which seemed related more to magic than to matter.

The papers which Ramdatta had given him to read were *hundies*, or notes of hand, to the tune of uncomputed sums. The thin sheets of native paper bearing signatures in English and in Hindu—all up-to-date, businesslike and unmistakable—were proof enough to Jacques that his mother had pledged herself far beyond the limit of her resources. He thought : " Possessions, like numbers, are infinite ; they begin in a man's flesh and work outward through his clothing to every artifice of his incorrigible brain." And he studied his own hand, his sunburnt wrist, the hard contour of his knees in their riding breeches. Were his flesh and blood his in fact ? Or was his breath and the tide which pumped in his heart pledged, likewise, to Ramdatta the moneylender ?

Ramdatta had explained, sonorously : " Years ago I promised your mother that I would not reveal the truth to you. She hoped, as I did, that by the time you were grown she might have managed to pay off these obligations. There is no one whom I admire more than Madame. We have always understood each other, for we are, in a remote sense, of the same *jat*. I kept my promise faithfully until to-day. But what can it profit Madame, or yourself, for you to remain in ignorance any longer ? Should creatures like Abdul Salim succeed in wrecking my livelihood what recourse would I have but to call upon you to fulfil your obligations ? Alas, this is not a new situation, Sahib. We all must live."

Jacques listened, his voice garnering the expected, the ordinary, the dry crumbs on which all mice must feed. He wondered why he was not more surprised, why this moment came to him rather as a vague, distant memory.

" We are in the same boat, Sahib. You, however, are in a position to help yourself and by so doing to help me. In the first place because you are a Sahib, in the second place because you are a friend of Hardyal and Ganpat Rai, both of whom exercise considerable influence over Abdul Salim. Men will sometimes do for love what they would scorn to do from other motives. Not that I expect wonders —I know that Salim ! He and I are old enemies. We were enemies before we were born. Yet, were he brought to realise that your fate must, in a measure, depend on mine, who shall say that he would not think twice, or even thrice ? "

Jacques spoke without glancing up from the papers. " He has threatened you, then ? "

" His very existence is a threat to me."

" But your friends the Police, what about them ? "

" Yes, there is always the Police. But Salim knows that as well as I do. He has his methods, and subtle ones they are. You must remember that the Police can step in only after a situation has been created."

" True, I was forgetting. And in the meantime your house might be burned over your head and your crops trampled into the ground."

Ramdatta winced. " We deal with unscrupulous men ! "

" True. Salim has a determined nature. Suppose I were to approach him as you suggest, and he refused to hear me. What then ? "

" It is a chance, a hope only ! I know men well, I have known them to do remarkable things out of affection and chivalry. Ah, I could tell you stories ! " He moved his glossy shoulders. " But do I need to tell you ? You are yourself young and full of illusions. Salim speaks well of you in public. He likes you, trusts you."

" You hear much."

" I hear everything ! "

" So you would have me go to him and tell him of these . . ." Jacques tapped the package on his knee. " And say to him, ' Salim, my friend ! Ramdatta has me in his clutches. He can in the wink of an eye deprive me of my

home, my factory, my very shoes ! Stay your hand, Salim,
my fire-eating friend. Do not breathe brimstone into the
ears of Ramdatta, nor try to inspire courage in the breasts
of his miserable victims—for by doing so, see where you
will land *me* ! ' ' "

Ramdatta stared at the young man, and round them the
silence seemed to settle, to thicken, as if the whole village
had become conscious of something extraordinary taking
place in its midst.

The moneylender said at last : " You misunderstand
me. I am not trying to blackmail you. I too have a code
of friendship. Have I not for twenty years kept my word
to your mother ? Have I once come to her with whinings,
with a single demand for what, after all, are my just dues ?
Come, Sahib ! A little while ago you spoke scathingly of
attitudes. It is not necessary that you strike one now, with
me."

When the young man remained silent he went on
urgently : " Jacques ! Work with me, let us be friends !
Let me serve your interests as I have always served Madame's. This war will bring wealth to many—why not to
you and to me ? Salim is an obstructionist, a troublemaker,
a fool. He thinks that this is the moment to oppose men
like myself and to force concessions from the Government.
He cannot last long, but he can do much harm while he
lasts. Is it not better for us to try and win him over to our
side—rather, to shame or to frighten him into retreat ? I
don't demand that you succeed with Salim, I merely ask
that you try, that you use your good offices through Ganpat
Rai and Hardyal. If you fail, then no matter. We shall
be no better off and no worse off than before."

While Ramdatta was talking Jacques reflected on the
familiar pattern of all accepted themes, all normal pre-
occupations. He replaced the *hundies* in their oilskin cover,
and rising, flung the package on the cot beside Ramdatta,
who looked up at him eagerly, like a child.

" Well, Sahib ? "

" No."

" Ah, come ! That is sheer foolishness."

Jacques stood under the flickering shadows of the mango
leaves and his stillness was matched by that of Ramdatta's

son, who appeared in the doorway and watched them with big, inquiring eyes.

" Sahib," Ramdatta repeated in a voice which had lost most of its resonance.

Jacques glanced at the boy. " Tell them to fetch my horse."

He turned to Ramdatta. " Salim is your enemy, not mine. As for this other affair . . ." He shrugged. " It has rested in your hands for a long time. The decision is yours. I leave it to you."

The man rose in agitation. " Then give me your word that you will never tell Madame ! It would blacken my face before her were she to know that I have spoken of this to you."

Jacques looked at him curiously. " For a man of substance you are full of quaint humours ! Why should I tell my mother ? What has this matter—any of it—to do with me ? "

He left his horse at the stables and walked round the end of the house to the garden, where he found his mother walking with Father Sebastien. Madame leaned on a stick ; she still limped slightly from her injury, but it was with eagerness, almost with anxiety, that she greeted her son. " It has been so hot, and you were gone for ages."

He had taken off his hat and the brown hair clung to his head, giving him for a moment, in that afternoon glow which holds all the humid tints of evening, an air of something bronze and permanent. His beauty troubled the priest, who looked away as some men look away when confronted by just this conjunction of youth and perfection in their own sex.

" I missed you," said Madame, her eyes fixed upon him.

Jacques said nothing.

48

A LATE October somnolence hung above the Terai jungle ; once in a while the hint of a breeze strayed down from the mountains, themselves invisible in the haze, and overhead wheeled a few kites, alternately black and brilliant in the sun. The Government rest-house stood in the shade of a sal grove that did little to soften the glare which rose off the empty ravine a few hundred yards away. Beyond the ravine stretched a level plain of plumed grass and beyond that again the jungle and the farther crouching forms of the lower hills.

A woodpecker was hammering in an old stump and green pigeons kept up a ceaseless whistling in the sal trees. Bertie Wood, lying in one of the Government's long veranda chairs, stared from the dazzling stones of the ravine to the wheeling kites, and reflected that here was an air, a place, which made speculation difficult but which with every breath and every mutation of light and shadow, stirred afresh the slow pain of realisation.

Pale, inert from the heat, she found herself at the mercy of her own discontent, which had settled like a sullen fever in her bones. Part of the pathos of intelligence is its impotence before such moods, and as she listened to the subtle overture which in India heralds the changing hour, she thought bitterly : " Every note of the pigeons' whistle, every answer from the kites, the whisper of wind in the grass and the savage dance of sunlight on stones, used to mean something—once ! Even as late as yesterday they meant something. Now they don't. My mind and heart are closed up tight like an idiot's."

Her features had the drawn look of a child who has cried itself to sleep, and this thought occurred to John Macbeth as he stepped from a room farther down the veranda and came towards her. Bertie heard him and turned her head, meeting his gaze with the false directness which he had learned to interpret.

" Pat and I are taking a stroll. Coming ? "

" In this heat ? "

" It will cool off. We'll take the elephant if you like."

She shuddered. " God no ! I had enough of the elephant yesterday. So did Diana."

Macbeth leaned against the veranda pillar. He looked cool and comfortable in khaki shirt and shorts, the little fringed tassels of his garters showing under the ribbed tops of his stockings. Sinewy, slender, he had at such moments a stillness which belied a capacity for sudden unerring movement. Bertie's gaze rested on him with a sort of gratitude for his appearance, for his calm.

She said : " I'll go if you really want me to."

" Better not. Pat says Diana won't move. She's lying down, full of aspirin and moans. Hadn't you better do the same ? "

" Moan ? "

" I meant, take some aspirin."

" No, I'll just lie here and wait for you."

" That's nice. I'll remember it."

She looked away. " I may go for a little walk, later."

" It's quite jungly, but there's a good path which takes you towards that little village we saw yesterday. It's shady most of the way."

" Don't worry, old boy. I'm all right."

" Honestly ? "

" Honestly."

He came close and bent over her. " Bertie ! "

She caught the clean smell of his clothes and his flesh, and when she lifted her hand to touch him he took it and pressed his lips to the palm. " Bertie," he murmured. " Bertie, Bertie ! "

There was a disturbance down the veranda and a young man appeared, walking clumsily on tiptoe. " Hallo ! " he exclaimed. " Bertie down and out, too ? "

" It must have been that shandygaff after lunch, yesterday," said Macbeth. " That, and the sun."

Captain Harding shook his head. " Diana has her own theory. In the first place it isn't her fault, in the second place it's mine. But this time I share the blame with that damned *hathi*. She says it had a motion like a Messagerie Maritime steamer during a storm in the Bay of Biscay. Never again will she ride a pad elephant, never ! "

A crew of orderlies and gun-bearers appeared round a

corner of the house, and Macbeth glanced at Bertie. " Sure you won't come, after all ? "

She shook her head, and Captain Harding nodded approval. " If I wasn't sure that this time next week my Sikhs and I will be en route in quest of different game, I'd stay and bear you company."

Bertie watched them stride away across the compound followed by their retinue. They disappeared over the edge of the ravine ; then she saw them again, the sunlight leaping off their gun-barrels. As the sound of their feet died away she became aware once more of the recurring diminuendo of the afternoon and felt, on her face, a breath from the invisible snows.

" Bertie, are you there ? "

Bertie rose and walked down the veranda to the Hardings' room. A dark-haired girl lay on one of the beds. She opened her eyes as Bertie came in. " I suppose I should have gone with Pat. There is so little time left, and I hate to be unsporting."

" You're not in the least unsporting," said Bertie. She sat on the edge of the bed and gazed at its occupant. " Feeling better ? "

The other stared at her with troubled eyes. " You know, it wasn't the heat that upset me. It wasn't the shandy either, nor the elephant."

" I understand. It's the baby."

" No."

Bertie waited. She had met the Hardings a month before at Gambul, where Captain Harding was spending his leave before going to France with his regiment. It had been Macbeth's idea that they come to Lal Bagh together for a few days' shooting, for he knew that the soldier was an ardent sportsman. " Hardly the season for good shooting—grass too high, foliage too thick, sun too hot ! But it's all you'll get for some time."

Diana went on : " It's the war. I try not to think about it or about Pat going, but there it is, all the time. When I wake up and when I go to sleep, whenever I start to feel happy." She stirred uneasily. " I'm a coward. Pat would hate to hear me talk like this, he'd hate me to have such thoughts."

Bertie touched the dark hair gently, but found nothing to say. The other continued : " There are actually times what I catch myself wishing that there was something the matter with Pat, that he might have a game leg or something, so he'd be unfit for active service." She looked at the girl beside her. " That's sinking pretty low, isn't it ? "

" I think I understand."

" Well, there's nothing the matter with him. He's young and strong and fit. He's exactly what they want."

Both were silent, listening to the faint crepitations of the house, to the voices of the pigeons outside. Both felt the presence of an irrelevant, almost an irresponsible peace, and it was Diana who remarked :

" When I'm able to keep the thought of war out of my mind for just a minute everything that used to be, everything warm and friendly, everything familiar, comes back. Like the uninterrupted sound of those birds, who have been singing for hundreds of years . . . singing on the same note, among the same kind of trees. Then it seems as if nothing could happen to interrupt my life, that it is still here—the past and the future—the hope . . . the hope . . . the hope of all known things going on quietly until one dies as one has a right to die, as all gentle things die. Although at such times one doesn't even think of dying."

" Don't think of it now."

" I'm Irish, you know. That means I'm full of presentiment."

" And imagination ! " Bertie tried to sound rallying.

" And hate. I'm full of hate. You don't have to be Irish to hate, you just have to be a woman. Pat doesn't hate the Germans. He just wants to kill them without making too much mess. It's left to me to hate them."

Bertie thought of her uncle, who had left India six weeks before with his Indian regiment. Diana was staring at her. " Yesterday, out there in the sun, in the jungle, whenever I looked at you I was conscious of your vitality, your happiness. You looked as if you expected joy to fall from every thorn tree or to come stepping from behind every tuft of grass. And I remembered that it was only a little while ago that I used to feel the same."

Bertie said impulsively : " You will, again ! "

" No, it won't be quite the same. Nothing will ever be quite the same for any of us."

Bertie left her, and went back to her own room. She found her leather writing-case and drew out Jacques' last letter which had come the evening before, brought with the three-day-old newspaper and other letters, by runner from the post office at the nearest railway junction. Macbeth, glancing at the envelope, had handed it to her without comment, and she had carried it to her own room to read. She stayed there a long time, and when she emerged at last he asked no questions, nor did he look at her. It dawned on her then that he had learned to dread Jacques' letters almost as much as she was learning to dread them herself.

She returned to the veranda. The sun was draining towards the farther grasses ; it bathed the ravine in a flood of greying light beyond which the tallest plumes rose in a host of spears. Bertie sat down and re-read Jacques' letter. He wrote briefly, almost brutally, of his financial predicament, and as she read, Bertie understood something of the savage spirit in which he had forced himself to state the bleak truth.

" God knows when, if ever, we shall be able to marry. You will suggest, as you have before, that we live off your income ' until ' and ' unless '. If it were merely a question of pride I wouldn't hesitate, for pride in money matters is the attribute of *banias* and to my sorrow, and perhaps also to yours, I am not and never will be a *bania*. However, until I have brought some sort of order into my life I cannot—in fact I will not—ask you to share it. Nor can I ask you to go on forever waiting and waiting for something to happen. Neither of us asked for this. Neither of us has done anything to deserve it. It all began a long time ago, before we were born ; in a way it's like this bloody war. Someone was planning it while we were innocent and happy. But what's the use ? There you are and here am I . . . and I suppose that the priests and the politicians, the bunglers and the *banias*, all have their explanations. You and I just don't count."

Bertie did not finish the letter. She laid it on the arm

of her chair and sat staring before her. The flashing light ignited, it seemed, an equivalent fire in her veins. Far away stood the little dark hills and behind them she thought she glimpsed the mountains tipped with ice, but it must have been her imagination, for as she stared the sun gathered itself together and struck her between the eyes, so there were no longer mountains, nor the cool breath of mountains, but instead the lesser figures of malevolent hills beyond the harsh plain. India ! The name held everything that had been important in her life ; it had taken her up in its dark hand, caressed her, enchanted her. It had exacted from her every impulse of fervour and generosity and she scarcely knew when the loving grasp relaxed, when her eyes first began to clear of their childish dream, when the hills ceased to be miracles and became, instead, beasts which stalked her along the horizon. She thought of yesterday before Jacques' letter had reached her, and a line from the Persian poet recurred to her : " To-morrow I may be, myself, with yesterday's seven thousand years." A trite sentiment, but truth and triteness seem always to be one and the same thing.

Perhaps what burned and blistered more than anything was the knowledge that what had happened to her and to Jacques was an ancient story ; they had simply not been able to muster sufficient force or sufficient originality to evade a commonplace fate. She had believed that because one lived in a different country one's life could be different too, that it could approach nearer to the dream, the vision.

Yesterday, hunting cheetul from the back of an elephant, the will to happiness, like the will to beauty, had palmed itself off on her as the real thing. She felt like a goddess as she stared down at the tall grass which waved above the elephant's knees, and watched a covey of peafowl scuttling with outstretched necks. The elephant had carried them past small sandy openings covered with the tracks of wild pig ; it stopped, and with its trunk plucked a green bough with which to fan away the flies, while its passengers climbed down to examine the pugs of a tiger in the soft sand. Then from out of the sal jungle crashed a cheetul herd and fled like ghosts under a splitting volley which left one of them kicking and twisting in the grass. Life, thought Bertie, has

its special, its personal direction—there could be no other ;
and her happiness faltered as she stared for a moment at
the creature's brilliant, dying eyes.

49

THERE was still an hour before sundown as Bertie crossed
the compound to the path Macbeth had indicated. She
heard a shot in the distance and decided that by skirting
the little village she might waylay the hunters on their way
home. The light in which she walked was no longer per-
pendicular ; it lay on acres of plumes of grass or struck a
tentative note on a twig, a leaf, a stone. The pigeons had
fallen silent at last ; the woodpecker uttered its terse note
and darted down the path before her, leaving a trail of
blue. She heard something pad away into the brush on
the other side of the trees, and a slight qualm assailed her.
Life was everywhere, she felt its breath, she was aware of
its unseen eye, and for a moment she thought she heard it
talking to itself under the crisp sound of her own feet among
the dry leaves.

The peace of the hour and of her surroundings struck
her even more forcibly than it had done a little while ago
in the bungalow, for the indifference of nature had never
seemed more irrelevant in face of human realities. It
spumed up from the earth, it whistled with the pigeons,
it was implicit in the paw which had left its seal in the mud
beside the drinking-pool. It was a mood, too, which dwelt
in the flimsy huts of the villagers and which keyed and
coloured their flimsy lives. Certainly its indifference bore
little resemblance to the mood of her own world, stumbling
towards eclipse and spitting blood at every step. One does
not require the approach of death to see pass before one's
eyes a retinue of departed days ; one needs only to come to
the end of a vital experience, and with this confession Bertie
repudiated, not her private universe, but this other, this
monstrous, terrestrial indifference.

Before her the path stretched in a stream of golden dust
and presently she heard goat-bells and caught a glimpse of
a woman striding through the grass, carrying an earthen

pitcher on her head. The village was out of sight, but now the path widened and the land on either side had a cleared look. The sun struck fire from something beyond the frieze of sal and cactus, and Bertie saw a temple so small that a child might have built it. It seemed deserted and for a moment she wondered whether some shy god—perhaps the genial Ganesh himself—had melted into the jungle at her approach.

Then she saw him, or rather his image. Made of stone painted a deathly white, his red hair plastered with cow dung, he sat cross-legged under a baobab tree, the shadows playing over his stony nakedness. At his back the trunk of the baobab hung in smooth pachydermic folds, like the sheltering knees of a vaguer, vaster deity. Bertie pushed aside the intervening leaves and stepped to the edge of the clearing. No one challenged her and for a long time she stared at the stone god, motionless under the caressing shadows. A chain round his loins supported a sort of tray, and on this reposed the godly genitals amidst an offering of jungle fronds and flowers. The silence was complete, but as she stood there Bertie imagined that the shadows whispered together in their evening dance over the god's breast and shoulders. The fantasy lingering in her mind inspired wonder as his painted eyelids opened and he stared back at her with drugged and crimson eyes. Fantasy completing itself, the stone came to life and rising to its feet made a rush towards her.

Bertie turned and fled through the screening leaves to the path. Light-headed, she flew down its glistening channel and saw her cousin walking towards her. Macbeth stopped and held out his arms and she flung herself on his breast, clinging to him like a creature distraught. " Hold me . . . hold me . . . hold me."

" Bertie, what on earth ! "

" Don't let me go, don't ever let me go ! "

He stared at the path stretching innocently before him. Somewhere along its empty length a woodpecker hammered, then ceased. Could that sudden sound have frightened her ?

" Bertie, what is it ? What happened ? "

But she clung, shivering and muttering incoherently,

and he led her to a patch of grass. There he sat, drawing
her into his arms. He stroked away the hair which had
fallen across her eyes and his own hand trembled against
her warm skin.

" Tell me, Bertie, tell me."

She tried to explain in hysterical sentences, and presently the light broke on Macbeth. " Oh, good Lord, that
saddhu ! I forgot all about him. He's supposed to be mad,
so the villagers keep him tied up to his tree. But he's quite
harmless . . ."

Bertie was not listening, and presently, frightened himself by this hysteria, Macbeth laid her down on the grass
and leaned over her, cradling her head on his arm.

" Don't let me go. Swear that you will never let me
go."

" I swear I shall never let you go."

She opened her eyes and he saw himself reflected there,
leaning down as though to drink. " Bertie . . ."

She lifted her arms, drawing him down to her breast.

50

As Madame St. Remy stepped from the church door into
the light of the church compound she felt that she left
behind her, like a forgotten cloak, the charmed oblivion of
the past hour. All the emergencies of her life seemed to
wait for her in the brighter air, already tinctured by
winter. Behind her rose the voice of Father Sebastien's
native choir practising a Christmas hymn, and in Madame's
mind there lingered a prayer which she had just uttered,
a prayer for the return of peace to the world. She felt the
weight of the unanswered appeal lie heavy on her heart,
for the Battle of Ypres was just ending, but not the war.
Yet here in the oleander-bordered compound was peace
indeed. Difficult to believe that its grace paused on the
fringes of the land, difficult to acknowledge that upon all
the earth those nasal voices were not singing " Noel, Noel ! "
to the surging optimism of the church organ.

Father Sebastien emerged from the vestry. " Shall I
send for your carriage, Madame ? "

"It is waiting for me at the gate."

"Then I will walk there with you."

As they fell into step she said : "Jacques has gone to Mrs. Lyttleton's funeral. They tell me she desired to be buried in her garden, near her husband and child."

He nodded. "I called at her house, out of respect. I found her servants weeping."

Madame said grudgingly : "No doubt she had her virtues, but it would be hypocrisy to pretend that I care one way or another." When he remained silent she exclaimed : "All I care about is Jacques ! He has been hurt enough. If her death is to hurt him more, then I shall find it harder than ever to forgive her."

He said in a low voice : "Ah, Madame, let the dead past bury its dead. She can do you not further injury, nor you her. And as for Jacques, you have news which will, I imagine, divert something from his sorrow for Mrs. Lyttleton."

"I know, I know ! I have thought of little else, and all day I have felt like a coward, all day since I read the announcement of Bertie's marriage in the *Pioneer* and knew that Jacques had not yet seen it. Why must these things always fall to a mother's lot ? No, I don't mean that. I'm glad, happy that it should be my task to have to tell him, and to be with him when he learns of it. But I dread it just the same." Her eyes hardened. "One would have supposed that people who call themselves civilised might have found a civilised method of conveying such news. Why did Bertie not write to Jacques himself to tell him about her marriage ? Why didn't Macbeth write ? "

"It was Jacques who asked to be released from his engagement," the priest reminded her, gently. "Under the circumstances one can hardly blame the Macbeths." When she said nothing, he asked : "Jacques has never explained to you, has he, why the engagement was broken ? "

"Never," said Madame bitterly. "Never ! He explains nothing. He asked me not to speak of it, and naturally I have respected his wish. But I, his own mother, am told nothing, nothing."

As she bade the priest good-bye and drove away she felt more than ever conscious of a fading of that solemn charm which never failed her in the house of her God. Faced, now, with a return to her own house, foreboding descended on her. The thought of meeting her son, a thought which used to bring its special delight and anticipation, brought instead the pang of some mysteriously acquired bruise. A month had passed since the day when he came to her with the news of his broken engagement, and remembrance of that scene was still vivid. She had thrown her arms around him, and he stood in the circle, submitting but not responding to her embrace.

" Jacques, my poor child ! She has deserted you."

He looked at her then and through the blur of her own tears she saw that his eyes were hard and clean as stones. Gently, he freed himself and led her to a chair, and in a voice which somehow matched his eyes he said : " Bertie has not deserted me. It is I who have deserted her. Please understand this, then promise me that you will never speak of it again."

For Madame the weeks had passed in an atmosphere of bewilderment and incredulity. Every morning Jacques rode to the factory and stayed until afternoon ; then he changed his clothes and bicycled to Hardyal's house where he played tennis and often stayed for dinner. It seemed as if his whole nature had suffered some catastrophic change, it had become elusive, elliptical, at no point could she grasp it. He no longer offered to kiss her nor did he display any more the charming little attentions which she had learned to expect from him. When, rather timidly, she tried to force them upon him he submitted with averted eyes.

" One would suppose," she confided bitterly to Father Sebastien, " one would suppose that it was all my fault ! "

" Give him time," urged the priest. " He is young and he has suffered. Give him time and he will come back to you."

Madame did not voice the thought which sprang into into mind : " *You* gave him time, but he has never come back to you ! "

As confusion increased, hope diminished ; unable now, to win a word or a glance of tenderness from him she began to brood on her wrongs, to recall with tears the hundred and one griefs and sacrifices which she had endured for his sake. Right was on her side, God was on her side, and if the world only knew, the world itself would be on her side. This exercise in self-pity assumed a curiously familiar pattern, but Madame's subjective intelligence barred her from the recognition that here was an experience almost identical with one she had suffered years before on discovering that Auguste no longer loved her. What followed was to follow inevitably the lines laid down for it. Denied possession, her vitality sought its only expression, and she dwelt with a sweet and secret satisfaction on Jacques' physical and economic handicap. She felt increasingly secure in the knowledge that she had lost her two most formidable rivals, Bertie, and at last and forever —Mrs. Lyttleton.

The carriage stopped and she got out, making her way slowly up the steps to the veranda. It was not yet dusk and the lamps had not been lighted. She heard her servants talking as they went about their evening duties, and the sound of her carriage as it rolled across the compound towards the stables. At the door of the drawing-room Madame paused. The room was empty, vagrant flickers of light touched familiar objects—the ormolu clock, a bowl of flowers, the gilt frame of her husband's portrait. She stared round her, affected by the stillness and the air of expectancy which hangs about an empty room. Then the bead curtains moved and Jacques appeared, his figure in its white suit slender as a shaft before her. They stared at one another, then Madame inquired gently : "When did you get back, my dear ? "

"An hour ago." His voice was colourless.

"Were there many people at the funeral ? "

"Just her friends."

"You, Hardyal, Ganpat Rai . . ."

"Ganpat Rai has not returned from Agra."

It might have been the conversation of mere acquaintances. Madame removed her hat, stabbed the hatpins through the crown, and laid it with her gloves on a chair. Both continued to stand in the curious indecision which beset them, nowadays, when they found themselves together. She said, presently : " I wonder what will happen

to her property. She had no relatives that one ever heard
of, unless there are some in England."

"Ganpat Rai handled her affairs, and I understand
that there are cousins in England."

His voice sounded absent-minded, and she asked, with
a tentative smile : "Tell me, Jacques, would it have pleased
you if I'd gone with you to Mrs. Lyttleton's funeral?"

"I think it might have amused Mrs. Lyttleton, could
she have known!"

Madame flushed. "So, in spite of your expressed disbelief in such matters, it did occur to you that Mrs. Lyttleton *might* know . . ."

He shrugged. "She was always so much alive when
she lived, I now find it difficult to believe that she is dead."

"Nevertheless, she is dead."

"Yes." He stood at a little distance, the oval of his
face somewhat darker than the rest of him, his wounded
hand in his pocket. There was something apparitional
about him, and Madame's heart beat with a sudden frenzy.
"She is dead, Jacques, dead! She has gone out of your
life, as completely as though she had never come into it."

He shook his head. "No, for I shall never forget her.
Nor shall I ever feel my conscience to be clear again."

She started. "*Your* conscience!"

"That I should have neglected her in the end . . . that
I should have listened . . . believed ill of her . . . allowed
myself to be persuaded."

Madame St. Remy controlled her emotion with a visible
effort.

"So, both the women you professed so to love have left
you!"

He made no reply. A servant came into the room carrying a lamp and hung it on its ornamental bracket against
the wall, then withdrew. Silence, that immeasurable silence
which she knew of old, deepened between them. Madame
clenched her hands. "Jacques there is something I have
to say to you. . . . You must find out sometime, and though
it hurts me . . ."

He interrupted calmly : "If you are trying to tell me
about Bertie's marriage, she wrote and told me about it,
herself, two days ago."

Madame felt flow back on her all the heat and exaltation of this prepared moment. " She told you ? You know ? And you said nothing to me ? "

" What did you expect me to say ? "

" I would expect you to behave like a human being . . ." She struggled to repress a detestable shrillness. " I would expect you to show a decent indignation . . . feeling . . ."

" If you were looking forward to telling me, yourself, then I'm sorry I deprived you of the opportunity."

Her passion flared into fury. " Mon Dieu ! You speak to me in such a tone ? You, who have squandered your affections and are now paying for it. . . . Bankrupt in your love, you turn against me, your own mother ? "

He looked at her steadily. " Must we use the language of *banias*, Maman ? If so, have you ever considered what might happen were Ramdatta to take it into his head to press for payment of his bills ? "

Madame grasped the back of a chair. " Ramdatta ! What do you mean ? "

Jacques hesitated, then in a few curt sentences told her of his interview with the moneylender more than a month ago. He felt a vague astonishment at the sound of his own voice, but was powerless to check himself ; the things were there, they uttered themselves. Inside him all was darkness, a continent obscured by a new climate. He finished at last, coldly : " And that is why I broke my engagement with Bertie. I might have asked her to share my poverty, but you'd scarcely expect her to share my penury ? "

Madame felt crumble within her the fantastic structure which she had been twenty-five years in building. She broke into breathless explanations while he stood impassively before her : Some day the factory would take a new lease on life. Indigo would come back as it had come back in the past. And after all, had she not been right ? The war was not her responsibility—God knew how long and how passionately she had prayed for its end. But war had come and with it a renewed demand for indigo. Ah, could she but find a few paltry thousands of rupees she would put the factory back on its feet ! At the end of the year Ramdatta would be paid back. While she talked, eagerly and at times incoherently, Jacques stared at the floor. When she paused for breath and he made no move to speak, to comfort her, she cried in despair : " Whatever I did, I did for your sake ! If I made mistakes they were no worse than any you might have made in my place. One cannot read the future, one cannot give up just because circumstances are temporarily against one. And what would you have had me do ? Let the factory go ? Sell the property ? What would we have lived on ? If I've kept the truth from you all this time it was not because I was ashamed. It was because I wanted to save you anxiety."

" You should have told me when I left school and came home to work for you."

" And what could you have done that I was unable to do ? "

" At least I would have known where I stood. I would not have become engaged to Bertie."

" Ah ! " Her voice was charged with bitterness. " Bertie ! Because Bertie has shown that she has not the strength of character to share your misfortune, you blame me ? "

He replied in a gentler voice : " No, I don't blame you."

She stammered : " Oh, Jacques, if you would return to God . . ."

" Let us not speak of that, Maman. I realise how fortunate you are in your faith. I understand how people can be persuaded into any belief. Perhaps to be constituted as I am is a sign of stupidity ; I don't know, I can't be sure of anything any more."

" You would live on air," she retorted angrily. " You are like your father. He, too, despised *banias*. He thought money was mean and vulgar. He gave up his wife, his children, his church, everything, because he acquired instead a pride in what he was pleased to call his free intelligence."

" You would prefer that I give up everything even before I have attained it, then ? " He turned to look at her and she saw how pale he seemed, how remote. " Sometimes it seems as though my father's problem and mine are the same."

At a loss, she hesitated, and he went on : " You have

explained that he hated meanness and vulgarity. Perhaps
his hatred taught him how little choice a man has, and he
chose the little for whatever it was worth to him. Well,
I choose it too, but for myself only. It is far too meagre
to ask someone I love to share it with me." When she remained silent he added : " You are quite right . . . the
women whom I so professed to love have left me. You
should now be quite content."

" Do you realise to whom you are speaking ? "

" I know very well that I am not speaking to Mrs.
Lyttleton or to Bertie."

" Ah, yes, with them you would use a very different
tone ! "

He murmured distractedly. " One loves . . . one loves
. . . irresponsibly. It's the only love. I can't explain and
you cannot understand. Let us not discuss it."

" I shall discuss it ! " The passion which had been
generating in her breast broke free at last ; her face had a
distorted, sexless look. " I shall discuss it ! You cannot
deceive me, it has never been in your power to deceive me,
in these matters which you now say you cannot explain
and that I cannot understand. I understand very well.
You already know that your father was unfaithful to me
with Mrs. Lyttleton. Perhaps you do not know that he was
her lover before you were born. Ah, you did not know
that ! You cannot believe it ! Well, it is true. Before you
were born. And I think that in his diseased mind he formed
some hideous notion that you were in a sense—ah, in what
a sense !—his and Mrs. Lyttleton's child. They had their
way, but I was resolved that their way would stop short
of my children. Gisele's case was easy, she was naturally
mild and virtuous. You were not, you never have been.
When Auguste died Mrs. Lyttleton tried to appropriate
you as she had appropriated him. Perhaps she shared his
monstrous idea that you were, in that sense, her child too.
She did her utmost to make you so, but she reckoned without your true mother. And when I saw Bertie that first
time in Gambul I saw in her something of the look of Mrs.
Lyttleton. They had that same air, that frightful pride
of the English, that sinister force which makes them
believe that there is nothing they may not appropriate if

they so desire ! And Bertie, your loyal and beautiful Bertie, coming here to stay under my roof when you were both hardly more than children. Do you imagine that I was blind to what went on ? Do you think that I was ever taken in by your cleverness and by the complicity of the servants ? "

He said harshly : " Then why did you not interfere ? It was your chance . . . we were young, what could we have done ? "

" I refrained because I loved you. I loved you more than any stranger could have loved you. I wanted you to trust me, I wanted you to feel that I trusted you. It seems that I was mistaken. And Bertie . . . ah ! Bertie. . . . In the years after Mrs. Macbeth ran away from her dolt of a husband, what sort of life did Bertie live, unchaperoned, with her uncle and cousin ? Your father had taught me to be suspicious—nothing that has happened has gone unobserved by me. One loves irresponsibly . . . what a delightful idea ! But not always, not always."

The breathless sentences came to an end and in the silence which followed, it seemed as if the servants, the whole house, must be waiting tensely for what was to come. Outside, dusk had fallen ; it crept into the room, but its freshness had no power over their human fever.

Madame said in a calmer voice : " Let us not talk of love or understanding since you seem to have so little need of either. Let us confine ourselves to more practical matters. You are still my son, though no doubt you consider yourself to be fully a man. You scorn a man's natural responsibilities, and it does seem rather as if they, in a manner of speaking, scorn you."

She broke off, distracted by his silence, by his almost spectral stillness. He had remained like this throughout the strange interview, unconscious of the clock's faint strokes. Madame waited for him to speak, to move, and when he continued to stand motionless she was taken by a storm of shivering. " Jacques, Jacques, forgive me ! " She held out her arms. " This is fantastic. . . . Don't look like that . . . don't stand there like that, like a ghost ! My dear, my son . . ."

He made no move towards her, and, denied the impetus

which such a move would have invited, she gazed at him
with a sort of terror.

" You cannot treat me like this, you cannot ! "

His figure against the glinting beads which, years ago,
Gisele had threaded on linen cords, blurred and melted
under Madame's eyes. When her vision cleared again he
had gone, and the bead curtains trembled slightly, giving
off little spurts of colour and light, their faint music the
only sound in the room.

51

" I HOPE," said Abdul Salim, " that your father will not
be angry with me when he learns that I have taken you to
Berari to hear a political speech ! "

Hardyal was amused by his friend's misgivings ; the
fiery Mohammedan cared so little, as a rule, for another
man's anger.

" Abdul Salim, must I remind you that I am no longer
a child ? Besides, Father has too much affection for you to
be angry."

" He has, however, little affection for Jagnath Singh."

" You think, then, that there might be a row over this
speech ? "

Salim hesitated. " I understand that he has obtained
permission from the magistrate, Mr. Sheldon, who is one
of the most liberal of our Civil Servants. But one can never
be sure even with the best of them . . . nor," and he laughed,
" nor can one always be sure with Jagnath ! Government
is now embarked on a policy of forgive and forget. The
loyal response of the Princes and of our rich industrialists
has rather gone to the Government's collective head. It
feels that it can afford to be lenient with men like Jagnath,
the Ali brothers, and the rest—not to mention such insignificant fry as myself."

There was nothing insignificant in Salim's appearance ;
tall, rugged, with an iron grey beard, he looked more like
a distinguished soldier than like a struggling pleader of the
lower court. Both men wore native dress. They had a
second-class compartment to themselves and reclined on a
long leather-covered bunk, smoking and watching the

shadow of the train hurtle alongside. The green plain unfolded like a carpet, villages and mango groves loomed and faded, camels grazed and children capered derisively.

Hardyal was glad to be with Salim, glad to lose himself for a little while in the Mohammedan's restless existence which seemed so impersonal, so divorced from everything that was self-centred and stale. They were on their way to Berari, a city twice the size of Amritpore and a day's journey distant, where they were to hear Salim's friend Jagnath Singh discuss the Government's recruitment policy for the Indian army. Jagnath Singh was a barrister of great ability and an old enemy of the Raj. He had in the past served several terms in jail, but remained uncompromising, and it was largely due to the Government's recent policy of conciliation that he was not now languishing in prison. Salim spoke of the man with admiration, even with veneration. "The truth is, Government would give much to have Jagnath's support of the war effort. They have done everything except offer him bribes. They would welcome, in him, recreance which they condemn in one of their own skin ! Now, because their existence as Englishmen is threatened by Germans, they demand that an Indian forthwith rush to the English side. In other words, Jagnath Singh must conduct himself like an English patriot—after he has three times been sent to jail for preaching English logic to the English."

They talked of politics, of the war, and their conversation seemed strangely at variance with the traditional, peaceful landscape which unrolled before their eyes. Presently, Salim asked why Hardyal had not asked Jacques to accompany them, but Hardyal shook his head.

"You know that Berari is Macbeth's station. It would have been embarrassing, should they have met."

Salim agreed, then added impatiently : "These intimacies bore me ! Macbeth has married the charming Bertie. Jacques, I expect, will eventually marry someone else. The world is full of white women dying for someone to marry them. What does it matter ? There are more important things in life. You know, there is in your Jacques a disillusionment which I cannot understand." He went on quickly : "I do not understand, nor do I condone. He refuses responsibility. He has denied his religion, he declares that he has passed beyond persuasion. What now? I tell you, he is an example of the dry rot which has infected the European spirit."

Hardyal said sadly : " It is what he believes, himself."

" Yet these are the people who profess superiority ! Allah ! But I feel sorry for Jacques. He, at least, has honesty. He knows."

" Yes," Hardyal repeated. " He knows."

" Poor boy ! Did he not even have a chance to sleep with his lovely Bertie ? Ah, to know, now, that his friend is in possession. That must be painful, it must be unbearable. But they are a disorderly lot, these English and French. Unable to manage their own lives, they turn on each other. Let them bleed to death, who cares ? "

Hardyal stared out of the window. The train was passing a big *jheel*, glassy under the sun, and as the engine sang its hollow song, birds rose, clamouring and glittering, into the air. Only the *sarus* remained motionless, studying their black-and-white images in the water.

Presently, Salim drowsed and Hardyal turned to his own reflections. He was coming closer and closer towards sharing Salim's ideas and attitudes, and the knowledge brought him a peculiar thrill, half fear and half surprise at himself. He knew that this impulse must have resided in him for a long time, that it had been growing silently, unobtrusively, like some tough and fluid sea-plant. Nevertheless love, which Mrs. Lyttleton had once said transcended politics, still held him faithful to the few whom he knew well. It held him faithful to her memory, faithful to the spirit which he had seen in her. But now the great war had swamped individual concepts, it made personal considerations appear as mean and slight, it thrust past glories into a background lighted only a little by nostalgia ; it imposed distance, like a no-man's-land of dreams, between generation and generation. Perhaps he should have gone back to England and finished his education, then gone into English service, or studied for the Bar as his father had wished him to do. Instead, he had chosen his own way, in his own country, among his own people. What troubled him now was the suspicion that the choice had not been his own, but that it had been forced upon him by accident, and that he had reacted to the accident by striking an attitude at once defensive and defiant. Mrs. Lyttleton argued as women argue but the bitter truth remained : love never has and never will transcend politics . . . not until politics have broken down the barriers which transcend love.

He began to think about Mrs. Lyttleton. Like all Indians, he was profoundly affected by death because he saw it as void and expressionless. Coming home after her funeral he had gone to his piano, and, moved to pay her some secret tribute, he sat down and tried to play. But his talent proved too small for his emotion. What was the use ? Getting up, he stood frowning at the keyboard and a song began to run in his head, a tune half remembered : he thought of the Fair at Amritpore and the garden party at his father's house, of Mrs. Lyttleton asking him for Aubrey Wall's letter. There were Chinese lanterns hanging in the trees and the musicians had played their *zitars* and rice-bowl drums, and one had sung :

> Love with his hand shall part the sacred water
> And revive you with showers from his hair !

That night, Jacques' servant Hanif had been stoned to death, and now Mrs. Lyttleton, herself, was no more. Hardyal understood at last why he mourned for her : she had been part of his innocence, part of a vanished time.

In a few weeks he would be married. He had not seen his prospective bride, but prayers and purifications and the terrific excitement of all his female relatives, were beginning to affect him. Day and night the house trembled with preparations, with snatches of song, laughter suddenly stifled, sibilant whispers, jinglings, tinklings, heady scents. Every day there arrived gifts and deputations, and strange circulars from medical firms in Calcutta and Bombay, documents offering marvellous elixirs for the restoration or promotion of virility. Hardyal laughed when he read them, but his blood was already stirring, a strangeness opened before his eyes, and he knew that his life would no longer be what it had been.

The train jolted over a level-crossing and he sighed, glancing at his bare forearm where it rested on the sill. Suddenly he wished that his grandmother had lived to see his marriage and to receive his first-born son into her arms. His son ! Hardyal's hand clenched. His son ! Strange that at this moment the woman who must bear that son was unknown to him as a creature of flesh and blood, one he would hold in his arms, one whose hair would lie warm as woodsmoke round his throat. He had been told that she was lovely ; he knew that she was young, much younger than himself. He was far from ignorant in matters of sex, for, as he had told Jacques, he had not denied himself the essential experience. But the idea of marriage with its august ramifications had seemed remote enough. He knew that it would be decisive, that it would seal him away, forever, from his childhood. Happiness ! He closed his eyes and at once the mysterious image of his wife appeared under his eyelids. Motionless, he waited, feeling her presence increase, feeling her breath against his face, her breath scented with cardamoms as he had once smelled them on a woman's breath a year ago at Allahabad. He saw the shape of her face with the little red tikka between her brows, the thin arch of her nostril with its turquoise stud, the unbearable slow lifting of her lashes under his own.

He opened his eyes to find Abdul Salim watching him with friendly amusement. " Wake up ! We shall be in Berari in a little while."

52

BERARI PLATFORM was large and imposingly modern ; there were no monkeys and very few beggars, and the red turbans of the police bobbed like flowers among the drab and dust of the crowd. Europeans in khaki or pipe-clayed helmets appeared and vanished, and everywhere squirmed the ubiquitous pedlars whose cries sounded like birds' or like frogs' during the monsoon.

Missionary ladies were buying *The Tatler* and the *Illustrated London News* at Wheeler's big roll-top book-stand ; a palanquin containing a sick begum swayed towards the

exit on the shoulders of four staggering bearers, and a troop
of Eurasian school children home for the holidays chattered
shrilly like a troop of mynas. Salim and Hardyal were
jostled and butted by the stream of passengers disembarking
from the train and an opposing stream clambering on to it.

"I will find a tonga," said Salim, elbowing his way
through the mob. "We will go straight to Jagnath's
cousin's house. It is Number Three Tamarind Road,
behind the European quarter."

Hardyal followed the tall Mohammedan but he had not
gone far before his arm was touched and he was saluted
by a police orderly, who handed him a note. "This is the
son of Ganpat Rai of Amritpore? A letter for you from the
Captain Sahib of Police."

Hardyal stopped in surprise. "For me?"

"For you, from Macbeth Sahib."

Salim, missing him, had fought his way back. "What
is it? What has happened?"

The orderly stood a few paces away, respectful and aloof,
as Hardyal tore open the envelope. With Salim peering
over his shoulder he read the letter:

"Dear Hardyal,

"I have learned that you are expected in Berari and I
thought that with luck I might catch you as you got off
the train. I do not wish to interrupt your plans, but if you
can spare an hour will you come and see me? The orderly
who carries this note will direct you to my house. I should
like very much to have a talk.

"Yours sincerely,
"John Macbeth."

"Wah!" Salim's exclamation was full of jealousy
and suspicion. "Had you told him you were coming to
Berari?"

"How should I? We have never corresponded."

"Then Jacques . . ."

"Hardly, under the circumstances."

They looked at each other, and Salim's eyes hardened.
"I made no secret of our plans. Every one knows that Jagnath Singh is to speak this evening. However, you and I

are not such exalted persons that we should be followed
with this devotion."

"My servants knew where I was going," said Hardyal.
"I, too, mentioned it casually, here and there."

"The Police were intrigued," muttered Salim. "No
doubt we were watched from the moment we left our
homes." His lawyer's mind was working swiftly, and he
turned to the orderly. "Tell me, brother, how it happened
that you recognised my friend? Had you seen him before?"

The man answered respectfully: "His appearance, and
yours, were described to me by the Sahib. To make sure,
I inquired of the guard."

It could mean but one thing: they were objects of
official surveillance. Suddenly, Salim laughed. "Go,
Hardyal. Call on your friend the Captain Sahib. Convey
my salaams and congratulate him on his efficiency."

"He means no harm. This is a friendly invitation."

"Is it so friendly? Why then did he not write to you
at Amritpore? Why does he have you accosted thus, by
a police constable, on a public platform? Nay, you cannot refuse, for this is a command, my boy—a command!"

For the first time in his life Hardyal experienced the
shock of knowing that his actions were under a mysterious
scrutiny. His privacy had been invaded, he was no longer
an anonymous figure. He stared about him with a new
feeling, encountering glances which a moment before had
seemed merely inquisitive or casual, but which now became
sly and inimical. He turned to Salim. "I will do whatever you say."

The other's hard face softened a little. "I would rather
you did what your father would have you do. Go, my son.
Perhaps, after all, Macbeth's intentions are friendly. You
will soon find out."

Followed by the policeman they made their way through
the crowd out on to the broad courtyard behind the station.
Here Salim hailed a tonga, and turned once more to
Hardyal. "For the time being our ways lie in opposite
directions. When you have seen Macbeth, come to Jagnath's cousin's house. Do not be late, for the meeting is at
six, and it is now four o'clock."

They parted and Hardyal climbed into another tonga with the police orderly. They rattled out of the courtyard, and left to his own reflections Hardyal's spirits began to lift. Salim always affected him powerfully ; the man's optimism or his pessimism was alike contagious. But now, reading Macbeth's note for the second time and judging from the deferential manner of his escort, it was far easier to believe that nothing particularly sinister could be afoot. After all, Macbeth was an officer in one of the most efficient police systems in the world ; all kinds of information must reach him, and the merest accident might have put him in possession of the fact that Hardyal had taken the train from Amritpore with Abdul Salim. And in any event, although Jagnath Singh might temporarily enjoy the good graces of the Government it did not follow that his movements or those of his admirers were ignored by the authorities. Learning of Hardyal's destination Macbeth might easily have acted on a friendly impulse. Hardyal began to feel much better. He wished now that he had thought this sooner and spoken of it to Salim ; it might have spared that irascible person an hour or two of anger and anxiety.

His mind more at ease, Hardyal looked about him with renewed pleasure and curiosity. He had never been at Berari, and he decided that he liked its trim and prosperous air. As they swung into the main channel of traffic the orderly pointed out the line of the distant barracks and parade ground, the Municipality buildings, the woollen mill, the new High Court with its lawns and flowers. Flags floated from their turrets and cast leisurely shadows on the white streets. There were palms and oleanders and a fountain in the little park which served as a boundary between the commercial side of the city and the beginnings of the residential quarter. A car with its hood down whisked past, and Hardyal had a glimpse of rugged soldierly faces.

" Look, Huzoor," said his companion suddenly. They were seated at the back of the tonga ; from a side-street at right angles to their path a troop of horsemen appeared, Indian lancers in the khaki of battle dress, with their lances at rest and pennons fluttering. They drew abreast of the tonga, and Hardyal gazed at the erect and magnificent

L

figures led by a young prince whose saddle-cloth was a leopard-skin and whose profile under his tightly wound turban might have come off a coin discovered on the upper reaches of the Indus valley where, once upon a time, Alexander the Great had paused.

The troopers drew away and Hardyal exclaimed : " I did not know they were in Berari."

" We had a regiment of Punjabies, but they have gone. The cavalry came last week. They, too, will go, but others will come. While the war lasts there will be soldiers in Berari."

That glimpse of warriors had an odd effect on Hardyal. They had, inexplicably, engraved themselves on his mind, and he knew that it was one of those vignettes, of no particular importance, which sometimes lodge in one's memory and which are never forgotten. He wondered what passed in the minds of those men. Dare he claim them as brothers ? He would have liked to touch them, to have looked for a moment into their aloof eyes, for he had the conviction that men who look like that, who ride like that, do not come home from battle.

They left the busy precincts of the town and turned off down a side-street bordered with trees, beyond which he caught glimpses of big, attractive houses. All this was familiar enough, the ekkas and hired rattletrap carriages, the ayah wheeling a white baby in a pram, the figure flying past on a bicycle.

Would Macbeth ask for Jacques ? Instinctively, Hardyal dismissed the question ; Englishmen do not as a rule discuss one another before an Indian. He wondered about Bertie. Would she be there, would she greet him as a friend ? He was filled with a pleasurable stir of excitement and anticipation.

The tonga turned in through a pair of handsome gates and rolled up a neat driveway, accompanied by a flock of barking spaniels. It stopped before a deep veranda furnished in chintz and wicker. On a table were books and a bowl of flowers which no *mali* could have arranged. A woman lives here, thought Hardyal, remembering the bleak quarters inhabited by bachelors, white or brown.

He commanded the tonga wallah to wait, and got out,

giving his name to the sentry who stood beside the steps.
But Macbeth appeared at once from a door farther down
the veranda. " Hardyal, this is good of you ! "

Momentarily embarrassed, Hardyal said simply : " I
came."

They shook hands, each observing the other with a
sense of relief. He looks less secretive, less arrogant, decided
Hardyal, and wondered whether Bertie was responsible for
the change.

Seems damned decent, as he always did, thought Macbeth. Aloud, he said : " Let's go into my *duftar*."

The *duftar*, the official sanctum . . . Hardyal suffered a
momentary recurrence of suspicion. Why the *duftar* ? Why
not the drawing-room or the veranda ? But Macbeth put
a hand lightly on his shoulder and they walked down the
length of the veranda into a large bright room furnished
like an office. A native clerk was typing at a desk, but at a
word from Macbeth he gathered up his papers and left the
room.

Macbeth offered Hardyal a cigarette, took one himself,
and they sat down on cool leather-covered chairs. Macbeth
looked at him and smiled, his eyes friendly and tranquil.
" How are you ? It's ages since we met."

" The last time was two years ago."

" It seems longer."   There was a tiny pause, then he
added : " I hear you are to be married. Congratulations ! "

Hardyal smiled.   " Will you accept mine ? "   Then,
before Macbeth could speak, he said, lightly : " There
seems little you do not know about me—about my forth-
coming marriage, my departures, my arrivals ! "

" My note must have surprised you. But the explanation is really quite simple. You were travelling with Abdul
Salim, and you must know, as I am sure he does, that his
movements are more or less under official surveillance.
But as far as you are concerned my information was purely
fortuitous."

Hardyal persisted banteringly : " But my marriage !
Who could have told you of that ? "

" My dear chap, Amritpore isn't on the other side of
the world. One meets people, occasionally, and one ex-
changes news. As a matter of fact I learned of your mar-

riage from an old and mutual friend—Ramdatta the moneylender."

"Ramdatta?" Uneasiness returned, but vaguely.

"The old scamp did me a good turn once long ago, and we correspond occasionally. If you should see him when you return to Amritpore, give him my salaams."

Hardyal thought, Yes, but first I shall speak of this to Abdul Salim. So Ramdatta is in communication with the Superintendent of Police of Berari. They are friends, they exchange news, information. A gleam, still not clear, touched the edges of his mind.

Macbeth went on : "Tell me about your father."

"Father is well. He has been in Agra for several weeks, on a riot case."

"And I take it you have come to Berari to hear Jagnath Singh?" It was put lightly, almost absent-mindedly, and without waiting for an answer he went on : "I am told he is a fine speaker, though I have never heard him."

"Perhaps you will hear him this evening?"

"I dare say." He dropped his hand on the head of the spaniel which had come in and lay at his feet. In a tone which was somehow unexpected he asked : "Did your father know that you were coming here with Salim?"

"I don't think I mentioned it to Father." This was the simple truth but it sounded like equivocation in his own ears.

"Had he known, do you think that he might have tried to dissuade you from coming?"

"Why should he? Salim and I are not children."

Macbeth laughed. "Right you are ! And all this must sound to you like prying, but honestly, I speak out of friendship for your father as well as for you. I've often thought of those long rides and the games of tennis and the garden parties at Amritpore."

Hardyal, feeling that he had been churlish, replied : "I, too, think of them. I appreciate your motives in asking . . ." He did not, quite, yet he felt that he had to say it.

"As a matter of fact," Macbeth continued, "there is no reason why you shouldn't go to hear Jagnath Singh, provided he *does* speak. What I wanted to discuss is your association with Salim. He is unquestionably heading towards trouble. You could not prevent it, nor, I imagine, could he, at this stage of the game. That is why I was sorry to hear that you had travelled to Berari in his company. Duty, if nothing else, would compel me to speak of it to you."

Hardyal hesitated, then began confusedly : " But you know that Salim has been our friend for many years ! And as for Jagnath Singh, the authorities have agreed to let him speak, have they not ? Where, then, is the difficulty ? You said just now ' provided he *does* speak ' ! May I ask what that can mean ? "

Macbeth stroked his spaniel's smooth brown head. " Since we talk as friends I may as well tell you that a difficulty *has* arisen. You probably don't know our Magistrate, Mr. Sheldon. He is in many ways a remarkable man, what people call a liberal, a dyed-in-the-wool sympathiser of—of Indians, a stickler for free speech and all that sort of thing. Perfectly all right, of course. He is immensely popular as a consequence, and that is undoubtedly why Jagnath Singh selected Berari for his speech-making."

To Bertie, an hour before, Macbeth had unburdened himself of a more forthright and exasperated version of the situation : " Sheldon, the infernal idiot, will end by getting us all into the devil of a hole before we know where we are. He's so full of his brown-brotherly notions, prides himself on talking their *boli* even better than they themselves, likes to imagine that he thinks like them, hobnobs with them all over the place, and generally inspires them with the belief that there is nothing they cannot say or do while under his aegis. But if things get out of hand and there's a row, I shall have to go in with my men and stop it. Damn Sheldon ! "

To Hardyal, he continued with a friendly, confiding air : " You know we have troops stationed in Berari. Their commanding officer, Colonel Gordon, has of course nothing to do with the civil administration. However, he is a friend of mine and of Mr. Sheldon's and he has privately expressed his disapproval of public controversy in the neighbourhood of troops at such a time. You can't blame a soldier for having little patience with such things, for while Jagnath Singh talks and talks, Gordon and his *sowars*

go out and do the fighting and the dying. To put it in a
nutshell, Colonel Gordon is not a bit keen on having his
men filter into Perron Park to listen while a fellow-Indian
lambastes the Raj which they are pledged to defend. He
could, of course, confine his men to barracks, but that
would rather take the edge off Mr. Sheldon's gesture of
confidence, wouldn't it ? "

It would, as Hardyal perceived instantly and vividly.
He was flattered by Macbeth's friendly candour. No
matter what one's own view might be, here was a situation
too delicate, too implicit with danger, to be lightly shrugged
off.

Macbeth went on quickly : " The speech itself is harmless enough—I've read it, so has Colonel Gordon. It's
quite innocuous in fact."

" Well, then . . ." murmured Hardyal, hopefully.

" That's just the point—it's too damned innocuous to
be worth giving. But you don't know Jagnath Singh, do
you ? He's a genius in his way. Once he starts to talk it
will be in the vernacular, full of twists and turns, images,
innuendoes—all idiomatic and impossible to pin down.
His presence by itself rouses a strong response in the crowd.
Berari is literally overrun since the news got about that he
was coming. And those who have come to hear him are
hardly going to be content with milk and water from such
a source, are they ? Questions will be asked, challenges
flung by men like your Abdul Salim. And that is exactly
what Jagnath hopes for . . . someone to throw him the ball
so he can throw it back, weighted. Whatever has been
forbidden or agreed upon between us will go by the board,
and it will, of course, be nobody's fault ! "

In the pause which followed, Hardyal, feeling suddenly
important and responsible, smoked and pondered while
Macbeth reviewed the argument in which he had joined
the night before, after dinner at Henry Sheldon's. Colonel
Gordon had suggested that Jagnath Singh's speech be
arbitrarily called off, that notices be pasted on every wall
and policemen posted at every strategic corner. " They
won't like it but they'll have to lump it, and once you've
made a decision there's damned little they can do about
it."

Sheldon had replied without hesitation : " You simply can't do things like that."

He was a scholar, a man of mild appearance, but obstinate, idealistic, visionary, immovable in his conviction that East and West are one and that individuals alone barred the path to reunion. Indians loved him ; his own kind, with but few exceptions, regarded him as a lunatic when they did not stigmatise him as something much worse. " Sooner or later," they prophesied with bitter satisfaction, " sooner or later Saint Sheldon will pay for his sentimentality and will make the rest of us pay with him."

" Sooner or later," thought some Indians, with an equivalent bitterness, " sooner or later he will let us down. It may not be his fault. He won't be able to help himself."

But for more than twenty years Henry Sheldon had let no one down. How should he have bargained for the complexities and contradictions of a vast European war ?

Macbeth had volunteered, mildly enough : " As a matter of fact, at any other time it wouldn't make any difference, would it ? Jagnath Singh could talk his head off, as usual. But now . . . with the Turkish-German mission at Kabul, under our very noses . . . the possibility of spies, enemy agents and all the rest of it . . ."

" Precisely ! " interposed Colonel Gordon. " It's all the purest rot, Sheldon, the purest rot, allowing the swine to talk against us at this stage of the game ! "

Sheldon looked at them mildly. " What do you want me to do, rescind my permission at the last moment ? "

" Why not wire Government House and put up to Sir William ? "

" Why should I ? "

" Damn it, man ! It's an emergency, isn't it ? " The Colonel was nervous and angry. He had been nervous and angry for several days. " If Sir William backs you, naturally no one can have anything further to say." He did not add his private hope that the Lieutenant Governor would refuse point blank to back this amiable crackpot, that Sir William would telegraph his immediate and unequivocal demand that the whole business be called off. It should never have been called on ; no one but Sheldon would have dreamed of carrying tolerance and conciliation to such lengths.

It was with maddening good temper that Sheldon replied : " I don't see it as an emergency. We've all read the speech. There is nothing in it to provoke a row."

" Then why does he want to give it ? "

" God knows. He's probably no different from other men who like the sound of their own voices."

" Just the same," objected Macbeth, " I'm thinking of the audience. We all know the sort who'll gather to listen to him."

" Yes," exclaimed the soldier, angrily. " It's the audience that I'm thinking about, myself."

" Jagnath Singh has given me his word . . ."

" His word ! "

" . . . His word," Sheldon repeated, equably. " I foresee no trouble. Had I done so I certainly would not have been fool enough to give my permission in the first place."

There was a brief pause, then the soldier said, heavily : " There will be Mohammedans present. Someone will ask a question about Turkey : Why should Indian Moslems be expected to fight against their co-religionists, in a foreign war ? "

Sheldon shrugged. " Moslems have volunteered to fight and are now fighting, in such a war. Isn't that your answer ? "

Colonel Gordon ignored this as mere quibbling. " Damned if I see why you don't put the whole thing up to Sir William."

" Damned if I see why you should expect me to. This is my show, you know."

" Oh, good Lord, I know that ! I'm not trying to barge in where angels fear to tread. On the other hand . . . under the circumstances . . . with troops quartered next door . . . I think you'll find that Macbeth agrees with me."

Sheldon turned to his young colleague. " Do you ? "

" Afraid I do, rather."

Sheldon heaved a sigh. " You sound like a pair of old women. Will it set your minds at rest to hear that Sir William *does* know ? I had a letter from him last week, and I answered at once, telling him about Jagnath, and I stated that, considering the remarkably loyal response we have received from all over the country, there could be little risk in allowing these public addresses. Since then, I haven't had a word from Sir William. I think it's safe to assume that he shares my views."

They looked at him. " Why in the devil didn't you tell us this before ? "

Sheldon merely smiled. " And that," Macbeth observed afterwards to Bertie, " is his idea of humour."

53

HARDYAL broke the long silence. " I do appreciate your confidence, although I don't quite see what I can do about it. I'm a nobody, after all."

" There's precious little any one can do about it now, except perhaps where oneself is concerned."

" You mean, it would please you if I were to absent myself from this meeting ? "

Macbeth met candour with candour. " It would please me. I'm pretty sure that it would please your father. I, too, can do little, for I'm hardly more of a somebody than you. One can only stand by or advise one's friends, to the best of one's ability."

He has changed, decided Hardyal. He carries force and authority, but love—and perhaps war—which embitter many, have sweetened him. He was silent for a moment, and Macbeth was thinking : " If I can keep this one from becoming infected it will be something. Little enough, God knows, but something."

" You realise," said Hardyal, with a smile, " that the implications of your request are not exactly flattering ? "

Good-nature flowed between them, making it possible for him to add, with a laugh : " I make no promises ! "

" Nor would I dream of asking for one. Cigarette ? "

They smoked and talked for a little while about the war and its problems. Macbeth, grateful that Hardyal had not brought Bertie's name or Jacques' into the conversation—grateful for the considerate restraint on many subjects whose mention he'd dreaded—leaned forward and said : " Would you care to hear my point of view ? It isn't very great or very grand. As a matter of fact, it's almost entirely a personal one. My father is a man of sixty-five. He is now in France with his regiment. At an age when most men look forward to peace, he is fighting, simply because he held an idea, or an ideal if you prefer it, which has tried to bar the path of unfairness and indecency all over the world. It has tried to bar it here in India. I see this not so much as a problem of race or of government but as something far more important. I see it as a question whether or not a fundamental sense of decency should be allowed to grow and prevail. Personally, I couldn't breathe without that sense. There are lots of things about us that are not so very decent, but these things do not happen to be fundamental."

Hardyal was moved by this frankness, by this sincerity. He realised that he must often have misjudged an earlier, inarticulate Macbeth. Somehow, somewhere, a miracle had taken place, making a new man.

He said in a low voice : " You and I would not disagree about those ideas."

" No. But one of us might, out of a confusion of values, acquire substitutes. They might be palmed off on one, like fake emeralds."

" Not when one has known the real ! "

Instinctively, now, both relapsed into Hindustani. Macbeth said : " To know the real, one must first have experienced the false, and that is far more difficult in the realm of ideas than it is in the matter of gems."

" Nevertheless, both have reality. What it all comes down to in the end is, as you say, value . . . value . . ." His eyes became luminous. " Not the real or the unreal, for there is nothing unreal in that sense. There is but the true and the untrue . . ." He felt, powerfully, the force of this idea, of this difference. " And I have known both, yes—both ! "

" You mean the personal and the impersonal," said Macbeth, watching him curiously.

The tensions of the past hour, indeed of the past few weeks, were working towards expression. Hardyal, with extraordinary intensity and with the voice of one who conjures up a spirit outside himself, repeated : " Both, both ! I have seen them, I have known them ! "

" Name me one, for I, too, should like to know ! "

" Mrs. Lyttleton."

" That queer old lady ! "

" She is dead." He had forgotten, but now he remembered and a protest rose in him. He saw her quite clearly, a strong and limpid presence declaring itself in the very teeth of that falsehood, Death.

" Dead ? " exclaimed Macbeth. " I hadn't heard. I wish I'd known . . . another friend was asking about her just the other day. Aubrey Wall."

Stillness fell on Hardyal. One spirit had conjured up another, and if he had asked for any proof of his vision, here it was.

" Wall ? Aubrey ? Aubrey Wall ? "

" One of your old pals, wasn't he ? He's been stationed at Berari for the past few months. His wife and child are here, too, for the winter. He retires next year."

" He has children ? "

" One, a little girl."

Macbeth felt the tension of the past minute without understanding its cause. He went on conversationally : " Wall spoke of the old days at Amritpore. He asked for you and for the—for the St. Remys, and of course for old Mrs. Lyttleton. I'm sure he will be saddened to hear that she is dead. But she must have been quite old."

He became increasingly conscious of a coldness interposing between them. There was something new in Hardyal's silence ; his eyes, once filled with intelligent animation, were now veiled in the obscurity one sometimes sees in the eyes of very young children or of Orientals. At a loss to account for this changed mood, Macbeth persisted in his easy, friendly manner : " You stayed with Wall's people in Sussex, didn't you ? "

Hardyal nodded. He stared at his feet, thrust into light sandals which he had not remembered to take off before coming into the house.

" Wall wondered—and so, as a matter of fact, did I— why you never returned to England."

" Did he talk about that ? "

Macbeth hesitated. Wall's remarks had not been complimentary : they were the remarks of a disappointed patron turned indifferent.

" Well, he just wondered."

Hardyal drew a deep breath. " I came home for the holidays. I felt, then, that my place was at home."

It was not convincing, and Macbeth had the impression that it was not intended to be. But he went on, agreeably : " Well, what have you been up to since, anything important ? "

Hardyal answered without looking up. " Important ? What could I do that might be considered important ? You know that when I came back from England I studied with a tutor. He was an Eurasian, and clever. Then I took my B.A. at Calcutta University. It was easy . . . everything has been fairly easy. Since then I have helped my father somewhat with his work."

" And soon you are to be married."

" Yes."

" And the future, have you thought about that ? "

A slight tremor passed over his dark, impassive features. " I have thought of it, often, often ! "

" You've never considered getting into Government service, I suppose ? A nomination to the Police . . ."

" It does not appeal to me."

There was another silence and Macbeth thought : Mentioning England was, somehow, a mistake. I wonder what happened. Could he have fallen in love with some girl, and it ended unhappily ? That was the usual thing. . . . Hardyal sat before him, silent as a clod, and Macbeth, who had seen other natives go through these strange metamorphoses, knew that there was nothing to be done about it. He asked gently : " How long will you stay at Berari ? "

" I return to Amritpore early to-morrow."

" With Abdul Salim ? "

" With Abdul Salim."

So, it was ended. Not by words, not by declarations and gestures, but by the incomprehensible accident which at some unguarded moment had come between them. It was Hardyal who rose at last ; he could not have borne, now, to be politely or even kindly given the hint that it was time for him to go. Macbeth, grateful for the other's initiative, rose too, rubbing out his cigarette on a silver tray.

" Well, Hardyal . . ."

He tried to meet the other's eye, to accost without peril of direct inquiry, a spirit which for a little while had seemed to march with his, but instead he met a darkness in which his own cheerful glance was swiftly drowned.

The trivial preoccupation of navigating chairs and tables brought them safely to the door and there, for a moment, they stood.

" Whenever you are in Berari . . ." said Macbeth, his friendliness straining for survival, " do come and see me."

He held out his hand and Hardyal took it, his own nerveless. He did not look round as he walked down the veranda to the steps, but he felt that his body, like his spirit, was suddenly unclothed, that he took upon his flesh the stab of hostile glances, the harsh breath of unspoken summations. Memory winced under its old, tight scars.

His tonga was waiting and when he walked down the steps he was sure as he would have been had his eyes guaranteed her, that Bertie's eyes followed his departure. She must have known that he was with Macbeth in the *duftar*, yet she had not come out to meet him. She had eaten his salt, she had walked in his father's garden, she had, without doubt, slept with his closest friend, Jacques. But now she let him come and go without greeting.

" Whither, Huzoor ? " asked the tonga wallah as his passenger climbed in beside him.

Hardyal made a vague motion of his hand. " Drive a little way, and I will tell thee."

54

As THEY drove through the gates and into the road the tonga wallah looked once more at his passenger. " Which way, left or right ? "

Hardyal clasped his forehead. " Drive . . . drive . . . till I tell thee."

The man whipped his pony and settled back contentedly. So long as he had a fare what did he care how far or how long he drove ? The young man had a prosperous and respectable air, he was evidently in the good graces of local officialdom. All would be well, with probably a handsome baksheesh at the journey's end. They struck off down a side-street.

Hardyal lifted his head and stared about him with superstitious eyes. Aubrey Wall was here, in Berari. Wall, whom he had not seen for years, whom he had hoped never to see again. Wall was here . . . within reach, perhaps within a few paces of himself. He might now be strolling behind that clump of oleanders, he might be the figure reclining in a chair on the veranda of that house just visible between the trees. Perhaps this white man bicycling towards him in grey flannels and sun-coat . . . Ah, if they should meet and their eyes encounter ! Hardyal's muscles were rigid as an Englishman pedalled by. Their eyes met fleetingly—but it was not Aubrey Wall.

Hardyal sat back and tried to reconstruct the half-remembered, rather colourless figure of his old friend and patron. But what recurred, what Macbeth's casual reference to the Engineer had sharply revived, was the memory of Mrs. Lyttleton and the finality of her death. A little while ago that death had seemed to set a seal upon his youth, now in an aching second it ripped bare the knowledge that he had inherited the full weight of a terrible responsibility. Aware that he and Wall, now, stood together in the baleful light of that responsibility, Hardyal felt at one and the same instant threatened and threatening. He was caught up in the contradictory impulse of longing yet dreading to meet his unconscious adversary, not to talk with him or to be seen by him, but to catch him unawares, to scrutinise from a safe distance the enigma that was Wall. This is an instinct shared by lovers and enemies, the fatal attraction which seeks to shatter an unbearable suspense. Yet in all this the pathetic figure of Jalal had not once intruded ; he was as lost to Hardyal's memory as he was lost, now doubly lost, to Mrs. Lyttleton. He had emerged but once from his brief and inconsequential existence—an obstacle, a stone against which a man stumbled and fell. But the thought of that fall and of what it had brought down with it excited a sort of delirium in Hardyal. A sweat of fear broke over him and he turned his face aside, seeking the unknown wife who would comfort him, who would receive him into her heart, believing him supreme among men. He would lay his head between her breasts and generate a son who would be different from himself and from her, different from his own time and from his fate : he would generate a hope, a future. To be thought supreme, to know oneself supreme, to rise once in one's life above all others, to breathe into one's nostrils the promise of one's own tried and trusted gods ! Forget the Walls and the Macbeths, forget—forget ! He closed his eyes and felt the warm sea washing his feet, he saw the white moon above Arabia and the offerings to Varuna moving out with the accepting tide. He heard, somewhere, the faint sweet sound of a woman's laughter.

" In that house," said the tonga wallah, pointing with his whip, " resides the District Magistrate. The other, the big white one, is the house of the Deputy Commissioner."

Hardyal's fever broke ; the conscious world thrust itself before his startled eyes. " Driver, what time is it ? "

The man consulted the air, sniffed, meditated, then replied, with reasonable accuracy : " Going on six."

" Oh, good heavens ! My friend . . . I must meet my friend. Turn and let us go back as we came." He racked his brain. The number and name of the street which Salim had given him had completely vanished from his memory. He stared at the tonga wallah. " Where is Jagnath Singh staying ? "

The man started. " Jagnath Singh ? He who is to speak this evening ? "

" I was to meet my friend at the house of Jagnath's cousin."

The driver, with Jehu's dry wit, suggested that they drive to the nearest jail. " If Jagnath and his cousin and all their friends are not already there, they will be shortly."

Hardyal hailed a man trudging along in the dust with a bundle of sugar-cane on his shoulder. The man stared, shook his head, opened his mouth and made a mewing noise.

"He is mute, he hath no tongue," said the driver in disgust.

"Then let us drive to the city and make inquiries there."

"Better to go straight to the park. Jagnath is to speak there in half an hour. If your friend is with him, you are sure to meet."

Hardyal thought confusedly : Suppose Salim waits for me and misses the speech ? Suppose he imagines that I have been arrested and goes to Macbeth's house to make a scene ? It would be like him. . . . No, they must somehow find the cousin's house. He searched his memory in an agony of humiliation. Salim had told him clearly enough. . . . Something Avenue . . . Something Road. He stared anxiously round him as the tonga wheeled and headed back as it had come.

"Someone is sure to know where Jagnath Singh is staying. Let us ask a constable."

The driver spat over a wheel. "Do not be sure that a constable will tell you anything." He glanced at his passenger. "I would not be too sure that Jagnath will speak, at that."

"What are you talking about ? "

"Do not be impatient with your humble servant. While you were with the Captain Sahib, I listened to his minions. Those flatfeet know everything and they cannot resist showing off their knowledge if it suits them to do so. It seems there is a chance that Jagnath's speech may be called off. There is disagreement in high places."

"Called off—at this hour ? " scoffed Hardyal. He was obsessed by the thought of Salim waiting for him, perhaps fuming and disgusted, perhaps darkly suspecting the worst. "Drive to the city. I shall ask at the post office."

The driver had taken a short-cut down a dusty ally, and they now emerged on the main thoroughfare which ran in a straight line from the railway station, past Perron Park, towards the European Club.

"Look," said the driver. "All these folk are going to the park. Let us go with them."

A stream of traffic flowed along the main channel— ekkas, carriages, a motor car or two, bicycles, people on foot. They were in holiday mood, raising clouds of dust,

some lifting their voices in a half-defiant, half-jocular shout :
" Jagnath Singh ki jai ! "

The tonga wallah smiled dourly. " They better take
care. Here come the Police."

With the eerie suddenness of their kind, a company of
khaki-clad, red-turbanned figures appeared riding bicycles,
led by a short, powerful, red-faced English sergeant. The
crowd made way for them, genially or timidly according to
their separate natures or consciences.

" Let's ask them," cried Hardyal. " Stop, let me speak
to the sergeant."

He leaned out and shouted as the Englishman pedalled
alongside.

" Can you tell me, please, where Mr. Jagnath Singh is
residing ? "

The man did not answer, nor did he turn his head.
Grim, thick-necked, he flashed past, followed by his retinue.

Hardyal subsided on the shabby seat. " Drive to the
park," he said, his voice not quite as assured as it had been.
" Hurry, hurry ! "

" Be calm," urged the driver, gently. He had, with the
peculiar sophistication of his calling, already gauged his
young fare's innocence, which inspired a protective con-
descension. " Let them go. Perron Park is no distance, and
without doubt that is where you will meet your friends, or
someone who will direct you to them."

The tonga merged with a flux of vehicles and pedes-
trians, and was forced to slow down. The city lay directly
behind them, and Hardyal saw the bright green of the little
park which he had noticed when he drove from the station
to Macbeth's. The crowd was orderly enough, and he saw
numerous policemen armed not only with their truncheons
but with the brass-bound *lathies* which come as close as
anything can to being India's national weapon. Once, he
caught sight of the white police sergeant and thought :
Undoubtedly that one has not changed since he was born
. . . that face, incapable of expression, was cast in stone
rather than in flesh.

" Jagnath will speak from the bandstand at the farther
end of the park," explained the tonga wallah. " It is wider
there, and there are benches."

Hardyal watched the crowd, knowing that many had come from a distance, others from the suburbs, from the bazaars and alleys of the city itself. Members of an amateur band straggled by, wearing the cast-off tunics of some long-demobilised regiment. The late sun struck gold from a battered trumpet ; a drum, cheerfully thumped by some urchin, emitted a thunderous growl. Voices and the rattle of vehicles, the tinny warnings of bicycle bells, all rose on a mounting wave towards the higher, clearer air.

"The world and its wife are here," observed the tonga wallah. He interrupted himself to engage in foul genea-logical compliments with an ekka driver whose near wheel threatened to tangle with the tonga. "Well, perhaps I heard wrong there at the Captain Sahib's. Or else his chuprassies were talking through their turbans. No one would prevent this gathering at this hour."

A policemen pressed through the crowd. "Vehicles may not proceed nearer the park. You will have to walk from here."

Hardyal paid the driver, adding a generous tip, then got out and was instantly swallowed up by the crowd. Pushed, jostled, his feet stepped on, his cap knocked off, he felt exhilaration well up inside him. Here was the same sweating, craning, genial crew which brought to the scene of political controversy the incorrigible *tamasha*-loving spirit of the country. They came with minds and hearts prepared for anything, for everything. Such occasions were all too rare in their lives ; what matter if this turn out to be a dull party, nothing but vague chit-chat and impossible visions presided over by the police, with nothing to buy or to covet, and little to look at except one another ? Take what the gods offered . . . and be happy.

A casteless man bumped into Hardyal, and recognising their separate stations, backed away with abject salaams and muttered " Maharaj ! " Hardyal saw groups of students in the black coats, white trousers, and red fezzes of the Moslem High School, others in the less formal haber-dashery of Hindus. Everywhere moved the red turbans of the police, enlivened here and there by dashes of braid and the bobbing gold fringes of subordinate officers.

Agile and athletic, he had little difficulty in making his

way through the congestion to the park gates. The enclosure was shaped roughly in the form of a square, bounded by an irregular masonry wall of perhaps five feet. He saw at once that he had no chance of reaching the bandstand from which Jagnath Singh was to speak, so he decided to wait until after the speech before going in search of Abdul Salim. Perhaps Salim would accompany Jagnath to the speaker's stand, in which case, thought Hardyal, it might be possible somehow to attract his friend's attention.

55

TREES grew at intervals along the wall nearest the main road ; boys swarmed up their trunks and swarmed down again when their dangling legs were spied by the police who, however, offered no objection to people taking up positions of vantage on top of the wall itself. Someone gave Hardyal a hand and hauled him up, another steadied him when he was almost precipitated over the other side. He felt their excitement, their good humour. "We may not hear anything, but we'll get a good view," observed one, philosophically.

The whole scene might have been a circus or a pantomime. Hardyal, longing for a sight of Abdul Salim, studied the milling and leisurely crowd. The bandstand was a couple of hundred yards distant and he could see little beyond the ornamental palms and the European hats of some of its occupants.

"Will Jagnath Singh be in European dress ? "

"Never fear, you will recognise him," declared a neighbour. "He is tall and stout, with white hair. He always wears European dress. He is said to have observed once, that in a scuffle the police might find it child's play to steal one's dhoti, but it would be less easy for them to deprive one of one's trousers."

"He hath a tongue, that Jagnath."

"I heard him once, in Lucknow. He can make a stone laugh or a tree burst into tears."

"Aye, and he has been known to raise blisters as big as plovers' eggs on the police, before now."

" What will he tell us to-day, know you ? "

" About Turkey and the great war."

" A thorny subject."

" Nay, he is to explain about the new taxes."

" Why should he waste time on such matters ! It is more likely that he will explain why the Raj needs our sons to wage war against the Germans."

" You mean," drawled a sour voice, " why we should refuse to send our sons anywhere to wage war against any one."

" Let us wait and listen."

Hardyal felt happy among them. The man who had given him a hand on to the wall was youngish, with a leathery black face and sparkling eyes. He wore an English jacket with his dhoti and clutched the rough stone wall with bare, muscular toes. From his pocket he now extracted a piece of sugar-cane, chewed the rind off it with his teeth, and offered a fragment to Hardyal, who accepted it with thanks. They champed, enjoying the sweet liquid, spitting the pith between their feet. Hardyal could see various comings and goings on the bandstand, but there was no sign of Abdul Salim nor of him whom they had described as Jagnath Singh.

" It is early yet," said the man in the jacket. He was a clerk in the Municipality. Now, with a self-conscious flourish, he produced a nickel-plated watch and consulted it. " Ten minutes. These affairs are always late."

Hardyal watched the evening crows fly in squadrons across the deepening sky. Where, where was Salim ?

Behind him in the road a carriage bell shrilled imperiously. He heard important shouts from the police, cries of " Hut jao ! Hut jao ! Make way for the Sahib's carriage."

Craning round, Hardyal had a glimpse of a smart dog-cart driven by an Englishman. The police were clearing a way for its passage. The Englishman looked as though he was keeping his temper with an effort, but he was also keeping his foot on the bell, which shrilled and shrilled. Behind him on the syce's stand his groom brandished a horsehair switch over the heads of scurrying urchins.

" Hut jao ! " bawled the policemen, shoving people out of the way.

"Dolts, owls, brothers-in-law of untrustworthy women, make way for the Sahib's horse!"

"It is the Engineer of Canals," volunteered the clerk at Hardyal's elbow. "It is Wall Sahib himself."

Hardyal's heart grew huge, he was almost stifled by its sudden pounding. Aubrey Wall, intent on keeping his horse and his temper under control in this melling, milling mob, saw no one in particular. They were natives, heterogeneous, unmannerly as usual, a bloody bore . . . and he was on his way to the Club for a game of billiards and a drink before dining with friends.

"Hut jao! Hut jao!"

The bell shrilled again, insistent, imperious, then the dogcart and its occupant disappeared and the crowd surged upon the space where it had been, as the sea surges upon the site of a dislodged pebble. Hardyal's eyes were blazing. He was possessed by an emotion which seemed to fill his veins with light. He put his hand on the shoulder of the Municipal clerk, and steadying himself thus, stared across the shifting throng. Then he lifted his voice in a shout which carried high above the muted uproar:

"Jagnath Singh ki jai! Jagnath Singh ki jai!"

The cry, evocative, traditional, first stilled, then stirred the fickle mob; it harnessed their disorderly limbs, focused their attention, channelled and directed their ready emotions. The clerk put his arm round Hardyal and added his own undistinguished voice to the plangent cry: "*Ki jai! Ki jai!* Jagnath Singh ki jai!"

Accented like this, the words surrendered their purely evocative appeal and became at once militant, emphatic, intense. The crowd took it up, took it up with a roar as only people reared and nurtured in the single current of tradition, religious or otherwise, could take it. The amateur drummer lost somewhere in the mass rub-a-dub-dubbed wildly, a trumpet squealed, small boys concealed among the higher branches gave themselves away with shrill cries. Then all these human throats instinctively discarded whatever was trivial or individual: Moslem and Hindu, and the outcastes among them, settled as marching men settle into that throbbing primordial chant which for force and rhythm depends on the upward, outward stroke of the heart's concerted beat. " Ki jai ! Ki jai ! Jagnath Singh ki jai ! "

By the gates, the policemen moved towards each other, forming up two by two or in fours, slipping their truncheons from the leather holsters. Those who carried *lathies* held their right palms against their mouths for a second before grasping anew the polished bamboo staves topped with brass.

The people nearest Hardyal had taken their stroke from him and relayed it to others farther along. It travelled, not in eddies and trickles, but in an increasing wave, as one voice and then another—waiting only the penultimate note —came crashing home on it. The young, unknown voice which had struck the note where and when a forgotten carriage bell left off, now merged and became one with the larger, the growing, the formidable voice of the mob.

Light flung its final spear among the trees ; falling, it dazzled for a moment the eyes and the hearts of the multitude. This was the heroic moment, and they acclaimed it, every one poised on the brink of instant, obedient silence should their hero show himself. But he did not show himself. Instead, the bandstand suddenly swarmed with strangers, like a piece of sugar with ants.

A figure wearing a dark suit and a white topi detached itself from the group and walked quietly to the edge of the platform. As he held up his hand for silence those nearest him, recognising Henry Sheldon, their Magistrate, became silent, and that silence rolled back as the sea might have rolled back for King Canute—had Canute been lucky.

Hardyal craned forward in a passion of concentration, but he caught only a word or two of an utterance which lasted, at most, not more than three minutes. The gist of it reached him several minutes after Sheldon and his companions had left the bandstand and disappeared. It reached him through exactly the same channels as news reaches the unlettered and the far-away—it reached him strained and modified through the minds and mouths of a hundred intervening human beings.

" Jagnath Singh will not speak to you to-day. A difficulty has arisen which makes it necessary to postpone his speech. The Lieutenant Governor himself ordered the postponement, but in due time the public will be notified as to the reason for this delay. Until then they will be so good as to disperse with the least possible disturbance of the general peace."

The pause—the indecision rather—which followed the collective digestion of this announcement endured for a few minutes, then a ripple passed over the crowd, another and yet another—the loud formless, humble characteristic of surprised and disappointed citizenry. In a vague, unhurried fashion they began to drift towards the separate exits. Packed fairly tight, they still maintained proportion, density, and centre, and it was from this centre that a voice, hoarse with rage, suddenly yelled : " It is a put-up job ! Shame on them, shame ! Shame ! "

The new voice, as Hardyal's voice had done earlier, carried no farther than the depths of ten or fifteen standing men, but that was far enough. Tempers were ignited or extinguished by the sheer heat of contact and example, and a tremor shuddered through the single sympathetic nerve which Hardyal's voice had first touched and set quivering.

" They don't dare let Jagnath Singh speak to us ! " This from one of the Moslem students.

" It's the truth ! Jagnath was going to tell us that we have no quarrel with our brothers in Turkey."

" He was going to tell us how Government backs the Marwaries and the *banias* against us . . ."

" . . . Things which he felt we should understand . . . but they prevented . . . they prevented ! "

" They gave their word, then broke it ! "

" Cheats ! Liars ! Cowards ! "

Hardyal stayed on his wall. The tumult poured in and out of his veins ; he shivered a little from excitement, although his brain worked fast and clearly. Jagnath Singh and Salim had not come to the park—of this he was increasingly sure. It was hardly likely that the authorities would allow the speaker and his entourage to appear before an angry and disappointed audience. No, if they were not already in jail they must still be at the address which Salim had given him at the station. Something Road, Something Avenue . . .

A voice near him yelled : " Let Jagnath appear before us and explain ! "

" Let us see him, and we will go quietly."

" See him ? What do you wager the police had already hustled him off to jail ? "

A gruff voice spoke suddenly behind Hardyal. " Move on, move on."

It was the police sergeant, mounted now on a tough cavalry charger, carrying his wand of office—a short, stout leather quirt.

" Move on, I said. *Chello*, you ! "

Those below the wall began to move a little faster. Children scuttled like frightened beetles ; women, pulling their veils over their eyes, clung silently to their men.

" *Chello*," repeated the rasping voice, its Cockney lending an indescribable accent to the vernacular word. " Go on, go on ! "

One by one, the people on the wall began to jump down and mix with the crowd. Hardyal gave a final sweeping glance over the massed heads. There was just a bare chance that Salim might have come in search of him.

A voice muttered : " The whole thing is a police trap. They've put Jagnath in jail."

" If you ask me, they got us all here so they could arrest us, too."

" Better get out. They've sent to the nearest *chauki* for more men. You know what happens when they start picking people up. All they want is a couple of dozen innocents to swell their bag and maintain their reputation ! "

The voice behind Hardyal reiterated : " Didn't you hear what I said, you cheeky swine ? *Chello !* "

The Municipal clerk, who had been addressed thus, leaped swiftly from the wall and disappeared into the crowd.

" You too," said the sergeant, staring at Hardyal. " Get down from the wall and move along."

Hardyal answered mechanically in English : " I am looking for a friend."

" Then look for him somewhere else. You can just bloody well *chello* off that wall and hurry up about it."

Hardyal climbed down—he dared not jump because of

the congestion. Nor did he see what happened immediately afterwards. He did, however, hear a sudden scream as the sergeant's horse, pricked by a vicious spur, reared and brought its iron-shod hoof down on a man's foot.

"God blast your soul! Why don't you get out of the way?"

There was the sound of a scuffle, blows, shouts. Somewhere a police-whistle shrilled and was answered, mockingly, by a terrific thumping on the band's invisible drum. Hardyal pushed his way along the wall and presently found himself pressed up against his friend the Municipal clerk. They exchanged grins. "If we get out without broken heads, we'll be lucky," murmured the clerk, quite cheerfully. "I just had a glimpse of the Captain Sahib himself. They're afraid of a riot."

"Then let us give them one," muttered an infuriated voice close beside him. The speaker was a strapping man with the look of a Pathan. "Jagnath Singh is right—they herd us like cattle, like cattle!"

Hardyal pushed ahead and when he believed himself to be out of reach of the sergeant, hoisted himself on to the wall once more, realising that to make his way along its undisputed length was his only chance of rapid progress. But the noise of the scuffle seemed to dog his heels. A voice cried passionately: "They even train their horses to kill us!"

"He's not dead, you fool! Pick him up. Make way there, make way!"

The whistle shrilled again, and he saw coming towards him a phalanx of constables led by Macbeth on horseback. His face under the severe brim of his helmet wore an assured expression; he was talking quietly to the people, who crushed aside to give him and his horse ample room. Pale, erect, he bored through the mass, with his constables shouldering their way behind him. The light was now almost gone; it struck the gilt spike on Macbeth's helmet and the metal knobs of the police *lathies*, it ran eerily along the battered trumpet of the native bandsman and lost itself like quicksilver in the drab and defeated mob. Hardyal, momentarily arrested by the sight of Macbeth, saw something fly through the air and for a split second took it for a frightened bird or a bat. But it was a shoe which, hurtling over the intervening heads, struck a red turban. Then something viperous whipped out, struck, vanished. The turbanless constable fell, with blood spuming from his nostrils. On top of him, his head split like an egg, lay the big man who looked like a Pathan.

Hardyal was caught in a sort of trance by the sheer unexpectedness, the sheer perfection of this detail set in a generally formless and indifferent whole. Perhaps a dozen people had actually seen the thing happen, certainly very few more were to witness what so swiftly followed. As Macbeth rose in his stirrups and began to lay about him with his riding-crop, a figure leaped on to the wall and Hardyal saw the uplifted hand which clutched, for missile, a green, broken, jagged bottle. Hardyal's warning cry reached Macbeth, who ducked as the murderous glass flew past his face, but the sound of that English : " Look out ! " never reached the ears of the white sergeant and his escort. They struck Hardyal from behind, and he and the thrower of the bottle went down together under a rain of *lathi* blows and the high, thin piping of the whistles.

56

THREE days later Jacques left his bicycle on the gravel of the driveway and ran up the steps of Ganpat Rai's house, where Krishna, the old servant, came to meet him. The man's eyes were inflamed, his voice harsh from weeping. " My master will receive you in his study."

The barrister, wearing a kurtha and dhoti, rose as his visitor appeared in the door. For a moment they stared at each other, then as Jacques went to him the older man clasped the younger to his breast.

" Ganpat Rai, why in God's name didn't you send for me at once ? "

" There was little time, and much confusion." Gently, Ganpat Rai released him. " Let us sit. I am very tired, I feel old." He smiled, but his face had a worn, yellowish look. " First let me set your heart at ease : Hardyal was badly hurt, but he is out of danger. In a few days he will be out of jail."

Jacques felt that they moved, spoke, listened in a dimension which had somehow lost all its familiar characteristics. " In jail ! "

" In jail. It was there that he recovered consciousness, it was there that we found him—Salim and I—two days ago."

As Jacques stared, unable to speak, the older man went on heavily.

" I was at Agra when Salim wired me of Hardyal's disappearance. I took the first train to Berari, where I arrived on the morning after the affair. I went at once to see Henry Sheldon, who has always been my friend. He is in very bad odour with his colleagues and with most of the European community, who hold him directly responsible for what happened at Perron Park. You know that two men were killed and several badly hurt, among the latter, Hardyal." His eyes moved in a troubled way, as though he were trying to peer through a veil. " From the chorus of ' I told you so ! ' and ' What can you expect ? ' one would suppose that they are really delighted at what occurred. It justifies their attitude."

Looking at him, Jacques realised that here was a wound that would never mend. " And Hardyal ? " he murmured, sick at heart.

" There are certain formalities, but he will be released within a very few days. Sheldon has promised, so has Macbeth."

" Macbeth ! "

" We had a long talk. I found him sympathetic. You see, he is convinced that it was Hardyal's shout of warning which saved him from serious injury. Others have testified to this, among them a clerk from the Municipality, who saw the whole thing."

" Then," said Jacques, drawing his breath, " Hardyal has a clear case ? "

" As far as that goes, yes. But there are things which I myself do not find so clear. Salim and I spent hours making inquiries and questioning people. If, after leaving Macbeth's house, Hardyal had gone straight to the address which Salim gave him, he would have found Jagnath Singh and Salim there, for Sheldon had already notified them of the Governor's last-minute intervention. But when I questioned Hardyal about this he was very evasive : he declared that he had completely forgotten the address which Salim gave him. Realising how such an excuse might sound in court, I protested that such forgetfulness was foreign to him, whereupon he turned away his face, saying : ' It was fate.' "

Ganpat Rai laughed. " Fate ! To speak of fate to me, who have learned that there are but two implements to human action—intention and accident. However, I did not want to disturb him then with arguments and expostulations. But when I was leaving him I tried to cheer him up by saying that Macbeth himself had interceded for his speedy release—that it would be a mere matter of days before he was free. At that he gave me a strange look and replied : ' There is no hurry. Let me lie here and get used to these walls. I have a feeling that I shall see them again, often, often.' "

" What did he mean ? "

Ganpat Rai hesitated, and Jacques sensed his deep disquiet. It expressed itself at last, haltingly. " I think we both know what he means. Some men are born into the path of revolt, as Salim was. Others are thrust into it by accident—or by another's fault. I can tell you, who have known him all his life, who have always loved him, that I find myself wondering whether we have lost Hardyal."

" Lost him ? "

" You must know that more than his body suffered at Perron Park."

" Yes, I understand." Then, afraid lest the understanding contribute to the other's distress, he added : " But if the whole thing was an accident . . . surely he will see it that way for himself ! "

" What is happening in Hardyal's mind and spirit is no longer accidental. It is, I believe, the culmination of something that has been long in coming. I don't know when or where it had its beginnings. I have often wondered, but he has never confided that secret to me, and I have never brought the technique of the courtroom into my home. Once, years ago, Hardyal and I quarrelled. I was eager for him to return to England to finish his studies, but he refused. He gave as excuse the fact that he could not bring himself to leave home again. Although at the time I was sure that there was more to it than that, I said no more. I hoped he might one day come to me with the truth, but he never has."

" Nor," said Jacques, " has he confided that mystery to me."

" Then you, too, feel that there is a mystery ? "

" I have been sure of it for a long time."

Both were silent, then Jacques asked : " What can we do ? There must be something."

Ganpat Rai shrugged his tired shoulders. " We must wait. I think that just now he moves in a sort of darkness. He has ceased, temporarily, to see men as friends or enemies. The shock has numbed, in him, the faculty of discrimination —he is aware only of forces, immense, impersonal, and hostile. He sees himself caught up by these forces, victimised by them, even aggrandised by them. I have seen it happen to witnesses and to men whom I have defended in court. By identifying themselves with a cause, or with a friend or a lover, they succeed in depersonalising themselves to such a degree that they can endure any situation. It is this detachment from himself which moves one man to confession, and which breeds impregnable silence in another."

" Is that what you meant when you said, just now, that we had lost Hardyal ? "

" Yes, and it is what I mean when I say that Hardyal must not lose us."

Jacques exclaimed unhappily : " But if he should no longer want us ! "

" Remember, he is the wronged one, the sufferer. He will make demands he has never made before, demands on our love, on our patience, on our understanding. On you, perhaps, more than on any one."

" Why on me especially ? I should think that he could take me for granted."

" I do not think that Hardyal will ever again take a man for granted."

Jacques gave him a straight look. " Tell me what it is you really mean, Ganpat Rai."

The older man stared at his hands, folded on the desk before him.

" I mean that he may never again bring himself to take a white man for granted."

" As a friend ? "

The other bowed his head a little, and Jacques thought : This has brought the years upon him ; he looks twenty years older.

" As enemies ? "

Ganpat Rai made a sudden despairing gesture. " My God, how can I say ? I do not know . . . I cannot see . . ." He clenched his hands. " I cannot resign myself ! Do you know what they did to him ? Macbeth himself told me this when he was trying to explain how it all happened. He never saw Hardyal, he thought he must have disappeared into the crowd after that warning shout. But there was good reason why no one saw Hardyal, for the police had beaten him senseless behind the wall. They broke his arm and his teeth. They manacled him between two others, and left him all night chained to the floor of his cell, without water, without attention. They did this, to Hardyal, to my son ! "

As swiftly as his composure had deserted him, it returned. " Excuse me. It is stupid to lose one's temper."

Jacques rose impulsively. " Ganpat Rai, my friend . . ."

Ganpat Rai rose too, and put his hands on the young man's shoulders, staring into his face. " We are friends . . . friends ? " It was asked wonderingly, and Jacques was made to feel the full weight of his own misery with this additional, vicarious shame.

" Can you doubt it, Ganpat Rai ? "

The other dropped his hands with a sigh. " No, for you and I are the same kind of man. We are not like Hardyal, not like Salim. We were not cut out for faith or for destiny." A glimmer of his old humour appeared for a moment on his face. " For that reason, perhaps, we shall always remain friends—loving, but incapable of illusion ! "

Jacques said gently : " Take me to Berari with you, when you go to see Hardyal."

They exchanged a long glance, then Ganpat Rai's face cleared.

"We will go together and bring him home. But in the meantime, here I have sat talking, talking only of my troubles, when all the while there is a matter which concerns you and which I had almost forgotten. I would have written you from Agra if all this had not happened to drive it from my mind."

He crossed the room to a small green safe set against the wall, and returned carrying a large brown envelope. "This is Mrs. Lyttleton's will."

Jacques scarcely heard. He was thinking of Hardyal.

"She did me the honour of entrusting me with her affairs. I felt bitterly that I was not in Amritpore when she died, that I was unable, even, to attend her funeral." He opened the envelope and withdrew its contents. "This was written five years ago. In it she has made you her heir."

Jacques stared at the document which the barrister spread before him on the desk. "There are a few bequests to her old servants. Everything else—and there is a great deal, for she was a wealthy woman—everything else goes to you."

Jacques picked up the crisp bluish paper and examined its elaborate phraseology with almost casual attention. Neither surprise nor pleasure moved him, only a sort of painful mirth, as though he'd taken a draught of slightly poisonous nectar. Ganpat Rai was watching him. "This will make a difference to you. It will take a little time for you to get used to the idea that you are now . . . independent." He smiled. "I, for one, shall observe the outcome with interest."

So, thought Jacques, shall I.

Both men were silent, meditating on a future whose sudden, sumptuous contours even Madame St. Remy could scarcely have visualised, let alone have achieved ; on a revenge so exquisitely contrived that it must leave her, irretrievably and to the end of her days, to the subtle mercy of her dead rival.

"You are not going to refuse ? " Ganpat Rai asked at last, puzzled by his companion's long silence.

"Refuse ? " Jacques repeated. "No, how could I refuse ? "

How could he refuse his old friend her long-delayed

triumph, or deny her, from this distance, the rewards of this ironic moment? And because he glimpsed, now, the first bright outlines of this moment which she had long ago conceived and foreseen—a moment whose eventuality must intensely have amused and sustained her—Jacques began to laugh, convinced in his heart that from somewhere on her point of vantage she laughed with him.

"Good!" said Ganpat Rai. "Take it, my child. Take it, use it, be happy."

"Happy? I'm not sure about that . . ."

"Yes, I understand. If only there were no war, if only we could carry forward into life the innocence and the generosity of childhood!" His brown eyes filled with light, like pools at evening. "You are young . . . you, Hardyal, Bertie, Macbeth. Whatever the future holds will belong to you."

"I wish I knew!"

"One must go on living, Jacques. For you children, as well as for us who are old, the end remains hidden."

THE END